ALETHEIA

J.S. BREUKELAAR

Let the world know:
#IGotMyCLPBook!

Crystal Lake Publishing
www.CrystalLakePub.com

OTHER TITLES BY J.S. BREUKELAAR

American Monster

PRAISE FOR *ALETHEIA*

"Family and small town desires and secrets simmer in J. S. Breukelaar's melancholy and affecting mix of literary, noir, and horror by the lake. *Aletheia* is a compelling 21st century ghost story. Don't lose your Gila monster!"

—Paul Tremblay,
author of *A Head Full of Ghosts*
and *Disappearance at Devil's Rock.*

"Sometimes the monster lurks within us, and sometimes it prowls the world we inhabit, made flesh. Both reside in this unsettling, moving, and haunting story about family, loss, and the dark shadows that loom at the edge of our perception."

—Richard Thomas,
author of *Breaker* and *Tribulations*

"In *Aletheia* by J.S. Breukelaar the prodigal children of a strange lake come home, their return dredging up old enmities and reopening barely healed wounds. Breukelaar's prose is as warm as blood and sharp as a scalpel, and even the smallest moment is made miraculous. By turns unsettling, terrifying, and uplifting, *Aletheia* is a stunning examination of the intersections between memory, love, life and death."

—Angela Slatter,
World Fantasy Award-winning author of
The Bitterwood Bible and Other Recountings

"J.S. Breukelaar's *Aletheia* is simply a masterpiece. Drawing on elements as different as folk-horror, mythology and symbolism, JS Breukelaar weaves a terrifying, yet beautiful psychological and metaphysical patchwork that reads like a dream. J.S. Breukelaar is definitely the next huge name in horror fiction, right along King, Koontz and Straub. Mark my words."

—Seb Doubinsky,
author of *The Song of Synth* and *White City*

For Michael

BEFORE

NOSE **ISLAND WAS** a glacial booger sneezed up by Funes Lake, five miles to the north of town. Most people you asked swore that it had always been there—first an Iroquois graveyard, then a potters' field, leprosarium, orphanage, or toxic dumping ground during the Eerie heyday—but how and when it came into the Zabriskie family no one exactly knew. Some said a poker game gone sour, others said a favor owed or interest paid on some unimaginable debt—there was even talk of a curse. Over time, subsidence and falling water levels created treacherous structural currents around most of its perimeter—the lake-effect weather that was a feature of the area, along with various other environmental anomalies meant the island itself was mostly invisible and all but inaccessible. Being private property, of course, no one had set foot on it for decades.

Or if they had, they couldn't remember.

PART I

1. ARRIVAL

WHEN OLD MAN Zabriskie got sick and privately offered his manor house, including its very own island, to the first man who would shoot him in the head, it was Frankie Harpur who stepped up to the plate. Frankie Harpur—shell-shocked war veteran one minute, Lord of the Manor the next.

It would be five years before Thettie Harpur would hear about Frankie's change of fortune. They'd moved away by then, of course, and how she heard about cousin Frankie was through a one-eyed girl called Bryce, whose inflatable took a bullet a mile upriver, and who Doc found drifting face-up in the current, her good eye open and blinking. Back at The Landing, an abandoned hamlet along the Susquehanna, where they'd been in exile for almost a decade, Doc told Thettie that there was something familiar about the girl. As far as Thettie could see, she was just some no-account water-rat, but Doc was right, as usual. It turned out the foundling knew Frankie, or said she did, and had even claimed to have been to the island—so Doc decided to keep her. By then, the Harpur boys were falling all over her, but it was Archy who won her in the end, fair and square—even if his brother, Grif chose not to see it that way.

'We ain't taking her back with us,' Grif said. 'What kind of a name for a girl is Bryce, anyway?'

'Bryce with a 'y,'' said Archy.

'I don't give a god damn what it's with. You don't know where she's been.'

'She's from Little Ridge, same as us.'

'How comes we never seen her before when we was there?' Grif bit down on his cigar and spat out the tip in the direction of where Bryce was sitting alone on the dock fixing her lines. Nothing but a dark blur against the white Pennsylvania sky.

'She's younger than us,' Archy said.

'Too young.'

Maybe it was that. Or maybe it was her narrow waist and uncomely boy-hair, not to mention the fact of the missing eye. Or maybe it was that Bryce-with-a-'y' did have news of Frankie and some new mix he was cooking up alone on Nose Island—a rock whose very existence had been in contention for as long as Thettie remembered. Maybe it was her uncanny knowledge of all the hidden currents and inlets that would get them there—but whatever it was, Thettie, like Grif hated the girl on sight.

'She's been there her own self,' Doc claimed. He described to Thettie what the girl had told him about the deep narrow harbor that spilled out beneath a high nostril-shaped outcrop, and Frankie's new lab supposedly in one of the old engineer huts.

So, after ten years away from Little Ridge, they were going back, and if Thettie had her doubts as to where or what 'back' was, she kept them to herself.

'Let bygones be bygones,' Doc said. 'Forgive and forget.'

ALETHEIA

'Harpurs don't do either,' Grif said, under his breath. 'And if he was one of us, he'd know that.'

***

It was first light when they finally pulled up to the shores of Little Ridge—their return in the same formation in which they'd fled: Doc, on point on the deck of his Craigslist cruising yacht—the one difference being the two parole absconders he recruited learning about the Yankee security system Frankie had rigged up—Grif close behind on his beloved Lund, and Thettie with Archy and the water rat on the old Black Crown that had been in the family for years. The rest of the clan—aunts and cousins and boyfriends—taking up the rear. Everyone's stomachs were so full of lakers and muskies, all they could talk about was pizza and burgers and fries and Taco Hell. And how, given half a chance, they could murder an Oreos McFlurry—kill it twice.

The stars had begun to fade over the expanse of lake and Archy and Grif were already toe-to-toe in the shallows. Thettie leaned against the rail of the Black Crown, worn out from her boys' non-stop yammering and bickering all the way up the river and across the state line and then some. Their ongoing feud a dream-like voice-over to the three hundred miles of rush-lined streams and riverside shanty towns, jostling tapas bars, office parks, summer-camp sites, gleaming Mormon tabernacles, families fishing off retaining walls, and fake antique water pumps.

Despite her exhaustion, Thettie's heart was flopping like a fish. She didn't know what to expect after being away from Little Ridge for so long, but she didn't expect to feel like this—a stranger. She couldn't look at what was left of their settlement at the edge of town, nor at the genteel Village roofs still shrouded in night. Instead she concentrated on trying to spot the island in the mist, wondering if in fact the girl was right and Frankie was still there. Because it wasn't just the leaving. And it wasn't just Frankie left behind to die. It was the never coming back.

'Fucktard say what?' Archy gave Grif a shove.

'She's not staying.' Grif shoved back.

Frankie would say, 'never say never.' Grif lost his footing on the lake stones, his nose bleeding onto his soggy cigar. He asked again, 'What kind of name for a girl is Bryce, anyways?'

'The name of my girl, not yours, is what it is.'

'It's a boy's name, fucktard.'

'Not with a 'y'.'

Archy, Thettie's real son, was the quicker of the two but the giant, motherless Grif packed a harder punch. Archy, winded, lost his grip and Grif jabbed the space between them with his damp cigar. 'Which you had to spell out for her. FYI, most folks don't need someone else to tell them how to spell their own fucking name, fucktard.'

Frankie would say that she and her boys were a three-headed monster, like Cerberus, hound of hell. The hair on Thettie's neck prickled. She peered into the mist for the island. Frankie?

The fog brought a cold that burned breathing in. The familiar reek of rotting lake weed and bracing pine made her know she was home. Thettie coughed and lit a cigarette to cover the smell she'd been dying to return to for almost ten years. She was a girl then. Inhale. What was she now?

ALETHEIA

Archy's hood fell off his pretty eyes and he lunged. Grif swung, and took his brother in a bear hug, and they continued their tussle beneath the grunting stars. Mist aureoled their long Harpur hair, and water streamed down their filthy thermals. Thettie climbed up from the rocking trawler onto the jetty. To her thinking, the truth was a devil in lacy disguise. Doc may or may not have had a piece of the water rat between pulling her from the creek, giving her CPR, and towing her back to the Landing—but the fact remained that none of them really knew where the girl had been.

Archy was going to have to get rid of her.

'Get rid of her.' Grif burbled and jerked his hips from beneath the slops, his ability to read Thettie's mind acquired after following her around from the age of ten, like on an invisible leash. 'She's not one of . . .'

'We need her,' Archy's rings gleamed dully in the early light. 'Doc said she knows where Frankie is. She knows how to get to the island.'

Grif, splashing to the surface, spoke the words Thettie didn't dare to say. 'No one knows how to get to the island.'

Archy's eyes glowed like planets, the pupils submerged in glittering spheres of blue.

'Bryce says he's there, asshole. Frankie's there now!'

'Yeah but how . . .' Grif's question drowned in gurgles while Archy held him down in order to silence a possibility not worth thinking on. The bigger man's arm punching through the surface of the water, tattoos on his giant knuckles running like stains.

Thettie looked across the ruffled lake, but Nose

Island—part of some founding father's estate, which according to Bryce, Doc said, belonged to Frankie now—was wrapped in time and Frankie with it. Doc's squeaky brogue was suddenly and without warning behind her like an ambush, his rubber-soled combat boots having a lot to answer for.

'I'll send someone to see to renting us some cabins, girl. You go on into town to get us supplies.'

She nodded and took a step toward the shore, but his hand clamped over her wrist in a guerilla grip. With a sideways nod, he sent the two parolees at his flank to break up the tussle in the slops since joined by any number of Harpur sons, nephews, and brothers. The boats had churned the water into yellow curds, the mist alive with the eerily familiar click of invisible Bics and Zippos. The last of the light from Orion's belt caught in the pink-tinged droplets that fanned off the swinging ropes of Archy's pretty hair. Dawn was slow to come over the eastern ridge.

'Not what I expected,' Thettie said. 'So quiet.'

'Well, it's a tad early for a welcoming committee and all,' the words spat out of the good half of Doc's mouth. He drew her toward him, the stump of his trigger finger brushing against the inside of her wrist. The unforgiving sting of the hemlocks on the back of her throat made it hurt to swallow.

'There'll be one soon enough,' Thettie stiffened in his embrace.

'Home, girl. Feel good?'

'Feels cold,' she said, wriggling free. 'Barely October. I better see to breakfast. Stores will be opening soon.'

Lights had begun to wink on along the shore.

ALETHEIA

Thettie dropped down off the jetty and winced at how her wet sneakers chafed at the hollow of her ankles, the sound of her footfall on the stones like a fingernail raked across a blackboard. Her knees buckled but did not give way and she felt the urge to pee but did not let go. Instead she stood up straighter, tried to pull everything back into herself, everything lost somewhere between here and the Landing and back again. Behind her she heard Archy and Grif submitting to Doc's toughs and dropping their squabble to follow her. It was with an effort that she kept her spine rigid and her back to them, signaling by the length of her stride that this was not about them. Not this time.

Her vision was jumpy from lack of sleep and there were dark flakes like ash at the edge of her eye. She shivered in Archy's cast-off sweater. Between the lake shore and the woods was a row of new solar-paneled log cabins behind which ran a scraggly line of budget-priced trailers for retirees and fishermen, invalids and itinerants who came back year after year or who never left. A face jumped into the window frame of a listing double-wide trailer and Thettie's flesh rippled. A scarf or veil obscured the face as it followed Thettie's progress, and she heard the strumming of a distorted guitar. She knew those chords! Thettie jerked away fast and just as quickly looked back—she didn't want to— but the face was gone and the music, too.

Word of the Harpurs' return had started to spread and a small posse of locals and lawmen began to gather in the parking lot. She felt their eyes on her. Thettie fluffed out her hair and unbuttoned the top button of her sweater. The ridge behind the Village blocked the rising sun and blurred the outlines of the waking world. Headlights floated slowly down Main Street like eyes without a face. New smells drifted in the air. The unfamiliar grind of an espresso machine from where the drug store used to be, rosemary in the fresh-baked bread from a new bakery at the end of the block.

'I'll be damned.'

Ten years since they'd left Little Ridge, and it had transformed from a forgotten lake town into something from the future.

Her body remembered, before her mind could argue, to avoid a wedge-shaped crack that had been in the sidewalk, but was no longer there. When she stepped over where she was sure the gap had been, fine lines began to web the new mica. She froze. At her feet, small fissures widened as she watched, like something trying to push up from below the surface, like something come up to meet her. At this spot—she was sure this was the spot—had been a deep vertical slit that Cassie and Frankie always said it looked like a giant mouth—it was just here, she was sure of it. It had cut all the way down to the soil and was tufted with weeds and crowded with chunks of asphalt like broken teeth—and it always tripped one of them up, either by accident or on purpose. Could turn a spectacular wheelie into a dramatic lose, cross-bar slammed into pubic bone, that old cement mouth with its broken teeth laughing at their pain. Thettie held her breath, like she was on thin ice instead of six inches of brand new asphalt. Don't make any sudden moves, she told herself. Only when she no longer could feel or see the cracks in the sidewalk getting any bigger, and was washed in sweat, did she carefully step away.

ALETHEIA

Yes, her boys were right not to follow. This time it was all about her.

She passed the old post office and the newspaper rooms where they'd once printed *The Dawn*. Instead it was now a gift store and gallery filled with paintings of the lake.

Art in Little Ridge—for real? She walked on toward the Inn, trying to slow her drumming heart. A once shabby throwback to the Fargo days, the Village Inn had grown too expensive to run and was beyond the means of Sullivan college, who owned the property, to repair. Thettie had been inside its dim, musty interior only once before they shut it down. It stood before her now, immaculately repainted like a Disney castle. White columned balconies, green shutters on all four stories. Lilies and delphiniums grew in planters on either side of a limp flag. A doorman discretely sipped coffee from an Eco cup and Thettie's mouth could taste the fresh-ground smell.

Granted, the smell of the lake was still as oppressive as a wet sock. She wiped a drip from her nose with her sleeve. The lake would always be there. She could see it behind the rolling lawns of the Inn, stretched out beneath the mist like a sheet of burnt tinfoil. The college bell tower pealed the dark hour. 7:30 am.

To either side of Main Street, grandly restored Georgians and Revolution-era manors faked sleep while watching her approach through beveled windows closed to any notion of second chances beyond their own. So that it was Thettie who felt herself disgracefully aged, though she was only forty-two (give or take) whatever her pale reflection in the window of the Little Ridge Market said to the contrary.

Thettie hadn't really expected the store to be open yet. That was just a ruse to get free of Doc, put herself right in the head before she set the clan to order. She remembered it as an IGA—an understocked, overpriced country store keeping random hours. But even as she approached the new beveled glass corner shopfront and got her hand to the door—repainted in a shade of green that looked more authentic than Little Ridge ever was—it opened. Out spilled a slender man, grocery bag in one hand and texting with the other. The phone, his groceries, and her purse hit the sidewalk at the same time. Her crushed cigarettes, coupons, tampons and make-up among trays of rose-red hamburger meat as far as she could see, glowing against the sidewalk like it had just been butchered.

'Bait or barbecue?' she said, letting the man apologize and hand her up her things. Cassie would say to let men think that you like them on their knees, even if this one looked a little young. Thettie wondered what anyone could possibly want with so much hamburger meat. Best to stay away—it was Frankie who taught her that. Townies aren't like us, he said. Who knew what they wanted, or why?

'Neither,' the man said, getting to his feet and passing across her purse. 'The hamburger is for Vernon.'

He had paint on his fingers, which brushed hers and a smile that looked older than the rest of him. Buying hamburger meat for his kid? She scanned for a wedding ring.

'How old's Vernon?'

'Almost thirty.'

Her eyes lifted to his, indistinct behind the smeared glasses. No, not too young at all probably, and not a townie, definitely. Not the usual condescending townie smirk. Nor a farm boy either. Man was far from home. She tore her eyes away from his. Paint on his sweats, too. 'Your roommate?'

'I guess,' he pushed up his glasses, tentatively stepping back over a tray of meat without dropping his gaze. 'In the wild, of course, he'd be lucky to make it to twenty.' The man seemed to be playing a game he knew too well and had grown weary of. A desert drawl to his vowels.

'What is it, for Christ's sake? A bobcat? A badger? My cousin Frankie had a raccoon called Rocky who used to try and hump the cat . . . ' Thettie fumbled in her purse for a smoke.

'Vernon's a Gila Monster.'

Thettie brought the Parliament to her lips with a shaking hand, and his eyes followed her every move. 'A heelah-what?' Except she knew.

'It's a lizard,' the man said. 'A big one.'

This she knew also.

'Don't they eat mice and such?' she said, trying to ignore the cold thrill of terror at the mention of the word, lizard. Her knees wobbled a little, steadied a little by those far-from-home eyes.

'My vermin guy has gone into rehab.'

He smiled a little crookedly at her, like the game was up and he was the reluctant winner.

'I thought they ate like twice a year.' Inhale

'So, this is one of those times.'

'Hamburger meat doesn't sound right.' Pockets of

bright blood had begun to pool at the edges of the Styrofoam trays scattered on the pavement. 'But that's just me.'

'He's not really going for it, actually.'

'Try pizza.' Exhale. 'It's a cure-all according to my cousin Frankie.'

'The raccoon guy,' he nodded. 'Thanks. I'll give it a try.'

They looked awkwardly down at the flung packs of hamburger swimming in the bright blood.

'How big is it?' she said.

He blinked at her.

'Your lizard. How big?'

He flushed a little like he'd see the way she looked at him and raise it. 'Big enough.'

She went all in. 'Big or small. They make me sick, literally. Hives and shortness of breath. My one fear.'

'You're lucky,' he said. 'Having only one.'

Yells and crashes drifted up from the shore. It'd be all over town by lunch time. How those hick Harpurs had pulled back into town in their shitty boats, and how the boys were at each other's throats over pussy before they'd even tied up.

'We're back,' she said, blowing smoke. 'Lock up your daughters.'

'A little late for that, isn't it?' The man didn't back out of the smoke but he wasn't smiling any more either. 'Your homes are all gone.'

He didn't need to tell her. From the little news that made its way down to them at the Landing before Bryce showed up, she knew that Parks and Recreation had come in soon after they left ten years ago. Pulled all their float homes and grandfathered shitholes off the banks of the creek and smacked an Eminent Domain claim on the land to prevent this very occurrence—the Harpurs coming back with their hard-ons and chain-swinging vengeance.

'Except here we are,' she said, and the place looked like a theme park with its fake façades and false scents. So maybe the lizard guy was right. And maybe not. 'It's never too late.'

She ground the cigarette into the shiny new mica and pushed past him into the store.

***

Things were quiet but tense back at the camp ground when Thettie returned. The sun had pulled itself up over the low eastern ridge and blinked damply down at the lake shorn of its veil and dead as an old nickel. The rental office remained closed but some of the Harpur women had fired up the barbecue for the children. The reek of weed and coffee drifted from the boats. The posse at the camping grounds had grown and the sheriff's truck was now among the parked trucks and cars. Doc would have had words with him, words that Thettie could only guess at. Maybe the lizard man was right after all. Maybe it *was* too late for the Harpurs. Maybe their time had passed.

But what choice did they have? It wasn't just because they burned bridges the way some folks burnt coffee—though there was that. It was that during those terrible years of exile down at the Landing, she would wake up in a frigid sweat, the guilt of what she'd done sitting so heavy on her chest she couldn't breathe. The weight of knowing that to keep her boys safe, she'd left as much of herself behind as she'd taken. Maybe more.

Even before they left Little Ridge, Frankie had

warned that their sell-by date was passed. ' 'Send not to know for whom the bell tolls," he'd say at the pealing of the college bells. "It tolls for thee." There had to be room made for old clans like theirs in this new America, Frankie had said, unless your idea of a new America was an underground bunker somewhere in Georgia. 'Folks of Little Ridge need us. We're all that stand between them and nothing.' Thettie wasn't paying Frankie's hand-wringing much mind by that time, though. She had her own problems to deal with, namely survival. But what she never bargained on was that a price of that survival was having to leave her own blood behind. And had she really survived—entire?

Bells pealed the hour but they didn't sound the same. Would Frankie know her now? Would he say her name?

Archy was sitting on the deck of the trawler with his head in his hands. Heavy ink glistened on one arm—a floppy eared rabbit, a needle toothed Buddha, a twinned tree. His fingers bristled with silver rings. She touched a band on his thumb, a gift from Grif, battered from all the times Archy had cut it off and soldered it back together again.

'Me and Bryce might break up,' he said.

'Maybe for the best,' said Thettie. 'What happens down river stays on the river. When I was a girl, we'd all load up into Frankie's Zodiac and head downstream to Buckport and hang out at this pizza place there near a chop-shop. There was this one mechanic, jeans so tight—'

'Shut up, ma.' Archy's dark blue eyes were thunderheads. 'If it wasn't for Bryce, none of us would of known about Frankie. Show some respect.'

'Hush,' Thettie nudged him with a paper cup of coffee. The steam rose in the unseasonable October chill, and his eyes—when he lifted them—were her eyes. Blue as steel and just as indestructible. A shiner beginning to bloom.

'Grif went too far. I swear. I was like, now's my chance. Just drown him. Bam.'

'He's your brother. Once you've lost that, you've lost everything.' Like I lost Frankie, she thought.

'He's not my brother. He's my cousin.'

'Same as Frankie is to me,' she said. 'Blood's all that matters.'

Archy had her serious mouth and thick wheaten hair, although his was tobacco-colored with streaks of rust. His jeans were still soaked, and he was trying not to shiver. His huge hand unfurled and she rummaged for her smokes.

'He's just watching your back,' she tried. 'You'll be good again tomorrow. What kind of a name is Bryce for a girl, anyways?'

'Shut up momma, okay? Just shut up.'

She watched him light up, the cigarette cupped in both big hands. He passed back the pack, smoke curling from his lips and around his delicate moustache and fine nose.

'What do you want me to do?' she said.

'What makes you think I want you to do anything?'

But he got up wearily and, careful not to spill the coffee, held the little cabin door open for her. Thettie stepped in and down, pausing to cast an eye out first to the rubberneckers on the shore and then to her own clan. Electron-eyed nieces and cousins in their cut-offs. Bored and mutinous on the jetty where they hung about in twos or threes. Aunties in lawn chairs on the rocking decks, dreaming their OxyContin dreams. Grif's voice wafted across, organizing a party to reel in some lakers for lunch, which was a good thing, she thought stepping down into darkness, because the Village Market had been clean out of hamburger.

2. VERNON

VERNON SAT IN his tank, motionless as an idol.

Lee wiped off the last of his brushes with a rag, tossed them on the table, and walked across the studio to the bar fridge. He leant in and took a piece of cold pizza out of its box and closed the fridge. He chewed carefully, not taking his eyes off the Gila, who fixedly ignored the mouse-shaped hamburger patty Lee had placed there earlier. Vernon's black-banded hide looked to Lee more apricot than pink today, and hung loosely from his frame. A single faraway light glimmered in his black eye.

It was true what Lee had told the Harpur woman outside the store. September wasn't a good month for Vernon, but this year it had been worse, and Lee would have liked to have taken Vernon home to die. He chewed the pizza and tried to figure out why he told her about Vernon. He recalled the white space between her unzipped collar, luminous in the first light and sprinkled with freckles like stars.

'Hang in there,' Lee told Vernon through a mouthful of pepperoni. 'Next year, I promise.'

An Ilium dealer planned a big show around Christmas, featuring Lee and some other local artists. He hated that term, 'local artists.' It brought up images of easels in man-caves and soccer moms with stretcher-bars. Lee bit into an olive. Buyers and bloggers had been invited from Buffalo, Jersey and New York. Lee was headlining. He'd already been promised a spot for his lakescape on the front page of the brochure. But the way the Harpur woman's eyes hardened when Lee said it may be too late for them, made him wonder how much longer he too could rely on the lake alone for his drama—plumbing it year after year for its secrets and its lies.

He just had to finish the painting. It was of the lake after a summer storm. Lightning scrim-lined the horizon. To the right, knuckled at the edge of the frame, was Nose Island. Or islands, if you counted the secondary hunk of rock, which was all but subsided, like the fist of a drowning man.

Vernon's tongue-tip flicked out, and the blue light in his eye, the one on Lee's slice of pizza, pulsed for an instant and then dimmed. The blue was paler than the Harpur woman's and Lee felt a flush of heat across his chest, thinking about her.

All he needed was a couple of good sales and he could afford to get his old station wagon fixed for the trip back to ABQ, or that was his excuse this year. He and Vernon could be there in the spring, when the flowers of the mesquite would be fat, yellow allergy bombs—a childhood affliction left behind with numberless others.

'So. You'll be fine,' he said aloud, getting a phantom whiff of hard liquor. 'What's that smell?' He'd dreamt last night about drinking—he hadn't had that dream for months now, maybe longer, the one where he was so drunk that he couldn't find his hotel room and kept knocking on the one next door, demanding that they let him in. It was always the same dream. But Lee had been sober for five years, so Vernon just turned his huge head away and the temperature in the studio dropped a notch.

Lee had converted it from a decrepit greenhouse built by the previous owner. Lee's actual house sat fifty yards up the hill, but neither he nor Vernon went in it much anymore. The studio had everything they needed. A couch for sleeping, a coffee pot and a fireplace—and Vernon liked the light.

When Lee had chewed down all of the cold pizza but for the crust, he tossed it into the tank.

'There you go, kid. I hear it's a cure-all.'

He wiped his hands on the paint-spattered sweats he cringed at seeing reflected in the eyes of the Harpur woman, whose jeans were clean and whose hair smelled like apples beneath the cloud of tobacco smoke she blew at him. He'd bumped into her at the exact moment his phone signaled an incoming text which had simply said, 'They're BACK!' and when he looked up, there she was. Staring down at his spilled meat with eyes like the lake. Cold and blue and almost indestructible.

Back in his studio, Lee found himself unable to put that blue, an unnerving shade he'd never seen in a paint tube or in nature, out of his mind.

***

Lee pulled his sweats off and rummaged around on the couch for a pair of jeans and a leather belt his wife had bought him from Seneca Village outside of Henksville. The text that came in when Lee collided with the Harpur woman was from Sam Habib, Lee's one-time

PhD supervisor. Lee had followed Habib east from New Mexico to take up a post-doc and assist in the new memory lab to be set up at Sullivan College, a declining liberal arts institution in the remote town of Little Ridge.

Most of what Lee knew of the Harpurs was from Habib, and the rest he'd filled in from the internet. The Harpur people claimed to be descended from a lawless union between the Revolutionary soldiers and the Iroquois who fought against them. Despised by both sides and deprived, for their sins, of the spoils of war, the clan flourished like disenfranchised rural groups everywhere, at the edge of things. Fishing and hunting sustained them—along with their famous yams and moonshine—plus various potions and cures and selling all of the above at Farmers Markets and more recently online. One of Lee's art students swore that Sarey Harpur's Shine Youth Serum was, hand to heart, a miracle.

So why had they come back?

The Harpur woman outside the store seemed unsure. She wasn't young but she wasn't old either and she had good hands. Her mouth was grave behind the flirty mask. Her hands trembled a little around the cigarette, but it wasn't age and Lee didn't think it was drugs—her fingers were strong but slender—no ring as far as he could tell—the fingernails unvarnished and gently curved. She had looked at Lee as if there was in him something still possible.

The clan had made a killing during the Prohibition years but slid downhill after that. Got into spare parts for bikes and boats—more junkmen than mechanics— mixing meth in decrepit cattle sheds and running mash through car radiators. Over the years their numbers diminished and dispersed, until their crappy little operation went down in a raid, and the whole family—what was left of it—just up and disappeared. But as Habib liked to quip, it's not the trip, it's what you do with it, that counts. And what the clan did was to head across state lines, leaving a war veteran called Francis George Washington Harper to take the fall. After his release from jail, Frankie's rage became a part of the scenery of the Village, the broken eccentric's vendetta against the family who betrayed him, gibbered all up and down Main Street to anyone who'd listen and especially to those who wouldn't.

Lee poured coffee from the paint-smeared pot, more to buy some time than because he needed more caffeine. He took it outside and drank it standing on the threshold of the studio, looking across the lake. The land sloped steeply down to the rocky beach, past an ancient maple where a frayed rope swing hung from black branches, the wooden seat above the fist-sized knot splintered and warped. A memory of summer remained in the stillness of the foliage and a whisper of goldenrod exhaled from the shore, calling to him.

You could still find an ossified peach or plum stone between the roots of the indigenous orchard that stood between his and the neighboring property—a twenty-six room sprawl which had belonged to Eli Zabriskie. Habib had explained to Lee how the Zabriskies had been canal industrialists with mills on every shore, now converted into tourist sites or ruinous squats for itinerants and runaways. Zabriskie himself made a fortune in ladies' underwear, but his pet project, a maternity bra with a cooling component in the cup, almost bankrupted his father's firm. Geese honked overhead in flight. What was it the woman had said when she'd stormed past?

It's never too late.

Lee took his jacket from the hook just inside the door and headed down to the lake.

His upturned canoe was tied to a tree beside a weathered picnic table that looked to be growing out of the rocky shore. The water undulated to the horizon line. To the north lay a low headland, and most people in Little Ridge could point to that vaporous irregularity just on the other side of that. To where Frankie Harpur cut out in Zabriskie's Zodiac Avenger from his hellfire days, and from where he'd never come back.

Until today, the island was Lee's obsession, an obsession that had nothing to do with Frankie. But today its indistinct lines were overlaid by the Harper woman's face, her wounded eyes and grave mouth. Lee put his empty cup on the picnic table and turned south toward the Village dock. If you knew what you were doing, you could make it the mile and half from Lee's beach to the town without getting your feet wet. Lee knew what he was doing.

He crunched around shallow pools filled with brackish water, passed head-high stands of rushes and stooped under leafless branches. In a few months, the entire shore—pools, stones, branches, reeds—would be covered with a layer of glittering ice and the ceaseless drip of winter.

He got to the Village dock, skirted its pylons and kept going south until he got to a smaller jetty eaten away by rot and poking out into the lake like an accusing finger. He stepped upon it and the lake sighed and sucked at his feet. A crowd of locals including the sheriff and his deputy, had gathered in the campground parking lot. Harpurs in hoodies and hunting jackets milled outside the rental office. Girls in short denim skirts lugged Disney suitcases into the budget trailers behind the new cabins on the shore. Looming above the bobbing Jet Skis and all the sad and shabby cruisers and speedboats and pontoons, Lee noticed a larger old-model Sundeck yacht, thorny with fishing poles and towing a small barge laden with bikes, batteries, tires, engine blocks, oil drums, and coiled rope. As he got closer he registered the surveillance cameras on deck and inhaled the burn of weed. A fat man waddled around the corner of the helm. He was huge, wearing a filthy wife-beater under an open shirt, with short curly hair and a bushy beard. His neck ended in a fold of fat around his ears, and was ringed in a ragged razor-wire tattoo. There was something about the tattoo, a savagery that Lee couldn't place. The fat man swung an unzipped Steelers' sports bag over one shoulder and Lee glimpsed a pistol shoved into his waistband.

Lee's glasses were splattered with lake water. He took them off and cleaned them with the greasy corner of his painting shirt. When he put them back on, the huge man with the gun was blurred and distorted. Lee felt a shiver up his spine. As his glasses cleared, he saw that the fat man's prison tattoo covered but could not conceal a ridged necklace of scar tissue that circled his entire neck.

Lee turned back to the campground. There looked to be a small and noisy party at the picnic area, and the musk of grilled fish dipped in cornmeal made Lee remember that he'd had nothing to eat except a half a slice of cold pizza. He scanned the camp grounds for the Harpur woman, feeling guilty as a teenager. There was a lone figure moving near the new-growth tree line by the parking lot—its gender cloaked in a puffy parka and a hat of some kind, a beanie maybe. Lee squinted through smeared glasses. The figure stopped moving but looked to be shrinking before his eyes, decreasing in both height and girth, as slender as the black saplings that sprung around it like a cage. Lee blinked, eyes fried from fixative, oils, and charcoal dust. At the sound of a human sigh behind him, he spun and almost slipped off the jetty, but there was no one there. When he looked back to the trees, the figure was gone.

A battered Lund roared in from the lake and spilled out a party of half-drunk men in hoodies and Goodwill Levis, wielding fishing rods and sloshing plastic pails. Lee stepped to the edge of the jetty, but if they saw him, they ignored him like he wasn't there.

A lone hooded man remained near the speedboat, casting a line and judging by the plume of ragged smoke around his head, enjoying a quiet cigar. Before he could think better of it, Lee began to walk slowly along the slats. He turned back only once, and the shore seemed further away than it should be, and some dark thing surfaced in the sucking water beneath the weathered boards, and slithered along in the shadow of his feet before it dived in and disappeared.

Lee neared the end of the jetty. He saw now that the man wore a leather biker jacket over his hoodie. A totemic cigar smoldered from between tattooed fingers. The halo of smoke hovered around his head like his personal heavy weather.

'Hey,' Lee said. When the guy didn't answer, he said it again.

A tackle box at the man's feet bristled with stickers and street-wear logos. Crushed cans of Keystone floated in a Styrofoam cooler.

'Any bites?'

The man finally turned around and pulled the wire from his ear. His black hood cast shadows across a haunted, raw-boned face. His eyes were the same tensile blue as the woman's at the Market, and Lee's throat turned dry.

'Not yet,' the man said.

He was probably in his late twenties, although his face looked older, and he was a giant, easily six and half feet tall and a yard across the shoulders. His cheeks were bruised and scratched from a recent fight, and a premature frown-line bisected his heavy brow. The sun had passed its zenith. The fishing line was a silver scribble against the blue-black lake.

'I'm Lee Montour. I live at the other end of town.'

'Grif Harpur.'

'Welcome home,' Lee said.

'Some welcome,' Grif Harpur cocked his head at the hostile crowd. 'And they pulled down all our homes.' His hands were huge, and baroque letters were inked on his fingers—black on one hand, a dirty red on the other.

'Maybe they didn't think you'd come back.'

'We were here before anyone. There's even a waterfall named after us.'

'Harpur Falls dried up,' Lee said gently. 'I think you'll find it's just a trickle now.'

'Still there on the map, last time I checked,' and Grif's voice was anything but gentle.

The lake hissed at the boards beneath Lee's feet. The ridged leather padding on the shoulders of the man's biker jacket jutted wide as the pauldrons of old and just as lethal.

'Watch your step.' The cigar-and-whisky growl in the man's voice sounded less convincing the more he spoke. 'Water's deeper than you think.'

'Well no one knows how deep it actually is,' Lee began, but Grif had already turned back to his line. 'The shifting bedrock beneath these glacial lakes makes accurate measurement problematic.'

'Supposed to be a monster down there,' Grif said. 'Beer's in the cooler.'

Lee reached into the icy slush and tossed a can of Keystone across. Grif caught the can without turning his head. In the uncertain light, Lee made out two of the red tattooed letters on his fingers—F, and A.

'You ever heard that?'

'What?' Lee eyed the beers in the cooler, his pulse racing.

'Whatever's down there.' Grif Harpur brought the can to his mouth and drained half of it. 'Ma always said it was more afraid of us than we was of it.'

A hawk wheeled high overhead, screaming. Grif rocked back and forth on giant boots. 'I expect you've come looking for her.'

Lee felt his face burn. Grif drained the rest of his beer, crushed the can into a golf ball-sized mass, and dropped it at his feet.

'Wouldn't kick her out of bed for eating crackers?' he said, the bar room growl returning to his voice. 'I knew you weren't here to talk about the fish. Sooner or later, there's always some townie who comes looking for Ma. Sees her at the store or out the window of their car, can't get her out of their heads. Take a number, Townie.'

The beers swam lasciviously in their icy stew. Lee hadn't had a drink in half a decade. The echo of the hawk's scream came back to them in a diminishing falsetto.

'You're her son?'

'She took me in when I was ten. Her biological son's the one who did this.' He swiveled and sulkily pulled down his hoodie so Lee could see the fiery bruise on his neck.

Behind him the fishing line jumped and quivered against mountainous rain clouds, like it was searching for something.

'The place has changed a lot since you left,' Lee said.

'No kidding.'

Abruptly, the vapor to the north parted to reveal the nostril-shaped outcrop with its inner grove of bestial nose-hair and the ruin of a lighthouse hugging the rock, once needed to alert traffic to the dangerous rips produced by water sucked into the caves that riddled the rock walls below.

'I noticed new warning pylons out there,' Grif said.

'Sheriff Boyle had them put in after Frankie . . . after your cousin took over the property.'

'You ever been there?'

'Close,' Lee said. 'You?'

Grif shook his head and pointed with his cigar, its tip glowing against the raspberry sky. 'You take a big enough vessel around the perimeter, drop an inflatable into the still water just north of the strait, pick up enough speed, I wager that the momentum'd take you in.'

'You aiming to try it?'

Grif Harpur motioned for another beer, and Lee tossed it to him.

'Not a drinking man?'

'Not any more,' said Lee.

'Married?'

'Not anymore.'

'Girlfriend? Boyfriend?'

'I have a Gila monster called Vernon, if that counts.'

'Whatever hones your bone,' said Grif, laughing, low and melodious, as befitted a big man. 'Some of us are throwing a coming-home party Sunday night at the tavern out on the Interstate. Ma'll be there, if Vernon can spare you.'

Lee pointed just as the line went taut. But when Grif reeled it in, the bait was gone and so was his smile, and the laughter that echoed back to them was as cold and empty as his eyes.

3. PRIZE

CHICK WAS HOT, chick was smokin'. Her boys could pick them, Thettie had to give him that.

'She can't stay, Arch.'

Archy sat across from Thettie at the fold-down table in a corner of the galley. His broad back slumped like a question mark. Tears clung to his dark lashes and his blue-blazes eyes followed the girl from ring burner to sink and back to the slab of melamine he'd fashioned for a counter top. Thettie's face hurt from lack of sleep and her eyelids felt dry. She tried to ride the gentle movement of the boat, but she was at odds with it. Her legs twitched beneath the table. She tried to focus on the girl who looked to be wearing nothing but one of Archy's shirts, and her eye patch.

'Doc wants her to stay,' Archy said, 'to get us to the island.'

'What about Grif?' Thettie said. 'He never did give two hoots about what Doc wants, and neither did you.'

'Grif doesn't know shit. Should have drowned him when I had a chance.'

Was that what it was, a chance? Half-drowned beneath a wet-cement sky, the whole world narrowed down to two brothers' hands around each other's necks—no way of telling where one ended and the other began—what chance was there in that? What choice? But then again, she'd never been very good at picking out the real chances in life, except in hindsight.

'*This* is our chance, Arch,' she said, with an urgency that made him wince. 'Coming back for Frankie.'

'If we can find him.'

'We don't need her help.'

'That ain't your decision to make. He's my blood, too.'

The girl clattered at the stove in her all-together, acted like she hadn't heard. Maybe she hadn't. Archy turned his coffee mug slowly in his huge hand, the silver rings on his fingers eating up all the light.

'You hurt your back in that scuffle?' Thettie asked.

'Some.'

At the edge of her eye, a flash of buttocks from the girl at the stove.

Thettie sighed louder than she needed to. Was that a sign of her getting old? It was true— more invisible you became, the more noise you felt you needed to make. No. She wasn't that old. Not like Aunt Sarey, whose sighs would scatter the crows.

But Archy was right. It didn't feel like home anymore, not without Frankie. Maybe that's why the boys went at it this morning. Maybe they had to. Because here they were, and all that was left of home was this fight, this enmity between them that defined them and held them in a drop of blood, kept flowing with their non-stop fucking and fighting and yammering and low-born brutish smarts. Because if not that, then what else? Where was home if not in the blood they carried in their homeless souls?

'Place has changed some,' Thettie said. 'I'll admit it.'

'Easy to see that now after ten years and a state line between leaving and coming back,' Archy said. 'Smells the same.'

'You were twelve.' Thettie shook out a cigarette.

'Almost thirteen. And Grif was sixteen.'

The only place left for a person in the end, Frankie had said, was the island. In this whole bullshit lake with its hostile shores and overfished waters and sad addictions, nowhere else to go.

'You got some of that MiraKil cream for Frankie's foot?'

Thettie blew a messy stream of smoke to hide the sudden gush of tears. Archy's hand reached for hers, his tattoos gliding down his forearm in the uncertain light. 'You did good, Ma. Frankie wouldn't have wanted it any other way. Would of been the end of the world if you'd stayed. You would have gone down as an accessory, and me and Grif'd be in foster care changing the batteries on some bearded lady's dildo, instead of taking care of you.'

'Mine uses a USB so keep your hands off it.'

Ice broken. Archy laughed a little too loud, and Bryce ignored them both. Her skin in the watery light looked translucent. A shudder gripped Thettie then, and left her in a cold sweat. She must have caught something downriver.

'But Doc? Maybe now's our chance, Ma. Get Frankie from the island and bail.'

'Hush,' said Thettie, sliding her eyes toward the girl.

'Bryce is okay,' said Arch. 'She knows about Doc.'

Thettie recoiled. 'What does she know? How Frankie let him in, but I was the one who allowed him to take control of our family? How everything's all my fault?'

'You did what you had to, Ma.'

A small muscle in the girl's shoulder-blade bunched as she dipped fish in flour. She kept her back to them. Thettie bit her lip hard enough to draw blood, and leaned toward her son. 'I didn't do what I had to. I did what I wanted to. And our story is not yours to tell to all and sundry river-pussy. Hey, you. Bryce with a 'y''. Thettie pulled her hand away from her son's. 'Where'd you come from anyway? Where are your people? What happened to your eye?'

And just like that, the gulf widened again between her and Archy, with Thettie yelling from one frozen precipice and her son backing away from the other.

A red sunset filtered into the cabin's high, narrow window and lay on the girl's faintly bruised flesh like a hand. A real prize this one. What man doesn't love a bit of damaged goods? Your work half done, you can wear her wounds like your own—better than your own, because a wound from an unknown source would never heal.

And a missing eye would never know what it missed.

'None of us would be here if it wasn't for Doc,' Thettie said evenly as she could. 'Doc saved us and that's on me.'

'It hasn't been a picnic for you, I get it. So, let's just move on, Ma. Okay? Get Frankie and get the hell out of here. She can help us if you let her stay.'

'And what if Grif takes off?' Thettie said. 'That'd be on you.'

Archy's mouth started to quiver and he pressed his hands to his temples. 'I just want it to stop.'

'I'll go,' Bryce cut in without warning and without bothering to turn around. 'I was going to tell you after breakfast, Archy. Better that way.'

Archy looked down at his hands and the girl continued, 'No harm, no foul. I'll be gone soon as the weather clears.'

The girl turned around with her son's shirt flashing open over her small high breasts and it occurred to Thettie that Archy seemed a little encumbered with them both there, his momma and his woman—for all intents and purposes—naked at the stove.

'You got yourself a real prize here.' Thettie's face felt hot.

It looked to her as though the girl needed a shave down there and it surprised her somewhat that Archy hadn't seen to it. Archy was known to be particular about personal hygiene and appearance. He liked his women neat and clean. Thettie, riding the swell of the lake, swallowed a tight lick of revulsion at the sight of that dark stubble around the liver-colored slit. She recalled, without meaning to, how the girl had turned up that day with water streaming down her face, her breasts and her boyish thighs, pooling at her childish feet. No matter that she said she was eighteen—she could have been ten years younger than that the way she carried on, a regular mooncalf. Could barely read and write. None of that mattered. What did, Thettie now saw, was how she'd come to Archy and soothed his rage.

'Ma,' Archy's voice was husky, his eyes wild. 'She knows the lake. She knows Frankie.'

Thettie shuddered at the thickness that had wrapped itself around her son's speech but she knew enough to see she had fallen away from this moment. Whatever she'd come to say to her son, or hear, the chance—like numberless others in her life—was lost.

'Fine. She can stay,' Thettie said. 'Help us find our kin, Bryce-with-a-'y', and you can stay. For now. Get your own trailer, is all. That's on me.'

Tears clung to Archy's lashes, and he shook his head, but no words came.

'Whatever it takes to find Frankie. Alive or dead. Deal?'

But Archy had already turned back to Bryce with a cold and alien thirst. The cabin had filled with the smell of fried fish and coffee and her musk. Archy pupils were like atolls in a sea of blue, and Thettie could hardly stand to witness it. She dropped her cigarette into the girl's coffee and stood up.

Bryce turned toward the table with a plate of eggs in one hand, coffee pot in the other, her belly curved and her nipples hard.

'Cunt needs a shave,' Thettie said, and banged out of the cabin.

4. MEAT

SUNDAY WASN'T A good day for Lee.

The piece of pizza that Lee had put in Vernon's tank was gone, unlike the mouse-shaped hamburger patty, which had dried to gray grizzle. A fly buzzed over the tank, trying to get at the meat and Vernon's obsidian eyes ignored it disconsolately. Lee's bar fridge was full of packets of hamburger, another half-dozen crammed into the tiny freezer.

'What am I going to do with all this meat?' said Lee. But Vernon didn't answer.

Lee pulled out his phone, and brought up the number of Sam Habib. Habib might know what ailed Vernon, and in all of Little Ridge, he'd be the only one, beside Lee, who cared. Vernon had gone on hunger strikes before—pining for the buttes, Habib said— although never as dramatic as this one.

But Lee had another reason for wanting to go see Habib today. Since retiring from the lab, the professor had taken an almost obsessive interest in local affairs— everything from youth soccer to house hauntings to genetically modified alfalfa strains to Haudenosaunee history—it all fascinated him in equal measure. *They're back*, Habib had texted, and Lee suddenly wanted to know as much about this prodigal return as

Habib could tell him—anything to explain the cold blue fire in the Harper woman's eyes, the whiteness of her knuckles on her fine hands, the haunted laugh of her adopted son, and why Lee couldn't get any of this out of his head.

He looked up from the screen. On the other side of his smeared lenses, lakes floated into view. Lakes everywhere. Lakes on the chair, on the TV set that he rarely watched. Lakes stacked on the shelves, and miniatures of the lake jumbled into a big yellow Tonka Truck under the desk. The lake came to him and gathered in this place of light, surrounding him. There was half a cup of cold coffee on the desk, and he threw it at the canvas on the easel. Coffee dribbled down the painted sky, carved dirty ruts in the pure blue eye of the painted lake. Lee got a rag and wiped it off, trying to draw breath around the pressure in his throat. A dirty mark remained on the canvas like a bloodstain.

Vernon watched him from his tank, a bleak world of Home Depot sand and potted mesquite, complete with a heating component and dish tray filled with water.

Habib's memory lab closed down almost six years ago. They all lost their jobs and grants. The lab technician wept as he sacrificed the cannibal mice and diabetic rats and cancerous pigeons, yet there remained the question of what to do about a thirty-year-old genetically modified Gila monster whose venom contained an enzyme that would open the door to the secrets of memory.

Maintaining a reptile enclosure wasn't cheap. Local zoos didn't want a Gila—Komodos were sexier—and flying Vernon back to UNM was beyond the defunct project's budget. Teaching art in a small room above the Village library and occasional work as a substitute biology teacher at Little Ridge High was not going to get either Lee or Vernon home any time soon.

The Gila inched a huge claw to one side, curved his thick body toward the weak light washing in from the window.

After the shut-down of the lab, it took most of the Memorial weekend to rig up a reptile tank for Vernon in the converted glasshouse. Lee could not have done it without the reluctant assistance of the technician, Jason deGroot, whose resentment toward Lee for claiming Vernon, manifested itself in a phlegmy sniffle and a tick-like twisting of his bleached blond hair. The deGroots—who claimed to have ancestors on Hudson's first ship, *De Halve Maen*—knew how to hold a grudge. Even after Jason left, the smell of his filthy trench coat and tooth-rot lingered beneath the slightly intestinal musk of the Gila.

The previous tenant of Lee's house had been a classics professor at the college. At the edge of the spruce and black walnut woods behind the studio, was a small graveyard where her kids had buried their pets. Broken crosses made from twigs, and shale markers bore faded names in spidery script—Zeus, Aphrodite, Hector, Helen. To these sad plots, Lee had added those of three experimental pigeons with advanced dementia and two male Wistar rats (Thing 1 and Thing 2) with induced Korsakoff's syndrome.

It wasn't anyone's fault that Lee's animal hospice inevitably ended in death. The animals had already given their all to science. And the most Lee or Jason or any of them could offer was comfort and dignity, a few more weeks of life—couple months' tops. Sometimes the animals actually recovered and lived to endure more water-maze training or hippocampal lesioning or neural electrode insertion, but Lee no longer knew which was worse.

Vernon was his second chance. Like Lee, Vernon had made the journey east with Lee, from Navajo to Iroquois land, and would always be with him. If the Ilium show was a success, they could head back to warmer parts. In his mind, Lee had already fashioned a travel tank for the back of the station wagon.

'We need to get out of this place,' Lee said. 'While we can.'

He left a text with Habib saying Vernon was sick and he'd be around in half an hour.

Since the scandal at the lab, Habib rarely left his lakeside villa, except to coach his youth soccer teams, among whom he was known—not very originally—as the smiling assassin. Before coming east to start his own lab in Little Ridge, Professor Sam Habib had been head of the School of Neurobiology and Behavior back at UNM, where Lee met him as a graduate student. Habib had run over Vernon in his Prius one cool summer night on Navajo land outside of Albuquerque, brought him to Lee, who happened to be doing his PhD on the distribution, habitat and behavior of *heloderma suspectum*—the Gila monster. Habib had worked with spiders and reptile venom before, but there was new research to suggest that Helotide, a peptide in Gila venom, had unsurpassed power to augment memory and learning in everything from fruit flies to Fisher rats. Vernon had unusually large venom glands.

ALETHEIA

Lee's grandmother had died in a dementia ward at Presbyterian Hospital, believing herself to be running poker games with Bill Clinton in a rig off Kodiak Island. It didn't take much for Habib to convince Lee to switched his area of study from biology to neuroscience. Habib became his doctoral advisor, and a compensatory father for the one Lee felt he had been assigned in error. When Habib left UNM to come east and take over his own lab in partnership with Tantra Pharmaceuticals, it was pretty much a given that Lee would come with him. What wasn't a given was that Tantra would fold under a cloud of scandal and take the lab down with it.

Lee reached down into the tank and scooped Hamburger Mouse up into a paper towel. The white star in Vernon's eye flared and gleamed with a cold intensity.

'I'll tell him you said marhaba,' Lee said. 'I promise.'

He carefully placed a whole slice of cold pizza into the tank. Vernon moved his blunt head and inched glittering claws toward it, an incongruous figure with his pink and black banded hide, against the backdrop of endless silver lakes. He held the crust in his jaws, and tore off the rest like fresh kill. Lee picked up his Polaroid and took a picture. He waited for it to process while running a finger up and down his old friend's studded hide. The alien turgidity of Vernon's body, like something neither alive nor dead, still made Lee's flesh crawl.

'I'll be back for the movie,' Lee said. It was the only time Lee used the TV. Pizza, beer and a movie, him and Vernon. Just like every Sunday. He was about to say he promised, but something stopped him.

Five years. And the Sundays never got any easier. This one felt a little different. Maybe it was Vernon's appetite for pizza in conjunction with the Harpurs' unexpected yet inevitable return. The false hope in the tinkle of their dirty boats.

Lee left the studio and hurried past a rusty and lethal looking metal swing set beside his empty ranch house. Dark woods ran all the way to the headland. Within the woods were the ruins of an old schoolhouse—now a make-out place for kids, hobos' squat, dopers' den. He backed the station wagon out of the garage, checking the time on the dashboard— almost four o'clock. He'd have time to visit Habib and be back to put another coat of sealant onto the painting before Netflix time. He eased the car up the steep driveway onto Main Street. Steered south through the Village past an exhumed water pump, retroactively verdigris-streaked, and other relics of an imagined past. One of his painting ladies looked up from her raked leaves, anachronistically clutching her purse. Outside the Village, silos shouldered each other beneath a white expanse of sky.

Lee slowed past a dirt access road posted with a charred signpost that said, 'To Triangle Creek.' He heard a car pull up behind him but when he glanced in the rearview, the Harpur woman's eyes sputtered back at him instead. He blinked and they were gone, the road empty in both directions.

Lee's mother fostered Siamese rescue-cats and Lee had always been convinced she'd loved them more than him. They over-ran the small house and yard at the edge of Indian land, on a street with no kids to play with, no neighbors to speak of. The cats, attuned to

Lee's resentment, blinked cross-eyed at him down their flat noses, yet trailed after his mother in a skittish mewling wave, hissing at Lee over their shoulders, until he gave up and hid in his room.

When Habib employed the troubled Jason deGroot, Lee had felt that same stab of panic, that same certainty of being sidelined for something much more exotic. Although the Harpur and deGroot clans were historical enemies, Jason deGroot's alliances were never that rigid, a flexibility exploited by Habib without apology. But Lee thought it was more than that, and the more the boy wore his punk heart on his sleeve, the more Lee hated him.

Lee had been to the old Harpur compound once when he first arrived in Little Ridge. It had been on one of Jason's many days of unexplained absence. Habib had sent Lee to pick up some emergency methyl-amphetamine for his memory project—'Mice on Ice'—from Jason's dealer, Frankie Harpur, a connection that flourished in the space between the feuding families. Lee had come away with the crystal and a nasty bite on his arm from one of Frankie's dogs, and he had not been back.

He accelerated past the dirt access road and stayed on the highway until he got to Habib's gravel driveway, a new security measure in the wake of the lab's scandal. A speed boat slowly rotated on the lake behind the villa, reflecting a cold and silent explosion of light.

Professor Habib was a short but punchy sixty-nine years old, deep in the chest and spare in the belly. His eyes were espresso brown, the lashes extravagantly curled. He had dealt intel along with black-market antibiotics in Rashidieh from 1967 to 1972, watched death fall from the skies when an Israeli airstrike buried his father, uncle, and three cousins under a city block of rubble. He had said to Lee that life as a man was impossible without recourse to either science or the Almighty, just not, he liked to joke, at the same time.

Over organic single-origin coffee, brewed with filtered water in Habib's office that overlooked the lake, and with an Italian walnut desk between them, Lee told Habib about Vernon. Habib sat back and ruminatively crossed his arms over his chest.

'You could give him some vitamins. He needs sunshine probably. Fresh kill.' His voice was as warm as blood, still virile, a veteran of TED talks and Ivy League lecture halls.

'My supplier's gone AWOL.'

'Have a cookie. They're gluten free. What about hamburger meat?'

'He's not going for it,' said Lee.

'Have you shaped them into mice?' The professor cupped his two hands together in the form of a heart.

'He seems to have acquired a taste for pizza,' said Lee. 'Maybe it's the nitrates.'

'How long has this been going on?' Habib said. 'The pizza thing.'

'Just today. I mean he's gone off food before, but never for anything else.'

Habib stood up to make some minor adjustment to an impossibly fragile looking standing telescope that pointed over the lake. He wore his soccer coaching kit with compression tights beneath satin shorts. When he excused himself to make more coffee, Lee got up and went to the telescope. It was fashioned from some golden wood, oak probably, and held together with delicate brass chains and fittings. The afternoon lake had gone as dark as a bruise ringed in angry, red foliage. The island, with its ruined lighthouse like a splinter of bone and veiled in pearlescent mist, was just visible with the naked eye.

Lee slid his glasses off and bent into the eye piece of the telescope. He recoiled as if bitten. He wondered if the lens had cut him, or maybe the brass eye piece had scratched his cornea. Through his good eye, he saw that the island had retreated once again behind its veil of vapor, and the indigo sky had become stained with yellow. At the swish of the professor's silks Lee turned around with one hand over his eye and his heart pounding.

'Spying on someone?' Habib said.

'I think I banged my eye on the lens.'

'I hope not. It's a bitch to recalibrate.'

'Well it could be me, but I can't find the island through it.'

Habib placed Lee's coffee cup carefully down on Lee's side of the desk.

'Let me see,' he said.

Lee excused himself to use the bathroom, still covering his hurt eye. He wasn't getting much sex lately, not since he'd allowed Sunny Weeks, head of the Little Ridge Progress Association, to dump him again. The urine dribbled out into the bowl and he remembered Habib complaining a few years ago about his 'stream.' When Lee finished, he wiped the sweat off his brow with his sleeve and tried, unsuccessfully, to blink away the angry knot of blood vessels that had burst in the corner of his eye after looking into the telescope.

Habib was standing by the telescope, and fluttered dark lashes at Lee over his shoulder. 'It's just you,' he said, pointing at the lens with his coffee cup, professor style. 'I can see it fine.'

Lee collapsed back into the library chair that Habib managed to pilfer along with who knew what else when the lab closed down. Habib regarded him for a moment and seemed about to say something but changed his mind.

'Vernon will live,' Habib said. 'But that's not why you're here, is it, my friend?'

When Lee shook his head, Habib wagged one arthritic finger at him and pointed to the flotilla bobbing at the jetty to the north. 'I knew it. The return of the repressed. As surprising as it is inevitable.'

'You wouldn't have any eye drops, would you?'

Habib put down his cup. 'You've met one of them. Haven't you?' He left the room and returned a moment later. 'I can tell. Didn't your mother tell you not to talk to strangers, Lee? Ah, the pretty one . . . ' He put an unopened bottle of eye drops down in front of Lee.

'They're all pretty from what I can see,' said Lee, thinking about the giant Grif with his leather armor and gentle laugh. He leaned back and squeezed some drops in his sore eye. The drops felt like acid.

'True. But I'm guessing it's the one with the Greek name you've come about—Thetis? Haven't seen a spring in your step like that for years.'

The flotilla bobbed soundlessly below the high double-glazed window like a flock of exhausted and uncertain water-fowl. There was no point in asking

Habib how he really knew about Lee's collision with the Harpur woman, and Lee eyed the crouching telescope with loathing. His eye hurt to blink.

'I met two Harpurs, seeing as you've asked. I met her son, also. On Friday, the day they arrived. You mustn't have been at your little spyglass then.'

Habib raised his eyebrows, a single parabola of fur. 'Archy Harpur? Why he was just a child when they left.'

Lee savored the rare moment of knowing something his mentor did not. 'Grif. He's her stepson. Or adopted or foster, or something.'

'Ah yes! She took him in when his father, a second cousin or something, went to jail and never came out.'

The overheated room was the only sign so far that Habib was getting old, and Lee began to sweat again. 'Okay, I give up,' he said. 'Why do *you* think they're back?'

Habib stood with his back to the window.

'Frankie Harpur. The man they left behind. I think they've come back for him.'

'Why?' Lee said. 'Why now?'

Habib ran both hands through his silver hair, made it stand up like sheet metal. Lee wondered again, with a twist of love, how many times his Nutty Professor used himself as a test subject for Vernon's memory-spit. 'There were always rumors about her and Frankie. The usual thing about cousins.'

'They're cousins?'

Habib sipped his coffee with the same calculated pause that he used to ambush grant committee meetings, student advisory committees, board meetings, Zoom interviews. 'What do you think of this brew? It tastes a little off to me. Single origin Ethiopian. I think I'm a blend man after all.'

'I remember how Frankie used to carry on in town after he got out of jail,' Lee said. 'Talking to everyone and no one at once.'

'That awkward dance at the edge of things.' At that Habib grew thoughtful again, the mask slipping to reveal the original mentor, the serious man who persuaded Lee to follow him to the ends of the earth. 'No one knows exactly how Frankie came to mesh so strongly with Zabriskie. They both fought for their country and lost. So there's that.'

'What?' Lee said. 'Zabriskie was in Vietnam?

Habib nodded. 'Frankie in the Middle East, of course. Or maybe it was because our founding father felt sorry for the wayward son with his war wounds and squandered smarts.'

Lee forced a laugh. 'I remember how Frankie would tell anyone on Main Street who'd listen how a man's war was never in the one place . . . '

'One hand saluting the flag and the other on his balls in a practiced maneuver so as not to over-balance on his rotten foot,' Habib said. 'Whatever transpired between the souls of this mismatched pair, it was enough for Zabriskie to trust Corporal Frances George Washington Harpur with his passage into the hereafter.'

'And for Frankie to trust that the suicide note and the old man's will and testament would all be duly witnessed, authenticated and pronounced in good order,' Lee said, some of the rumor and hearsay coming back to him now. 'Why did his people leave him behind in the first place?'

Most of the townies, Lee included, had even forgotten that the man prowling down Main Street in that rusted out Pontiac with his dogs and his coons, and that stink from his wounds that hung in the air wherever he went, was even a Harpur.

'It all went down soon after I got here, and before you did. '04, must have been. There was a big raid on the Harpur drug lab behind the compound up at the gully. Just a few chemicals and a ring burner in a converted shipping container behind the settlement. Rumors of a set up. A leak, what have you. Anyway, so everyone managed to get away except Frankie because of his bad leg. He took the fall, did five relatively easy years without squealing, and got early parole because of being a war hero.'

Lee peeled a leaf off his shoe, crushed it between his fingers and dumped it in the waste basket. 'I'd be more surprised that Boyle screwed up a raid on a crappy little operation if I didn't know what Little Ridge's finest were already capable of.'

'Of course. Sorry. Well of course there were rumors of a set-up. Being in the pay of a local hydroponic marijuana empire can be surprisingly good for a Sheriff's career.' The sun made a halo of Habib's silver hair. 'For every vial of meth the Harpurs mixed, or blister pack of OxyContin they bagged, there's a metric ton of weed drying beneath the deGroots' rolling alfalfa acreages and no law enforcement operation has ever come near it. Devil's Bud, I think is the name on the streets.'

'Devil's Butt,' Lee squeezed some drops into his sore eye, blinked away the tears. 'Is what Frankie used to call it, remember?'

Habib gave an exaggerated shrug. 'So to get re-elected, what Boyle had to do was shut down the Harpur's meth operation—make room for the deGroots. Poor Frankie.'

'You'd smell him coming.'

'And hear him, too. The perpetual rot-gut lament. Traces of Afghani shrapnel working its way from his heel up.'

'A cerebral abscess, undiagnosed?'

'Don't get me started on all the crap they pack into those IEDs, Lee. Rotor parts, nails, feces. Subdural, too, maybe, judging by the stink.'

Lee recalled how after his parole, Frankie lived with an aging aunt in what was left of the Harpur settlement on the shores of Triangle Creek. Forced to watch government flunkies pull the float homes to scrap, leaving the planks and window frames to drift off out of the mouth of the creek and into the lake where they got sucked down into the depthless cold like everything else. Abandoned and ill, Frankie would take the occasional trip into town to mutter rank words of vengeance and ill intent to whoever would listen. Canted over that grin-like crack in the sidewalk, townies giving him a wide berth. Cracking his knuckles. Snot crusting on his lip. And that stink.

'He'd stopped cooking crystal,' Habib said. 'Partly because kids are into different drugs these days. Smart drugs . . .'

"Nootropics?'

Habib nodded, his hair waving up and down. 'That and also the fact that he and his aunt revived the family line in salves and liniments, partly to try and cure Frankie's infection, partly to survive.'

Lee's mind flashed back to his meth-scoring venture at Triangle Gully, dirty lace curtains fluttering from a trailer, new forest growth already pushing through from the plots where their homes used to be. 'You two became friends?' He felt that familiar, unbidden stab of jealousy.

'I'm not sure if I'd call it a friendship. Somewhere between impossible colleagues and plausible competitors, I guess. Soon after his release he enrolled in night classes to brush up on his chemistry. He'd come into town from the Gully for supplies, that old Pontiac crawling with beasts, and he'd mutter about peptides and enzymes, hop up and down and spit equations at me. Smart drugs, he told me in a lucid moment. The way of the future.'

The drops seemed to have made Lee's eye worse. He could hardly see his mentor in the darkening room. He got up and walked to the window, looking for the lake as if he wanted to make sure it was still there. Plus, he needed to pee again, but he wasn't keen to face the dribble. Lee wasn't even forty yet. Too early to be experiencing issues with his stream.

'He ever ask you about the Helotide?'

Habib ran his finger along the edge of his laptop and didn't say anything.

'Seriously? You gave him some samples?'

'Improbably. Plausibly?' Habib's smile was so sweet that you wanted to pluck it right off his face, keep it for a rainy day.

'Jesus, Sam. We were looking into memory! Frankie's looking into getting high.'

'Same difference. Besides, I'd been retired—no lab,

nothing. Frankie had a lab he could use for free at community college . . . '

'And in return he, what? Passed on his quote-unquote findings to you?'

'For a while,' Habib said very quietly. 'And then nothing. Not once he left for the Island.'

'Which he came into by shooting a man's brains all over the walls. There's that.'

'That always cheered me up,' Habib sipped some water from a sports bottle. 'In the hard days after the lab closed down, just knowing what a mess Frankie and old Zabriskie made on the Utrecht drapes gave me a lift. You don't mind?'

Lee minded like hell. 'Getting back to Frankie. And his cousin.'

Habib wiped his mouth. 'The only threat poor abandoned Frankie ever posed was to himself. He was a cutter. He'd cut himself a dozen times in one weekend. You'd see him every day and then you wouldn't see him for a month, and he'd be covered in cuts, some infected, his limp worse and stinking like holy hell. But what really cut was the betrayal. Your Thettie Harpur and Frankie's best friend.'

'My Thettie Harpur? Wait . . . she doesn't seem the type to . . . '

'Run off with a man's best friend? People are like the island, Lee. Most of us is below the surface. He goes by the name of Murphy. A medic he met in Afghanistan. Murphy ended up here, became part of the family—he'd saved Frankie's life in the war, or something. Then the raid happened. Frankie's wounds meant he couldn't get away like the rest of them. He was a liability. Murphy took over the family after that.'

The clear eyes and serious mouth of the Harper woman, Thettie, flashed into Lee's mind. 'Are you sure these drops are in date? They're burning like fuck.'

'That's how you know they're working.' Habib bent down to rummage in a desk drawer, came up with a blister-pack of penicillin and tossed it to Lee.

Outside the windows, the clouds parted and a red slice of sun fell on the one picture frame Habib kept on his desk. Two men sitting on a couch looking at each other, and a woman entering the room, turning toward the camera but not looking at it. The woman's hair falls over one shoulder and a boy comes toward her from the opposite direction. A slice of light that now had to stand for four lives. Gone in the blink of an eye.

'So, okay. Frankie survived. Banging around in a twenty-six room Early Republic manor, complete with a Georgian rotunda and its own island—that'd be enough to help you forget.'

'He lost everything, Lee. His family, his livelihood, his health. No forgetting. Could you?'

Lee's eye burned and his bladder knifed and he felt the whole story catching up with him now. How Frankie Harpur had lived next door to him for a while. The dogs shitting all over the rolling lawns, Frankie's Pontiac roaring up and down the paved driveway. Unable to follow his family down to Pennsylvania because of his disability, and unwilling to send for them because of the conspiracy of corruption waiting for them back home.

Habib got up and put his hands on his hips, stretched to one side then the other, a lithe ghost beside the predatorial outlines of the telescope. 'While

Frankie was still mostly coherent, he would say that the deepest cut was Doc legally adopting her sons, too. Frankie said he loved those boys like they were his own, blamed himself for a near drowning when they were younger. Told me once that's why she let Doc take over.'

'It doesn't make sense. Why she'd leave him here? Why not send for him?'

But Habib didn't answer, maybe because Lee wasn't asking. Instead, Habib looked at his watch and said something about having to be at practice. He reached for the eye drops and the antibiotics and tucked them in Lee's jacket pocket.

'Frankie liked to stand near the Village dock where the sidewalk was cracked and local kids did wheelies on their bikes and skateboards before the Progress Nazis gave Little Ridge its face lift. He'd stand there straddling that crack in the stone with that crazy grin on his face. Remember? And he'd tell you about how she'd promised to come back for him one day.'

They both turned to the window and pointed to where the island had once again dropped beneath the mist, and where Frankie said he'd be waiting for her. Always.

*****

The steering wheel felt rubbery in Lee's hands. The station wagon driving itself, seemed like, off the highway and down the dirt road to Triangle Gully and the old Harpur settlement. The day's outlines had begun to lose their integrity and it was difficult to gauge whether the car would fit through the weeds and briars that had long closed over the road. Lee steered it carefully down the purplish descent. The car had filled with mosquitoes. A shack materialized, cow parsley growing by a fence. Lee could smell the creek but not see it. More outbuildings and a trailer. Finally, the matte green stripe of water flashed below, along with some disused shacks, the moorings and docks empty of the float homes and houseboats that had for generations been home to the Harpurs.

Lee got out. From the trailer by the side of the dirt access road, lace curtains dropped shut. There were animal pens beside the trailer. A lone sow rooted. Raccoons dragged a lumpen plastic bag across the dirt, and an albino mastiff-cross slinked toward him from around the wheels of a Ford F-150.

Lee took a step back, heard an unmistakable click.

'I suspect you've come to the wrong place.'

He turned slowly to face a woman of advanced years in possession of a Mossberg rifle aimed at his heart, and because of that and the way the dog's pale lip was pulled back from grooved yellow teeth Lee agreed that yes, he probably had.

5. GUNS

BOOM-BOOM-BOOM. Thettie stood down by the lake and listened to the lake farts. She needed to get her head right before seeing Frankie. The setting sun made the water bloody between her toes. The campground would throw them out in a month—the season ended on Halloween— management needed any excuse to get the Harpurs gone.

In point of fact, the Harpurs included many families bound by blood or marriage—Thettie herself was related to the Tullys, the McCormacks, and the Webbs—who, like Thettie, could trace their line all the way back to John Washington, George's great-grandfather. John W. was a rich planter and slaveholder who the Iroquois called 'Conotocaurious,' which means destroyer of towns. And years later, George W. earned the same name on account of the Iroquois villages *he* destroyed during the Revolution. Frankie would say that Thettie's people owed their existence to the big guns from both sides and it was just a matter of finding room to move between bad and worse.

She lit a cigarette and curled her toes around the smooth pebbles beneath the crimson water. Tried to think but the lake farts made that hard to do. *Boom-*

boom. The lake farts were also called lake guns, and this Sunday afternoon, guns were what they sounded like. It seemed like a stretch but Thettie thought she recognized the report of Frankie's own Winchester, the beautifully restored .303 that Sarey bought for him with the savings from her salves. Thettie closed her eyes and the sunset blossomed on the inside of her eyelid like an opened vein.

The sooner they got Frankie from Nose Island and moved on, the better. She didn't care where. California maybe. But that had been Cassie's dream, not hers. Since leaving Frankie behind Thettie hadn't dared to dream much.

Boom-boom-boom.

Doc had a fancy word for the ghostly guns, but she just knew them as lake farts. Underwater caves collapsing. Trapped bio-gas or the Lake Monster blowing raspberries or Frankie firing off his rounds—you used to be able to buy Lake Monster merchandise at Mack's Drug Store, before it became Maxine's Pie Kitchen. Before the racks of porno magazines gave way to jars of organic jams swinging from their nooses of curling ribbon in the store window. She'd noticed that on arrival, among all the other changes in Little Ridge. Arrival—two days ago, Friday, the day she ran into the cute guy with the hamburger meat. Boom.

Some shadowy lake weed slithered near her ankles, fleet and dark as bacteria. Peering into the water, she thought it might be a shoal of minnows. She overbalanced leaning forward, tried to scoop one up in her hands and recoiled. It wasn't lake weed and it wasn't fish either. It was as slimy as an oil slick but shadowy across her arm, like something had come between it and the sun. Greasy, too. And alive. It wormed through her fingers and up her arm and she had to shake it off, flip it into the lake.

Boom-boom.

'Mistpouffers,' said a high-pitched brogue over her shoulder.

Thettie wheeled around splashing water, but couldn't see him at first. Her chest squeezed. The sunset reflected pale arrows of light from between the trees and between them emerged a black shape against the light, a null space. Thettie could swear for a moment that something was burning, but she always smelled burned flesh around Doc. Must be the scars.

'You scared me,' she lied to the shape. Thettie wasn't scared of Doc, at least not as scared as she was of herself. But don't tell him that.

'Boom,' said Doc.

She always knew there was something wrong with Doc Murphy, some malformation of his spirit that had nothing to do with the war, with the burns. But as he traded tree shadow for the soft light of the shore, he just seemed travel-worn like the rest of them. He wobbled for a moment on his feet like an aging bull. Her skin rippled at his approach—like hackles on one of Sarey's dogs. She felt her toes grip the lake stones. Struggled to keep the revulsion from her face.

'Mistpouffers,' he said, aiming a gun in the direction of the island. He was up at four a.m. every day of the year, but he didn't seem to sleep. How many times had she woken in the night to find him sitting on the edge of the bed staring at her? 'Mistpouffers.'

'We used to call them lake farts when we were kids,' Thettie said, shaking a cigarette from her pack.

'Of course Grif told Archy it was the lake monster popping off because he was hungry for little boys. Half scared him to death.'

Doc leaned in and she could see in the flare of the Zippo he held out to her, how he had his work face on, which meant he was focused on hurting something other than her. Doc wasn't a monster. He was just hungry, and over the years the hunger had emptied him out until that's all he was.

'You think Frankie knows we're here?' she said.

Doc turned and looked to where she was looking. Out at the island.

Doc and Frankie had met in Afghanistan in '01, cut their palms and mashed them together between dawn patrols in Bagram Province. *Boom*. Doc was the company medic—had the fake degree to prove it.

Frankie told her and anyone who'd listen how Doc saved him for Thettie. Pulled him out of a burning school because of a picture of Thettie on Frankie's computer—Doc always said that picture was what did it for him, made him know that what was between Frankie and Thettie was something special. So when Doc turned up at Triangle Gully a year later—'02 or '03—his face thorny with a savior's scars, Frankie expected all of them, but Thettie especially, to give him a hero's welcome. The savior comes to Earth. Didn't matter that Frankie's frag wounds never healed and started working their way from his foot to his brain via his heart—he was alive was all that mattered. He was saved.

'Some savior,' Sarey said with her lips tight.

Doc saving Frankie changed everything, the way it would change her if Beyoncé gave Thettie a clipboard and a monthly paycheck. You'd be so grateful that a part of you would become lost in the rearview mirror. That gratitude, that sense of being saved from the worst part of yourself would carve you out and you'd project whatever you had left onto that other person. And that's what Frankie offered Doc.

Doc took it too, because every savior must have their pound of flesh.

Sarey just said Frankie was Doc's bitch. Frankie moved out after that. Slept in the car, or on the floor of the shed where he and Doc cooked their drugs. Thettie tried to get Sarey to take it back, but some things, once said, can never be unsaid.

Doc this and Doc that. Well, it was true. Thettie'd be the same with Beyoncé. Yes, Queen B. No Queen B. Except Doc wasn't Beyoncé. He was self-made in a way Thettie couldn't fathom. Sarey said he was like something jacked-off into being. Like one of those Greek Titans Frankie was always telling her about—offspring who ate their dysfunctional parents to save on therapy. Doc was that. Even walked and talked like a Titan, like just fixing his eye on something could make it his.

Doc was a master of spin, an independent fixer to the power of n, Frankie claimed, his blue eyes shining with love. In other words, Doc brokered an alliance with the deGroots and made Sheriff Boyle go away. If Doc was the spin doctor, Frankie was the mix-master, ran the joke between them. Welcome to the Dream Team. Frankie cooked and Doc distributed, mainly to the armed forces via Fort Drum, via a complex and hidden network of connections. Smooth as silt, Sarey said, spitting a fat loogie into the dirt with a plop that scattered the crows.

'I wouldn't be here if it wasn't for Doc,' Frankie insisted, like it was a good thing.

But Frankie sold himself short, even then. Because he was one hell of a chemist.

Problem was what Doc wanted from Thettie. Like he had it all planned before he even left Bagram. Thettie told him from the get-go that she wasn't that kind of girl. That she had commitment issues and whatnot—what he saw was not what he'd get.

'I never want just what I can see,' he said, taking her in his hungry arms. 'Why limit myself?'

Boom. Doc didn't scare her but he chilled her with his smarts and his will. She'd have been an accessory if she stayed and a fugitive if she returned, Doc said. And he was right. Mostly. After the boys nearly drowned that time, Doc never let her forget it.

'I pulled those boys out of the lake time and again with my own two hands,' he would say.

'You pulled them out once,' she corrected him, except Doc was smart enough to know that in Thettie's mind it was the event that never stopped happening.

'Once was enough,' Doc said. The point being that he hadn't raised those boys—with an emphasis on *raised*—like his own, just so he could see them fostered out. So she stayed away—from the sheriff, from the Feds and from Frankie. And she got lighter every year from the pounds of flesh Doc ate, like a true Titan, until there was barely nothing left of her at all.

***

'You think Frankie'll see you?' she said. 'You'll think he'll see any of us?'

Doc said with a flutter of his lashless eyes: 'That's where you come in.'

'I was never out.'

'You're the key to Frankie,' he said. 'I brought you back just like I always said I would.'

That was another lie, but Thettie knew the thing was to keep Doc focused. Keep his eye on the big picture. 'Ten years but okay. We're back.'

'I heard you already got yourself another secret admirer. Arty type with a strange taste in house pets.'

'Facing my fears.' But her mouth grew dry. Not at the thought of Lee's lizard, but of how Doc had made it his business to find out about it this time—she'd had a lot of secret admirers he didn't stop to care about. 'Back to Frankie. How am I the key?'

Something moved across his gray eyes like dirty slush sliding across a windscreen. 'He'll forgive. Once you tell him I brought you back like I said I would if he kept quiet, he'll be ready to put it behind him. We all will.'

Another one of those shadowy black things swam across her feet. She took Doc's maimed hand, tried to lead him away from the lake, but he held his ground. 'Frankie wouldn't rat, Doc. But the girls tell me things. He's got some security system rigged out on that island, is what my girls say. Mines and dogs, Doc. Big-ass dogs.'

'Christ on a crutch, girl, you have a mouth. How does a low-down piece of ass like you get a mouth like that?'

Archy would say that the only thing Doc hated more than dogs was himself for hating them.

She braced, smiling a little, thinking—maybe even hoping— he was going to hit her for trying to use his one fear against him, but that would have been like admitting he had one. It would have been like giving it a name (dogs) and he could never do that because the only thing a Titan fears is fear itself. But he didn't hit her. Just took the cigarette from her fingers, and breathed the smoke out through his burned-off nose.

'Sorry, Doc. Don't shoot the messenger. My girls are my eyes and ears.'

'You think give a fuck about your slag bitches?'

The Irish insults were reassuring. Like being hit without the actual bruises. Meant he'd let off some steam and was recalibrating. Because behind the scheming and the eliminating and the rubber-gloved secrets, what kept Doc going was what he couldn't see. Total vantage point, Frankie called it, the Big Picture— until he was the one who got lost in it. Doc pointed out to the lake with his amputated trigger finger.

'Forest Path,' he said. 'Shortie told me what Frankie's doing out there. The killer mix.'

'Bryce? On the island? That what she told you?' Thettie tried to cast her mind back to that bend in the river where Doc had found the girl struggling with her stricken inflatable. Thettie had made Grif take her back there, searching for signs of the poachers that had supposedly brought the girl down. The water wasn't even a meter deep. 'You believe her?'

His eyes, focused at an invisible point behind Thettie, said he did. Totally.

'Doc, Frankie might not even be there.'

Except she knew he was.

'He's giving us a warning,' Doc jutted his chin toward the lake. His brogue rose to a rasping whine around his fire-damaged vocal cords. 'That's what you're doing, right, Frankie? Testing the mines.

Sending us a message. Surprise, surprise, that ain't no lake fart!'

Thettie listened but all she heard now was the lap and tinkle of the boats, and the soft muffled sounds of her people getting ready to call it a day.

'What kind of killer mix?'

'Like DMT but no cooking. Christ on a crutch, girl, I can feel it in my bones. A new day, a new dawn.' He puffed out his chest, his combat boots spread wide across the stones.

'If he's got security, how're we going to get by it?'

A black tongue of lake water licked her heel and she stepped out of its reach, which brought her closer to Doc.

'Let's have a party,' Doc said. The chemical smell of his cologne and the detergent on his clothes—he'd been to the laundromat already—made her eyes sting. He pulled out a wad of cash and stuffed it down the front of her jeans, his finger-stump digging beneath her panties and her naked toes jammed between his combat boots.

'That old tavern on the highway. Tell everyone the drinks are on me. Make a crowd so's the locals know we're back, and word gets to Frankie. Draw him out. Only one who can do it is you.'

Thettie tried to stay calm. 'You can't tell me that place isn't closed down by now.'

'Who knows? Maybe your secret admirer'll be there.'

And then he was gone, his combat boots crunching across the stones until there was silence again, not even the lake guns. Just the impure beat of her heart.

6. THE WAY

LEE GOT BACK into his car, no longer in the mood for a Henksville pizza but not ready for a hunger-striking Gila monster and Netflix either. Instead, he remembered two things. That the Way also sold pizza—and Lee could get one to go—and also what Grif Harpur had said about the welcome-home party. That *she* might be there. Lee had not stalked a woman since college. He had not wanted to.

He pulled into the small dirt and gravel parking area in front of the Way Out Tavern off of the Interstate, which—thanks to the Harpurs—was in full swing.

Lee had not been in a bar for five years. He'd dreamt about them. He'd sat outside. He'd driven city blocks around wine bars and basement bourbon clubs. He'd driven county circles around Motel 6 lounges and college juke joints. In some of his memories, bars were velvet arcades, fragrant with fleshy secrets and alive with the melodic tinkle of ice. In others, he was alone at noon in an upstairs room that smelled of black lace and brown shoes and the dregs in the glass were webbed with blood, like an eye.

Lee felt like he'd come home. The line at the bar was five deep and grumbling. Plenty of time for Lee to change his mind. He did not. He ordered a beer and a shot of Grants. He turned to survey the crowd, which was clearly divided into Harpurs and nons.

The Harpurs were rowdy but small in number. There were fifteen or twenty of them, but noisily and in great gulps they drank up all the air in the room. A grim quietude was all the locals could muster in response—mainly deGroots—rangy, toothy alfalfa barons and their sons lined up against a wall, watching and waiting for someone to make the wrong move.

But no one did. Because tonight it was all about the Harpurs, mainly the women. It was what they did with what they had. It was how they knew when to let bad blood flow and how to keep it at bay, and tonight was all about the latter. They slunk through the crowds in their strappy dresses, denim jackets and boots, ropy in the arms and narrow in the waist from those hungry weeks on the river. They went about the business of cadging drinks and feeding the juke and keeping conversation flowing. The pizza was terrible but that didn't stop them eating. There wasn't a dance floor but that didn't stop them dancing. The passage between the main bar and the pool tables thronged with slim hips and bare shoulders. And if their flesh was firmer, or their gazes more lingering than the farm girls or scattered co-eds slumming in from the town, it was more than that. It was how they moved with an alien grace that carried with it a promise as uncertain as it was irresistible. Something half remembered and desired in full.

Lee scanned the crowd for Thettie Harpur. He told himself that as soon as he saw her and said hello he'd leave. He told himself he just wanted to apologize for banging into her at the store, his mind on Vernon. His pulse raced with the things you could say to a woman like that, and his blood sang with the liquor. And then, he heard someone calling his name.

It was the man he'd met on the dock, Grif Harpur, waving him outside toward the looping bulbs hanging from the sycamore trees.

Lee bought another beer and went outside.

'Fallen off the wagon, Lizard Man?'

'Thought I'd walk alongside it a while. Take in the view.'

Grif wore semi-clean Levis and the same biker jacket he had on earlier. The smell of the lake clung to him and to the rest of the men with him. They were tall and strangely pale, with dull hair of all colors that stuck out from their heads or fell down their shoulders. Lee got glimpses of Norse blades sheathed in leather through the smoke, the cold steel of Saturday night specials and dull-looking saps of hide and lake rock. But they kept their talk on the fenders they fixed or brownies they'd caught or girls they'd left behind. They drank and smoked and kept to themselves, febrile and lethal, content to leave the hard espionage work to their women, because for the men, information was gleaned with a different kind of exchange.

Grif passed him a joint and Lee drew on it and passed it on, lifting his stinging eye to the looping lights blurred in October foliage. Grif did not mention his mother and Lee did not ask. He finished his beer and told himself yet again that it was time to leave. After five years sober, the only effect of the weed and the beers, it seemed to him, was to make him want to piss. The rest-room doors banged open and shut and there was a steady stream of men and women in both, hands in their pockets as they went in and sniffing as they went out. Lee was prepared to bet that this many women under fifty with all their own teeth, hadn't been seen at the Way since the moonshine years. The college girls and the townies mainly patronized a dive bar in the Village called the Pump, or the Lakeview, or the Inn for date nights, or they drove down to Ilium. The Way Out Tavern wasn't for townies. It was for hicks and hands and truckers and traders. The haunted and the hunted and the end-of-the-liners. All here in force, being worked by the Harpur women tonight. Worked for drinks and juke money, for rumor and speculation and hearsay. For information about what happened to their homes, why they'd been pulled down and by whom.

And mainly about Frankie. About where he'd gone with his wounds and his grudge. About who was with him, and who against.

And the island. Had anyone been there? Had Frankie really laid mines? Were there dogs or just men keeping the watch? What kind of men?

The floor felt far away, and the scent of perfume in the air made Lee cry a little. The Harpur girls' eyes were oceanic but their laughter was warm and a little throaty with a song at its ragged edge. They laughed with each other and with the farmhands and the alfalfa barons as they slunk around like cats, all cheap perfume and dirty purrs. Their IDs were as fake as their Columbia jackets, but they knew their way around a pool cue and a Levi zipper, their dirty talk less from an intent to spin a web of lies than to catch in its tensile threads a wing of truth.

ALETHEIA

Because all around him, Lee could see the locals scratching their heads as they tried to think when the last time it was they saw Frankie Harpur.

Lee overheard a pizza delivery boy trying to describe to a Harper girl, the grandeur of the big old manor house Frankie inherited. But the pizza boy could not tell the girl if it was Frankie who answered his knock or someone else. Father-and-son firefighters bragged to another girl about the trip wires and mines Frankie was supposed to have laid around the island. The Harpur girl listened, all eye shine and push-up bra—trying to pick pure gospel from a can of worms. And Lee began to wonder if the truth, when and if you finally found it, was poor compensation for the years lost in the hunt.

A young man walked through who looked so much like Thettie Harper that Lee wondered if it was her brother. The same pretty mouth and shaggy head of hair, the same delicate bone structure. Silver rings on his fingers.

Lee stumbled after the man into the pool room but what he saw there arrested his pursuit, arrested everything. It was a girl playing pool. Her hair was shorn like a boy's and she had one eye. She wore red lipstick and her eye patch, more harrowing than piratical, seemed to eat up all the light. Her skin was pale like the rest of the Harpers, but with the cool, slightly impure quality of petals or bone. Her good eye, heavy lidded, narrowed as she bent to take a shot. A matted black sweater flapped around her narrow waist, and she wore unfashionable camouflage-print jeans. Her feet, naked in sandals despite the season, were as slim and smooth as a child's.

Lee felt something cold spill through his guts, and there was a sudden shift in the atmosphere of the room. The younger Harpur man had disappeared but Grif had come inside, his wide mouth wrapped around a dead cigar, and his gaze glued to the one-eyed girl's reflection in the bar mirror. Other men joined him, pasty and nervous behind the flap of cigarette paper. They stood ill at ease against the wall, and their glances arced between her and him.

'Take a number,' said a familiar voice behind him.

It was a nice voice. Without turning around, Lee said, 'She's too young for me.'

'Bullshit,' Thettie Harpur said. 'Men act like gentlemen only when they have to.'

She stepped up beside him. She wore a white sleeveless sweater that showed off her figure, and a tight skirt above black boots. She had on a shimmer of lipstick. Freckles dusted her high cheekbones like fool's gold. He asked if he could buy her a drink and came back with two beers. He said he'd met one of her sons, Grif, and she said he wasn't her son but might as well be. Her born son, Archy, was somewhere around. Sulking, because the one-eyed girl had dumped him.

'That was your son?' Lee said.

'For my sins,' Thettie Harpur answered, only half joking. 'He's never taken it so hard before.'

'First cut is the deepest,' Lee said.

'Second one stings like hell, though,' at that she laughed, a warm, prickly laugh that took the chill away from him. 'I'm Thettie Harper.'

'Lee Montour.'

'I know.'

A waitress came by and they ordered more drinks.

Lee asked how long the Harpurs were staying.

'We have some business out on the island. You ever been there?'

Lee regarded the one-eyed girl. 'Close.'

'Well Frankie's made it all the way. He's my cousin.'

'I know.'

Thettie cocked her head at him. 'You seen him?'

Lee was about to explain how he'd scoured the lake in all directions in Frankie's old canoe and every time he got close to the island, some current, some squall—something—got him all turned around. But Thettie stopped him with a sideways flick of her eyes. Lee turned to see Jason deGroot walk in.

'Who's that?' she said.

When Lee told her, she blanched, looked another question at him that she decided against asking, and her cut-glass eyes softened. 'He looks sick,' she said. 'What's wrong with him?'

'Borderline schizophrenia,' Lee said. 'Possibly related to his abuse of the family crop . . . .'

'Devil's Butt,' she said with a sad smile.

'Levelled out with Xanax and speed,' Lee said. 'Which your cousin Frankie allegedly supplied back in the day. After Frankie left for the island, I think Jason missed him.'

'That makes two of us,' she said.

Lee got what people saw in Jason deGroot, that punk-metal adaptability, a refusal to be one thing or another. The trench coat and backpack stuffed with Borges, his hair stuck up around his blue eyes in a toxic orange double Mohawk—like a chimera, Habib would say. An impossible dream.

'Anyway,' Thettie said. 'Soon as we get what we came for, we'll be on our way. Place is not what it was. And they tore down our homes. So there's that.'

Jason caught sight of Lee and his mouth bunched around a gap in his teeth. He hitched up his backpack and started feeding the juke.

'You have the Progress Association to thank for the new-look Little Ridge. Sunny Weeks is its director but she's backed by the college. She wins, the town wins, is how they see it.'

'Everyone a winner except the ones whose homes they pulled down,' Thettie said.

Then Grif came over, nodded at Lee, and Thettie asked if he'd seen Archy. He said he was here somewhere, and did she want him to find him? And Thettie said, with a sudden shudder, best leave him be. Grif reached across and gently pulled a strand of his mother's hair from her face and said someone must be walking over her grave, and then he swaggered off, throwing Lee a lewd wink.

'What do you paint?' her voice soft and warm.

Lee said, 'Mainly the lake. And the island.'

'Not people?' her words slipped into each other.

Lee shook his head, 'I paint Vernon.' He pulled out his phone. 'If that counts.'

'Your monster?'

But when he tried to show her a picture, she pushed his hand away.

'I'm not a fan,' she said. 'Remember?'

There was a brief cold wind as someone opened the door. Thettie's expression hardened and Lee turned around. A man stood before the closing door, his clean-shaven face looking like it had broken fingernails growing from it. One corner of the man's mouth was fused closed by a puce flap of flesh. Powerful shoulders beneath a great-coat squared off against an unseen enemy. Desert combat boots braced for impact. The bar staff looked chastened. Some of them saluted. Others blinked away tears. The man was flanked by two other creatures; the bearded flabby man with the scars around his neck Lee had seen on the boat, and a smaller guy, damp-eyed, covered in facial tattoos, jittery as a burnt-out boxer.

'Doc Murphy,' Lee heard someone say. 'The war hero.'

And when Lee looked across at the mask now drawn across Thettie's face, he knew that must be the man she left Frankie for.

The wall of deGroots stiffened but no one made a move. Doc Murphy walked unencumbered to a table, and his fat minder called over a waitress. And then it was as if a laser beam had newly triangulated between their table, and the deGroots along the wall near the door, and Jason, alone and feeding money into the pinball machine beside the pool table.

Thettie shook a cigarette from a pack with her fine hands and talked Lee into going outside with her. She asked him, swaying a little beneath the fairy-lit sycamore, what else he did for fun besides paint his lizard. The yard had begun to empty, just a few dark shadows mumbling at its edges. Stars tumbled through the cloud.

'I paint the lake, too,' he said. 'Mainly that.'

'How long have you been here?' she passed him her cigarette and he shook his head.

He told her ten years, ever since he'd followed Habib to the lab.

Habib?'

'My PhD advisor. We set up a lab here.'

'To study what?'

'The neural mechanisms of memory,' he said. 'How it works in the brain. Habib was somewhat of a big shot in the area once. Nobel finalist, NY Times bestseller . . . '

'That was right about when I left,' Thettie said, swinging her boots back and forth above the ground. 'Maybe I should have stayed.'

'I guess that's what I'm afraid of, too,' he said. 'Like the Clash song.'

'Me, Frankie and my cousin Cassie—we each had our favorite band. Frankie's was the Stranglers. Cassie was Patti Smith. Everything Patti. I was the Clash. '*Should I stay or should I go?*" She smiled sadly. 'I forgot the rest.'

"*If I go it will be trouble, if I stay it will be double.*"

Her mouth trembled and she seemed to fight for control. 'So, these paintings of yours. They're your ticket out of this place?'

'They're my ticket to somewhere.'

'Somewhere is good,' she said, looking through the crowd. Maybe, to see if the war hero was still there.

Her wheaten hair caught the colored bulbs from the sycamore tree. A few locals made out with Harper girls in the shadows at the edge of the yard. Doc Murphy came out to the yard, holding court with some local toughs, his slippery vowels carrying across the yard. None of them were deGroots except for Jason, who stood there rapt, like he'd looked in the early days of the lab whenever Habib had walked into the room—

like the sun had just come out. Doc Murphy's handlers stood facing out to the crowd.

'You want pizza?' Lee said.

'I'd kill for some,' she said softly.

They moved back inside and sat on the edge of the pool table. She entwined her fingers around his. Dancers clutched each other near the juke box. Some of the alfalfa farmers remained by the wall. Talking about reservist training, or reciting crop reports in booming voices, barflies fixing their gaze on the late-night fights.

'Tell me, why the lizard?'

The juke surged then, some keyboard riff Lee remembered from his college days. He leaned in closer so he wouldn't have to yell. Her hair felt coarse against his lips, like the mane of a colt. 'Vernon came to Little Ridge with us from UNM. He worked in the lab with us.'

She waited. 'And?'

And Vernon waited alone in Lee's studio, far from home beside the animal boneyard and the fathomless lake.

'And we found that Gila monster venom has a peptide we called Helotide that can open doors into neural paths that we didn't know were there.'

'Can people take it?' she said.

'We never got a chance to find out.'

And then she took his hot hands in her cool ones, and said, 'About that pizza.'

Lee went up to order but the kitchen was closed. Avery said he'd dig around for some peanuts. Lee went to the restroom. On his way, he saw through a window out onto the parking lot, that Jason deGroot and Doc

Murphy's minders had moved outside and were talking beside Jason's truck.

Lee peed next to a huffing deGroot, one of Jason's uncles maybe, or maybe his old man. Lee leaned against the mirror to inspect his eye. The angry nest of burst capillaries had faded to a pallid scrawl and it didn't hurt as much anymore. The deGroot man pushed out of the bathroom without washing his hands. Lee would be forty on Christmas Eve. He splashed water on his face and cleaned his glasses. He had paint on his corduroy shirt, which he'd bought from SEARS for the buttons. They were smooth tiered disks with three thread-holes stamped into an inner tier. They were made from a vegetable ivory material patented in Rochester, NY. No two buttons were alike, not exactly, to mimic something carved from real bone.

When he got back to Thettie, she was combing shadows into her hair with her fingers, and working her way through a packet of Funyuns from the vending machine.

'You married?' she said.

'Not anymore.'

'Kids?'

'Not anymore.'

Thettie's grave smile froze as she watched him.

Lee had forgotten to tuck his shirt back in. The two bottom buttons were undone, one hanging by a thread. He pressed it against the corduroy, held it there between his thumb and forefinger.

'My son was kidnapped when he was seven, but they never found his body. My wife killed herself a year later.'

Thettie stopped with a Funyun halfway to her mouth.

'Let me guess,' she said. 'It was a Sunday.'

She put the Funyun back in the packet, then she bought another round. It was the last call. The bar emptied and the chairs went up. The bite of Lysol overlaid the sell of spilled beer and cigarettes and the only light that remained was a midnight sun above the pool table. The only sound that of Avery counting the takings.

Lee stroked Thettie Harpur's fine-boned hand but could not meet her eyes when he asked her to come up and see his etchings.

'Vernon's in a tank,' Lee said. 'He can't get out.'

Three's a crowd, she told him, at least when it comes to venomous lizards. So instead she took him back to her trailer nestled beneath a pine tree with a bed at one end that looked over the lake. And when he finally made it home at dawn, Sunday was gone and so was Vernon.

7. LAKE

DAWN'S **YELLOW FINGER** scratched at the window of the trailer, and Thettie shrank from it.

Thettie's parents were maybe first cousins, or maybe brother and stepsister. She never knew which 'uncle' was her actual daddy. Her Uncle Ellis was hands everywhere, whenever he thought Thettie's mother wasn't looking, until one day Thettie's mother put some special powder in Uncle Ellis' oatmeal to make one of his testicles blow up the size of a melon and grow a mouth so it could eat the other one. Thettie overheard Ellis' girlfriend screaming at him to get his giant hungry ball sack out of her face or she'd leave him, which she did anyway. Men were blind, Thettie's mother always told her. The trick was to make it work for you, find room to move in their blind spot.

'You're all lucky you got me,' Doc liked to tell them.

Every man had a blind spot and Doc was no exception—but Thettie hadn't found his yet. So in the meantime, Yes, Doc, she said. They *were* lucky to have him. He saw to it that she didn't forget it.

Doc wasn't a monster, not exactly, and maybe that was the problem. At least with the thing that took Lee's child, you knew that what you were up against was some kind of thing it'd sear your soul to think on.

ALETHEIA

Speaking of monsters, Lee seemed in a hurry to get back to his lizard, and Thettie listened to his station wagon leaving the parking lot, smiling to herself. She would like to just lie here and wait for him to come back. To believe he would.

What that monster did to his child. In Thettie's thinking, that was the difference between monsters and men who, however much they dress up like monsters, are underneath just men. Men like Doc who want to take over worlds more than creating new ones to rule. Doc and his ilk just don't have that creative bent. They prefer to leave their kills whole like trophies you mount on a wall. Or scalps. It's a different kind of a hunter that chops up its prey in little pieces so no one can find it, so it's just their little monster-secret—no. Men in the real world prefer to get the credit for their kills. And the best way to do that was to have a body count you could brag about. A body count in whole numbers, not fractions.

Poor Lee.

His scent was still on the pillow and she hugged it to her breasts. She sickened at the little that he told her, how pieces of his son's body were still missing somewhere in the lake, an absence that pinned him to this place like a butterfly on a board. She recalled how Doc had pulled her boys from the lake, too, saved them from another kind of monster—a mother—and in saving them had pinned her to a different kind of place. But it was still a pin, just the same.

Doc would tell her to look at him, tell him what she saw.

But you can't see a man in a monster mask, she discovered, especially one who doesn't know it's a mask.

It took a lot of explaining to the boys when they were young why Uncle Frank couldn't come with them to Pennsylvania. It wasn't because he didn't want to, she said. It was just because he was sick, she said, but he'd be here when he got better. Except it wasn't Frankie that had to get better. It was her.

She listened for sounds of the Harpurs rising, but the campground was silent in sleep, and the light coming in through the window still uncertain, still not committed to the day.

'See you soon,' Lee'd said. He had to see to Vernon and then he'd be back.

Actually, Frankie wasn't a real uncle, more a distant cousin. Not that it didn't make him as much a father to Archy and Grif as they'd ever know, but Harpurs didn't have much truck in fathers. Archy's father had been a migrant worker on a dairy farm at Forge Grove, upstate. Half-Mexican, half-Greek, he said. She'd never seen him again. But Arch had the herding streak in him, a feel for the four-legged. Had talked about becoming a vet, could break anything that ate. Cats, snakes, horses, dogs. One day, jealous over the attention she'd been lavishing on the mute interloper Grif, Archy came home bearing a hatful of skinks that had crawled into it for some unexplained reason. Thettie made Archy toss them off the porch into the lake. He did what he was told and then ran away from home for three days. It was Grif who found him along the leaf-clogged railway tracks halfway to Canada. Archy said he was going to find his father. Grif brought him back to Triangle Creek, stood back to let Thettie sweep her runaway son up in her arms, until she pulled Grif to her too, and he finally let himself be caught up in their three-headed embrace—from then on, always both their hearts that Thettie would feel racing against her own.

Thettie thought she heard a footfall outside, wondered if it was Lee coming back as he'd promised. She swung her legs off the little bed at one end, and shook out a cigarette. The Winnebago was separated from the rest of the campground and stood by itself on a slight rise that hugged the tree line. From the wind-scraped window over the bed, you could see all the way to the island, almost visible through the mist. The larger outcrop breached the water like the blunt muzzle of a primeval beast, behind it the smaller rock poking up through the black water looked like a spine, or the tip of a tail.

She waited for the knock on the door, but it didn't come.

Like she told Lee, Frankie was the only one she knew who'd ever been to the island or so he claimed. Managed to push through the squalls and lake-effect weather that surrounded it like a force-field, he said. The blueberries growing there had been the juiciest he'd ever eaten, he said. And the sweetest. Aunt Sarey whooped him firstly for trying to get to the island, and secondly for eating anything that could grow on such a god-forsaken place, contaminated with leprosy, radiation and what all else, she said. And Frankie's eyes, when he snuck out to meet Thettie and Cassie at Harpur Falls to tell them all about it, *were* a little radioactive that night. It was like a drug, he would say, like heroin, actually setting foot on the island. Steering his inflatable into the tiny access inlet. Total reality, he said, arcing a circle in the dark with the glowing flat of his hand. Everything unconcealed.

'Bullsheet!' Cassie said, took out her guitar, and started playing the chords from 'Space Monkey.' Frankie liked the Stranglers, but with Cassie it was always Patti Smith.

Frankie never talked about the island again.

Forgive me Frankie. I always said I'd be back and here I am.

The lake was a strangled blue. The sun hesitated atop the ridge, like it was scared to go any further. But abruptly it did, and the yellow light of morning peeled across the lake to the island, and the guns rolled in, boom-boom-boom, and the island dove beneath the surface once more. Thettie's cigarette dropped from her fingers. Her legs grew cold. Through the window she saw something begin to snake across the lake toward shore, a black flattened shadow side-winding across the surface, feathering out in scrolls of black that seemed to be flowing in at the same time as they slithered out.

Thettie's flesh crawled. She remembered the oily slick or strange weed that had stuck to her wrist the day before, was gripped in a cold unease, and determined to walk it off. It was Cassie who got the skeevies, not Thettie. She slipped into her sneakers and unhooked Archy's cast-off pea coat from its nail. She pushed out the door of the cabin through the slumbering camp ground toward the tideline. By the time she got there the snaking slither was gone and all that was left was the water churned up and the smell at the back of her throat of something she couldn't place—vaguely pukey but metallic too. She visored her hands over her eyes and scanned the lake for the thing she'd seen dragging through the water. She searched the area where it had carved its path. The surface was a paler blue than the rest of the lake, and flecked with a dissipating black foam. The foam ended five hundred yards past the jetty where Triangle Creek emptied into a deep basin of lake, where her boys had nearly drowned all those years ago before Doc saved them.

Satisfied the lake was empty once more, she turned to go back to the cabin but caught Bryce at the edge of her eye, like something just winked into being. She was fishing on her belly off the end of the jetty and dangled a hand line into the water. As Thettie watched, the line grew taut and she shoved her fists into the pockets of the coat and felt her feet moving before she could stop them. Bryce tugged at the line, trying to pull herself upright. It tugged back and the girl had to hang onto the edge with one hand and hold the line with the other, wrap her legs around the post like a space monkey.

Thettie froze. One more tug and out it came.

It was a baby. Thettie's hand flew to her mouth and she screamed between her fingers, couldn't stop screaming. The girl stood and dangled the thing off her line. Black goo dripped off its body. The hook in its eye. Thettie started running along the jetty, slipping in her sneakers and still screaming. Pulled up a ways behind the girl, who turned and smiled, her little teeth carnivorous in the dark hole of her mouth and her eye patch askew, pushing her short hair up in clownish tufts. She called something out to Thettie, who didn't realize what she was saying until she got right up to her.

'It's a doll.'

Lake weed snaked in one eye. The hook pierced the

empty socket of the other. 'Oh my God,' was all Thettie could think of to say. 'It's got a ding-dong and all.'

The little rubber penis nestled in the swollen sack, half torn off by some groper. The reptilian mouth crammed with lake trash.

Thettie clenched her teeth in rage. 'That has to be the creepiest goddamn thing I ever saw.'

But it wasn't just the doll, it was what had got to it. Half its bald head had been clawed away, and a bite was taken out of its tiny chest. It was smeared with the same creepy goo that had leeched to Thettie's flesh the day before.

Thettie looked down the pale channel of black-flecked water to the island, and she felt the rage in her building, rage for the water rat, rage for Little Ridge for its false hopes, rage for Doc. Even rage for Frankie over being left behind. There was a part of her that could have easily pushed both the doll and the girl back in, watched them sink, watched this all go away.

Instead, all she said was 'For God's sake, throw it back.'

Thettie turned around so she didn't have to see the hook come out of the empty eye socket, and so she could find her smokes, which she must have dropped along the way.

***

'You're all lucky you got me,' Doc liked to say to her on starless nights down at the Landing, lying beside her on his boat and lighting up one of her cigarettes. He didn't scare her. A man is only as good as his tools, he quipped, like it was ironic. He carried a medic's bag around with him when he called on the girls, Thettie included. He'd get out his rubber gloves and speculum. His scalpel, too.

'Be afraid,' he would say to her girls. 'Be very afraid.'

Thettie wasn't afraid. But she hated how he scared her girls, made them come crying to her more than once. That filled her with rage. Because they were her girls. She loved her sons like there was no tomorrow, but the Harpur girls, the Webbs and Tullys, her nieces and second cousins and goddaughters and sometimes lovers, were the daughters she'd never have. They were the women she'd never be, the sisters she'd fight for to the death.

Thettie shuddered, walking back to the shore. That one-eyed water rat could never be one of them.

The lake looked calm once more—the water as cold and clear as it should be. Her cigarette pack floated in the shallow water and Thettie stepped out to retrieve it while it was still in reach. She stood up and shook one out, actually managed to get it lit, while her white sneakers magnified and refracted beneath the water. She had nice feet, and good ankles. Trying to calm her breath, she closed her eyes and imagined her ankles wrapped around Lee's slim hips. He was older than he looked and gentler, too. And that cooled her rage.

8. MACHINE

THE FLIERS INCHED out of the machine. They showed Vernon in full color, the round black nostril holes and beady eye in the black face, a piece of pizza crust hanging from his scaled lips.

MISSING.

Lee had returned to the studio from Thettie's trailer to find Vernon's tank empty. No sign of a struggle beyond the crushed markers in the pet cemetery behind the house. No sign of anything else missing.

Lee's little family always planned to move once their son got older, once the cottage on campus became too small for the three of them. So, when a ranch home by the lake became available at the beginning of the semester in '05, soon after their arrival in Little Ridge, they took it. The yard sloped down to the shore and had a rope swing hanging from the big sugar maple, and the three of them took long walks in the woods behind the house with the ruined schoolhouse-turned-orphanage at its heart. There was a disused wooden shipping container dumped in a clearing from the previous family, who'd shipped their belongings from Athens, Greece. Lee and his wife converted the shipping container into a clubhouse for their son to play in. Lee sawed square holes for windows and helped his son attach scraps of material to the makeshift window frames with thumbtacks, for curtains.

Lee's wife joked that it looked a little like a trailer home, and now was their chance to learn how the other half lived.

They had cookouts on the shore, burgers and marshmallows roasted on a stick, and ate at the little wooden table, just the three of them. They took Frankie Harpur's old blue canoe out, snorkeled and fished. If there was one thing his wife said she missed in New Mexico, it was the lake. Since coming back, though, she'd become anxious about living so close to it with her own small child. She insisted that he wear a life jacket, and looked askance at how the water seemed to solidify at dusk, become purple and bloated like an over-ripe plum. But Lee reminded her that their son was nearly eight years old, and already, like his mother, a fearless water rat.

The house was at the northernmost edge of town, where the last homes gave way to the wooded headland. Their southern neighbor was Eli Zabriskie until Frankie Harpur blew Zabriskie's brains across a John Lafarge stained glass window that depicted the fleeing Goddess of Dawn. Frankie Harpur and his dogs lived there for a while after that—another source of anxiety for Lee's wife—until he abandoned the manor to live out on the island, at some point someone setting his old blue Indian canoe adrift to wash up on Lee's shore.

Lee had tried to return it to him numerous times.

On the other side of their house, half hidden in the

woods, stood the ruined schoolhouse, a mecca for unofficial Halloween partiers, truants and squatters. But Sunny Weeks, head of the Progress Association, had other ideas. She wanted Zabriskie Manor for her vintage toy museum, and Peachtree School for a function center. It was all part of her plan to save Little Ridge, she claimed, and she, Sunny Weeks, would be the one to save it.

Across the highway, a gas station sat on a lonely corner, and after that, nothing, unless you counted a small clapboard farmhouse on the other side of Main Street, set back all by itself in a field. The farmhouse had belonged to Bud Wallace, war veteran and ham radio nut and occasional wearer of women's underwear, but not, according to Sheriff Boyle, a kiddie snatcher.

The machine stopped. A red light flashed on the side. Lee took out the paper tray, slid another ream in and it started up again.

'Kiddie snatcher' was a terrible term and Lee wished they would not use it. If evil had a name, if you could specify and label it according to its various attributes, like a peptide or a protein, then it was hierarchical, which simply meant that some evil was purer—truer—than others.

Evil, eviler, evilest.

Meaning that some of its forms mapped more or less onto an ideal uppercase Evil—the Whole—while others were only a dim approximation. But then you had to ask, was evil better or worse, the further it got from its pure form of Evil—the Whole thing? And if it was purer in form, did that make it more forgivable or more damnable?

ALETHEIA

A ghostly report rolled in the distance and rattled the brushes he kept in a jar, yet the sky was clear and it wasn't thunder.

It was the Guns of the Seneca.

'Lake farts', as Thettie called them back in the little trailer where they had lain together like endangered creatures. She'd lit a candle in a wooden holder that she said her cousin Frankie had carved for her. It rolled waves of light across the walls and ceiling, like the cabin of a ship. There were no curtains across the window, and there was a skylight cut into the trailer ceiling above the bed.

Lee had come great distances to end up here in Little Ridge, but Habib would say that was just a matter of perspective. 'You can cut distance in half, and then in half again, and again, without ever actually reaching your destination. So, when you say distance, it's hard to say whether you mean from, or toward, a destination.'

Lee looked up from the machine at Habib's voice, but it was just in his head, a habitual source of comfort all the same. Habib was right. Lee had met his wife while doing her masters in biochemistry at UNM. But in a strange twist of fate, she had been born right here in Sullivan County. They'd gotten married at Habib's house in the Albuquerque foothills, and when Habib asked Lee to come east with him, right back here to Sullivan College, it surprised Lee how his wife didn't want to.

'I thought you were homesick,' he'd said. 'I thought you missed the lake.'

She'd shuddered. 'I miss it,' she said. 'But I don't know if I want to go back. It's cold. The winters are terrible. I don't know, Lee. You can never go home.'

They argued, which was unusual for them. Lee said she was being unreasonable, that it was his chance of a lifetime to make a real difference. To solve the mysteries of memory at a purpose-built lab—just him and Sam Habib. She accused him of loving Habib more than her, of loving his career more than their son. Lee stormed out. She apologized. He apologized. In the end, she agreed.

They found a good school for their son in Little Ridge. His wife connected with some biochemistry people at Cordell University. But for Lee, there was the lab. Working with his great friend, Professor Sammi Habib—his hero, a father to him, an uncle to his son. They had dinner together twice a week. They introduced Habib to Lee's wife's parents, and to her grandmother from whom she inherited her scientific mind. The grandmother and Habib played scrabble together. Habib tried to teach Lee's son his way around a soccer ball, helped the boy build a bird-feeder. Habib who was going to crack the secrets to memory. Habib, who was going to rid the world of forgetfulness, surely the greatest evil, if evil could be said to apply to a God who continually forgot what was in His heart.

Vernon's tank yawned empty as a grave.

The reptile lab had been part of shared venture between Sullivan College—propped up by Sunny Week's money—Cordell U., and Tantra Pharmaceuticals. Soon after opening the lab, Sami Habib began extracting a novel peptide called helokinestatin-5 from Vernon's saliva. They called it Helotide (patent pending).

Who could have taken Vernon from his tank, and why? Lee didn't think Vernon had broken out this time like he had twice in the past. There was no sandy trail on the floor, for one thing. And there was the matter of the crushed markers in the animal cemetery. Lee was no detective but the damage was not as extensive as it might have been from, say, a gang of drunken ghost-hunters on their way to the ruined schoolhouse. No, it looked to have been done by a lone trespasser, someone who possibly knew where he or she was going.

Lee had, while considering all this, wandered out to the animal graveyard. He knelt down beside an upended popsicle-stick marker that said, 'Thing 1.' He tried to stick it in the ground again, digging a hole with his finger until he made contact with the squelchy remains of the Wistar. Lee sprung away. A pale bone gleamed from the bottom of the indentation he'd made—possibly a tiny rib or a vertebra. Lee dug no further. He got up, dirt clinging to his knees, and went back inside to the grinding Xerox machine.

In lab and pre-clinical trials, Helotide dramatically improved learning in rats. There was strong evidence to suggest that it was both neuro-enhancing and neuro-protective by acting on unknown pathways in the hippocampus—a narrow ridge (two in humans and other mammals) located in the medial temporal lobe of the brain. Helotide demonstrably opened up untraveled neural pathways in the rat hippocampus by (hypothetically) activating protein-producing genes that enabled memories to be recorded.

From the six-figure salary Tantra Pharmaceuticals paid him, Habib was able to buy himself a boat, although he hated water, and a modern lakeside villa on the southern shore of Funes Lakes. Lee and his little family rented on campus for the first few years before getting their own dream house on the northern headland.

At the time of his child's disappearance, Lee had been supervising Jason deGroot's repair of the Morris water maze. Lee was training Sprague-Dawley rats in the maze, administering Helotide nasally and recording the extraordinary results. After ingestion of the peptide, the rats made it to the platform submerged beneath the surface of the milky water in half the time it took without it. There had, of course, already been conclusive evidence with foot-shocked mice in operant chambers, and fruit flies whose memory became photographic after ingesting Helotide, but Lee's work with rats clinched it. His career seemed assured. Secrecy was crucial of course, because of the competition—the race to solve the secrets of memory was as ongoing as it was brutal— but the remoteness of Sullivan College provided the perfect cover. For five years, Little Ridge seemed like the center of the universe—everything Lee needed was finally in the one place. If that wasn't home, then what was? On the rare days that he remembered the desert, when the dry bite of sage flicked out from the cold lick of the Hemlocks, when Vernon's eyes turned dim, he told himself that he could always go back.

The MISSING fliers looked good and Lee congratulated himself on them. If North America's only venomous lizard had a shot at looking cute, then Vernon, caught with the pizza crust between his scaled black lips, nailed it. Except for the outsized claws on his feet, which glittered like tarantulas in drag.

It was the word 'kiddie-snatcher' that got Lee

stuck, or unstuck, especially on a Sunday, and he tried not to think about it. He tried to think about who might have seen him and Thettie together and would know that the studio would be empty and that he'd left Vernon unprotected.

As he had his child.

Thettie didn't want to talk about it much, which was probably a good thing. She and the rest of the Harpurs had gone or were on their way out by the time Lee's son disappeared in October '05—so there was no point in talking with her about where kiddie-snatching fell in the hierarchy of evil. About where it lay in relation, for example, to granny-snatching or hostage-taking, hyphenated abominations that lay on an exponential series beginning at MISSING and ending at DEAD. What about what happened along the way as the series, MISSING, intersected with other series, like RAPE or TORTURE? In the end, was dead just dead, no matter what had been endured along the way?

Do the dead remember?

Lee hadn't slept much. His skin still tingled from Thettie's touch, every nerve-ending a sweet heat, his cock waving like a flagpole. His fall-off-the-wagon hangover epic.

He poured another coffee and squinted through greasy glasses out on the mist-veiled lake. The coffee was making his headache worse. The Xerox machine grinded away, viciously spitting out Vernons.

What if, after you went missing, but before you ended up dead, you were dismembered past the point of being recognizably human? What form would you remember to assume in the next world? That bothered Lee more than anything. The image of his son wandering alone without a form, or trapped in a shape that didn't know itself.

That was the worst evil of all. Or was it? Could evil keep getting worse, or did it reach a point where it was all it could be? Lee didn't know, and neither, it was a safe bet, did evil itself. Isn't that the point? That it would always want more? Evil, like the lake, was hungry and even at its deepest point, five hundred meters, it could always go deeper. A subterranean cave could collapse, or an underground geyser could blow. The last continental glacier made sure of that. Hanging on for life, its frozen claws scratched a wound on the face of the earth that would not heal. That would only get deeper until it reached some point where it was no longer a wound, no longer a deformity, but was the very essence of form itself.

Lee decided to hang the fliers in the Village. The sooner the better. Maybe some kid (one of the Harpurs—her sons?) had just done it for a joke or for the reward. He would not shave before he went out to hang the flyers. Lee shivered, suddenly freezing. He would not brush his teeth, or wash Thettie's taste from his mouth, but he would shower, just to warm up.

While the machine was churning out its missing Vernons, Lee stepped out of the studio and wandered, as if in a frozen dream, past the rusted swing set and back to the old house. The chill rose from the black woods and wrapped itself around his bones. There was a chance Vernon would have crawled there for warmth, or company, or fear. Lee had never stayed out the whole night before, never left Vernon alone. The studio must have been freezing.

He opened the front door of the small house where

he'd lived, all too briefly, with his family. The family smells—wet bathing suits and books and toasted Eggos—hang trapped within. But the inside of the long shut-up house was even colder than the outdoors. The cold curled out from the walls, like a dream escaping the net of consciousness. A part of him told him it was the hangover—alcohol lowered your core temperature. A part of him told him it was the shock of Vernon's disappearance. A part of him told him it was guilt.

The hallway had never been so narrow, never so long. Lee held his breath. He swam across a lazy slice of dust motes toward his son's room. Lee nudged the door open, stood at the threshold. A Spiderman blanket lay folded at the foot of the bed. His son's solar system lamp stood eternally still. A stack of picture books: *Good night, Moon* on the top.

Lee backed out of the room with his hands raised like in a stick-up. He turned and stumbled stiffly down the suddenly foreshortened hall and across a stray branch on the welcome mat. Holding his breath until he got to the studio. He grabbed the lukewarm coffee, spat it out. Exhale. Steam plumed from his nose and mouth. He refilled a spray bottle with pheromone concentrate he'd taken from the lab. Outside he liberally sprayed bushes and flowers around the yard, all the way to the shoreline, ducking through black brambles and crimson leaves and then he went back up into the woods to his son's club house and squirted the synthetic musk around that, too. Just in case. He then squirted a path of lizard musk through the fruitless orchard at the property line, and down the path to Zabriskie's moss-covered porch.

After Frankie Harpur quote-unquote mercy-shot

Zabriskie in the head, and inherited the property, he'd rattled around there a while, with no one but his and Zabriskie's dogs to keep him company. Bud Wallace, the radio operator who lived at the farmhouse and with whom Frankie had gone over for Operation Enduring Freedom, visited Frankie once or twice with supplies—medicine and dry-goods, toilet paper and two-by-fours, drums of water and chemicals. From the studio, Lee had watched Frankie loading up Zabriskie's Zodiac, heading out on the lake and staying away longer each time, until one day he left and stayed there for good. Wherever *there* was.

Lee pounded on Zabriskie's door but there was, of course, no answer. He pounded again, yelled once or twice, his voice coming out cracked and frozen. He walked to the rotunda near the shore, where Vernon had in fact escaped to once before. Lee sank down on one of the benches and lifted his face to an abandoned wasp nest on the vaulted ceiling. He tried to think at what point, during his night with Thettie, the intruder had broken into the studio and stolen the lizard, and why. He tried not to think of Vernon cold and alone in the trunk of some car, or worse. He would ask Thettie—that's it. He would ask her, outright, if anyone she knew, any of the Harpurs—even her sons—could be behind this. She would understand. Not take offence. He left the rotunda, kicked a path through the drifts of fallen leaves and flinched from a rotten peach branch that crumbled on contact. When he got closer to the studio, he could hear the urgent ding of the Xerox machine. It had run out of paper.

The point was whether evil could differentiate amongst itself.

Or maybe it needed to defer to some Higher Authority, some precedent or arbitrary hierarchy. At the annual Evil Oscars, for example, was the Best Kiddie Snatcher Award interchangeable with the Worst Kiddie Snatcher Award? Was the Kiddie Snatcher Award in a different category than rape, like Comedy-Musical from Drama, and were there subcategories marked by hyphens, like Date-Rape Award, or Child-Molestation Winner? If there were a Lifetime Achievement Award for Evil, would it be called the Adolf Hitler Award or the Pol Pot Award or the Saddam Hussein Award? And when the winner took the stage with his or her gushing list of demonic influences, sincere reminiscences of babysitters who locked them in closets, priests who interfered with them, regimes that destroyed their hopes and wars that took their worlds, would the triumphantly raised idol be an offering to the gods or their demons? Would it matter?

Lee loaded his safety razor with a shiny new blade, its edges guilty as sin.

Because innocence was just an illusion, a way to find or lose oneself in the frame, depending on your vantage point. And evil knew that. That's what made it so. It saw itself and knew its name, and knew it was form and function. It was all there was, a collective solipsism, nothing left to believe in. It began at the tail and grew fat on the exponential consumption of itself, the never-ending series of Evil, as far as the eye of the mind could see, and the tongue of the world could speak.

So Lee preferred to think of the man who took and used and photographed his child, who hid the dis(re)membered body where the sun couldn't shine, and who further investigations found to be Bud Wallace after all—and not a weed-addled farmhand, subsequently released—as the Thing itself. As Evil's own hole. As being able to claim no distance from the idea of itself and its true form. No room to move. It could hide its victims, but it could not hide from what it knew itself to be. Bud Wallace liked to wear a pink plush G-string that stuck up over the top of his jeans, and when Lee would meet him at the gas station in the weeks after his child had been taken captive, but was still alive, Bud would ask about the boy he had tied up in the cellar beneath his own farmhouse. Once he even baked a spinach lasagna for Lee and his wife.

They ate the lasagna, feasting on it for a week—the spinach, Bud claimed, grown from his own garden. Above the cellar where their son lay dying.

When the Feds finally caught up with Bud Wallace, it was not because they'd found the body of Lee's child, but that of another one, in another state. Wallace was charged with *that* murder. But all the authorities could pin on Bud Wallace regarding Lee's child, was kid(die)napping, based on photographs and other evidence they found in the cellar of the farmhouse across the highway.

Lee's wife refused to believe the pictures. Wouldn't credit her own eyes when she saw them. Unmistakably parts of her child. She had giggled uncontrollably at the Ilium police office, and had to be sedated in the psychiatric wing of University Hospital.

Bud Wallace was transferred to an undisclosed prison. Lee's wife told whoever would listen that she would track him down and kill him. Definitely. That would be a small 'k'-kill, one that did know its own power and therefore had none. She would.

A born Catholic, she whispered prayers for Bud's parole. She would find him, make him watch her slice off his cock an inch at a time. She would feed it to the fish until he told her where he'd hidden her child. Her baby. She would. Or she would paint her mouth in a rictus of lust and then she would nail his ball sack to the floor of her kayak and she would ride him down to hell. She would.

In the meantime, she combed the lake looking for her dead child. And when she didn't come back one bright October morning, a year after he went missing, the trap, for Lee, was complete. He was held in place no less than a bug in amber. Because although his wife's body did wash up and was laid to rest in her family's plot at Henksville, the dispersed and displaced parts of their child was, five years later to the day, still missing.

Lee gathered and stacked the Xeroxes. It was Thettie he needed to ask and only she who could answer. He quickly lathered up at the little mirror beside the toilet. Halfway through shaving, he stopped. One side of his face below the mask of his eyes was white with foam. The other oozed blood in dendritic strands of Sharpie red. He extended a hand to the mirror to wipe away his own reflection. He needed to think of evil as mortal because Bud Wallace needed to think of himself as not. It wasn't, as the poets said, that the mind was its own place— making a heaven of hell or a hell of heaven—but more a matter of who got there first.

9. RUNAWAY

'**H**E HASN'T TOUCHED me,' Bryce said. 'Not a finger.'

Thettie shivered in the ghostly noon. Bruised purple and yellow leaves blew against porch trellises, more than a few of which looked like they had not kept up with the famous Little Ridge Progress Association Thettie had been hearing so much about. She was on her way to the drug store for some baking soda when she came across Bryce reading a flier taped to a power pole.

'You got yourself a trailer? You looked like you slept on a couch.'

'Grif let me stay with him last night but I got me my own trailer now, like you told me to. A little one in the back row. He never touched me.'

There had been four fights the previous night. Two between the Harpurs and some townies over women, one between the Harpurs and a local they accused of slashing the inflatables. Another between Archy and Grif's dueling homies over whatever men fight about at that dark hour. A rash of diarrhea broke out in the campground after some college kid threw a dog turd on the barbecue grill. The tension in the camp was too thick even for Thettie to cut through it. There were those who wanted to stay. Who were willing, or curious, to see if Frankie could be found, and if there was anything to be gained by that. And there were those who were ready to be gone, who were afraid that whatever was to be won by staying would be outweighed by what would certainly be lost. Thettie didn't know which side she was on any more.

'Missing,' said Bryce, pointing at the flier with a slender baby finger.

She was so young.

Thettie became instantly self-conscious of her own broad-boned hands. Hands that had done things the heart would forget if it could. Her fingernails were still discolored with black by whatever had been in the lake water this morning.

Bryce now wore a bulky parka a little small for her, and smelled like wet dog. Thettie tried to remember the reason for her hostility toward the girl, who had, judging by the missing eye—and Thettie as a rule tried not to judge—been places God would forget if He could.

Turning to face the flier, because in the end she had to, Thettie saw the word, 'MISSING,' in capital letters, and beneath that, an image of a black-banded pink lizard, almost two feet from tail to nose, eating what looked like a piece of pizza. This was almost certainly Lee's pet, Vernon, and explained why he had not been back to see her.

'What's it say?' she asked the girl. 'Read it to me.'

"Missing," Bryce read, tracing the words on the flier with her bruised fingers. 'There's a list.'

'Well?'

"One," she read hesitantly. "Missing . . . . Gila monster . . . .' something something 'Vernon. Two . . .'

'Mooncalf,' Thettie muttered loud enough for Bryce to hear. 'I'll read it myself.' She squinted to blur the image of the lizard and read out loud. "Aged and in need of medication. Three. Venomous bite. Four. Does not generally attack humans . . . "

"Generally?" Bryce said. 'What does that mean?'

"Five. Do not handle. Do not harm. Six. Place a cardboard box or similar item over the lizard to immobilize him, and call this number immediately. Six. Reward for any information/assistance leading to Vernon's return . . . "

'What are they?' Bryce said, pointing to the sign.

'Dollar signs. Lots of them. 'Seven. No questions asked."

Was it the claws? Or the smile that made Thettie break out in a sweat? Its studded hide was an impossible pink, the body ringed in a bizarre black band in a pattern that resembled links in a chain. Its black face and a broad nose as blunt as a python's. The eye facing the camera was both bright and dead.

'It must have got out while he was at the bar,' Thettie said.

She clicked away an itch in her throat. Her temples thudded, and she remembered that she hadn't slept much. She lit a cigarette to steady herself.

'I don't creep easy but those things creep the hell out of me.'

The girl did not say anything, still turned toward the flier.

'Where is everyone?' Main Street had emptied out and had taken on the look of a sepia picture of a forgotten town from which even the pale leaves were fleeing.

ALETHEIA

***

After whatever Thettie had seen this morning out on the lake, she'd gone back to the trailer to try and sleep it off. She gave up trying to scrub the black from her hands and crawled back into bed, the sheets still warm from where she and Lee had lain in them. A candle, burned down to the wick, sputtered in the filigree sphere Frankie had bought for Cassie at the Henksville swap-meet years ago. Cassie had given, or Thettie had taken it when Cassie ran away from home, never to return. Thettie's eyes closed on the flickering wick and she dreamt of a grown woman seen through a window with a fish-hook in her eye. A hand held open the curtain at the window, and in the dream, the hand became a giant tongue, and licked the glass of the dream-window until it was painted black.

Thettie woke up to the sound of Grif slamming the door open. He marched in, flushed and wild-haired from being out on the lake—the glacial burn he let in made her shiver. He dumped three-four trout on the table and told her he'd help her move her things into Doc's cabin. He wore fingerless gloves over his hands that hid the tattooed red and black letters.

'Since when?' she said, holding the comforter up to her neck.

'Since that's what Doc wants, and for once, him and me are eye-to-eye on that, Ma. This trailer's too cold, and it's too far away. And the lock doesn't work.'

'So?' she said.

'Better for you to be behind four walls with a door that locks, close to me and Archy. Natives are getting restless, Ma. Best not to take any risks.'

He'd picked up her bathrobe from the end of the bed, tossed it over to her.

'We won't be here long enough for the natives to get too close,' She grabbed the bathrobe, put it over her head, and rolled away. 'I like it in this cabin. It's got a skylight.'

Grif eyed the grimy patch of Perspex fixed into a square hole cut into the trailer ceiling. 'Hell of a skylight. You hear the lake farts?' The smoke of his cigar drowning out the last of her lover's musk. 'We was right on top of them.'

Thettie sat up in bed, hooded in the robe, the black dream-tongue fading. She asked how far they got, and Grif told her halfway to the island before the weather picked up and the boat was held in a hard and blinding fog. He shook his head and grinned, but the crease between his eyebrows remained.

'We figured the island was dead ahead, but visibility was zip. Turned the fog lights on, but got turned around in the current and found ourselves a mile up the lake, almost at Tinkers Glen. Pulled up for a few beers and by then it had lifted.'

Thettie shivered. The trailer was freezing, and the wind pulled the surface of the lake into mean little peaks.

'Don't see too many Octobers like this in Pennsy,' she said. 'I didn't miss them.'

Except that, too, was a lie.

'Before the fog came up, we heard the dogs,' Grif said. 'A shitload of them. Barking and howling like hell. It was like the mist grew fangs and a throat. And something shot at us, into the water in front of us.'

'You shoot back?'

Grif drew off his gloves and ran inked fingers through his hair. Thettie caught the letter S. 'What if we hit Frankie? Nah, we held our fire.'

Thettie reached for her smokes. 'Archy go with you?'

Grif's smile turned sour. 'Just me and couple of my boys. Archy bailed.'

'What's Doc going to do?'

'Try his own self, I guess. When the weather lets him.'

'You'll go with him?'

'Okay.'

'Archy, too. I don't want it to be just Doc and his two psycho body guards going after Frankie.'

Grif switched his cigar to the other side of his mouth and sniffed. 'I ain't Archy's keeper anymore, Ma. I think he made that clear.'

***

Grif was four years older than Archy, ten pounds heavier, and an inch shorter—six foot five. Grif was a Tully. He'd become hers when he was almost ten and Archy was six, and Thettie moved them out of the float home to a small house on the banks of the creek where she felt safer with two little boys and no man to speak of. Grif came with a leg broken in one place and an arm broken in two—he'd still had a grimy fluorescent-green cast on his left arm. He wouldn't speak, wouldn't sit. Stood against the wall plugged into an old Walkman, the one thing he'd brought with him from a life that, unable to be spoken of, left him with nothing to say. She let him be, hoping that Archy would win him over.

The year after Grif had arrived in '02 or '03 maybe, two things happened. Frankie went to pick up his war buddy, Doc Murphy, from the Greyhound Station in Tinkers Glen and Archy—accident-prone from day one—slipped on a rock while they were gathering herbs at Harpur Falls and cut a long gash in his leg from knee to groin, nicking his femoral artery. Most of that day was dark in her mind except for a tunnel of light in which she was forever running with Archy held in her arms, soaked from neck to knees in blood. She'd left Grif in his room plugged into the Walkman but he came out when he heard her yelling—his eyes taking in the tourniquet around Archy's leg that she made from her bra—and Sarey already had her truck halfway up the switchback for her to jump in. Once Archy was safely home with ten stitches in his leg beneath a stark white bandage, Grif drew a three-headed monster on it with a green Sharpie and never let either of them out of his sight after that.

***

'I don't want to move cabins. I like it here.' The lake filled up the big square of window. There was a texture to the air in the trailer like gauze, grainy with memory.

'Not up to me,' Grif said. 'You're the one who made Doc the boss.'

Her fingers curled so tightly around the edge of the covers that her knuckles whitened. 'This is all my fault?'

Grif wrinkled his nose over the cigar against the lingering odor of Lee's sex. 'I'll let you get packed, Ma. I gotta crash.'

'I hear guitar from somewhere. Is that someone singing?'

Grif ran both his hands through his hair, spilled ash in it and made it stand up on end. 'Ma, jeez. I don't hear nothing.'

'Sounded like that song Frankie and Cassie used to play. Space Something.' How could she forget?

'Ma, the big trailer has a bath. You'll like it there. You can rest after the trip.'

'Grif?' she said, with a resigned stretch of her arms over her head. 'Remember Frankie's Mohawk?'

'Like a picket fence. Green as one, too.'

'One that needed a good lick of paint,' she smiled, and Grif smiled too. 'Came home from the war bald as a badger. Never grew back, not fully.'

Grif chewed on his cigar. 'Anyhoo, Doc'll probably want Archy to come with, on account of the dogs Frankie's got out there.'

'Doc was never a fan,' said Thettie. She twirled a finger in the air, and Grif turned away. Thettie shrugged into the robe, swung her feet out of bed and walked past her son, over to the counter. She poked one of the trout—its skin neither silk nor leather, but something in between—then bent into the cupboard under the sink and reached for a pan. She filled it with water and then began to make coffee, slowly to keep Grif there—she didn't want to be alone with the black tongue. The birds outside had gone quiet and Thettie always hated these yawning hours, the middle-aged spread of the day, fat on the illusion that it could go on forever.

'I have a bad feeling about this place.'

Grif shrugged, 'It was always like this. You just couldn't see it.'

'I see it now.'

'Better late,' Grif said, 'then never.'

'It's never too late.'

'Dream on, Ma. Get packed.'

'Be the bigger man, Grif. Talk to your brother. Where's your Thermos?'

She poured the coffee in.

'When he had me under the water there when we first got here, I could have just reached up and pulled out his heart. I did it in juvie. Killed a rapist with my bare hands. You know that. Archy was there. He was the reason I did it.'

Thettie sipped her coffee. 'You would have burned down the house to save us. I know, baby. Go talk to him.'

'You don't really pull the heart out. You just make it stop,' he said. 'You could pull it out *then* if you really wanted to, but it'd be messy. The Korean librarian taught me. Just a jab in the right place, she said, and bam. I did the math under the water there, how easy it would be. Just end it all right there. Pull my brother's heart right out of his chest, teach him some respect.'

'You never used to be like that about each other. What happened?'

Grif picked up the Thermos. 'Doc happened.'

'Maybe this *is* my chance,' Thettie whispered. 'For real.'

Grif didn't answer, but he looked away too quickly and his eyes as they turned away, glittered like lake glass.

***

Bryce's gaze never left the flier with Lee's missing lizard. Thettie couldn't let that distract her, any of them, from the job at hand—getting Frankie. She straightened and snapped two fingers in front of the girl's face.

'Hey. Not our business. If you're going to hang

around, I want you to talk to Archy and Grif. Earn your keep.'

'What do you want me to say?' said Bryce.

'Tell them that as long as they keep up this bullshit squabbling, we don't have a chance.'

'At what?'

Thettie said, 'Back when we were living here, Frankie made the boys fishing pants out of an old fire-hose. Cut it in patches and sewed it all together with Sarey's pelt needle. Took them both out in the stream and taught them how to tickle trout. Archy caught more, but Grif's were bigger. So when he thought Frankie wasn't looking, Grif swapped a couple around. Took two of the smaller ones from Archy, gave him a couple of three-four pounders. Frankie told me about it later.'

Bryce chewed on her lip. Wood-smoke drifted in the air. A pretty young couple sauntered past, their autumn clothes bright against the sepia storefronts. The girl wore a yellow skirt and the boy was half an inch shorter than her, holding her hand and smiling at her face as she talked. High up on the ridge behind the Village, the pines swelled and darkened.

'All those years I blamed Doc for taking us away to Pennsylvania,' Thettie said, lighting another cigarette from the tip of the one she just finished. 'But I wanted to go. If I stayed, I'd be an accomplice and my boys would be taken away from me. No way I was going to let that happen. Only one thing was going to take me away from my boys, and I'd had to fight that demon off with a big stick more than once. Choice between going down with Frankie and staying with my boys was not a choice. It was a sickness, a poison. The whole time I was there I hated myself for what I did to Frankie, hated to think of him all alone, not right in the head, not understanding why I ditched him any more than an old dog'd understand, and that's what I had to live with. This is my chance to make things right with Frankie, but it sure as hell doesn't feel right.'

'Frankie knows.'

Bingo. Thettie waited but the girl's lips kept twitching, soundlessly following the words on the flier. 'You think I was born yesterday, like you? Frankie sent you to find us, didn't he? Don't think me and Grif didn't have you pegged from day one. You probably shot a hole in that inflatable yourself. What'd he offer you to lure us back?'

The lake jumped at her between the houses. The nicotine on top of her exhaustion and fear, made the blue water look swollen between the houses, and Thettie had forgotten how big and alive it was. Thirty miles of shoreline, hamlets like Little Ridge and Tinkers Glen and Union Falls and Henksville, cowering from the hungry mouth of the lake.

She leaned in towards the girl, so that Bryce's face was just eyelash and bone. 'Why'd he bring me back? Why now? He's dying, isn't he—or dead?'

Bryce shook her head back and forth, back and forth. The parka hood rustled. Scratched and hissed like some kind of animal.

'Listen to me, Bryce with a 'y.' You tell Frankie that I'll find him, wherever he is. Doc or no Doc. I'm not leaving without him but I'm not staying either, so tell him to get his shit together. Because those jailbirds . . .'

'Lomer and Hyle?'

'Whatever their damn names are. They'll need

dealing with, because Doc's only as good as his tools, and he'll need those tools to move in on whatever Frankie's into. But you're only here on my sufferance, because of Frankie and because I don't suffer tools or fools, for real. You want my protection, you got to earn it. Frankie gave you a job? Well here's mine. Archy and Grif. Make it right between them. Over you or under you, or one at each end, I don't care. You want shelter for the winter, that's how you earn it. By bringing together what you forced apart. Nod for yes.'

Bryce hiccoughed, but she stopped the crazed head-shaking. Her good eye stayed fixed on the picture of Vernon until they seemed to come to an understanding—the cold dead eye of the one and the living, broken eye of the other. Only then did she nod.

Thettie was suddenly starving, could seriously kill for a good square meal of eggs, fish and green tomatoes like Sarey used to make. She reached into her purse and pulled out the money Doc had given her, reached over and bunched the bills under the beanie, her knuckles brushing the dirty fuzz.

'Take that and get yourself some breakfast. And come by my cabin when you get home, not the Bago, the other one. I'm moving into the big trailer next to my boys. I got something I want you to give Frankie.'

Bryce said. 'For his foot?'

'Maybe.' Exhale. 'So, what's the deal with this runaway lizard?'

Bryce lifted narrow shoulders, kept them that way, all hunched up around her ears. 'Maybe it's not a runaway. Maybe it's stolen.'

'Well you better keep those thoughts to yourself, lady, you'll get us all in trouble—wait,' Thettie flinched as if slapped. 'You think it was one of us? You think a Harpur took that damn monster?'

Bryce turned to Thettie abruptly, her eye patch looking a little worse for wear and her good eye as dark as a wren's. And in it a fleck of gold, a kind of amber slice that hit Thettie with a strange force, the way it burned like something trapped behind a door—alive, and it saw her.

10. LACE

LEE KNOCKED ON the door of Jason deGroot's house, louder this time to be heard above the vacuum cleaner running inside. He'd driven to the campground, but changed his mind. Kept going south past the turn-off into the old Harpur settlement until deep in deGroot territory. Before he spoke with Thettie about the missing lizard, he decided to ask Jason. Partly because, besides Habib, Jason was the only other reptile handler in Little Ridge and might have some advice on how to get him back. But also, Lee didn't want to be *that* guy, the guy who blamed the Harpurs for everything that went wrong in Little Ridge. Leave that to the sheriff. The fact that Vernon disappeared on the first night Lee had gone with a woman in years, and that the woman was a Harper, was pure coincidence—hopefully had more than anything to do with Lee having left the studio unlit and unheated. And if Vernon had not crawled out of his own accord, the crushed markers and lack of any trail on the studio floor could easily be someone using the Harpur arrival as a cover. Someone who knew he had the lizard in the first place.

The only person who knew, apart from Habib, was Jason. But Lee could see no real reason for the boy to take Vernon—and disappoint Habib—so he planned to politely ask if there was anyone else he might have told about the lizard. He'd even brought along a six pack of beer as a sign of good faith. Science, as Lee knew, was in the details.

A gravel driveway wound past the farmhouse, new barns and sheds sat behind it. Gnarled hydrangea bushes grew along the garden bed below windows, on either side of the front door. Queen Anne's lace, gone to seed, straggled along the fence. A curtain moved in an upper window. A veiled or hooded head moved up to the glass, and as Lee watched, a tongue dragged itself along the steamy inside of the window and retreated behind the curtain.

'Vernon's gone,' Lee yelled at the fluttering lace. 'Thought you could help.'

He cursed his lack of self-control, blamed it on falling off the wagon. A rustling behind him made him pivot unsteadily on his heel. A boy stepped out from behind a hydrangea bush. He looked to be about twelve years old but with the wise squint of Down Syndrome. Lee felt a rush of cold to his guts when he saw that the boy was holding a newborn baby, also with Down Syndrome.

'This is Crystal,' the boy said. 'My doll.'

Lee reeled, thought he might vomit. An American Born doll, specifically, the brainchild of Sunny Weeks, who sold her doll company to Little Tykes for $17 million. She donated much of the proceeds to her favorite charities, one of which was the dying town of Little Ridge. The dolls were hand-molded in state-of-the art silicon rubber, life-size, able to simulate drinking and waste-production. There were, according to Sunny, thousands of molds for dolls in every hue and singularity in the history of human births. Not only dolls of every race, but also dolls with missing limbs, birthmarks, extra thumbs, deaf and blind. Lee looked at the boy's grubby arms wrapped around the doll. They cost two hundred dollars a piece.

Leonardo DaVinci—whose infants Lee had dutifully studied and copied in order to draw his son—recommended short, quick strokes of the pencil or brush in order to capture the perpetual motion and the dynamism of the infant. Otherwise, and in the wrong hands, children in paintings often came out looking like wizened little men or broken dolls. The American Borns were like that—faithful replicas but lacking in dynamism, in any sign of life. Forever frozen, instead, in reptilian stasis and liplessly screaming, their webbed toes curled in agony, the American Borns looked accursed, abominations doomed to relive a split second of infancy for all time.

'Hi Crystal,' Lee said, forcing a smile at the doll. 'Do you know where Jason is?'

After his son disappeared, Lee had burned every last sketch of his child—every watercolor, every oil, everything.

'You must be Jason's brother.'

At the word, 'brother,' the boy's face softened like damp dough, and his eyes slanted upward. He had a scratch on the tip of his nose, like a cat got at him. 'Jason,' he said.

'Is he home?'

The boy looked toward the fields questioningly. 'Gone to work?'

The vacuum cleaner fell silent, and in its wake Lee

heard a cawing, but the sky above was a blank canvas of cloud. Lee wrote his phone number again on the back of a flier, with a note to call him, gave it to the boy. He left the beer on the doorstep. He turned back once as he headed to his car. The boy cradled the doll in one hand and waved the flier at him with the other. Lee steered around the turnaround and down the driveway. In the rearview he watched crows settle on the boy's shoulders and on the doll in his arms, and as the boy waved and waved, more crows came until they covered his body like heavy brush strokes. Like scales.

***

Lee still had a bunch of MISSING fliers to post before he saw Thettie. It would give him a chance to work out what to say to her. At the south end of town, where Main Street became the Interstate, he put fliers up at the gas station, the feed store, Pottery Barn, Papa Johns, the refurbished Rod 'n' Reel, and the Old Motel 6 that was supposed to be haunted. He'd driven through campus and stuck them on the Student Union board alongside other notices; concert bills, bikes for sale and Yoga classes. He'd been to the library and through the Village itself—the empty Pump Bar and Maxine's Pie Kitchen and the Lake View. Vernon's blunt nose poked out from pay phones, store windows, stuffed in the mailboxes at the post office.

Habib would say that fear was just a story we told ourselves about the future.

Lee parked near the Village Inn. The lake flowed like quicksilver between the old homes. He would spray the pheromone fluid along the rocks and trees of the shore. He walked past the Village Market, and peered into the dark glass at all the non-Harpurs within.

ALETHEIA

When he was a boy, and even at college, Lee's crushes on girls had approached the level of obsession. He liked to think of himself as a romantic, not a stalker, and once, alluding to this, Habib had reminded him that the Big 'R'-Romantics had all been stalkers—more or less. Lee had played guitar in an '80s tribute band with two biology classmates at UNM. They called themselves Loaf Meat, and they were sometimes joined by a drummer from the chemistry department, a dark-haired woman from a remote town back east called Little Ridge. The keyboardist, Lee's best friend, fell for the drummer hard. She didn't fall back.

Lee and the band sat it out with the heartbroken keyboardist through an entire night and several bottles of vodka, out in the desert atop the roof of a goat shed, beneath the lash of Orion's belt. The keyboardist alternated between singing the chorus to Meatloaf's 'Bat out of Hell' and romantically throwing up, the roar of the desert bees closing in on the evening primrose. On and off through the long night, Lee could no longer tell where the roar of the wild bees ended and the roaring in his ears began. His mind neither able nor willing to tear itself from the image of the biochemist at her drums, her dark hair flying. Flying.

***

Back on Main Street, the wind pulled at the fliers in his ungloved hands. Crowds huddled in the steaming warmth of Maxine's Pie Kitchen, and around the tables behind the dark glass of the Lake View. He remembered when Little Ridge had been a forgotten college town, but since the renewal spearheaded by Sunny Weeks, it had transformed into a smug satellite community, all craft beer and Tapas Tuesdays. There was an alumni convention at the college. Sunny was the keynote speaker—Lee heard she was booked out for a year. Townies stopped to take in the shabby flotilla that rocked off the old jetty, the jangle from their moorings discordant and frenzied in the wind. The Progress Association, and Sunny Weeks in particular, must be apoplectic.

Lee's face felt scoured by the wind. Fliers flapped and slipped from his frozen hands. When Vernon had gotten out before, it was always in summer. He seemed happy to be found. Gilas are adapted to splash through the warm brown rivers of the Sonoran Desert or the arroyos of Utah, not the glacial lakes of the East. Lee stepped up onto the curb. Afternoon shadows seeped from doorways, and some of Lee's MISSING flyers had already blown off the telephone poles. He was just about to veer off toward the campground to find Thettie, when a square woman in her late fifties stepped out of the Inn. Her hair was cut into a chic auburn pageboy, and she dimpled as she greeted Lee.

'Well howdy there, mister.'

'Hey Sunny. How's your painting going?'

Sunny Weeks was, in addition to being Sullivan College's most sought-after alumni and philanthropist of the year, a student in Lee's painting class, and since Lee's wife's death, the occasional rider of Lee's lonely cock in the backseat of her Audi.

'I don't even have time to paint my nails these days. Hellooo.'

'Me neither.'

They stood there a moment with the backs of their hands outstretched toward each other but not quite touching. Grins on their faces and not quite smiling. Lee's wife had started a class action suit against Sunny's Progress Association. They hired NYC lawyers and wrote to *The Times* accusing the Progress Association of turning Little Ridge into Sunnyland, a Revolution-era theme park insensitive to the region's bloody history. They accused it of packing the board with various directors of Sunny's subsidiary companies—the owner of an interior design company specializing in reproduction textiles, for example, and building contractors specializing in fitting out historical buildings with modern amenities like spa baths and gas kitchens. They were right, of course, about everything. They lost anyway.

Sunny Weeks' generous contribution to Lee's wife's funeral costs had been anonymous.

Sunny's eyes flicked from her Audi back to Lee and then to her phone. 'I'm just heading off now to the Acres to interview a vegan chef.'

The Acres was a spa for Jersey brokers and Brooklyn wise guys remodeled from a three-hundred-year-old farmhouse surrounded by Six Nations orchards. Welcome to SunnyLand.

Lee shoved a wad of fliers into Sunny's peaches-and-cream face.

'I was hoping you could put one of these in your offices.'

She looked at the picture of Vernon, and flinched theatrically. 'You have a license for that thing, mister?'

'That's not a thing. He's a Gila monster called Vernon. I inherited him from the lab.'

Sunny's eyes widened like a debutante. 'You guys never got that patent, huh? Something to do with peptides? Monster-tide or something.'

Sunny, having sat on the board of the joint venture between Tantra, Sullivan and Cordell University, knew exactly what the patent was for.

'Helotide,' the sidewalk seemed both very far away and pushing up against his feet at the same time—Lee felt swallowed up in something beyond his control. 'An analogue. It's a synthetic equivalent of a peptide in Gila venom that augments memory and learning. And no. You never approved the patent.'

'Something about a tax scandal, right? One of the board members with his hand in the cookie jar. Did it work? I mean on anything besides rats?'

Lee was four inches taller than her. She once clawed his ass so hard in the back of the Audi that he couldn't sit down for a week.

'Golly jeez, mister. As a Psych major I know all about labs. Aversion shock therapy and what not. Poor widdle wats.'

The breeze licked the knife-edge of her chestnut hair. Her lipstick as thick as a wax seal.

Lee breathed in and held her peppery perfume in his lungs as long as he could. 'So, aversion shock training went out in the sixties, Sunny. These days with aversion learning, it's just their feet. A little less than two volts over three seconds.'

Lee's son had spent many happy hours after school on the floor of the lab playing, drawing with crayons on printer paper, or sitting on Lee's lap while he and the other researchers played *Legend of Zelda*. Jason deGroot let the kid help change the water bottles and feed trays. Jason showed Lee's son how the enriched mice played in their brightly colored tunnels and exercised on their whirring wheels. He let the kid give the rats chocolate chips. Except one afternoon they found a cardiac hypertrophy model lying on the floor of the cage with a gash in its chest, and the other rats eating their cage-mate's heart while it still beat. Jason had a rapt look on his face, his hands over the boy's small shoulders while the red eyes of the rat watched itself being eaten alive. Lee yelled, pulled his son away and covered his eyes. Jason's turned red as a beet and he went AWOL from the lab for a week. Lee gave his son permission to pick out a pup from a new litter of mice, and the boy name it after himself, but by the time they realized the mouse was a girl, Lee's child was already missing.

Sunny's jaw muscles bunched and jumped, leaving deep ravines in her make-up. She unlocked the Audi with a squawk. A male factotum stepped out of the shadows. She passed him the flier.

'Put these on the vending machines at the office,' she said. 'As an appetite suppressant.'

The afternoon sun limned the dark maples with a cold fire. As Lee hurried toward the campground, the lake began to seethe. He bent beneath the dock and doused the pylons with pheromone spray and remembered how he and his son would look for broken glass there. Amber beer glass, the edges rendered harmless by the tumbling stones. Fragments from old medicine bottles, blue and yellow, frosted with time. A strand of lake weed clinging to a frosted ruby shard. Lee would hold one up to his son's eyes and his own, to look at the world as though washed in blood, or green as an alien's tears.

Lee banged his head crawling out from under the dock. He knocked his glasses off in the slops and tasted metal. Through blurred vision he fumbled in the water, which left an unpleasant black residue on both the lenses and his fingers—he wondered if one of the Harper boats had spilled some oil from one of those drums. He wiped them as best he could and tried to orientate himself to where Thettie's trailer had been in relation to all the others. It was further away that he remembered, separated from the rest of the campground by a good fifty yards and nestled, half hidden beneath a straggly pine. It was on a slight rise and looked out across the entire lake, all the way to the island and beyond.

Lee walked briskly toward it, his glasses flecked with black from the water. He studiously ignored the electric stares of her people. Rancid smoke wormed from a barbecue grilling meat for supper. Beatboxes growled and a mockingbird yammered from a utility line running alongside the park. His head throbbed where he banged it. Harpurs stood in ragged groups, their blue eyes watching him as he passed, wearing last year's jeans and hoodies that reeked of weed and unwashable thrift store must. He walked past the bigger trailers and stopped at Thettie's trailer. A man emerged from the doorway and stood on the narrow stoop, one of the bodyguards Lee had seen with Doc at the Way. The older, skinnier one with the full-body tattoos. He exuded a strength more feral than muscular, his stress responses way out of whack. Lee knew it was the man by his heavy ink, but his face was hidden behind a Jack-O'-Lantern mask.

'Do for you?' the voice was muffled from behind the mask, but Lee knew a tweaker's twang when he heard one.

Lee said he was looking for Thettie. The man in the mask shook his head. Shadows moved around the inside of the trailer, their movements looked slightly off to Lee, lumbering yet strangely female. Lee flapped the fliers in irritation.

'I'm pretty sure she was here yesterday?'

Again, the man in the mask shook his head and pointed with a tattooed finger. Lee turned to see the one-eyed girl standing behind him. She smiled beneath a fuzzy beanie. Angled her good eye toward him, its amber lights stark against the silvery backdrop of lake.

'I'll show you where you can hang them fliers,' she said.

She took him back in the direction he'd come, toward the campground facilities. She slowed down so Lee could catch up to her.

'I'm looking for Thettie,' Lee wildly brushed hair out of his eyes. 'Thettie Harpur. She was in that trailer, and now she's gone.'

'She moved,' the girl said as soon as they were out of earshot. 'Doc and his two boys switched so they could see through to the island where Frankie is.'

'So she's not in the Winnebago anymore? Where is she?'

The girl pointed to a shabby trailer some ways from the Winnebago. 'That one. The one in the middle. Nearest to her boys. But I don't know where she is. I just went to get something but she wasn't there.'

Lee said, 'Who was that behind the mask?'

'That's Lyle. The other one is Homer.'

'The fat guy with the beard and the cut around his neck?' Lee traced a line around his own neck. 'How can they all fit in that trailer?'

He tried to remember the layout. The bed up

against the end window, a couple of day beds through a door into the main area. A dinette up the other end, by the woods.

She shrugged. 'Doc likes them close.'

Lee scanned the flotilla for the yacht, the one he guessed belonged to Doc Murphy. It wasn't there.

'He's on the lake,' the girl said, as if reading his mind. 'With Homer. Looking for the island.'

They kept walking and the electric eyes of the Harpurs sputtered after them like light bulbs about to blow. Their pallor and haunted expression—differentiated by an olive tinge to that one's skin, or high cheekbones on another, Norwegian full lips, nappy hair, or a Senecan curve to a nose—was of a muchness, and the trailer park had taken on the atmosphere of an extended family reunion with all the attendant disappointments. A bunch of teenagers standing on the dock stared at Lee and the one-eyed girl through rank clouds of weed.

'That's Marshall. And that's Marshall's woman and her friend Liz. And that's Emilio's cousin Strike and the girl he's dating.'

'She looks fourteen.'

'Fifteen. She's pregnant. He already has three kids. One of the ma's his stepsister but nobody knows but me. I'm Bryce with a 'y."

Lee itched in her presence. Itched all over his skin. Like something crawling under his thermal, like there were burrs stuck to his socks, and a dirty word on the tip of his tongue.

'I'm Lee with two 'e's." A dozen pairs of Harpur eyes turned toward him. He lowered his voice. 'When will Thettie be back?'

'Me and her were reading the signs. Your monster's stolen.'

She wrenched a thumbtack off the notice board outside the closed rental office. She turned to Lee, reached out a hand, and he passed her a flier. His fingers brushed hers, which were like ice.

'Thettie thinks he's stolen?' Lee's glasses had slipped and he pushed them up. The girl jumped into focus. 'That's what I came to ask her about. I mean not that he's stolen, exactly. I don't know for sure. Did she see something?'

'She told me not to say.'

She pinned the flier to the wall. There was a bruise on the webbing between her index finger and her thumb. And another, he noticed, to the side of her long pale neck.

'She told you not to say?'

'You can wait and ask her yourself,' she said, keeping her back to him. 'But she isn't there now.'

Dusk fingered the visible tufts of her hair. Some lights had come on in the town and winked behind the trees. In a moment, the college bells would peal the hour. A group congregated around the barbeque pit.

'I can't wait. Vernon—my lizard—might come back while I'm gone. Can you tell her to come see me? I have a studio at the edge of town, last house on the left before the headland. Or call me, or something?'

The girl nodded, and when Lee asked her where she was from, she shrugged and started to lead him away from the camping ground. Lee had the sense that he was being chaperoned, led away from the staring, hostile Harpurs.

'I just move from place to place. Like any water rat.'

Lee's wife had been involved with runaway teens. Addicts. Punks from the suburbs or lost in the cities, and who rode the rails and hitchhiked from state to state in groups or alone.

'You do seasonal work?'

She adjusted the strap on her eye patch. A ring of black, or darker brown circled the amber circle of her other eye. 'I do things for people on the lake and they pay me.'

They existed by stealing, dealing, and what his wife called 'survival sex.' Odd jobs, sometimes. Picking and yard work. The wind gusted around the fuzz of her beanie and the blunt tufts of hair.

'Does Frankie Harpur pay you? To do things? Did he tell you to take Vernon?'

An arrow of geese moved, honking, across the sky. The one-eyed girl lifted her head to watch their progress over the lake and Lee saw that she had more bruises on her neck. And a trickle of clear mucus from her nose.

'I've seen it,' she said. Behind her the island lay drenched in a molten goop of sunset. 'Out there.'

'Vernon? Out on the island? That's impossible.'

The wind snatched a flier, blew it under the dock.

'It's a tree.' Small gnawing teeth were just visible in the dark cavity of her mouth. 'The lake monster.'

Lee felt weak with relief. 'Oh, okay. The lake monster. I thought you meant . . .'

'It's a humongous tree. With a face. And arms out to here.'

She held her arms out wide, as far as they'd go. They stretched wider than they should, and the parka gaped over a thin sweater that showed her ribs.

'Sometimes, it goes deep and stays there. It sleeps in one of the underground caves or under a ledge. Then it comes up and that's what people see.'

Lee had maybe heard this before, but couldn't remember where. An uprooted giant white pine moved along by the current, year after year for centuries, maybe more.

'Listen,' Lee said. 'It's been good talking. But I have to . . .'

She nodded vigorously. 'It has a face. I seen it. I know its name and all.'

Lee began to move off, but the amber slice in her eye held him in place. 'What's its name?'

'Seek You,' she said. 'That's its name.'

11. MISSING

GILA MONSTERS EVERYWHERE. Clinging from tree trunks, utility poles, shop windows and mailboxes.

MISSING.

That cold studded hide. Those Kardashian claws. Thettie quickened her pace to get to where Bryce said Lee's studio was, but there were so many lizards blocking her way! Stuck in windshield wipers, pulped in piles of leaves. How had he put up so many fliers? She had to stop him. She needed to try and tell him that sometimes, gone is gone.

The lizard was stolen five years to the day since his child had gone. He said, 'my son.' He said 'my child.' Thettie didn't make him speak the name because she got that would make his child die all over again. Sarey would say that calling the name of the taken would summon the thing that took it. It would come out of the lake from where it had gone, answering to its name.

The smears across Lee's glasses, before she took them off, looked like they'd been made by a tongue. The waiting in his eyes for the monster to return had become a hungry, nameless thing.

A cardinal sliced across the whitening sky. Thettie

twisted the buttons on Archy's pea coat. She was always cold. Cold and hungry, too. The old trailer Doc had switched with her was full of chinks and holes, unlike the little 'Bago, huddled in trees that sustained its warmth, the skylight as grainy as gauze over the little world she and Lee had made their own.

Doc's army duffle bag and Homer's broken sports bag had still been in the trailer when Grif helped her to move her things in the kitchen area and he had to go and get Lyle to move that shit. But the smell was still there—Doc's cologne and some funk she couldn't place—Grif seemed anxious to be out of there, so she said she'd unpack later. Grif left to go find Archy for the expedition to the island, and Thettie went to the stores for supplies. Bryce had caught up with her again in the Village, told her that Lee had been looking for her.

One thing was now clear to Thettie. In coming back she'd crossed more than just the border between states. This memory-lane business was not all it was cracked up to be, that much she was sure. Some memories—you leave them alone for long enough, they get lonely and come back to bite you, and her skin was crawling with those little mites of time.

Everyone knew how strong she was. Everyone in the clan depended on her, knew what she was capable of, but ever since pulling back up to these shores she felt so incapable, and so young. Her mind's eye saw her skinny-ass girl-self standing under a tree here, taking a curve on her bike there, walking along the jetty, or hitching down the highway—wanting, hungry, gone.

The lake winked between the trees as she hurried toward the edge of town. The houses were further apart here, and the lake oozed and spread into the spaces between. She'd stopped at the drug store for some Pepto Bismol, but the unsmiling clerk told her they were out. Fake apothecary bottles swung in nooses from curling ribbon in the new plate glass window.

Her throat needled at smoke from an early leaf fire. A lone man in devil's horns raked leaves in his yard and watched her as she passed. At the Inn, townies and leaf peepers and alumnae tucked into their steaks and chowders. Their teeth so white. The glow of fine wine in their cheeks so golden.

If Little Ridge had ever been home, she must have been someone else and that bothered her. Thettie passed the last store window, a gift store selling candles and glass animals in which she saw herself in passing, windblown and arrested, looked half her age and not in a good way. Like she'd forgotten to grow up, and maybe she had. And what did that make her?

Trees grew close to the sidewalk here on Main Street, horse chestnuts and elms. Thettie stepped over a root that had pushed through the sidewalk, cracked and uneven like she remembered it.

She approached an abandoned car caught in a net of fallen leaves, some red, some yellow, some plum, stuck to its roof, its hood, the windows front and back, the tires. No other car on the street was covered in this way, and Thettie saw shapes within the web of leaves, people maybe, or pets, moving around—prisoners, she wondered—brailed in time. What fisherman had caught this family of drowned ghosts in his net? She veered away but a window shot down and an arm reached out to grab her. She jumped back and a yelp escaped her lips, and she could hear the laughter of whoever was inside following her as she hurried down the street.

She'd gotten her superstitious, story-telling side from Sarey, who, like Frankie, was a Harpur through and through—believed in ghosts and hauntings and doubles and all that bull. Her practical side, well, that she got from her own mother, a Tully.

***

When she was a girl and they lived on the shores of Triangle Creek, she and Cassie smoked some weed, faked their IDs and bought some beer. Cassie Tully was Frankie's cousin, or second-sister or something, musical like him. She worked as a maid at the Motel 6 and stole a credit card left there by one of the deGroots after a booty call. Cassie and Thettie put on make-up and false eyelashes and push-up bras they'd bought from Mervyns. They took Polaroids of each other in their bras blowing kisses, humping trees in the woods. Leaves in their hair. They rode their bikes into town, snuck into the Inn, and bought cocktails with their fake IDs and the stolen credit card. They ended up in the lockup with mascara running down their faces, peeing into a pail. The deGroot whose credit card it was had reported it, and the Inn turned them over to the Sheriff. Cassie was half-way through screaming how she couldn't go to juvie again, when they were abruptly released and sent home.

What Thettie found out later, much later, was that that Boyle—at that stage he was just another deputy on hazard pay—had an arrangement with the deGroots and saw where it might take him. Thettie recalled a new SUV for Boyle's wife a week after the deGroots dropped the charges. No one knew why until later. Thettie and the girls were sent home, let off on a warning. They thought that was the end of it. But they should have known better because that was the thing with the lake, it wasn't ever over. And no one got off with a warning.

One of the Harpur babies, the child of Grif's cousin Randall Hill, was seriously ill with diarrhea and his parents had taken her to County hospital. Thettie had not counted on the total absence of any kin or kind to lend them a hand, and it made her wonder if Doc knew something she didn't when he brought her back. No one to bring them meat or medicine or help with trucks or guns, a case of beer or cigarettes, some sugar, blankets. Nothing. All they had now was Doc, and he was neither kin nor kind.

Start over, he said, like he was the boss of time. This is our chance.

She hurried toward Lee's house. It had been a while since she'd had a date, if that's what this thing with Lee was. Well, no. She'd had plenty of dates. So what was this? She didn't care. It was what she wanted now. So hungry. So tired of eating herself. He'd started to say something a few times, about things she didn't want to talk about that. His dead wife. Lost child. His venomous goddamn *heelah*.

'No offence,' she whispered in his ear.

'None taken,' he said, arcing up to meet her.

Because in Thettie's experience, talking just wasn't something you did on the first date. If that's what that was.

Down in Pennsy at a titty-bar called the Landing Strip, Grif would proudly tell anyone who asked, that

Thettie was his mother and just as proudly tell them to keep their distance.

'Move along, boys,' he'd tell the drivers and mechanics lined up at the bar. 'She's out of your league.'

But Archy'd be all, 'Lock up your daughters, yo,' his own eyes as heat-seeking as hers.

Doc didn't care what she did or with whom as long as she was there for him when he needed her, and if that's what it would take to buy her some time, he could spread and poke at her all he wanted. Time was what she needed, time to find room to move in his big picture, a future for her sons and for the daughters she would never have. Teach them to fish, be nice to animals. Whatever it took. All she needed was time.

It took some explaining to her boys why Frankie didn't go to Pennsylvania with them. Frankie couldn't come because he was sick, she told them, and they'd see him when he was better. Except it wasn't Frankie who had to get better. It was her.

***

Main Street had emptied out on this late Monday afternoon, everyone inside their overheated homes getting ready for pork chops and *Game of Thrones*. She had the world to herself like a ghost, or a survivor. The lake flushed purple, bruised by its own loveliness, leaves dripped bloody from the trees. Monday, fifth of October. Month of masks.

A big yellow manor house came into view from the end of long curving driveway.

Lavender clouds raced across the surface of its zillion windows. The garden beds were choked with weeds growing around tossed newspapers and lizard fliers. The garage was tagged with alien scrawl. Mercy killing or not, how Frankie acquired the property was enough to give anyone the chills, and, whether or not Zabriskie's papers were in order, it would have been impossible for Frankie to stay in Little Ridge after what he did—if going to the island was a choice, it was the only one he had. Thettie craned her neck to see it in the distance behind the manor house, but it was hidden by some big-ass rotunda.

Before he'd fallen off the wagon last night, Lee said he had been sober five years—since the day his son went missing. For Thettie it had been a decade—since Doc had pulled her drowning boys from the lake and she decided to get clean. So that was another thing she and Lee had in common. Wagons.

She could murder a bourbon, though, kill it twice. Then she'd be ready to let Lee talk about his missing lizard, and she'd talk, too, about how the want in her was so strong, that sometimes all she wanted was not to want.

She reached the last house on Main Street before the headland. She side-eyed the wild orchard of curling fruit trees. Vernon's MISSING fliers flapped from the windscreens of the few cars in the lone Gas 'n' Go lot across the street. Thettie turned down a steep driveway to Lee's house and past an old-fashioned wooden garage. Webs flapped beneath its eaves. Behind it was a sparse wood and she remembered the old haunted schoolhouse in the middle of it somewhere—Cassie claimed to have lost her virginity there, and everyone said it was to Frankie, but Thettie knew that wasn't true. Cassie lost her virginity at the Motel 6 to something that called itself a man but wasn't.

ALETHEIA

The rusted bones of a swing set gave Thettie tetanus just to look at it. Twilight made black unlidded eyes of the windows on the little ranch house, and she hurried past it toward the studio Bryce told her about, a converted wrought-iron greenhouse patched in timber and sheet metal with a thread of silver smoke wisping from what looked like an old train chimney. It would have been an eyesore if anyone but an artist had put it together. But Lee had made the studio beautiful. He'd riveted overlapping sheets of metal to the steel frame leaving odd-shaped windows of thick glass between them, like a fairy tale home. It was like one of those drawings Frankie used to show her of the kind of magical house they'd live in one day. Her and him and the boys.

Inside the studio, with dusk threading around the windows, Thettie breathed in coffee and solvents, Lee's scent, and a familiar funk she couldn't place. The front door was flanked by shelves stacked with books—textbooks and glossy art books and creased science books with molecules and sandstorms on their covers. Some of the books had paint fingerprints on the spine and on pages left open at an image or an underlined passage. There were also sketchbooks and notebooks. She picked up a snow dome of Death Valley and put it down between a *calaca* mask and a plastic Spiderman.

Thettie stumbled over a giant Tonka pick-up truck, big enough for a kid to ride in, except that its yellow hinged bed was stacked with art books and canvases that caught her on the shin. It would bruise tomorrow. She hopped on one leg, looking for the source of the coffee smell. Shelves, running most of the way around the small space, served the dual purpose of storage and insulation. Lee had paneled the interior in more overlapping sheets of metal and wood around the glass and steel frame of the original greenhouse.

It was blindingly bright and felt wondrously warm. On the easel beside a central table was a painting of the lake. It was rendered in blocky brush strokes—grays, blues and browns, with threads of red and yellow. There was the island in the distance, like a hole in the canvas, or a piece of bone stuck to it. She had to bend down to see if it was, in fact, a hole or a rip in the actual canvas but it was painted on, a heavy glob of off-white.

She pivoted slowly around and around in wonder. Stacked canvases spiraled around her, bare and covered, finished and barely begun. Paint tubes and watercolor blocks, and jars of murk. Brushes lay drying beside a sink. Cattails teetered in an enamel pail of water. And so much lake. Everywhere, images of the lake in paint, charcoal, pencil, Polaroids, computer-printouts. The lake in summer, blue as a lie. In winter, all angel hair and dirty ice. The autumn lake ringed in blood, in springtime, a pink and yellow dawn. Warm and bright as the studio was, it was like something had flipped. There was an inside-out feeling to the space that began to unnerve her, the outer and the inner trading places. That and no paintings of people that she could see. No faces. None. Just Lee out there naked and searching for his son, the lake gathered and settled in here like some winged and nameless flock. Beneath the windows, on the table, beside an uneaten grilled cheese sandwich, the lake gathered and fed, crowding him out.

Thettie began to feel dizzy. The unsettling funk

clawed at the back of her throat and she saw that it came from a reptile tank on a low stand in the corner. It was a large Perspex box with a mesh cover, and there was sand and other things that looked like rocks behind the glass. It was empty, but emitted a vague stink like old vomit, and a low hum, probably from a heating element. Left on just in case he came back.

Vernon.

There was a part of her that knew Bryce was right and the lizard monster, old and ailing, must have been stolen, but by who? By what? Sarey would say that fear can create and fear can destroy. Fear is the most powerful emotion, Sarey said, more powerful than love or hate, because it has no life of its own but must imitate life stolen from other feelings. Fear, Sarey said, was a story we told ourselves about our future. Had the future stolen Vernon? Had Thettie's own fear scared it off? Was it, again, all her fault? And if she stopped fearing Vernon, and he came back, what would he want in return?

Thettie banged around loudly looking for coffee, wishing Lee would hurry back, and wondering how long she'd be able to wait for him. She looked down at the reptile tank. It was about the size of a child's paddle pool, or play pen. Had her fear driven off the only thing Lee had left to love?

Cassie would say that she was being a space monkey. It's not your fault, Thet. None of it.

As well as the paintings, there were Polaroids everywhere—of the lake, of the shore, of the sky, of a blurry blue-jay in a bird box—just no people. None of his son or his wife. No human faces. Looking around she began to get that dream-like quality of living through something twice. Once in the present when it was there and then again when it was gone.

She turned on the coffee pot. She went back and pressed a key on the laptop. The image of Vernon eating the pizza crust leapt out at her. She yelped and slammed it shut.

She could use a cigarette, would have to smoke it outside, but knew that if she stepped out the door, she wouldn't come back. The canvases pressed ever closer. Between them she glimpsed a couple of pictures of Vernon—more like scientific drawings than anything. But mostly the lake, over and over again, from both shores, and from a boat, all its inlets and coves. He must have traveled every inch of it. Frozen over, the shore blanketed in snow, fringed in fall flame, or giddy summers. In charcoal, oils, watercolors, chalks. Long dawns cauled in mist or cowered beneath sheet lightning. The island stood implacable in one, wreathed in spray. In another it crouched waiting for the unrisen sun. In another it shrank from a rascally moon.

'Holy shit! It won't let you leave . . .'

She picked up a new Polaroid camera on the table. The old angles had become high-tech curves. The dials were now LEDs. But it was still the same basic camera that had captured her and Cassie in their tree-humping innocence.

There was a quality to the Polaroid image, especially as it deteriorated, like memory itself, that Lee said he liked. She smiled for the birdie. A flash burst and she was blind in one eye for several seconds. When her vision returned, she depressed a button and out it came. Blank and sticky, and smaller than the ones from her girlhood. She watched her face materialize in the frame. Skinny and freckled, framed by strands of straw-colored hair. Eyes blue like a sign outside a titty joint—LIVE GIRLS!—a little too bright, and rough around the edges.

'Jesus H,' she said out loud. 'Talk about deteriorate.'

Something rustled in Vernon's tank. Thettie dropped the selfie like she'd been bit, and ran back out into the weather.

12. PUPPET

LEE WATCHED THE one-eyed girl disappear between the lazy swirl of leaves, feeling a tightness in his chest. Heavy weather came suddenly in these parts, as if everything the year had tried so hard to hang on to suddenly came unstuck. Lee shrugged his collar around his neck and left the campground to go back to his car and wait for Thettie back at the studio. Golden leaves sucked at his boots and flung themselves under the car. He pressed the remote. The lock clicked at the same moment that he registered Sheriff Boyle and Deputy Abbes in the truck parked a few spaces down. He carefully ignored them. He opened his car door.

'You looking for something?' a voice called out from across the parking lot.

Sheriff Boyle had rolled down the window of this truck, but the cheap shot had come from Abbes. Lee closed the door with a calm he didn't feel, waited for the sheriff to state his business.

Boyle wore glasses, heavy black narc frames. He flicked at his moustache with his finger. The department had mangled the investigation into Lee's son's disappearance, not realizing that it was Bud Wallace until too late. Lee had tried to bring Boyle down over his alleged connections with the deGroots, how they had their own reason for not wanting Wallace to be investigated too closely, and put pressure on Boyle to close the case. Lee set up interviews with the city papers, a lawsuit, official letters of complaint to the Police Commissioner in Ilium, implying an obstruction of justice on the part of Boyle, implying a conflict of interest involving the deGroots. It was an election year for Boyle, which meant that the deGroots had to call in some serious favors, and neither Boyle or the deGroots let Lee forget it. Any step Lee took out of line, even a parking ticket, would bring the whole department down on him, plus anything the deGroots could pull out of the whole Tantra mess, to boot. Lee stayed at the edge of town, took care of Vernon, kept out of trouble. Until now.

The college bells pealed 4 pm. Lee watched the men across the leaf-blown bonnet of the wagon. He felt a burning in his gut, like indigestion, but to the left, near his heart.

'Last thing I need with all this going on,' Boyle said, jutting his chin out toward the Harpurs campground, 'is a runaway poison lizard. Any idea where it got to?'

'You tell me and we'll both know, Sheriff.'

'Not the first time it's run off. You looked down at Zabriskie's pagoda like last time?'

'It's not Zabriskie's anymore, Sheriff, remember? Belongs to Frankie Harpur now.'

The deGroots paid Boyle to turn a blind eye and talk with a forked tongue. The less he knew about his bosses, the better. Lee recognized the sad blur of a man chasing his own tail, and for once it wasn't him.

Abbes started to say something, but Boyle cut in. 'All in order, far as we were concerned. Slightly irregular, I'll give you that, and I'll admit to being a tad concerned that Eli was of sound mind when he made the codicil. But Doc Burlington said the only thing wrong with Eli was the cancer, the rest of him was sharp as a tack. Besides, that old Frankie . . . '

'He wasn't—isn't—that old,' Lee said. 'My age, I'd say. More or less.'

'Man smelled like a shit that's taken a shit, young, old, or in between. That hunk of rock's the best place for him.'

'Out of sight, out of mind,' Abbes said.

'And Frances Washington Harpur was a war hero,' Lee said. 'You ever been out there looking for our very own war hero, Sheriff? Check to see if he's still alive?'

'It's private property,' Boyle said, leaning out the window. He looked exhausted—the veins on his nose tangled as an old road map. 'Four signs to that effect—one at each compass point.'

"Enter at Your Own Risk," said Abbes.

'You could get a warrant,' Lee said. 'Or apply for a government easement ... '

'Easier said than done.'

"Dangerous Waters," Abbes put in. 'We put up the signs ourselves.'

'The island is part of the history of Little Ridge ... '

'What history?' Abbes said.

Boyle turned back to the Harpurs milling around on the shore. 'Easy to get out of your depth if you don't know what you're doing.'

Lee clicked the remote again, opened the door so slowly it squealed. He picked up a nervousness in Boyle's voice, even fear, but whether of or for the Harpurs, Lee couldn't say.

'Hold on,' Abbes got out of the truck, sauntered around, theatrically brushing a headlight with his sleeve. Boyle rolled his eyes. 'We still got a missing venomous lizard to take care of. Wouldn't want anyone to get bit.'

Lee wondered if Bryce had passed on his message to Thettie. He felt time slipping away from him.

'Gila bites don't typically result in lethal envenoming, Deputy. Even if you do get bitten, you'd get to a hospital before the venom could kill you.'

'Make you pretty sick, though, right? Puking and whatnot. Asphyxiation I read on the Internet.'

'Kids running around,' Abbes said, 'Halloween and what not. We need to catch this fucker and quick. What exactly are we dealing with here?'

'A cold hungry reptile is what you're dealing with, Deputy. Pretty much immobilized in the cold I'd say. You could walk right up to him and give him a kiss and he couldn't make a move to save himself. The reward should help.'

Boyle fiddled with his side mirror. 'You think one of those Harpur's stole it?'

Lee said, 'Who said anything about stolen? Who said anything about Harpurs? You want something to hang on them, surely you can do better than that?'

His mind shot back to the studio, the undisturbed tank, the lakes crowding in.

'Just seems a little coincidental, don't it?' Abbes said, picking a tooth. 'Look at them. They're starving. They're cold. Kids are getting sick. A valuable reptile that'd fetch a good price on Craigslist goes missing right after they arrive. While you were fucking one of their women, according to the rumor mill.'

'Your wife was busy. Now, if you'll excuse me.'

Abbes pulled his hand away from his mouth, just ahead of a string of spit. He took a step or two toward Lee.

Boyle said. 'Get back in the car, Deputy.'

Lee lowered himself behind the wheel. Revved the engine and made a wide swathe around the Sheriff's truck.

'Maybe it's true!' Boyle yelled after Lee. 'Maybe that woman was just a distraction, keep you busy, so's whoever can help themselves to an exotic reptile. The old bait and switcheroo.'

Lee revved and skidded out of the parking lot, Boyle receding in the rearview, and the first of the Harpur barbecue fires just beginning to burn.

13. PROTECTION

SHE WAITED, PACING along the shoulder, for Lee to arrive. A watery face pressed against the dark glass of the Gas 'n' Go watched her from across the street. To its north, bald fields stretched out to a burnished tree line in the shadow of the eastern ridge that gave the town its name. A dirt-colored farmhouse hugged the woods—one of the migrant worker shacks from before Thettie's time. The shack was where Frankie's and Doc's army buddy, Bud Wallace used to live—a creepy ham radio nut used to run product for the deGroots. A bank of clouds dumped rain on the eastern ridge. Lee's studio was as far away from the town's bars as humanly possible, and Thettie wondered if that had been a deliberate move on his wife's part. After a while, when Lee still hadn't shown, Thettie decided to give up. She would walk back to the campsite and then head straight to the bar. She hunched into Archy's pea coat and started walking south, back down Main Street, glad to be out of the studio. Lee, seeing her calling card, would understand her meaning and come looking for her at the Way like he did last time. She'd meant to leave a note on the back of it, but all the ghosts in that damn place had scared her off. That damn Tonka truck creaking back and forth under the weight of all that time.

A little red Ford pulled up a few yards ahead of her. She jogged toward it, thinking it was students on their way to the city, but it was not, and by the time she saw who it was, it was too late. Old mangled-up Lyle was at the wheel, with fat tattooed Homer beside him. Doc sat in the back, behind Homer, whistling. She could see that his cheekbones were chafed from the wind, except for the skin grafts which were as pale and dead as ever.

'Nice ride,' she said, stepping away from the car. 'Where'd you steal it from?'

'Get in.'

Thettie shook her head, the wind gusting her hair. 'Thanks, but I'll walk.'

By which time Doc had pushed the door open and Homer had stepped out and was at her elbow, and Thettie narrowly missed landing her ass on Doc's clenched fist as she was shoved in.

She felt for her seat belt and smiled brightly. 'You get to the island? How's Frankie?'

The interior of the car reeked of cheap cologne and toe jam. No one said anything. Doc swiveled his head to the right, craned his neck down toward Lee's place, but really looking at Frankie's manor, taking it in—the windows and curved gravel driveway, the hundred-car garage and the lake stretching out behind it. Thettie could tell he was thinking that whoever lived in that damn manor'd be king of the world.

'That was some party the other night,' Thettie said. 'Just like back in the day.'

'Been making house calls again, girl?' Doc said. 'Bet there weren't too many dangerous reptiles at that Motel 6 you and Cassie used to work. Back in the day.'

'Worse monsters than reptiles at that old joint,'

said Thettie. 'You have no idea.'

Except she knew he did.

'Bet you wouldn't have gone calling on your new friend if his Gila was still there,' Doc said.

'How'd you know it wasn't?'

Lyle caught Doc's eye in the rearview.

'Signs all over town,' Homer cut in. 'That's how.'

Doc just kept whistling.

'*Come on Eileen*,' Thettie sang softly.

Homer joined in. No one else said anything, and after a while Thettie stopped.

'Tomorrow's another day.' She smoothed down her hair, and reached for her compact, her mouth dry as deadfall.

Doc said, 'How's the big trailer? Comfy?'

Homer's tiny mouth looked like a belly button on a hairy belly—his eyes small and pink enough to be nipples. The thick pad of his neck fat was inked with patterns of the special razor wire they used at The Hill, beneath it the rough necklace of scar tissue from where someone back in the Philippines tried to hack off his head. She hadn't worked Homer out yet. Maybe he was smaller than he looked, like a trout beneath the surface of a stream. Tickle it and its yours forever, Cassie would say.

'Look at the Inn, Doc. Remember when it was just all run down and whatnot and we use to—holy shit, look at the library, looks like Disneyland with those statues of book characters. Is that the Runaway Bunny? Someone sure has poured money into this town. Used to be the place was shabby, but whatever, it was real. We'd all pile into Frankie's ride, raise hell. That was before your time.'

Doc yawned, but at least he'd stopped whistling.

J.S. BREUKELAAR

No one said anything else for the whole drive through the shivery Village that looked in the tarnished light to be shrinking under the great weight of sky. Thettie counted half a dozen Jack O' Lanterns. She could already taste that first beer. But instead of continuing down Route 90, as she thought he would, Lyle pulled off and onto the dirt track into Triangle Gully. The familiarity of the old road stopped Thettie's breath and she pressed her face against the window. The Aspen grove was exactly where she'd left it, the green creek below that carved its way into the lake like a vein that she could feel pulsing at her temple. She knew, suddenly, that it had been more than not having had the means that had stopped her coming back—the wheels, the money, what have you. All the excuses hadn't ever been the only or even the real reason. It was this green pulsing threat that it would never let her leave, nor she it.

'Why're we here, Doc? I didn't want to come here,' her voice caught like a little girl's.

'I know.'

They bounced around some more in the little car and then it stopped. Lyle and Homer got out and stood by the hatch, smoking. But Doc remained in the back seat, whistling again, his shoulders bunched like grapefruits beneath his coat. He looked at Thettie and smiled through his half a mouth. Thettie felt woozy from the funk of the car. She put her hand on his thigh. He washed his hair with special shampoo and gelled it so it looked like a silver crown on top of his head. His deep-set eyes were so close together as to eliminate any peripheral distractions. Like he ordered them that way specially. Maybe he had.

'Why are we here, Doc?'

'You got me,' Doc said, holding up his hands in fake surrender.

***

One time Grif had gone to the Millersville library and had searched for Daylin Murphy, maybe hoping to find out who Doc was or had been before he immigrated to America. Before he became a citizen and wormed his way into the armed forces as a fake-papered medic. What Grif found was a man of the same name born 1954 and buried 1990 in a little churchyard in County Sligo, Ireland. Doc said it was true. Doc wasn't his real name, neither Murphy.

'You got me,' he'd said, holding up his hands like in a game of stick-up. 'Imagine this. Imagine you're not so much born as dropped out. Raised motherless, you get real good at kicking priests in the nuts and licking Bovril offa spoons and not much else. Someone picks you up off the streets, a right gentleman, shows you your future in the palm of his hands. Becomes a father to you, just imagine, and his name is Paddy the Hook. Imagine Paddy puts you through medical school and all he asks in return is a little clean-up job now and then. Hijinks ensue involving a pimp called Toeless Mears and a widow who doesn't take to being a widow, nor to newly having five bairns to feed so, with one thing and another it's time to exit stage left. Enter Daylin Murphy, not needin' his identity any more on account of being buried under six feet of Sligo sod, and there's your chance. Future belongs to the brave. Boom.'

Grif asked what 'ensue' meant, and Archy said wasn't 'bairn' a Scottish word, and Thettie said,

'Where's Sligo?' But when Archy asked Doc what his name was before, Doc just took him by the arm and said, 'What kind of a monster do you think I'd be, boy, if I could burden some mother's son with that kind of intel?'

Not the worse kind, Thettie knew, and maybe not even a monster, but close enough.

***

'It's Frankie,' Doc leaned back in the cramped seat of the car. 'There's been a hiccough.'

The windows had fogged over completely. 'Spit it out, then,' Thettie's roaring ears made the sound of her own voice faint. 'It's the drinking hour, I swear.'

Doc's minty breath filled the car. She patted him on the leg and pushed open the door, feeling like she was choking. Above her on the ridge, the Hemlocks greenly massed. Doc came out the other side, and they stood with the car between them, looking down the Gully at what remained of their little settlement. The float homes were mostly gone. A few of the docks remained. One or two had collapsed into the green and churning creek. Ancient trees holding onto the hillside by their exposed roots. The unhealed wound of the horizon opened to the west where Thettie could see the lake through a parting in the trees. There was a dirt-colored house in a clearing below. Torn curtains hung at the windows, and when they moved a little, Thettie bit her lip so she wouldn't cry out.

'Eastern Hemlocks,' said Doc, turning to sweep his hand at the forest that filled the valley to the east. '*Tsuga Canadensis*. You can tell by the dippy tip.'

If you followed a hidden path behind what remained of Doc's houseboat, you got to an old moonshiner's cabin in the woods, and a disused shipping container beside it. Frankie and Doc had cooked their mixes there until the Sheriff's department raided it on a dippy tip, ten years ago.

'I know the botanical name of every tree in the state and I still need a drink,' said Thettie. 'The DPR have the land now anyway, so who cares? My ancestors lived here, built some of the original log cabins they tore down. Some higher up in the valley are still standing, built out of Hemlock slabs. My woodsman great-great-great-granddaddy used the creek to float the slabs down into the lake, and to move them up and down the ice to all the other towns along the canal.'

'That was before crystal meth and Afghanistan and the downturn, girl. That was before Boyle and his men ran us off. What if we could have it all back again? You could be Queen Bee, just like before. Sittin' pretty with me and Frankie taking care of business.'

Sitting pretty?

'That why you brought me here, Doc? To make fun of me. Two words: Eminent Domain. Now how's about that drink?'

Thettie regretted forgetting her cigarettes in the car, regretted not waiting for Lee. Would he get her message?

'It wasn't just to make fun of you,' Doc snarled from the good half of his mouth. 'I brought you here so you could see it, remember what it was and what it could be again, if you play your cards right.'

Thettie felt eyes on her from behind the evergreen spines, and from behind the sumacs and maples, too. Like each leaf of every branch was and eye sending a message, blinking off and one to every other leaf. A jolt of unease ran up her spine. Lyle and Homer stood to one side. Lyle dangled a shotgun. Homer had a rifle over his shoulder and pulled a Steelers' cap over his bald head, his beard ruffling in the wind.

'How?' she said with one eye on the shack. 'How do we get it all back?'

Did the curtain flutter again? Did a sooty flash shoot out of the chimney, like one of the shadow things in the lake?

'Forest Path,' Doc said quietly.

Thettie looked from Homer with his rifle to the little dirt-colored shack with its torn curtains and pails for the dogs nestled in the hogweed, a triangulation that finally began to make sense. Geometry is fate, Frankie would say, and she never got that until now.

'This thing Frankie's cooking on the island,' Lyle was saying. 'This designer drug.'

'Devil's Butt?' she said.

Doc shook his head. 'Punters are looking to the next big thing, girl. Smart drugs. This one Frankie's working on is called Forest Path. The Killer Mix.'

'What's that got to do with me?'

Lyle muttered something making mock sign language with his finger, Homer trying not to smile.

'This just in,' Doc said. 'Frankie wants to see you, and no one but you.'

She stared at him. The wind had died down. There was no sound except for rain dripping from the trees, and Homer mouth-breathing behind his beard. 'You saw him? Frankie?'

'He shot at us, which is just as good. The old fire-hose effect. Frankie hasn't lost his touch—I'd know an old sharpshooter anywhere. But we couldn't get nearer than cooee.'

Behind Doc, Lyle's fingers flowered open and shut like explosions.

'It was raining like a bitch out there, girl. Hand to God. Island covered in mist and dogs barking and all. Couldn't see a damn thing.'

At a nod from Doc, Homer lit a cigarette and passed it to her.

Thettie's tongue felt thick. She drew on the cigarette to even her out but also to cover a new smell that had carried to her on the soggy breeze.

'Back up,' she said as slow as she could. 'How do you know that he wants to see me?'

'Just this messenger on a Jet Ski. Came out of nowhere.'

Thettie noticed Homer and Lyle exchanging looks. Homer mouthed the word, 'nowhere.' Doc leaned against the car, resting his forearms on the roof and gazing into the woods. 'Frankie's big Indian muscle on a big fucking Jet Ski. He had some beast on a chain riding pillion and all. The goddamnest thing you ever saw.'

'A wolf-dog,' said Homer. 'Big silver hound.'

Doc's eyes had shrunk to two tiny apertures. The apertures narrowed and the grey discs within slid to Sarey's shack, to the hemlocks beyond, to Lyle's handgun.

'He talked to you?' Thettie said. 'This so-called Indian?'

'You deaf, girl? He said Frankie wanted to see you and the boys alone.'

'Wait. I thought . . . weren't my boys with you?'

Doc smiled his half-smile, like Popeye but without his pipe. Lyle and Homer braced at a sudden rustle from the trees, raised their guns to nothing. 'At first they was and then they wasn't. We lost them due to currents, what have you. They might of got caught up in an inlet. How the hell should I know?'

Doc stepped away from the car, came around to pick up the cigarette she'd fumbled, passed it back to her. 'Nothing more to tell. Indian said you, Archy and Grif was to come in a small boat tomorrow. He'd take you to the island to see Frankie. Said if me or my muscle so much stepped on the shore, it'd be the last step we took.' Doc opened his close-set eyes as wide as they'd go and made fake tsk-tsking noises. 'After all I did for that boy.'

Thettie lifted her face to the dusk, feeling the fine mist sizzle on her hot skin.

'We don't really know if it's Frankie.' But she did.

'Only one way to find out, then. You tell Frankie I'm ready to let bygones be bygones. And once Frankie comes back to the fold, we got all this here just waiting for us.' Doc swept his scarred hand out to the ruins. 'You just leave the DPR to me.'

She almost believed he believed it. 'What's in it for him, Doc? Or me?'

What she meant, and they both knew this, was what would it cost her?

'I guarantee your protection. Your whole family's. No questions asked.'

'Are you for real?' She put one hand on her hip and cocked her head at him. 'Since when do we need your protection?'

'Since now.'

Lyle adjusted his gun.

'So this is how it is, Doc?'

There was a pause, and Thettie's kept her eyes fixed on the curtain in Sarey's window.

'Not this, but something. Not now but sometime. How it is, is up to you, girl. But by my reckoning I'm the least of your problems. Things have changed. You said so yourself. Between the Progress Association, Boyle, and the Dutch—make things right with me and Frankie, and I make them all go away.'

Frankie would say, A person's enemies are never all in the one place.

'Come on, girl. Frankie needs you. He's dying out there alone the Island. You're the only one that can cure him. And then who knows. Forest Path . . .'

Boom.

'Why's it called that, Doc?'

Find the blind spot, Sarey said—what they refuse to see for looking is what they're afraid of. Sarey would say that there's room to move in the forgotten parts of the big picture, room to grow like a wild rose behind an outhouse—all petal and thorn. All these years, and Thettie still hadn't found petals but there was still time. Wasn't there?

Lyle lifted his shotgun to chest level so he could pick his nose.

'Fine, if that's the way you want it.' The caw of distance crows drifted from the woods. Sarey would say that some men get so caught up in the sound of their own voices, they don't hear the caws for the crows. 'Why's it called that? Forest Path.'

'On account of what we got in our head,' Lyle said over his shoulder. He and Homer faced dutifully outward—Homer's back fat curving right up to his ears beneath a hunting jacket, and Lyle's crooked spine swathed in thermals, the sleeves too short for his long twitching arms.

'The way the nerves branch like trees in a forest.' Homer carved a path in the air with his tattooed hand.

'Means to an end,' Doc tried to spit from his half-mouth, making a mess of it. 'Nothing personal, Thet. Me and Frankie—*we're* the dream team. Always were and always will me. All you was, was what made that happen. Frankie would call you a catalyst.'

She looked into the next minute and the next, could see her and Archy and Grif and Frankie together again, maybe. On the island? Like a picnic. All the colors of the leaves, that yellow of the aspens, Frankie's favorite. Like lemon drops, he said. He'd forgive her. She'd bring him the salve for his foot. Her MiraKil cream. They'd bundle back into the boat—it'd have to be the Black Crown to fit them all—head north to Canada, put this place behind them. Never lay eyes on it again. The lake, the eastern ridge blocking the light. She peered into the glow of that moment, tried to see it, and mostly did, except for what was wrong with the picture.

'What makes you think I'd betray Frankie again? My own cousin?'

'What makes you think you won't?'

The first round sent a branch cracking down at their feet. The second took out a tire. Lyle returned fire, and Thettie spun.

A woman stepped out from the dirt-colored shack with a Mossberg rifle pointed up at them Thettie recognized the gun before she remembered the face behind it. The rifle was aimed at Doc. The woman's hair was like gray cobweb, and you could see the shape of her skull through the floss. Her eyes were electric blue, but they were haunted and unfocused and crying, too.

Thettie was crying now, stepped out from behind the car. 'Sarey, it's me!'

Sarey fired again. Doc's burnt-away nostrils quivered, and he raised the .44 he had up his sleeve the whole time, so she could see the *Semper Fi* tattoo looping up his arm. Thettie heard a shrill *caw-caw*, and saw in slow motion that Sarey had clipped Lyle in the rump. Something crawled in Sarey's tangled hair. Homer tossed the rifle in the car and hoisted his 9, but Thettie shoved her foot in the back of his knee, the shot going wide. She scrambled and waved her arms toward Sarey and ran toward her, slipping on the dry dirt of the descending road.

'Stop. Wait, I've come home.'

Sarey fired. The shot landed in the dead fall a yard from where Thettie was heading, sending up a spray of dirt and branches, and Thettie heard herself scream. She skidded to a stop, fell on her ass. *Caw-caw*, the crows shrieked, their caws echoing between secret stream and sky.

Sarey said, 'Mem-mem-mem.'

'Sarey!' Thettie screeched. 'Don't!'

Doc said, 'Nice to see you, Sarey.'

'We've come for Frankie,' said Thettie, waving feathers from her face. 'I came back Sarey, like I always said I would. I'm going to go across to the island and see him in the morning. And then I'll come back for you.'

The old woman cocked the rifle. She looked from one to another.

'A mem-mem-means to an end, Thetis Harpur, remem-mem-ber—' Blue eyeballs the size of quarters bulged in her seamed face. She lifted her head and stuttered a caw in answer to the crows.

There was a terrible mockery to her voice. *Caw-caw*. Something moved in her hair.

'Remember what, Sarey? What?'

'Remem-member n-n-not to die!'

And even as she said it, the curtain parted on that moment Thettie had tried to look into before. And she saw Doc, clear as morning. Why he brought her here. Not to show her what he was going to get back for her if she brought him Frankie on a plate, but what he would take from her if she didn't— how everything she had was his means to an end. He'll start with Sarey, holding her to ransom in case Thettie did not return from the island, but it wouldn't stop there. Her sons would be next. Then Frankie himself. And Thettie he'd save for last but not until she'd known the hell of having outlived them all—life, love and even death. He came here to show her one thing and it was all he knew. How, until you've stopped breathing, and even after that, there's always more to lose.

'Let her go, Doc! You got me. I'll talk to Frankie.'

'That you will!' Doc brayed. 'But you think I'd let you and them go off to the island alone without taking out some protection? It's for your own good, girl, and Sarey's to boot. Besides I always was a sucker for that soda bread of yours, Sare.'

'Aw Sarey,' Thettie's ribs knifed in a cramp, and sitting there in the dirt and the leaves, the sobs shook her like she was a doll. 'I missed you something awful.'

Sarey locked eyes with Thettie for a moment before

she started to laugh, soundlessly. The yellow branches alive with claw and wing. The wind tore through the ragged leaves, call of memory. Sarey's eyes widened. Her shoulders convulsed with mirth. *Caw-caw-caw.* She stopped abruptly and spat into the lightless dust between them.

Doc said, 'I'll get some men up here, Sare, to look out for you.'

He began to tee-hee, leprechaun-style, but Sarey's whistle stopped him short. Thettie saw a doubled flash of teeth and red gums and tried to pull herself up from the dirt, scrabbling to catch up with Homer who had already made it to the car. Doc was crawling into the back and Lyle screamed in the passenger seat. Thettie swung into the door, got in just ahead of a drooling mastiff—white as dirty snow. Its right eye seeped black gunk that left ragged streaks down one side of its muzzle, and out of its left eye-socket blinked the eye of a human with a perfectly round golden brown eyeball, set in creamy white. It barred fangs dripping with the same black goo that wept from its eye and when she slammed the car on its paw, it gave a human shriek of anguish.

'Stop!' Thettie cried, but Homer put the car into second and heaved it up the switchback, dragging the howling dog along by its paw, until she got the door open enough to kick it out, its crushed foreleg obscenely waving at her as it spun away down the hill.

At first Thettie was sure one of the crows had got caught in the car with them, but it was just Doc laughing again but not like he meant it any more.

'You kill me, girl. Always have.'

***

After they changed the tire on the highway, Homer got back behind the wheel. Thettie pressed her lips together in the back seat and refused to meet Homer's little piggy eyes in the rearview. Her throat filled with sharp tears. Homer had been running his eyes over her body ever since Doc had brought him and Lyle on board. Just waiting for his chance. She'd be ready. She was always ready. Wasn't she?

Lyle whimpered in the seat beside Doc spinning Sarey's attack like it was a comedy.

'See that old piece, Lyle, see the recoil? 'Most put her on her ass.'

'You okay, Lyle?' Homer said. 'He's hurting bad, Doc.'

'This is where I get off,' Thettie said when they pulled up at the Way, because it was Lyle's ass got a piece torn off it and Doc would need to see to it, and even Thettie could see the funny side to that.

The inside of the Way swam and twinkled, its surfaces reflected inward like a geode. Bottles, mirrors, pitchers and framed posters twinkled and crystallized through the tears and dirt in her eyes. She made a bee-line for the restroom. Her face in the mirror was masked with dirt. She pulled a black feather from her hair. It fluttered to the tiles and she watched it fall, then went and puked in the bowl. She had blood from the corner of her eye where a branch gouged her, and scratches on her arms, too. She shook a stone from her boot. Slammed the boot against the stall door five, six times, and put it back on. Weeping, she splashed her face with water, covered the scratches with make-up and smoked a joint, her gut in spasms. She pushed back out into the bar and there was a piece of herself reflected back in every mirror, nothing fitting together any more.

She bought a beer and a double shot of Avery's swill, and took a seat at a booth along the wall. The first sip burned her lips like a French kiss. She took another and kept her eyes open for her Grif and Archy. Somewhere on the inside, though, she let the lights go off and the curtains fall. From somewhere far away, the soft click of billiard balls counted down the years.

2012, Pennsylvania. The Landing Strip had closed down to make way for a new craft beer bar. The strippers all dressed up with nowhere to go. They hung around for a while at the new place, doing their best to lower its tone. Five, six inked lovelies, skirts too tight, broken heels and missing teeth, standing at the edge of the gentrified bar like dirt blowing in through a window. Minders not much older or tougher than the girls themselves spun in their orbit like ragged new moons. After a while they disappeared. Girls and minders both. One turned up as a congress woman. A few surfaced at a juke joint near the Landing. One of them, Joanie over there, ended up marrying Thettie's second cousin, Clay.

Because this is how it will end, this want at the edge of things.

Thettie's burning eyes blinked opened to scan for her sons. A truck driver and a soda salesman sat at the bar, both on their phones. The barman leaned across a newspaper and above him the TV replayed the hockey. The after-chore farmers and pool-addict crowd started to build, if you could call it a crowd. More like a few hair-of-the-dog truckers and the feed-store staff on their way home for some Dutch courage.

The Harpur girls—Joanie, Shelly, Leanne and the twins—sashayed in to work their wiles, but Thettie sighed, her heart slowing. *Hold your fire, ladies, ship has sailed.*

All the Pedialyte Thettie could buy at the drug store hadn't touched the sides of the gut bug rampant throughout the camp. Someone had vandalized the water vending machine and shat on the floor of the ladies' showers. Game over, girls. We thought we could come back home, but we'd gone too far. Like an overwound spring, a music box wound so tight that the ballerina just jerks on her toes. Dance of the dead, Frankie would say.

The lake with its freezing depths and weeping shores under the wash of sky, the scab of glacial rock that surfaced at will and where Frankie had gone to die—or to wait for her return, whichever came first. What did Doc really want? If she was Doc's key to the future, what did that say about her past? More important, what if he lost the key, or it lost itself?

Whose future would disappear, hers or Doc's and was there ever a difference? Or was that just another lost chance gone by?

The black feathers in Sarey's hair. Lord. That big white dog with the human eye and the stuttering crows.

Archy walked in and sat down next to her at the booth. 'You okay?'

'It's been a long day,' she said.

A nod from Thettie was all it took to get one of the girls over with a fresh pitcher of beer and clean glasses on the table.

'Where you been?' he said.

'Doc took me for a trip down memory lane, and Aunt Sarey was waiting there with a rifle and son of Cujo. Or daughter.'

'You hit? Bit?'

'You ever seen a dog cry?'

Archy, who knew everything about animals, said, 'Dogs can't cry, Ma. Not tears. They whimper, and sometimes they don't even do that. Most just suffer in silence.'

'Well this one was crying,' she said. 'Sarey clipped Lyle on the butt with that old-as-Moses rifle of hers.'

'Lyle ain't got a butt to clip, else I'd have done it myself.'

'Her stutter's gotten worse.' Thettie blew out a thin stream of smoke, glancing sideways to where her son hadn't touched his beer. He'd slept in his clothes by the looks of it, ketchup caught in the pocket of his jacket. His eyes were bloodshot beneath the low brow. The pretty mouth and patchy beard. She reached out and touched his hair, expecting him to flinch, but he didn't.

'Where is everyone?'

'You mean Grif? I thought he was with you?' she said, meaning she hoped he was.

'I saw Bryce coming out of Grif's trailer this morning, so I don't think so.'

'About that,' Thettie took her cub's big warm paw and wrapped it around the cold beer. 'It was just a matter of waiting until she could get her own trailer. He never touched her, Arch. She told me so herself.'

Archy raised the glass to his mouth, wiped the foam off his moustache with a calloused knuckle. 'I guessed. But I wasn't sure.'

'Well, be sure. Best keep a girl like that on your good side.'

Grif came through the door. Archy stiffened and rose to his feet, but Thettie got a hand to his arm, and he stayed put. Emilio and Dustin peeled off Grif like drones from a jet and he approached the table alone. Thettie motioned for him to sit down on her other side, poured him a beer. Grif shrugged off his leather jacket, unleashing the dark whiff of the lake. He lurched a little on the seat. A damp lock of hair fell across the crease between his eyes. He ignored his brother.

'I saw Doc's fools down at the camp ground, looking majorly worse for wear.' He took the cigar from his mouth, held it between his silver-ringed fingers. 'You okay, Ma?'

At that, Archy magicked up a bottle of Jack and some shot glasses, and then there they were. One of her hands brushed Archy's, the other wrapped around a cold glass of beer, Grif pouring shots, and Thettie sitting pretty between her two boys, with her heart full of feathers.

So long as they were by her side, she was safe, and so long as she was by theirs, they were, too. Let Doc think their futures belonged to him. She'd find another path. She let her eyelids dip for a moment and her head fell back against the headrest. Someone had hit the jukebox and it was playing a song she vaguely recognized.

'You okay?' Grif said again.

She nodded. 'Tired as hell.' But this wasn't tired. This was a chance, a choice. And she needed a moment to weigh the consequences.

'You get unpacked?'

'Not yet. Smells funny in there. I keep thinking I hear someone upstairs, but there isn't an upstairs.'

'We didn't like you stuck on the end, by the trees,' Archy said, by way of an apology. 'The double's bigger, right? Better bathroom, too. A closet. And closer to us.'

'Well, yeah,' she said. 'But the view's not as good.'

Bryce walked in and started chalking a pool cue.

'Weird,' Archy finally said. 'How she appeared out of the blue like that, back at the Landing. Either of you think that? I mean why then, just when Frankie got his new mix up and running?'

Archy the thinker.

'You think Doc knew her?' Grif said. 'From before?'

'Not Doc,' Thettie said, 'Frankie's running her.'

Archy's face twisted.

'Not for that,' Thettie took the cigarette from his fingers, brought it to her lips. 'For bringing him intel, supplies, running errands.'

'He sent her to come get us?'

'I knew there was more to her,' Grif said, but there was admiration in his voice now. 'You did too, Ma.'

'Is or was, you're to leave her be,' Thettie said, putting her hand to her heart.

'She belongs to Frankie,' Archy said. 'Weird . . . '

'She doesn't belong to anyone,' Thettie said. 'She's her own self. She belongs to the lake.'

'Frankie should of told her how to spell her own name,' Grif grinned at his brother.

Thettie shot him a warning look. 'What happened on the lake? Doc said Frankie shot at you and some big guy on a Jet Ski came out and said we were to come back tomorrow. Just us.'

'We never got there,' Grif lit his cigar and wearily

puffed on it. 'We were right beside Doc and his boys one minute, the next our boat near missed a warning pylon that came out of nowhere and then we were all turned around.'

'We could hear the barking anyways,' Archy said. 'And that rifle of his.'

They told her about the Jet Ski they saw over near Doc's boat, some big guy on it, hound riding pillion.

The lights had dimmed in the bar. Thettie picked up pizza smells from the kitchen, and her mouth watered.

'Wait,' Grif said, holding his cigar up between a thumb tattooed with a black star and a finger with a red R on the knuckle, and talking to the cigar the way he did when he need a listener dumber than he was, Archy would say. 'Why would Doc let you and us alone with Frankie? I mean what's to stop us just airlifting him outa there. Heading down to Mexico.'

'Canada's closer,' Archy said.

'Sarey,' Thettie said, breaking down into messy sobs that released something in her. They waited, Grif smoking quietly, and Archy twisting his silver rings. When she could talk again, she said 'He's got Sarey hostage, but he says it's for her and my protection. Just in case Frankie's got ill intent. We're to tell him that if we don't come back, Sarey's a goner. He says if we bait Frankie right, get him to parlay, Doc'll make sure no one can touch us. Not the deGroots, the sheriff, nobody.'

No one said anything for a while.

Archy said slowly, 'Protection from the protector.'

Grif said, 'From day one, the day he came out of the desert . . .'

'Bringing Frankie back to us, like an offering . . . '

'The deal was sealed. We were all goners.'

'I'm the bait,' Thettie, said, drying her eyes. 'The key to the door. The means to the end.'

What Frankie would say, was that these were each metaphors for the same unspeakable exchange. Except for one thing.

'What's the switch, Ma?'

'Me. It's all me.'

She was getting drunk too quickly, but at least she was no longer hungry. 'Forest Path. That new mix of Frankie's. Doc wants in.'

'What in the tarnation is Forest Path?' Grif said, getting his hillbilly on to make her smile. They all bent in close to each other, and Thettie wiped her tears away to think how, to anyone walking into the bar right now, they'd look like a three-headed monster.

Archy lined up their glasses, ran the bottle back and forth along the row, licked the excess off his fingers. 'Bryce told me about it. It's a new smart drug. Peptides and enzymes and herbs and such. Helps with learning.'

'Holy shit,' Grif said. 'What's the fun in that?'

Archy shook his head with mock pity. 'It's a rush, Bryce said. Some kind of hyper-awareness. Like speed but without the crash.'

Grif slammed his back into the booth. His eyes were like headlights from the future, staring at nothing. Archy shot a look at Thettie, the worried hunch of his shoulders unchanged since he was a boy. Grif leaned across and wiped a fine line of spittle from the side of Archy's mouth with the filthy cuff of his jacket.

'Maybe Frankie's running more than just Bryce, ever think of that?' Archy looked the question at his brother.

They both stared at him, Grif uncomprehendingly, and Thettie with a rush of hope. Grif sat back and puffed on his cigar, waiting for someone to explain the joke to him, too.

'All I'm saying is that Frankie knows Sarey's still at the Gully, and he knows Doc better than anyone. A man like Doc needs human collateral, always has. Call him a people person—man's only as good as the folks he thinks he's running. Frankie would be one step ahead of that, knowing Doc would stop at nothing to get what Frankie has. Maybe.'

The dream team, Doc had said. Thettie sat up straight and paid attention to her Archy the Thinker.

Grif puffed and listened, his eyes Jell-O blue. He waved across another round and then waited for the girl to leave. 'Are you saying that maybe Frankie's the one playing Doc?'

'Point is,' Archy said. 'Frankie's got it all. Everything that Doc ever wanted. A mansion, an island, the mix he's cooking up—that's one hell of a trap, seems to me. One hell of a lure for a big fish like Daylin McMurphy with cheese. You getting this, you dumb Fucktard?'

Grif nodded and puffed on his cigar like he was doing his damnedest. 'Except he don't have Ma.'

Archy fiddled with his rings. Grif flushed. Thettie began to say something but he cut her off. 'Ma. Forget it. Anyone would have done the same. You made only choice you could.'

'I got to make things right, Grif. I got to,' Thettie said.

Archy said, 'Grif's right. It's not 'just you,' never has been. We all have to make things right. This is *our* chance, too.'

Grif said, 'What if it's got something to do with the

island—hunk of rock subsiding more and more every year, so's you can hardly see it no more? Lake'll swallow it one day, and then it'll be Forest Sunk.'

She looked at him sharply and downed the shot he poured, the room beginning to spin. 'You see anything? Around those warning pylons?'

Grif made a spiraling motion with his finger—Thettie watched the black tattooed 'L' spin around and around. 'You can't see much. Rocks and trees through the mist is all. There's evil currents, too. From a trench of shallow water around the perimeter.'

And they all tried to see it, some cartoon island and the lake opening up its mouth and swallowing Doc whole and how maybe Frankie was trying to make it happen.

'Maybe,' Grif said in his thinking-aloud growl. 'Uncle Frankie brought us home to set us free.'

'Or maybe not,' Thettie said. 'Sarey's under house arrest, and I'm between a rock and a hard place. Doc's using protection as another word for deterrence, but I got to get to Frankie . . .'

The forked vein on Grif's high forehead began to pulse. 'For real.'

Archy extended his hand and pointed it like a gun at Emilio and Dustin at the bar. They acknowledged it by acting shot, and then went back to talking quietly amongst themselves. Emilio was a pale boy of mixed ancestry—part-Harpur-part-Creole—with a cowlick, and Dustin was lumbering and freckled with a deft way around old Norse weaponry.

Grif had gone thoughtful. 'That Homer and Lyle . . . you got to wonder what Doc's got over them.'

'Speaking of monsters,' Thettie mashed her half-smoked cigarette into the tray. 'Either of you see those signs in town. The missing lizard?'

Archy and Grif said they had.

She told them how five years ago, Lee's child had been killed, the remains hidden who knew where, so that Lee never found them, and couldn't leave until he does. After she blurted that out, no one said anything for a while.

'Whatever happens with Frankie,' said Grif quietly. 'I'm not staying in this damn hell hole.'

Archy banged on the table, the jukebox muffling the crash of his rings on the table. ''Member that time Frankie took us up river to get some trout and tricked us into believing that the trout were dancing to his guitar? Faster he played, the faster they danced?'

'They looked like they was dancing. I swear,' Grif said. 'Punk Muskies.'

'Iggy Trout.'

'And that old dog, Scrappy, used to hump anything that moved. Had a thing for Archy, remember? You were about nine years old. Dog was so in love with you, you're like, 'Look Uncle Frankie, he wants to play piggy-back.'' Grif makes like he's humping the table. Archy started laughing uncontrollably, trying to talk between gasps. 'Frankie lost his shit. I thought he was going to die. Piggy-back. He kept saying. Piggy-back.'

Tears streaming down all their faces. Three-headed monster tears.

Thettie blew her nose into a napkin. She said, more to herself than to her sons, 'The only reason Doc wanted me was because I never could be had. I belonged to Frankie. To you.'

'You belonged to your own self, Ma. There's men who'd kill for a piece of that.'

'Love is blind,' Grif agreed.

Archy's eyes went inky. 'Doc thinks he's the only game in town. That's his tell, Ma. Like he's the only one that can protect us, but he doesn't know Uncle Frankie, or what he's capable of. Never did.'

And he doesn't know, us, Thettie thought. He doesn't know the Harpers, a people sick with love.

Archy poured another round and they banged the glasses together.

'Freedom,' they said as one.

The rain poured down harder. The bar filled up, and Thettie let the events of the day recede. Her conversation with Bryce, the yawning lizard tank in Lee's studio. Sarey laughing at Thettie like some crazed crow, like maybe memory was a joke, return a lie and redemption just a shot away. Thettie opened her eyes to an unwashed knot of Rod 'n' Reel staff pushing through to the pool tables.

Grif brought a feather from her hair.

'Let's dance,' Archy said.

He led his mother to the dance floor, the crowd parting for the man-cub and the mother bear who could have been his sister, who should have been his sister but who danced like someone from the future— all elbows and neck. At the booth, Grif kept time with his feet from behind a haze of cigar smoke, some farm girl nuzzling his neck. And Thettie basked in the false hope that Lee would come by, any time now, and how good that would be for him to see how alive she looked in the arms of her son, how happy and so free.

14. NIGHT SWIM

IT **WAS A FOREST** of lake weed down there, elodea and hydrilla. Lee could part the stems with his fingers and swim between the hairy fronds. Beneath the surface, the water refracted a pallid column of light from the stars and Lee took care to avoid it lest it suck him up to who knows where.

His fingers closed around a stand of weed which came out in his hand, crimson roots and all. His gorge rose at the reptilian slither. From under the water, he tried to shake it loose. Time slowed to a crawl, and the root clung tighter and tangled around his arm. He kicked to the surface and sucked in sharp breaths of starless night. All around him the water was a caustic pink beneath the lowering dark. Lee swam around in a tight circle. Some breaststroke and then on his back. His skin burned. It would be close to midnight, maybe later. The lake weed still clung to his arm.

He'd wanted her to come back. He couldn't go to her in case Vernon returned, and so he waited in vain for them both. He stoked the stove and put on fresh coffee. Cleaned Vernon's tank to get rid of the funk. But she didn't come, and at first he blamed her and then he feared for her. And his fears grew legs, and a mouth, and grew hungry.

He tried to stave the fear off with alcohol, this monster of time. And the booze told him that it was time finally to meet this thing, whatever it was, on its own terms.

That there was no tomorrow. Only today.

He pulled himself up over the side of the boat, naked and dripping. A light rain fell. With a fishing knife, he hacked at the red weed bound around his wrists, nicking himself in several places. He worked against the numbing cold, swigging from the bottle he'd brought onto the boat, drawing blood. When the weed was loose, he tossed it over and the rain-pocked lake sucked it in. He pulled his jeans on and shrugged into a thermal, then opened another beer. Thettie wanted to think she could take care of herself. That with nothing left to lose, she was safe. That she was free. Lee had wanted that, too, after his child was taken. But even after the monster has taken everything you have, there's still more. Death is not the end, neither for the dead nor for those they leave behind.

His wife, even when she returned east, had swum every day of the year. She wore a wet suit in the coldest months, except in January. When the lake froze over she swam in the college pool. His wife's shoulders were broad, her belly flat and her thighs a full, long sweep of muscle. Between them the mound of her pubis pronounced enough to demand arousal, so that in his dreams he cupped it in his hand, worked one finger or two into the hot cleft that would dematerialize or turn cold on waking.

He tossed the empty can against the side of the canoe with the others. Above him, the clouds parted and the rhinestone jaws of Ganymede wheeled. Had he dreamt up his gods, hallucinated them all? His wife had rediscovered the old places from her girlhood in Little Ridge, finding turtles and crayfish in the lake, secret groves where gropers loomed and silently screamed.

'Look,' she said. 'The lake monster.'

Their son, who would not reach eight years in this world, would wave solemnly at some point out on the lake where there lurked a being conjured in the depths from the blood spilt by another mother. Blood that would engulf and drown the live issue unless *Aglaeca*—wolf-mother of the world—got to it first. To save her monstrous son and pull it from the deadly blood-lake of her own making, carefully lick the abomination clean. The maker-mother selfishly, slowly, measuring inch by inch what she had created in order to learn the secrets of its destruction, and how to avoid it. Danger and deliverance linked on the same chain of being and for interchangeable ends. His wife had two miscarriages before their son was finally born without complication. Because every god must create its little lamb, and every creation contains within the paths of its memory a dream of death because, upon the tender flesh, Father Time can always find another vein to prick.

The whole thing with the lake monster embarrassed Lee, but his wife and child wallowed in the extravagant possibilities of urban myth, as if beyond the bland curvatures of the lake and the imprisoning forests and orchards as far as the eye could see, there existed a world where monsters could be met as equals, and a simple exchange of terms would establish the rules of the game.

ALETHEIA

Even at seven, their son was serene behind his thick glasses, tall for his age but underweight. At times, he clamped his thumbs to the sides of his hands—the opposable abyss a place of unspeakable terrors. Mistaken as are we all in the belief that self-defense is a possibility in all worlds, including the ones that our hearts would not hold.

Lee had stood at the open fridge in the kitchen of their new home by the lake from which his son would be taken within a week. His wife bent over their son's latest drawing of some scaled mutation howling from the depths, and Lee watched her crayon in a warm and burning star in its dead eye. The refrigerator had a strange smell and he closed the door quickly, less afraid that it would suck him who knows where, than afraid that he wanted it to.

***

After his encounter with Boyle, Lee had driven back to the studio through an emptying Village. Fliers of Vernon fluttering. Instead of Thettie, he found her picture on the floor, like she'd left in a hurry. Maybe it was an SOS? A human face where previously there was none. All those Xeroxed copies of Vernon, still MISSING. All the canvases of the lake. Ditto. Lee would burn them all. And then he would find Thettie, ask her to dinner, whatever she wanted.

But first he started to paint. And then he started to drink. Or maybe it was the other way around. And then he started to remember and he couldn't stop painting. And he couldn't stop remembering and drinking. He drank and he painted in a fever dream of pale flecks buried beneath fecal browns and after-birth reds. At a half hour to midnight the sweat turned cold on his brow. The brush flew from his hand. He was suddenly gripped by an irresistible need to go out onto the lake. It would not stop calling to him, and there was no end to its want—to what it would seek.

***

'Here I am!' he yelled, trying and failing to come to his feet.

The turquoise blue canoe by now had drifted almost to the middle of the lake. There was a channel that cut into the lake floor—over five hundred feet deep out here—before it got dangerously shallow again near the island. He could see the warning beacon ahead, a canted monolith rising out of the water. The water police had added buoys with danger notices, and to these, Frankie Harpur, or someone else, had installed another that said, 'Private Property. Enter at your own risk.'

The canoe spun in a sudden tug of wind and Lee puked over the side. When he lifted his head, he was facing the Village again, pulled out backwards with the current so that the huddled houses on Main Street receded like on a fast-moving ice floe, and the bell tower blurred against the stars and the Harpur campfires were red welts on the shore.

15. WANT

UNTOLD HOURS LATER they were still at the Way. The windows had become mirrors, and Thettie was three sheets to the wind. She kept her eyes out for Lee, but he didn't come, and she felt herself beginning to spiral. Was it the Polaroid? Had he mistaken her intent? Read into the image a promise she couldn't keep, a plea he couldn't meet? The place was only about half full, a few deGroots she didn't recognize, some locals, and the rest Harpurs.

She and the boys talked about how Little Ridge had changed, about how fake everything looked. They talked about how they'd figure some way around Doc's threats and promises—even ways that involved dispensing with Homer and Lyle. They'd get Frankie and ride out the winter in the trailers if they had to, or if they had time to rebuild down at Triangle Gully. Then they moved back onto the stolen Gila Monster and how it had a thing in its venom that Frankie was using in his Killer Mix.

'I read about it,' Grif said. 'They've been using it with old people, making them smart again, and then the black market got wise to it, as per the way it always happens.'

'Promise me one thing,' Thettie said, trying to stay

in the spirit of the night, but feeling her soul grow cold. 'If I ever get old. No lizard spit.'

'No lizard spit.' Grif said.

She downed the dregs of her beer. 'For real.'

Grif, banging on the table. 'Lizard spit.'

Archy started banging too with his ringed knuckles and they stomped on the floor and a bunch of other Harpurs joined them and the whole place gave over to pounding and stomping and chanting 'Lizard spit, lizard spit' until Avery, the barman, had to yell at everyone to break it up or he'd call the cops.

Thettie's thoughts flew to Lee, and her eyes kept darting to the door, until Archy got impatient, which was understandable. What child isn't threatened or at least grossed out by their parent's love life? She hadn't wanted to know about her daddy's take on splits and tits but he'd told her anyway, and those were footsteps she didn't need to follow. Beside her Grif lurched and lit another cigar. He spilled beer on his wool jacket, had women all over him. And to her left, Archy levitated and glowed and talked up the future.

They ordered pizza. Thettie ate some because she was starving. Her mounting dread made her forget she was a pescatarian, forgot why or when she'd started with all that first-world bullshit. The pepperoni, or whatever it was, tasted as hot and spicy as home and just as lethal. And they bought more pitchers. Lots of pitchers. Thettie's spirit sinking with every one.

Doc and his muscle came in for a drink, Lyle limping, but Doc was chipper. He nodded at her, but kept a wide berth, as if to demonstrate that she could be her own woman now but only on his sufferance. His terms. As if to underscore that the choice he'd given her was no choice at all. Her despair deepened.

She had thought she was protection. Hubris, Frankie would say. False pride. Cassie would say, get over yourself, Thet.

Bryce won some money from the Rod 'n' Reel staff at the pool tables, sent them over a round of drinks. Grif went up to talk to her for a while but Archy just waved at her like a lovesick puppy, and Thettie's heart leaped at the sight of that missing eye, and at the false hope she saw burning in the good one. But the booze and the food slowed everything to a syrupy crawl one minute or sped it all up to the blink of an eye in another. And in the blink of an eye the girl was gone, and with it Thettie's hope for a second chance. And the juke box was still playing.

'The Stranglers,' said Archy. 'It just hit me. That song Frankie used to play is 'Golden Brown,' by The Stranglers. Remember?'

The weeping albino dog at the Gully with the human eye—golden brown—came to Thettie's mind. She started to tell them about it and stopped herself. It wouldn't do any good. Cassie and Frankie would play that damn song all the time. *Golden brown, texture like sun.* Boozy tears burning her throat. Frankie. Frankie would see no one but her, Doc said. She was the key to getting them all killed. If not, what was Frankie playing at, if anything? It had always been a private thing between them—forgiveness a given, forgetting a game. Hand to heart, Frankie, I've run out of moves.

She remembered Doc laughing in the car with Sarey firing on them, like the game was over from the start. But maybe the rules had changed, or she could change them. Instead of being a means to Doc's end, maybe she could be an end to his means. Was there a difference, Sarey? *Caw-caw.*

Sarey was right. Damned if you do, and damned either way. But in the end, you could do no more than what was in your heart. Maybe the only way to save her family was to set them free from Doc. Maybe Grif was right. That Frankie brought her back to set them free. And maybe she was key to that, not to Doc's future, but to their's—a chance to live free of all her rotten choices. Surely they would see—and forgive her—that it was her only chance to eliminate Doc's. That sometimes you have to burn the forest to save the trees.

But could she leave her sons? Would she? Is this my last chance, Frankie, to give them a second one.

Grif cut into her unforgivable thoughts. 'Fuck Frankie. I say we leave now. Right now. Get Frankie and Sarey and blow Doc off, just like he did to Frankie. Maybe get Bryce to help us. Water rat like that'll know the best way to the island, and then the best way to Canada across Ontario.'

Thettie looked away.

'Doc'll find us,' said Archy. ''Member last time? Doc always finds us.'

Archy made blinkers around his eyes and made them squint like Doc's. They laughed uncertainly.

Thettie took in the tavern with its neon-stained corners. 'You're right. I got to see this thing through tomorrow.'

If the boys took her to mean going to meet Frankie at the island tomorrow, she let it lie.

She reached across and took each of their hands

and brought them together in hers. 'I only wish it was just me. I never did win that mother-of-the-year-award, and now look what I've got you into. I wish it wasn't so. I fucked with my gods, should be just me got to pay.'

'Grif already said,' said Archy. 'There's no 'just you.''

'I'm going home,' she said.

'No booty calls, Ma. Promise?'

She promised.

'Remember where you are? Big trailer next to ours, away from the 'Bago.'

'Close to us,' said Grif. 'Instead of in the middle of fucking nowhere.'

'Where no one can hear you scream.' Archy made creepy crawly wiggles with his fingers. Thettie made them back. He laughed.

She would take a picture of that sound. The music of her boys laughing like children. Grif with his hair sticking out on end, and Archy beside him, making creepy crawly wiggles with his fingers. Grif lurched his glass across. Archy raised his to meet it, Thettie raised hers one more time, and the three sticky glasses met soundlessly and caught the light.

'Tomorrow,' Archy and Grif said, 'Tomorrow!'

And then she said it, too, just out of synch. *Tomorrow.*

She protested but they made Emilio take her on the back of his bike. No booty calls, she promised, and they were right not to trust her. Emilio took her to the porch of the double-wide, where she dismissed him. He saluted her, wandered off to his own trailer on the other side of Archy's and Grif's. She stepped on to the porch—half sunk into the dirt fringed by ragged geraniums—and looked wistfully back across the stretch of no-man's land at the small Winnebago nestled in the trees where the lake filled one window and the stars another. She longed to be with Lee still, floating somewhere in between.

The wind rattled against the flimsy windows of the big ugly trailer to which she'd been now consigned, like a jailer rattling his keys. Her throat stung as she stumbled to the door.

It was locked.

She didn't remember locking the door and no matter how hard she tried, the key skidded across the rain-slick escutcheon before she finally got it home. From somewhere high in the fir tree, an owl called.

Inside, there was a small living area—just a couch facing a TV on a stand—she didn't remember turning that on either, but someone had, and it was running a staticky channel, something foreign. The carpet was still scuffed from where Doc and his bodyguards had dumped and moved their bags, a messy trail leading off across the carpet like someone had dragged their feet. Behind the silently running TV, a little dinette, plastic tulips in a vase. She'd not yet unpacked, and her suitcase lay opened on the floor. She stepped out of her clothes and took a nightgown out of the suitcase, pulled it on. Doc had left a fifth of honey bourbon on the kitchen counter, as a house warming present. Her downfall. Doc knew what she wanted. She could still smell his cologne. He'd even left a towel in the bathroom—was he trying to tell her something? Make sure to dry off after a shower?

Daylin Murphy. A name taken from a man he killed

back in County Sligo so he could escape to America, free from the ghost of Toeless Mears, not to mention his hard-case widow. Thettie wondered, as always, who the real Doc was—the medical student who got thrown out for being caught up to his rubber-sheathed elbows inside a cadaver, or the child left orphaned behind a bingo hall? Lad with bad teeth and a monobrow.

This he'd told her: How he spent a day and a night in the old man's car behind that bingo hall. His old man had gone in to see some geezer called Haha Malone about some card money gone missing. The old man never came out. Instead it was Paddy the Hook who did.

'And the rest, as they say, is his story,' Doc always finished. 'Haha. Get it?'

Thettie poured herself the glass of bourbon that she didn't need and went down a narrow hallway with cracked paneling and last year's calendar hanging from a nail. At the end were two bedrooms. One that looked out between the fancy cabins in front of it across the lake, but at an awkward angle with a row of other trailers between it and the shore. The other bedroom had a window that faced the woods. She'd take the one looking out onto the lake. The light didn't work. She swore, but decided she could live with it. The open window let in a muted glow from the lake anyway. She considered closing it but there was an funk in the room, gassy yet earthy, that Thettie couldn't place, so she left it open. She got out her jar of Ambien and stared at it.

Fucking fine, Doc. Plenty more gas in the tank of her soul, and when she'd stop telling herself that was anyone's guess. Because Frankie. She lay down on top of the chenille bedspread, knobby beneath her hands. Bedspread smelled funny, too. She considered removing it. She rested her head on the board and sipped on the bourbon though she didn't feel like it any more. It was too sweet, a falseness she could taste in the not-real honey, nothing but a cheap flavoring you could order from homebrewdotcom. Nausea from the stink in the room dragged at the blanket of her weariness. She sighed with her whole body, not meaning to. Frankie. Waiting for her all this time on the island. Ten years. *From far away, stays for a day.* And what Doc was asking from her. Is that what it would take?

For if she was the means to a man's end, was the only way out to be an end to his means? She put the bourbon on the night stand. Picked up the bottle of Ambien and shook one out. Then another. Then some more. They pooled in her hand. Is this what it would take to be free at last, or was there another way?

Someone or something rustled nearby, and it sounded like it was inside the room. She thought about looking under the bed, but exhaustion weighed her down. Maybe it just was Emilio doing a perimeter check. Thettie ignored it, trying not to get spooked. Archy and Grif would be home soon and if they were her only hope, then what was she to them? Queen Bee, Doc? In *your* dreams, maybe but not mine, Doc. I am not the story you're trying to tell.

The lake behind the window grew dead flat before the upcoming storm, the sky above it paler than the water. She pulled aside the net curtains, peered across the no man's land between the trailer and the row of lightless cabins. The storm flashed, giving her a glimpse of the faraway island, the glimmer of red on Boyle's warning pylon.

Frankie, it's me, Thettie. I'm home.

From far away, stays for a day.

There must be a way.

Thettie smiled. Cassie always said Frankie was a poet, he just didn't know it. She put the pills back in the bottle.

Because there was no 'just her' anymore.

Doc was wrong about her betraying Frankie again but he was right about her never leaving them. They were her other selves, no way of telling where one ended and the other began. Whatever she was, she was neither a means to an end nor the end to a means. She was something else and there had to be a way to find out what that was. There had to be a way to be free from history. To be neither Queen nor Bee, but just to be.

You're the poet Frankie, not me. She shook out two Ambien, put a third on the night stand, just in case. She didn't need a monster's protection. She *was* the protection. Always had been, and Doc hadn't the power to change that. She let the curtains drop, washed down the two Ambien with the bourbon, and fell back onto the bed. She was asleep in minutes.

***

The bedroom was cold and the bed was small, so Vernon, drawn to the warmth of Thettie's body and the smell of pizza on her breath, did not have far to crawl from his hiding place under the bed.

The venom of Gila Monsters is lethal but the small amount produced, along with their unusual mode of delivery via the lower jaw, is such that it is not normally fatal. Considering all that Thettie had to drink plus the couple-three Ambien coursing through her veins and the fact that the lizard's recurved molars bit into the soft flesh of her lip where the taste of the pizza was strongest— the venom was more effective than usual. And as her esophagus began to swell, Thettie, feeling the nootropic effects of the gene-altering peptides, began to piece together memories from dismembered past. Memories such as her birth, the pressure of Uncle Ike's erection on her two-year-old bottom as she sat on his lap, Frankie with his sad goofy smile taking her by the hand and showing her a den of albino fox pups on the ridge above the falls— these unforgotten fragments of time floated through her mind on a tide of venom. Memories surged and crossed like currents and not all of them of the past, but also of a future yet possible. Unfamiliar nights, cold and fearful, reached out damp hands to circle her throat, and the room filled with a strange broken static like Morse Code, intercut by a child's tears. Her mind leapt forward—to a small boat pinned deep beneath the ice, and backward to the smell of burning waffles, and from somewhere between, flames and flying metal. It was an intertwining effect, this remembering, like branches growing into one another in the forest canopy. A path opened in the forest from which to stray—from far away, stays for a day. A melody clawed at her, snapping dendrites off like twigs so that new ones could take their place. Her flesh tore with wounds that would not heal, trees sprouted roots of tainted love—as her body arced and tore at itself in its final adventure.

ALETHEIA

So that by the time her sons found their mother drowned in blood and vomit—an overturned jar of sleeping pills and a bottle of bourbon upended on the side table—Vernon, too, was long gone. Neurons firing and headed west where he'd been born in a sandy burrow on Navaho land and where it now seemed a good place to go to die.

PART II

16. DARK WIND

THE ISLAND IS moving too fast. It arrows toward the canoe, the vertical mass of rock and moss coming straight at him. Water pours unendingly off its surfaces like that of a breaching Leviathan. The dark grove of trees in the chasm between the rocks strobes on and off in the lightning. Its ancient rocky nostril flares with more evil intent than even in his dreams.

But then the current yanks Lee's canoe like it's had a change of plan, and the island drops out of sight. Where it was, is now just empty night. The sodden wind lashes at him and black tongues of lake lap hungrily at the sides of the canoe, and does he have his lifejacket?

He stands panting over the paddle, can barely remember rowing out here, or why, except that the lake opened a door, and more than anything, he wanted to go through it.

He hears yelling back at the shore. He wrestles the canoe around, craning his neck to keep sight of the island. He stabs the paddle into the dark flesh of the lake, but the lake bites back. Lee is pinned in place, like a figure in one of his own paintings. Habib would say that even if you are physically capable of negotiating the structural current along that narrow strait around the island, you'd be talking terminal hydraulics if you don't know what you're doing.

Lee has no idea what he's doing.

An outlet current extends all the way from Triangle Creek. It begins to boil up and over the edges of Lee's canoe, pulling him through a terminal sluice. Or worse. The abyss on the lake floor is five hundred feet down or more, immeasurable in parts and pocked with caves and subterranean tunnels. Plenty of room for something like a petrified monster pine tree to hide, to disappear for a few centuries and bob to the surface, cursed for its sins to wander the lake forever looking for the door.

He can't stop shaking, feels everything about to spill out of him. He has been over every inch of this lake. Every inlet, every cove. Everywhere except the island. And now, spun full circle in the canoe, here it is, rising out of the night again at will. An eruption from the subterranean floor, a monster waiting for Lee, as he always feared it was, hoped it was.

'Where's my son, motherfucker?' Lee's howl devolves into a thin scream.

The face of the island, as far as Lee can see through his tears and lashing rain, leers in reply. Caves and canyons ridge its surface, against which the lake water surges and boils. He's never been this close, never been close at all, and now it's hurling itself at him with all the power of his disbelief, his desire, and all of his dread.

He had been able to wait no longer. Because of what he finally knew, and has always known. That the only way, in the end to beat the monster, is to join it.

The wind needles through his soaked thermal, the

heavy rain soaks his hair. The wind is continuous with the blinding dark and the faraway stars. He lifts the paddle and the night whips it away and he hears a distant, cartoonish thwack as it hits an invisible warning beacon. Lee screams but it's not just the paddle. It's what took it. He sees a flash of teeth.

Something pulls the canoe toward the red eye of the beacon. Just one eye, red and unblinking. He slips into an eddy and can see pale water ahead rising like a wall where the structure forms its own current, the legendary Z-water, that can—according to Habib—smash you against the rock walls or pull you under the surface to die wedged in a glacial smile.

Lee yells, 'Frankie, you son of a bitch, give me back my son!'

His throat burns but the roar of the storm makes his cries inaudible even to him. He yells again and this time is answered by the reverberating echoes of a crazed baying of dogs. The lake current thuds beneath the hull. It pulls and pushes at the same time, calling him with one voice and warning him away with another. The frenzied barking echoes on the corkscrewing wind.

Lee pulls out the spare paddle and jabs on his off side. Manages to push the canoe onto the lip of the current so he can twist in his seat toward the mainland. Yells coming from the shore carry clearly across the miles of lake, despite the headland in the way. Barking cuts into the cries from the shore. The yelling and the dogs sound scrambled together in the downpour—like heavy static. He paddles like crazy over the flare of the current, into an eddy in which he can rest and spin around just enough to make out tiny lights faraway in the campground. Some lights move fast and some are still. Blurry forms complicate the darkness. As Lee watches through the rain, one of these forms, bareheaded, separates itself from the lights and moves toward the dock, and it occurs to Lee that it's not raining on the shore yet, not like it is on the lake.

Lee may have pissed his pants. The solitary form on the shore is outlined in light. Lee's heart jumps, but the current has a mind of its own. It reaches with fingers of water over the eddy line into the channel current, trapping Lee's canoe between the two. He chops into the watery fingers with the spare paddle, hauling back into what he hopes is the center of an eddy, an oasis of upstream flow. If he can hold out there until someone comes to get him, or until the current changes, he has a chance.

The baying behind him becomes more frenzied. Ahead of him the vaguely human shape waves the flashlight again, or maybe it's a lantern. A camping lantern, like the one Thettie had in the little Winnebago—except it's not Thettie. She didn't come to him. Instead she came out here—for the door. Lee's thinking is murky, but he wishes someone could explain to him what he's doing out here, and what it has to do with her. Why, when she didn't come to him, he went to her—and what she wants now.

'What do you want?' he whispers.

And the lake doesn't answer, but something else does. Something that wants nothing but time and whose appetite is unending and will take until there is nothing left, and already has.

Screams erupt from the shore and carry faintly

across the lake, the howling of the dogs mixing with the human cries. Lee tries to call above the noise, but his voice, as in a dream, goes nowhere. A siren wails. The slim figure on the shore with the lantern, who is not Thettie but is both too far away, and so close that Lee can almost touch her, lifts the lantern again, like a wave—hello—and Lee, throwing caution to the dark wind, waves back.

Goodbye.

***

His wife had gone away for a weekend conference. Their son had awoken in the middle of the night for a glass of water, and called out but no one came. Lee woke up slumped in the living-room chair with an empty bottle of Jameson beside him, the TV running, and his son drinking from the dregs of melted ice and whisky in Lee's glass. Lee had snatched the booze back and covered the child's mouth with his own hand, saying, 'Shhhh. Don't tell.'

Lee screams again. He over-balances and the lake sloshes in. Something hard cracks against his head and tosses him into the lake. The water pulls him between its scales and into its watery lungs, inhales him with dark ecstasy, and the darkness below equals the darkness above and he is spinning in the ball of the world as it rolls on toward the void.

Lee flails and then surrenders. How long, how-how long now before the end? Ten feet down, twenty? The lake takes Lee's body down and his arms lift up toward the diminishing lights on the surface. There is a tickling sensation on his feet, at his ankles, spiky tendrils trying to gain purchase. He tries to kick them away. He doesn't want to be saved. before he can crawl through the door. He rudders frantically down towards the light. The panic in his chest has turned to fire. A door opens at the bottom of a well and he is spiraling down, the water tinged with bronze and swarming with shadow—with fleet and lethal black.

17. CHENILLE

IT IS AN adventure of the body, yes, all that pain and bulging eye business and she wouldn't wish it on anyone to see their own mother like that. Not just the bulging eyes but the bloody mess where her mouth had been and it was a nice mouth, too.

The befouled nightgown, well. You'd soil yourself, too, if some big old lizard tried to stick his tongue down your throat. But the pills upended on the table? The broken bottle fingerprinted in crimson, blood cupped in her palms like a chalice? *That* she could do without. Because of what her sons would think. Her boys, disrespecting her like that. Thettie can't abide it. She wants to tell them it wasn't how it looked—the sticky bottle of Beam and the upended pills, and with all of her will, she points at the monster with his giant tail who is nowhere in sight.

***

'MIA,' Frankie had said, rowing her out one full-moon night to the middle of the lake and pointing to the island, to where it should have been. But it was gone. And in the island's place the moon hung glaring and cratered and wild with loss. It hurt Thettie's eyes to look at the naked pain of the moon. They rowed away and she had looked back—for shame—and there was the island with its nose poking up through the water as always, the moon hanging over it all like a pill dissolving in water.

***

Because like Sarey used to say, bathing the fresh cuts on Frankie's arms, on his neck and legs, too, we never do it to ourselves—not entirely. Maybe cutting did run in the family, but that was never Thettie's *thing*. Because she wouldn't be doing it just to herself, would she? Like Archy said, there is no 'just you' any more. Any cuts she made on herself, she'd be carving on the flesh of her sons no less than if she took a knife to them also, and that she couldn't abide. No, she was definitely not a cutter.

***

Archy stands in the doorway of the room—her flesh with his delicate bone structure, the fetching overbite. Grif braces behind him, his knees bent as if about to buckle, his big jaw slack in terror, the man-boy she raised like her own. She wants to tell him how she loves him like a son—no less real for being another's— but something has got at her tongue. So she has no voice to tell him anything anymore. No voice to say what is in her heart.

If her lips were not a bloody mess, her tongue mangled and useless, this is what she would say:

That she'd thought about it. Truth be told, she had. How if women were a means to a man's ends then what was the way out? What chance in that? What choice except for being an end to a man's means, and that was no choice. But after Doc took her to the old settlement at Triangle Creek and told her how he was keeping Sarey for her own quote-unquote protection, and how Frankie would know that any wrong move on his part would cost him Sarey and Thettie both—her soul did darken with possibility. If she was Doc's leverage—his means to the island, and Frankie and total control of their family again—then the only way to close the door on that sick shit for good, was to throw away the key. So, truth be told, she wants to tell her boys that she did think about it.

But the monster stopped her, she wants to say. For real.

The monster saved her.

After the monster kissed her awake, she began to see another way.

She'd listened, with keener hearing than humanly possible, to her clan returning to the campground at some unnumbered hour—she could hear her sons stomping outside her trailer, laughing together like brothers again. 'Ma?' Pushing into the unlocked door and through the living room past her dumped coat and purse and to the bedroom door. Where they stand now on the threshold. Seeing her like that. The both of them, Archy the heart and Grif the soul—clutching each other like children—thinking that she'd started up with that self-ending business again when it wasn't that, not this time. Because one or two Ambien, or even three, washed down by a healthy slug of hooch is not starting up anything again, but a child always thinks the worst of their parent and a mother must know how constantly she is judged. Thettie looks cross-eyed down at her rag of a tongue. She would tell them. She would. That what took away her mouth and put this bloody smile there instead was not what they think. That the pills strewn and the booze spilled was not how it looked. She would show them while there was still time—before they called for Doc.

Because sprawled awake finally on the chenille bedspread in a trailer beside a forgotten lake, amidst the screams and sobs and her sons' roars and moans, and the thumping of feet and the window-rattle of the building storm—you feel time being sucked into some mechanism you can begin finally to comprehend. Your life consumed by some mysterious mouth like the cord on the Electrolux. Queen Bee one minute, hell's own chambermaid the next.

The other Harpur men and boys, and her girls, too—their glossed mouths tight knots of terror and shock—squeeze into the bedroom to get a better look. Some of them mill about in the little dinette with the TV shoved up against the wall. Has someone pulled its plug? She smells burnt wiring and thirty-six flavors of puke. She hears voices she can't remember.

'Call Doc!' someone says.

No! Thettie's heart flutters like the wings of a rain-soaked moth.

Not Doc. Not yet. Not that she doesn't owe him, big time. She wouldn't be here if not for him. Because it was just that one thing, the cold dread of her boys being left alone in the clutches of that old buzzard, that kept her alive all those years when it would have been so easy to end it. Fear—Sarey was right—is the lie we tell ourselves about the future.

One day at a time, Frankie said. Little Archy and Grif left alone with Doc? Never! It was what tore her away, finally, from addiction. One step at a time. At the AA meetings, they tell you there's just twelve of those goddam steps because that's a lie you can live with.

'See how far you get,' Doc'd say down at the Landing as soon as Thettie would get ideas, 'without me.' Without Doc, who'd saved her from herself, and as he liked to remind her, from her own limitations every time she tried to exceed them.

But still she'd kept one eye on the now, the other on the later, like there was a difference.

***

Grif has had more to drink than Archy, but he can hold it better. His bellows bring others across the campground to the trailer bedroom, to the rough and bloody chenille beneath her bare ass and no, this isn't what she wanted or had planned. But now that it *is*, her memories are as vivid as her perceptions, as hot and blue as stars, the past and present and future a Milky Way of possibility. She is unnaturally sensitive to lights going on around the camping ground. Her new senses go into overdrive as more Harpurs cram into the trailer. She tastes the fiery salt of the men's sweat, her helpless ears register in the amplified screams of the women, that Joanie will miscarry again, and that, because of Thettie, the twins will one day become famous horror movie directors. And in some immoderate, electrified new sense, Thettie sees Bryce running along the jetty, not towards the campground, but away from it. Holding a lantern and waving at someone on the lake.

Someone who is waving back.

All around her is the universal call for Doc to come back with his medic's bag—and will someone please tell me where that goddam lizard went to, the one in the flier. Because, it was here and now it's missing.

***

Years ago, when they all still lived in Triangle Gully, Grif waved in the direction of the island. 'The lake monster,' he said, and little Archy was all, 'Does it bite, Grif?' Grif nodded, 'Like a bitch,' and Thettie said, 'Watch your mouth, it's just scared is all,' and Archy had put one hand in Grif's and the other in hers and said, 'What's it scared of, ma?'

***

'Doc!' someone yells. 'Where the hell's Doc!'

Because after Doc came into their lives, and Arch grew too old *not* to believe in monsters, he wouldn't have to ask anymore. It was enough just to be there at school or on the streets, one eye on his ma and the other on Doc, never more than twelve steps away. And Grif, too, his teenage fists clenched between her and Doc at the dinner table, his already huge but as yet untattooed hands gripping knife and fork like weapons. So she wants to tell Grif that this wasn't his fault, either, but that he'd been right all along. It was the lake monster.

But they don't see it yet, and she can't blame them for thinking that she'd done the unthinkable. There is a strange smell in the room, monstrous, and another one, medical. Over these wash other sensations, exposing some secrets, annihilating others. The trailer is now filled with smells of the Way, sour beer and urine, and she listens to the sound of rain dripping from leather jackets and frayed hemlines onto the linoleum. Look, boys, the lake monster! The scattered precious Ambien, the color of sky, robins-egg blue, broken and gooey. The bourbon bottle smashed and the cuts on her body, the open window where the monster got out but not the same way it got in. She tries to crane her neck for it under the bed, but it has, like so many other things, disappeared.

For now.

She wants to tell them that it was and wasn't Vernon. Because to be misrepresented in life is bad enough, but in death it's hell! Thettie's heart flails. That anyone could think that this was what she really wanted—to be a key to some man's door instead of the light falling in through the window! She wants to tell them what Cassie told her the day she left for good. 'Listen to me, Thet. We live by leaving behind.'

She wants to tell them that she tried.

Her broken heart flutters one last time and is silent.

Grif's eyes darken in disbelief. Tears river down Archy's patchy stubble. Mama! A word you don't want to take with you when you go—the snot-streaked cry of your child left alone in this world.

The cold snakes in from the lake like a hungry thing. Doc will walk in any minute and will someone please pull her nightgown down over her landing strip before he does?

Grif, the mind-reader, tears off his coat to cover her. The wet wool chafes at her flesh. She concentrates on her fingers, wills them to entwine in his, red with the blood of his mama, and tell him one last thing, to hear for all time, what is in her undying heart.

Rain lashes, and leaves blow in through the window she smashed in the struggle with the monster after it crawled out from under the bed, impelled by some unnatural impulse she cannot yet comprehend.

Her eyes stare into the memory—the tentacular claws, the gnawing teeth. The monster's blunt nose and its dead eye looking into hers, unable to turn away from what, having been seen, can now never be unseen. Look! Her arm flung wide extends a finger, which she wills to move in the direction of her fleeing soul. The flesh on her face splinters in creeping paralysis. Look! But Grif can't and Archy won't. They will not look at the blood on their hands and hers.

Night pulses through the window like spilled milk. Footsteps pound toward the bedroom and the dry ice of Doc's cologne tickles her rising gorge.

'Look!'

She pulls Archy's gaze to her own with the last of her will.

'Look!' she wills his gaze to follow in the direction of her out-flung arm—three fingers curled back to where she's come from and one pointing to where she's gone. To the other escape, the door she would never have opened in herself. Homer and Lyle enter in front-and-forward formation. Someone has thrown up in a corner of the little bedroom overlooking the lake, and the smell of puke conjoins with the splashed bourbon and undercurrent of reptilian musk. The flesh torn by its wanting jaws. Think, woman! Because lying there on the befouled bed with her neck at a strange angle and her eyes unattractively popping—what matters now, what it mainly is, is that she's going places. So, think. Enough with the pain of the flesh and the heart. Can they hear what she hears, the ear-splitting drag of the Gila's belly on the floor . . . can no one else hear it? Can they see how the lizard's Ambien blue tongue still licks her hot blood off his lips? How his heart punches against his hide. Boom-boom. He hisses something in flight. Listen . . .

Boom.

Doc is in the room. Time slows down to a monstrous crawl. 'It was just a matter of when,' Doc's voice at the wrong speed. 'She was an accident waiting to happen.'

The prick. That medical sting beneath his cologne. The ever-present syringe. Tap. Tap. The little drop of fluid from Doc's dippy tip. The bedroom erupts in chaos. Archy and Grif lunge toward Doc and Homer and Lyle lunge back. Thettie is awash in perception, not just hers but Archy's and Grif's networking memories, raging even through their shock and grief that what is wrong with this picture is . . . is . . .

Doc—where is his luggage? It had been in the hallway. The army duffle and Homer's Steelers' bag, his pride. She remembers that. There has been a mistake and Doc will punish Homer for it, but she doesn't know how she knows that. And here is Doc with his little bag of tricks, the faded red cross on the side. Rain water running off his field jacket from where he'd gone to look for something he'd lost. Something. Gone. Missing.

Her eyes bulge with rage, and bloody teardrops stream down her face. She tastes them in the back of her throat, around the torn roots of her tongue. Her mind extends in the direction of the runaway lizard, while her finger extends to the floor. And the inordinate perceptions are each linked to a separate smell or feeling, in turn linked to memories faster than she alone can make them. Will they stop? She needs to think. To make connections between the same and different, to see reality where dreaming lies, because in the end it is all there is. Immortality is soul-vomit, and the point is to recognize the pattern. To seek connections between the sticky leakage she can feel from her own eye and that from Sarey's albino hound who grabbed her at Triangle Gully. What was the bitch trying to save her from? Or who?

Her mind is a forest. There is a river from her throat and a swamp in her ass. She extends one hand over the bed and tries to wiggle her finger. The sensation is seismic, and the room rocks. Her sons stumble and flail.

Brace yourself, boys, she tries to tell them. We live by leaving behind.

Death, Thettie now realizes, is an adventure of the body, but also—looking down on her eyes unattractively popping and Grif's coat thrown over her bits—an adventure of the mind, which she greatly prefers. Doc would flick her on the nipple and call her a thinker.

'You're a thinker, Thettie, I like that in a woman.'

And he'd take out his medic bag from the army and tell her how she had the best tits in the business.

Trust me, he'd say, tightening the strap around her arm. I'm a doctor.

But you can't think with your tits nor with a strap around your arm and feeling does you in. So, think, woman (with your brain) as hard as you can about touching your sons' hands one last time, the warmth of their flesh to take wherever you go. Because you are going places now, for real.

Grif tries to take Archy around the ribs from where he has thrown himself over you, to shield you with his body, his clothes heavy with rainwater and matter, ma, ma, ma. Grif looking wildly around the room to where his ma has gone.

ALETHEIA

There! There, you point with all of your mind and the last of your heart to where his fearfully comprehending gaze drops from the ceiling to your finger dripping blood, a steady stream onto the floor, where in a spreading pool of crimson lies a small reptilian tooth, pale and curved, and slick with venom.

18. RETURN

LEE COUGHS UP blue smoke from the inflatable.

'I pulled him out of the lake. He's alive.' Her voice sounds hoarse like a kid who's been crying for days.

Face up, Lee glides through the yellow morning. He sloshes in cold vomit and streaky lake water. His icy fingers make contact with a paddle—she must have found it in the lake. The sides of the canoe jut steeply above him like a blue coffin. The dawn vapors burn his eyes. He pulls himself upright, the shoreline stuttering in and out of view between breaks in the fog. The one-eyed girl steers the Zodiac toward a posse of shadows looming on the sunless beach. Lee retrieves his glasses, bent but miraculously floating in the puke and lake weed, and puts them on.

The Harpur men stand on Lee's beach, assembled in rough spearhead formation on the rocky shore. Hoods cover their heads. Black coats drag in the silver lake. Archy's moustache and patchy beard glisten with raindrops. His eyes roll up in his head like a blind man. His jeans are soaked in the rain and there is blood on his face like war-paint. The rain that runs off his hair is tinged with rust.

The one-eyed girl kills the engine.

The ghostly meep-meep of a thrush breaks the lapping silence and Archy's knees buckle in a faint. A giant separates himself from the right flank and takes Archy by the arm to keep him upright. That giant is Grif. His jeans are torn at both knees. His hair sticks up around the hollows of his temples and a forked vein bisects his brow. Grif takes a flapping canvas from his brother's hand. It is all that is left of the first human face Lee has painted, or tried to, in five years.

Thettie, her colors, gold and blue and green—earth colors—drain from the torn canvas onto the beach. The canvas flops like flayed hide in the hands of her son. Lee looks from the girl to the men and back again. Water streams from behind her eye patch. She wears only a dry sweatshirt and panties and there are bruises on her pale legs.

'He was out there till after midnight. I saw him row out, saw him go over.'

The men ignore her.

'He couldn't have killed her,' the one-eyed girl insists. 'He was out on the lake.'

Water gushes from Lee's nose, and when it pools in his hand, he sees that it is has a black grain to it, like small worms or parasites. 'Kill who?'

She shakes her head at him, and makes a little motion with her hand, *shhhh*. Then she turns back to the posse on the beach. Archy's pretty eyes are still trained at that high point above Lee, but they lack focus. He cants against Grif who leans back, counterweights against their combined fall.

'Who goes out on the lake at midnight in October?' a Harpur man says incredulously, looking at Lee.

'Kill who?' Lee says again, remembering the door.

J.S. BREUKELAAR

The Zodiac bobs and the canoe drifts parallel with it. The rocks waver beneath the surface looking bigger than they are and lake weed stews in the black-swarmed slop. Grif releases his brother's arm and Archy falters but holds his ground. Grif wades in, grips the side of Lee's canoe. Lee tries to get the rest of the way to his feet before Grif takes a first messy swing. A fraction of what he is capable of, but enough to splinter the yellow light, unloose blood from Lee's nose and piss from his pants. His teeth mash the inside of his cheeks to hamburger meat. Behind Grif, Archy's head swivels down and forward like an automaton. The hull of the canoe grinds across the stones and Archy snaps awake and lunges in for his turn. Grif angles out to make way for his brother, and in that instant, Lee sees his chance. Taste of metal in his mouth. He gets to his knees, swings the paddle at Grif's head. Misses. Makes contact mid-body. There is a crack but whether from the paddle or a rib, Lee can't say.

Grif says 'Oof,' and sinks down on the rocks.

His mouth hinges open. His eyes roll up in his head. From deep in the back of his throat comes a noise that sounds like clicking. He turns gray. Archy splashes toward Lee, and the girl fires up the motor, pulls the inflatable in reverse and tows the canoe out of Archy's reach. Lee lands on his ass in the blood and the puke.

'Wait.'

Everyone including Lee, freezes at the voice and it is as if the dawn hears it too and shrinks from it. A cloud moves across the hidden sun. They all turn to watch Doc Murphy make his way deliberately down the wooden steps built into the slope, swinging his medic's bag. His feral little bodyguard halts cross-armed at the top of the steps, wincing at some injury. The fat one with the slit around his neck, Homer, waddles after Doc down to the beach. Lee notices that Homer has a black eye.

'You're making a spectacle of yourselves, lads,' Doc's says. 'Keep this up and we'll all be in the brig.'

The one-eyed girl kills the engine. The rest of the Harpur men freeze, arrested hip deep in the water. Hick Vikings dripping leather armor and swinging chains. Doc puts the medic's bag down on Lee's picnic table and goes over to Grif. Lee searches one anguished face after another for answers. Thettie's portrait floats face-up in the shallows. Doc pulls Grif to his feet and gets him to put his hands on his knees. Grif sucks oxygen. Doc tells him he has a cracked rib, maybe two, a canoe paddle'll do that to a man, he said, even one weakly swung. He pulls a damp cigar out of Grif's shirt pocket, lights it and sticks it in the boy's mouth. The sour perfume of the cigar mixes with the diesel.

'What the hell is going on?' Lee's voice sounds alien. 'Where is Thettie?'

A pock-faced Harpur man picks up the canvas, his eyes brimming. He passes it shakily to Doc. Doc dips his head down and peers sideways at the dripping, defaced canvas. Thettie's low forehead, the electric blue eyes and overbite all melted like a Salvador Dali angel.

'Just because he fucked her,' Doc says. 'Doesn't mean he killed her.'

'What?' Lee lowers himself out of the canoe and, wielding the paddle, pushes through the water, one trembling leg at time.

Behind Doc's back, Grif makes a hushing motion to the Harpur man. Lee feels smothered in the dusty autumn exhalation from the brambles on the slope.

'We thought he might know something, is all.' Grif's voice is an almost indecipherable grumble.

Panic zigzags up Lee's spine and blood pools in his mouth. He spits it out. The blood blossoms in the water, snakes off in red tentacles.

Doc cocks his head at Lee, the unfused corner of his mouth twisted in a savage grin. 'You must be one hell of a sweet bone, Lizard Man, the way your women can't wait to kill themselves afterwards.'

Again, Lee looks from one face to another. Blue eyes drop to the ground. The pocked-face tough clenches his jaw.

'Thettie?' The water makes a dead weight of her name.

Doc turns to first Grif, then Archy. 'Don't look like he knows much of anything now, does he? Her wounds were self-inflicted, boys. You know that. We all know that. The Sheriff's already made up his mind and the coroner's going to say the same thing. Just another lowlife OD. One look at that trailer and they won't even do an autopsy.'

Lee brings a hand to his heart, sways and falls to his knees in the water but there is no one to catch him. The Harpur men step away from him like he's contagious. All except Doc, whose buzzard eyes burrow under his brow, seeking out believers and nons, traitors and allies amongst them.

'Didn't you know, Lizard Man?' He makes a slitting motion across his wrist. 'Runs in the family.'

The Harpur men kick at the stones and crack their

knuckles. 'Not Ma,' Archy says, humming low in his throat, like a refrigerator on the blink. Lee's shrink would say that humming was a stress-response.

'No, no, no,' Lee hums. Strings of red saliva whip around his face from his bitten cheeks.

'I think it has fuck-all to do with him. Don't blame yourself boys. You saw how gutted she was after I took her to Sarey. Seeing what they did to our homes and all. Frankie not there. That's what did it, you ask me.'

The Harpur men mutter beneath their breath, and Lee hears his missing son say, *shhhh*. The voice seems to be coming from the inflatable, but when he turns around all he can see is the one-eyed girl.

Doc visors a scaled hand over his missing eyebrows, the stump of his finger sticking out like a dead branch, 'I told her I'd get the gully back from the DPR, once Frankie and I get cracking on this new mix. I promised her, lads, and I aim to keep my word. Anyone got a problem with that?'

He juts a combative chin in the direction of the island, hidden by the headland.

'Forget it,' Grif says. 'Frankie's lost to the lake.'

'I brought him home once. I can do it again,' Doc looks from the canvas to Lee and dismisses them both. 'Just you watch me, and all.'

Lee lunges at Doc's knees before he can stop himself. Fat Homer appears from nowhere, but Doc kicks Lee backwards into the shallows, and the paddle flies out of his hands. Homer stands over him. Bryce inches the inflatable toward the shore but Lee gets to his feet, sliding on the black-slimed rocks. Homer looms. The forked vein in Grif's forehead bulges. Archy is a ghostly warrior in the swirling mist.

'Go home,' Doc tells Lee. 'You had her for a night. I had her for a thousand of them. Every which way but loose. And these boys have lost their ma. Now, take your bad art and bugger off. This ain't about you.'

The men's hard boots crunch away on the rocks.

'Come on lads. Time to bring back our Frankie.'

***

Long after he finishes cleaning up the studio they'd trashed, the Polaroid stolen along with the painting of her face, Lee stands at an unknown hour over Vernon's empty tank with a beer and an uneaten grilled cheese sandwich. He angles his head to the side, tries to assemble the events of the day and the night so that they keep happening over and over again. He angles his head the other way. Just plays it all over and over through the shattered lens of time—how the girl saved him. How she'd arrowed down at him through the bronze-tinged murk, pulled him from the abyss with both eyes open and her eye patch nowhere in sight.

19. BRIDGE

BRUSQUELY HE LEADS her along the dark rows. So lonely growing up among the guns and Dutch uncles, Jason's dog-eared copies of *Beyond Good and Evil* littering their shared bedroom. Thettie follows Jason's kid brother across the field, as best as she can, perceiving herself to be in a bad way, one leg angled and painfully dragging. The jagged stalks tear at her bare feet. She can't remember how she got here, or why.

'Look,' the little boy points toward a huddled barn with one blunt finger. In his other arm, he cradles a newborn baby doll like the thing Bryce pulled out of the lake. Thettie is almost fooled again into thinking that this one's a real baby, because its reptilian eyes blink at her from between silicon lids. The doll is wrapped in a dirty yellow blanket smeared with the little boy's boogers and what-all else, Thettie scarcely dares to contemplate.

'What's your name?' she says.

'Meat,' the boy says, looking confused and then, 'Blanket.'

She wonders if he's sleepwalking. He's maybe eleven or twelve years old, but is big for his age, like the kids with Down Syndrome who used to be in the special class at Clinton Elementary. His puffy red-ringed eyes blink furiously at her, and his mouth smiles and grimaces in unending tandem. From one nostril, a bubble of snot inflates and deflates with every ragged breath. The moon cuts a path along the edge of the field toward a Spruce forest behind a machinery graveyard. Beside the graveyard is the barn. He leads her through a swinging wooden door into darkness and the panicked flap of an escaping owl. Thettie looks up and instantly remembers why she came here—to find out what the lake monster was doing in her room.

Jason deGroot, was born in 1987, same year as Grif, which makes him twenty-eight, but you'd never know it from the wasted creature hanging from the barn rafters. Thettie stares up at the skinny chicken neck squeezed by the noose, the collapsed old-young face crowned by the fuzzy Goth hair. Jason deGroot's mouth opens in a soundless scream. He jerks on the noose, his trenchcoat flapping, and at Thettie's approach, lifts an arm to touch the brittle stars around his head. He's been beaten up, one eye swollen in a shiner, cuts and bruises to his forehead, across the tracks on the exposed forearms. There is blood on his hands, too, fluttering and swiping at the twinkling dark.

Thettie peels a barbed rope of cobweb from her bloody nightgown. The hay at the feet of the swinging schizoid stinks of piss and worse. Her tongue lolls, inescapably tasting other rank odors in the barn. Blood and oil and dung. And stinks not found in nature, too. Crystal meth and solvent and iodine-soaked bandages from a source that she cannot quite place. With a great effort, she drags herself closer to Jason deGroot, leaving a trail of blood through the old straw and droppings, until she is looking up at his shit-stained jeans. The little brother rocks his doll and sucks his thumb.

'Stop it,' she turns furiously to the little boy. 'You'll ruin your teeth.'

The little step-brother is not a Harpur. Not even in part. But Jason, on the other hand—well Thettie sees the mother Cassie, in Jason, clear as day. The high cheekbones and sloppy mouth—hanging as he is from a barn ceiling with no obvious way of getting up there by himself—unless you count an old oil drum dragged in from the scrap heap. It's the blue eyes mainly, Harpur eyes, even if Cassie was a Tully. Same difference.

'What about the lizard?' Thettie says, the words garbled around her chewed up tongue. She giggles at her flapping lips make the word lizard sound like 'sluzza.'

The little brother smirks. 'Sluzza, sluzza.' The baby doll's lizard lips stretch in a lewd smile.

'Shuddup,' Jason says, which is how Thettie realizes that he can hear his little brother, but he can't hear *her*, not yet. And he can't see her either. Through her heightened senses she feels that he knows she is there though, or that someone is.

Whoever dragged the oil drum in after beating Jason senseless, and stringing him up to the rafter, forgot to position it so that it actually looked like it was Jason who got himself up there, and not his attackers. It's too far away for Jason to have managed, by himself, to get under the rafter he's actually under. Fucktards. Thettie sniffs that iodine-soaked bandage smell again, its source on the tip of her thoughts.

'Ask him if he stole the lizard,' Thettie tells the little brother. His hands nervously clench and unclench around a fold of baby blanket. The doll hisses at Thettie.

'Tell him I'll cut him down if he tells me,' she says. 'Otherwise he'll have to stay here forever.'

She's not yet sure how things work, but if there is anything Thettie is good at, it's making it up as she goes along. Jason twitches on the rope and jabs with a broken finger at the stars flying in from all directions. The brown stain spreads on the ass of his jeans.

'Come down, Jason!' the boy whines. Jason begins to cry.

'I feel his pain,' says Thettie, which is not true, not exactly. She *sees* his pain, or the pain he can no longer feel. The pain of the beating he took, but also the pain of betrayal. The pain of not being able to save the one he loved. But whether this is the monster, Vernon, or his mother Cassie or the little brother Meat Blanket, Thettie can't be sure. These possibilities line up on the rafters, separate but interconnected like wrens on the wires of her newly networked mind.

Jason babbles something about a forest.

'Oh for fuck's sake,' Thettie motions to Meat Blanket, who helps her move the drum back under the body and Thettie hitches up her bloody nightgown and climbs upon it. She bites off a scream of pain as her dislocated arm flops at the shoulder. With her other arm, she pulls Jason over to her, stands on tip-toe and starts to gnaw through the noose. Even with her newly recurved teeth, it takes a while—hours or even years, it seems to Thettie, tasting grease and sweat and blood on the rope—but in the end Jason tumbles to the floor.

ALETHEIA

'Am I dead?' he asks.

'You are now,' she says. The brother bends over him. He reaches out to touch the crimson ring around Jason's neck. Jason bats him away, tries to sits up, but needs to lean against the drum. He cocks his head at the sirens and yelling that drifts up from the lake. Coming in from all directions, each note in the siren call separated from all the others. Even from here Thettie can distinguish the notes. And the voices, too. Archy's, Grif's, Doc's, the Harpur girls. The barn fills with wordless pain.

Jason and his brother clap their hands to their ears.

'Listen to that ruckus, you little 'tard,' Thettie says. 'What'd I ever do to you?'

Jason mouths some words, stabbing at the air, his bloody finger nail ripped off and hanging by a cuticle. Frankie liked to talk to the air, used to. Maybe it's a Harpur thing. Jason even smells a little like Frankie when his foot got bad. Like a shit that's taken a shit, Doc would say. Not even Thettie's MiraKil cream could mask the smell.

Thettie struggles to hold back the sobs threatening to spill. Every word comes back to her in memories, in dreams. Like the word shit. Every one smelling different from the next. She herself can, for her sins, now bring to mind every shit she's ever shat, from the first to the last—when she lay dying. The exact date and time every bomb was dropped, or if not hers, those of her children, or others. Smelled, stepped on, or wiped, for example from Jason's baby ass before Cassie lit off for LA.

Meat Blanket begins a hoarse but high-pitched keen.

'Shuddup,' Jason says. 'Shuddup. Shuddup.'

The kid rocks wildly from one leg to the other. Thettie lunges and grabs him by the shoulders, recoils in horror as her hands, not fully immaterial yet but the molecules of which are already compromised, pass through the kid's body. He shudders and the baby-doll bares its teeth at Thettie in a lizard grin.

'Sit down,' Thettie says, wiping tears and trying to regain control of the situation. 'Go over there and sit down next to your brother.' The kid goes over and sinks down against the oil drum beside Jason. That shuts him up a little. But Jason just keeps jabbering to himself, running through the events of his own death—she hears Vernon's name, and leans forward. But then he stops to play a tune on an air guitar, the killer riff. She rolls her eyes, which hurts enough to make her remember not to do it again.

Instead she tries to replay that night at the Way—the welcome-home party on Sunday night—and Jason deGroot skulking in all bleached Mohawk and army boots beneath a swinging trench coat, the one he's wearing now. She could smell it, she remembers, that Goodwill funk layered with the reek of cigarettes and meth. He'd shouldered a backpack that stuck in Thettie's mind—where is it now? There had been something familiar, even then, in his posture, in his bone structure, and it had made her shiver, and Grif had asked her if someone had walked over her grave. That brought her back to the moment, how these old-school manners of speaking bubbled up from nowhere when Grif had enough to drink. Expressions he never got from her, or anyone she knew, but from a time and place he liked to think he'd put behind him.

'Jason deGroot, all grown up. I helped changed your diapers,' Thettie says. 'When you were at Triangle Gully with Cassie. And this is how you repay me, by siccing . . . ' a word she now knows comes from the word, 'seeking,' ' . . . a lizard on my ass?'

'No!' the little kid says. '*Faux pas!*'

'I'll give you a *faux pas* upside your head if you don't shut up,' Thettie said. 'Ask him who he stole it for? And why?'

Jason deGroot looks up at some sonic signal he can't place. Not yet. But it gets his hands flapping again, swatting at the filaments of memory around his head. She sees them, too. One is a lab rat in a bikini. The other is Doc's men talking to Jason at the Way, buying him pitchers and shots. Another is his mother Cassie, absconded to become a rock 'n' roll star.

Thettie kneels down in front of Jason in the hay.

'Now we're getting somewhere,' she says. 'Why did Doc get him to steal the lizard?'

'*Faux pas*,' the step-brother says miserably.

'A *faux pas*?' Thettie leaps to her feet and hooks a thumb at what's left of her face. 'Is that what you call this? A blunder? A mistake? Look at me!' her arm has been yanked painfully behind her back, like a broken wing. Her tongue hangs by a thread and is already going blue. Matter runs down her legs. 'Look at *him*. Some mistake!'

The little boy has gone pale with fright. Her head is bursting with all of the associations unleashed by her outburst, like an unruly congregation in the Church of Forget. She lunges at Jason, flicking out her bloody tongue. She drops to all fours and skitters around and around the walls of the barn, and tells him she'll kill him again, Cassie or not. But he can't see or hear her and she's scaring the child half to death. He's stopped weeping but instead begins to chew the doll's hand, drool spilling from his loose mouth.

'Shuddup,' Jason says, hugging the boy tighter and rocking back and forth on the straw. The blood on Jason's face has slowed and his eyes are beginning to fade. She can feel the chill of his rigor mortis from here. She'll have to move quickly if she's going to get him out of here in time. It's the least she can do. For Cassie.

***

Cassie's Sweet Sixteen. The Motel 6 room strewn with bottle and pipes, Red Bull cans, crushed packs of American Spirit, and condoms. Thettie's thighs were sticky and there were crumbs between her breasts. She was crying and she heard sniffling from the other bed. Her thoughts sloshed with the effect of the roofies but she tried to find Cassie, and when she did, she wished she hadn't. An image she would take with her for all time. Cassie at her Sweet Sixteen, her brimming blue eyes pressed against a streaky motel pillow while Piet deGroot jammed into her from between her spread buttocks. Thettie looked away. She didn't want to see that at all.

The almost fifteen-year-old Thettie—desperate to forget what she had yet to remember—could see that the room was full of deGroots. Coming in from all directions. Some of them were naked. Other were in boxers. There were dollar bills rolled up beside bottles of *Jenever*. The men sniffed their fingers. The air was thick with the smell of weed and semen and Chinese take-out and blood.

Not actual blood but deep buried blood flowing through the cracks of time, flowing out and onward in slow motion like a dream for real.

*****

It's useless. She remembers seeing Jason with his backpack at the Way, and she remembers seeing him talking with Doc's muscle, Homer and Lyle, who took Jason outside to smoke a pipe or two. His downfall.

'Nice company you keep,' Thettie says. 'Just so you know, your new best friend Lyle got double-time for killing a teacher and a seventeen-year old warehouse clerk. How much they pay you to steal the lizard?'

'Backpack,' the brother says, and Thettie sticks her face in his. 'Where's the backpack now?'

'Stealer,' the little boy says, pointing toward the barn door.

'Shuddup,' Jason tries to cover his brother's mouth with his dematerializing hand.

Lee had given her his version of Jason deGroot's story—Lee's professor had taken him in out of some kind of social conscience, until Jason's illness had begun to affect his work. He'd forget sometimes to leave water for the mice or to set the timer for a researcher's protocol. How he worshipped the Gila Monster like a God and never forgave Lee for being the one to foster him after the lab shut down.

'Is that what this was?' she cries. 'A chance to get Vernon back for yourself? How'd that work out for you?'

Jason mutters something about Patti Smith, his mother's hero. Sea of possibility.

'See *this*!' Thettie waggles her broken tongue. 'After what that man has been through with his little boy? That damn lizard was all he had.'

'Doc,' Jason says. '*Faux pas.*'

'Wait.' A terrible chill creeps up her body from her twisted toes to the roots of her blood-matted hair. 'Did Doc put you up to this?'

Was this Doc's way of getting at her? Through Lee? That high-school romance stuff wasn't like Doc, and there was the small matter of whether he meant for the Gila to attack her or not. Seems a strange choice seeing as she hadn't brought Frankie to him yet like a sacrificial lamb—why would Doc have wanted to kill her before she got him to the island? She snorted, a sound that makes something shuffle and hiss in terror in the shadowy recesses of the barn. As if she'd ever give up Frankie—again.

What's up, Doc?

She howls and gnashes her teeth. Tears run down her stale make-up into the holes the monster tore in her flesh. The barn air is cold against her exposed jawbone. She could murder a cigarette.

'Jason!' the step-brother screams. 'Jason-Jason-Jason!'

Thettie freezes in the dark barn. His name wasn't Jason back then. Cassie had named him something else.

***

Piet DeGroot threatened a custody battle. At first Sarey helped take care of Cassie and the baby but Cassie knew that no court would rule in favor of a hick Harpur—single mama to boot—over a wealthy alfalfa farmer. Marrying her worst enemy was the only way she'd get to raise her son. So that's what she did. Piet deGroot loved her in his twisted way and gave her everything she wanted except freedom. But Thettie and Frankie didn't see her much after that. Until the day Cassie couldn't take the shame anymore, and decided to leave. Little Henry Jason—that was his name then—wasn't sick yet. He was musical by the age of twelve, like his ma, and she promised to send for him. The day Cassie left Little Ridge for good—when she was twenty-eight and still young enough to become a famous punk rocker—the three of them huddled the whole night together beside the Falls. Thettie, Cassie and Frankie. Frankie played guitar and Cassie sang 'Space Monkey' with him for the last time. And Cassie made Thettie swear to keep an eye on Jason, make sure he got through the teen-age years, and she'd send money every month into a secret account only he could access. Frankie was to tell him about it when he was ready. Frankie drove Cassie to the Greyhound Station at dawn, the three of them holding hands and singing in the front seat of the Pontiac: *To distant lands/takes both my hands/never a frown, with Golden Brown.*

'Look what you did, Henry Jason Harpur. What would your mama say? Look!'

Jason looks up at the sound of his real name. He runs his hands through his hair and it comes out in clumps. His lip splits open again from where Thettie can still feel Lyle's fist against it—she finally knows it was Lyle because she has managed to place the lingering smell of the bandages on his ass where Sarey clipped him with her old Mossberg. Jason's flapping hand makes shadow puppets on the wall and Thettie gnashes her teeth. She kicks the dirt floor with her bare and bleeding feet, howls in agony. The step brother buries his face in his dolly.

'Why? Jason, why? Why'd you take the lizard, and where is it now?'

The truth of it is that Thettie can't get past her own memories to get close enough to Jason's. The past is so overgrown, crisscrossed with conflicted recall— hers, Jason's, her sons'. She gets all tangled in it, the way her hands tangle in her nightgown, twisting it around her bloody thighs.

'*Faux pas*,' the brother says again sadly, nudging his brother and pointing at Thettie. 'Jason? *Faux pas*.'

'You're right,' Thettie says. 'It's useless.'

Jason tries to get to his feet, looks up fearfully at the shadow of a hanging man in a trenchcoat, against the wall. The little brother pulls Jason back down on the straw. Something rustles again in one of the hidden stalls.

'Forest Path,' Jason says.

Thettie stares. Her tongue finds a bleeding space of gum where one of her teeth has gone. And is still missing.

'Forest Path,' she says with her tongue on her missing tooth, and it comes out sounding like '*faux pas*.' Poison flows from the hole in her gums and there is more where that comes from. Not '*faux pas*,' a word she didn't even know she knew. No, not that.

'Forest Path.'

Thettie, Jason and the kid all say it together again, chanting it over and over again. *Faux pas. Faux pas.* Doves gurgle in terror. Spiders dance on their webs and from deep within the barn, a 'possum awakes and slinks past, hissing at Thettie as it goes.

Then it comes back to her slowly in filaments that smell like pizza. How Doc had told her about Frankie's

Killer Mix. How it was called Forest Path and it made you remember everything even if it wasn't yours to remember, and it was made of lizard spit.

The blue tongue down her throat, the dark-starred eye of love, kiss of life.

How long had it been sitting there in the trailer, crawled through some unnamable door to emerge in a slice of moonlight that fell on his banded hide, serious moonlight that expanded the bunched shoulders and transformed the clawed grip into a terminal caress? The monstrous head lowered in tainted love to hers.

Faux pas. A false step. The wrong move for the right reason. Or vice versa. Because you can't always save the ones you love, Jason. But she would try. For Cassie, she would not leave him trapped here. To swing forever from the noose of his own undoing. Stealing the lizard for love, another *faux pas* in a lifetime of wrong moves. Thettie understands. How can she leave a boy—who is after all a Harpur at least in part—here on deGroot land for all time?

'Say goodbye, Fucktard.'

Jason's stepbrother's eyes brim with gluey tears. His lips quiver, and he pats the baby, rocks the baby. 'Not goodbye,' he says. 'Jason, shuddup.'

The shadow swinging on the wall behind them is taking on dimensions, form. 'Hurry,' Thettie says.

Jason stands and pulls his brother to his feet.

'See you, little buddy,' he says.

Their fists touch in the dark, the material and the not, and will never touch again.

20. LEGEND

THERE IS AN unclean quality to death that Lee finds unsettling. It smells. It leaks. It stiffens and swells and falls prey to unclean things. It does not know itself but wanders needful and alone and calls to the warmth of blood to remember it. To call it by name.

It is Tuesday morning, the day after the one-eyed girl saved Lee back from the island. The weather-effect storms continue. He texts Habib repeatedly, wanting to ask him about the investigation, but Habib doesn't reply. The lake looks like it's levitating in the rain.

Deputy Abbes arrives at the studio, having dutifully made the rounds of everyone who'd seen Thettie Harpur in the days before her death, all just part of the process, Abbes assures Lee. Cut and dried case of self-inflicted death.

'The state of that trailer speaks for itself,' Abbes tells all and sundry. 'Doubt there'll even be an investigation.'

When Lee coldly asks Abbes what this is then, Abbes just squares his shoulders, spread his legs a little wider and tells Lee that last time he looked, this was America.

'What does that even mean?' Lee asks.

'It means have a nice day, motherfucker,' Abbes says.

Lee's phone beeps. It's Habib, finally telling Lee to come over right away. The message is punctuated by a sad face.

Lee drives south down Main street through the Village. His headlights bore vaporous tunnels through the rain, store-fronts surreally pixelated through the downpour. Harpurs rumble through the town on four wheels or two, stolen or bartered for, tail-gating Lexuses and Audis. The ghostly report from the bad mufflers and rusted exhaust pipes on the Harpur rides resounds through the Village like troops rebellious in defeat.

Lee stops at the Village Market to buy a six-pack of Habib's favorite beer, Moa, a New Zealand boutique brew unavailable in Little Ridge before the Progress Association stepped in. The store buzzes with rumor and hearsay. How the Harpur woman killed herself, and how her sons found her body, self-mutilated almost beyond recognition. Her mouth hacked into a bitter grin.

On a positive note, the checker tells Lee, it takes a tragedy like this to heal a rift. Why just earlier today she'd seen one of the Harpurs, the one who'd fought in Afghanistan, the war hero with the burns and missing fingers, talking to old Piet deGroot—the deGroots and Harpurs sworn enemies by tradition, even after one of the girls and Piet got married.

'Things did improve a little for a while, but then she left him,' the checker reddens. 'Not that anyone could blame her.'

It's the lack of an investigation that troubles Lee.

What bothers him is what is just assumed beyond reasonable doubt—the smug assumption that there are those whose lives matter even less to them than they do to the rest of the world. Lee presses Habib's doorbell, stomping the chill out of his legs. Habib calls out that it's open.

Lee goes in and shakes off his jacket, spreads greasy rain drops across his glasses with a thermal sleeve stained with Grif Harpur's blood. Habib, uncharacteristically unshaven and shirtless beneath a robe, is on the phone. The lake boils through the window behind him. Many of the trees have already lost their leaves, intermittent crimson foliage stark against the monochromatic shore. Habib's laptop is open and he is discussing Thettie's wounds with someone on the phone. The quote-unquote conclusive nature and location of the cuts on her body. Deep gashes on her arms and legs and face. How she tried to pull out her own tongue and so on, injuries more or less consistent with the most extreme examples of self-harm, such as under the influence of psychosis or crack cocaine. 'Well, why the gouges on her left side?' Habib asks and then listens to the answer. 'Surely that aspect introduces an element of reasonable doubt?'

Habib hangs up. He takes the beer from Lee with a sorrowful bow, and pours it carefully into a gleaming pewter Stein. He raises it and says, 'To Thetis Harpur.' Lee swigs his from the bottle.

'Where's the telescope?'

Habib looks baffled for a moment, and then he says, 'Oh that. It was hideous, wasn't it? And it didn't work. I had to take it back.'

Lee goes around the desk to the window and looks

down to the shore at his right where crime scene tape still flaps around the Harpur campground. At the edge of his left eye, two things. The framed picture of Habib's family, crushed under an exploding building in Lebanon, and on Habib's laptop, the coroner's report of Thettie Harpur's death.

'You got a backdoor man at the coroner's office, Sam?'

'I have backdoor men everywhere. Old habits die hard.'

'Refugee Gangster Number 1. What's that about wounds to the left side of her body? Is that why I'm here?'

'Any sign of Vernon?' Habib snaps the laptop shut and swivels his chair to Lee.

Lee shakes his head. 'He probably crawled away to die.'

'Mammals do that,' Habib says. 'Reptiles not so much, though that's more your area.'

'I went looking for Jason to ask him,' Lee drains half the bottle, peering down at a figure walking along the shore. It's the girl with the eye patch, the one Thettie called the water-rat. 'You haven't seen him?'

'Not for weeks, unfortunately. I paid him to help around the place occasionally—yard work and so on.'

'And so on?'

'And so forth. Last time I heard he was living in a half-way house in Ilium.'

'The little brother was at the farm, the boy with Down Syndrome. Jesus, that reminds me. He had one of those American Born dolls of Sunny's? It was a doll with Down Syndrome, too.'

'Self-validation is trending these days, Lee. You can't tell me that's a bad thing.'

The conversation, once again, seems to have branched off in some unintended direction. 'He told me Jason wasn't there.'

Lee goes to Sam's kitchen and brings back two beers. 'The old cryostat machine went missing that time, remember? From the lab. Remember how we found it in Jason's rented room above the gas station?'

Habib ponders the lake through the window. 'Jason was the only one who could fix it. He was brilliant with machines. I'll give him that. Something wrong with the wiring.'

'No kidding.'

Habib swivels back and forth, playing with a pencil on his desk. 'Who knows where he's gone this time? The boy's his step-brother by the way. DeGroot's first wife, Jason's mother, was a Harpur. DeGroot had no interest in Jason from the beginning. It was just a way to the woman he wanted, as children often are. In the end, he blamed Jason for driving her away. Or so Jason told me.'

Lee remembers his own father's indifference, and how Habib saved him, Lee, from disappearing in its wake. Lee turns his back to the lake, leans against the window and looks down at his mentor. 'I always wondered, Sam—what started the feud between the deGroots and the Harpurs?'

'You think a deGroot did this?'

'I don't know what to think.'

Habib doodles some calculations onto the condensation on his Stein. 'Who knows how these things start? The deGroots would beat up a Harpur, poison the creek. The Harpurs would retaliate by burning a car or a tractor. The deGroots would beat up some local tweaker, the Harpurs would ambush a truck full of weed at the border. And before that? The entire region was founded on rivalry—Dutch-Iroquois. Throw in the French, and then the slaves—the Harpers descending from all of the above. Quite a mix.'

Lee closes his eyes and listens to Habib drone on, a tremor to the older man's voice that Lee hasn't noticed before. 'And in recent times you've got the deGroots supplementing the depressed Alfalfa market with hydroponic weed, which they ship all across the state. I guess way back when, you could argue that Frankie's messy little meth and moonshine operations fueled the feud—they get rid of him, only to have him resurface with some new mix . . . ' Habib passes a hand across his face as if to dispel some unwanted thought. 'But I'm not sure what doing this unspeakable thing to Thettie Harpur would accomplish.'

'A warning, maybe?' Lee says. 'The deGroots concerned less about the competition than about the unnecessary heat it might draw . . . ?'

Lee's mind goes back to the grinding mulcher and Fie deGroot with his ax, and how no one knows where Jason is. Habib's still talking about feuds, saying something about Doc Murphy bullying his way into the Harpur family, playing the clans against each other.

'The fake Irish Doctor? I saw him at the Way,' Lee says. 'Talking with Jason.'

'Doc Murphy may be fake Irish and a fake doctor. But he's real gangster. Used to be part of a grisly protection syndicate in Liverpool—they hate the Irish, as you know . . . '

'Feuds. I get it.'

'Now *that* one goes back to the nineteenth century,

famine and whatnot—starving Paddies in their hordes sweeping into Slavers Bay . . . '

Lee sinks further into the library chair on the other side of the desk. He closes his eyes to stop the walls from spinning, and waits for Habib to come back to Thettie. To the present.

'Where was I? So young Doc works as a cleaner-fixer or what have you, for this Irish kingpin in Liverpool called Hook. Depending on where you get your information . . . '

'Where do you get your information, Sam?'

'Realcrime dot org, doesn't everyone? Doc goes behind Hook's back, tries to organize a sideline with a rival who goes by the name of Toeless Mears.'

'Jesus.'

'Doc has a super-villain's fear of dogs, so apparently, Hook punishes him by slathering Doc's fingers in dripping and getting the cute guard dogs to chew them off—just the index fingers, mind you—but on both hands.'

'I'm confused. What use could a gangster have for a Number 1 with no trigger fingers?'

Habib lifts his shoulders in a shrug. 'The logic escapes me, too, but I imagine it's something like that behind the court eunuchs of old. The point is that you adapt, as Doc proved by killing Toeless.'

'That's so sweet.'

'Paddy ordered him to, trigger-fingers or not. Unfortunately, the second honeymoon between Paddy and Doc was short-lived. Toeless's widow killed Hook in revenge and then went after Doc, who managed to escape by taking an assumed name—Daylin Murphy—and coming to America. Land of the Brave.'

Lee knows he should be paying more attention. Habib pushes the laptop toward him, but Lee just shakes his head and looks away.

'So you're saying he could have been doing the same with the Harpurs? Trying to organize something on the side with the deGroots?'

'There *was* a tip-off.'

Lee recalls the posse on the beach. How Archy and Grif Harper bristled under Doc.

'And now?' Lee says.

'You mean in regards to Thettie?'

'In regards to anything,' Lee says.

'Doc and Thettie were together,' Habib frowns. 'And then you came along.'

Lee's feels a jolt of electricity right down to his feet. 'I wasn't the only one. She told me.'

'Maybe you were different,' Habib says. 'Maybe Doc didn't like that.'

Lee thinks back to the spittle flying from Doc's mouth, the white scars protruding through the flesh of his face like little knuckles.

Habib fidgets with a Post-It note pad, opens a drawer in his desk and drops the pad in.

'Just to be clear,' he says haltingly, 'it wasn't me who took Vernon. I have enough Helotide in secure facilities to last me a lifetime.'

And if by secure facilities, Habib means a cryostat in his basement next to the dryer, then who is Lee to judge? The lab closes down and Habib grabs a stash of brain food for a rainy day. Maybe more than a stash. Maybe more than a day.

'She didn't kill herself,' Lee says. 'Accidentally or on purpose. I feel that.'

'Based on what evidence, a beloved's hunch?'

'It wouldn't be the first time.'

'I know. Sorry.'

Lee's grip is loose on his beer, spilling some on the desk, which he tries to wipe with his sleeve.

'Seems to me you haven't so much fallen off the wagon, Lee, as swan-dived?' Habib passes across what looks like a gym towel. 'You went out on the lake at night? In October. Again?'

It is common, Lee read once, for a person without a father to worship their uncle. Lee's father divorced his mother for a co-worker, but anyway had lost interest in him by the time Lee was fifteen. Lee didn't have an uncle. Until Sam Habib. They met over Vernon, and Habib wanted to know everything about Lee. Not only his research, but his sports teams, his friends. He arranged to go with Lee on his next hike, binge-watched *The Wire* with him, went to Lee's band Loaf Meat's terrible gigs. Lee—a stranger to his biological family and to his fellow grad students with their public boozing and desert philosophizing— recognized himself at last in the eyes of another. Sammi Habib, Palestinian-American activist, polymath and ground-breaking neuroscientist. Founding director of the Center for Matters of Mind, his popularized account of the mechanisms of memory awarded the 2002 *New York Times* Book Award, yet he found time to volunteer at reservation schools as a reading buddy, flirted with his students' moms and their dads, too. When he moved to Little Ridge, it was the same. He joined the editorial board of *Nature Magazine* and he read about rescued birds and attended clam bakes advertised in *The Village Dawn*.

ALETHEIA

He drank beer with clerks from the county coroner's office in Ilium, played masters soccer with a detective who he persuaded to reopen the investigation into the killing of Lee's child. He joined the choir. He participated in woods regeneration, the class action committee against Sunny Weeks' Progress Association, coached youth soccer and hosted visiting scientists for Sunday brunch at Sullivan Hall beneath the twenty-foot glass window of Veritas, Goddess of Truth.

Sometimes known as Aletheia.

The new electric bell tower 'peals' twelve times.

Lee wobbles to his feet. He feels his way around Habib's study like a blind man, touching the framed plaudits and awards. The photographs of Habib with Dennett, Kandell, Ursula LeGuin. It's not just the beer, although it mostly is. Lee doesn't need to cry because his head is ballooned in a sob, like a cell's nucleus in cytoplasm. He tries to trace back over the events of the last few days. The one night with Thettie, Vernon's empty tank, the smashed markers in the pet cemetery carving a path to the studio door, the water rat's floating eye patch. Her sons in their blind grief, but able, still, to see through Doc. But he doesn't get very far past the night with Thettie.

Habib's unshaven skin looks papery today, like a Greek mask, somewhere between comedy and tragedy. His robe gapes over the sparse gray fuzz on his chest. 'Maybe you should go home, Lee. Sleep it off.'

'She admitted to pills—Ambien and all sorts of things in her past, but she never gave the impression of being in that kind of mood. Of being in that kind of place.'

'What kind?' Habib's voice is gentle but probing.

'I tried to save her. I went out onto the lake to close the door.'

Except he knows that's not strictly true. He went out on the lake to maybe crawl through the door himself—while it was open—thinking that was the kind of sacrifice it would take. An exchange of kind.

The rain pounds on the windows. 'How did that work out for you?'

'Something stopped me,' Lee says. 'The girl, the one with the eye patch. She pulled me back.'

'Frankie Harper's water rat?' Habib says. 'Whatshername.'

'I think it may have been too late. I think whatever I was trying to keep out, or offer myself in exchange for, may have already crawled through.'

'Spoken like a true scientist, Lee. Go home and sleep it off, my friend.'

'That's what the Helotide is for, Sam, isn't it? Why you kept a stash for yourself? To help you get to the island before it gets to you?'

Habib straightens, his kinky hair more salt than pepper.

'Sometimes the ones we love are the hardest to save, Lee. I'm so sorry.'

'She was the key,' Lee hears the crack in his voice. 'From the first moment I saw her outside the Market, I felt it. Vernon felt it. And now they're both gone.'

Habib says slowly, 'The key to what?'

Lee leans forward, his words slurring. 'Her one fear? Lizards.'

'Herpetophobia.'

'Her favorite food? Pizza. And now it's Vernon's, too. Was. Is. Whatever.'

'Science is in the details, Lee, not in the whatevers.'

Lee's voice cracks and he pushes himself back from the Italian walnut desk. 'I thought we were gangsters now.'

'Go home and finish the painting,' Habib's voice is firm. A coach's voice to a choking player.

'Ever heard of Seek-you?' Lee contemplates another beer, but he doesn't want to risk trouble with the Sheriff, and he's got some miles to put in today. The painting can wait.

'Who?'

'The lake monster. The one-eyed girl who is with the Harpurs, she told me it was a tree.'

'But she's not one of them—and damned if I can think of her name,' Habib says irritably.

Lee's face burns. 'She said it was some big old pine that's been floating around beneath the surface for hundreds of years.'

'Ah, that,' Habib points to a book case across the room. 'Forth shelf, halfway across.'

Lee goes across to the shelf and pulls out a broken-backed book in a cloth cover.

'I picked it up at the Village fair, years ago.'

Lee reads the cover page. It is James Fennimore Cooper's *The Lake Gun*.

'It's an Iroquois legend,' Habib leans back in his chair and puts his arms over his head and crosses a knee over the other. Lee looks away as the dressing gown gapes. 'Or a James Fennimore Cooper legend, at any rate. Some rabble-rousing Haudenosaunee demagogue called See-wise got greedy and speared a huge salmon out of season, which was forbidden by the great Manitou. In the struggle with the salmon, the greedy demagogue lost and was pulled into the lake, never to be seen in his human form again, but condemned for his false pride, to float among the salmon and the trout and eels for a thousand winters in the form of a huge sundered tree trunk. Kind of phallic when you think about it.'

Lee flips through the soft pages. 'What do lake guns have to do with it?'

Habib stifles a belch. 'If I remember right, the noise of the lake guns is the voice of the great Manitou, the thunderous ring of truth, reminding the ravening See-wise, and everyone else, of the dangers of fishing out of season. Of not only trying to turn the tables on the natural order of things, but thinking you can get away with it. I wonder why she said his name was, not See-wise, but Seek you?'

Lee carefully replaces the book on the shelf. He doesn't answer Habib, because Habib is not asking.

Why the gouges on her left side?

Because there is another.

21. GOING PLACES

'**I DIDN'T MEAN** to kill you,' whimpers Jason to the noisiest thrush of all.

'Doesn't matter if you did or didn't,' Thettie says, making it up as she goes along. 'You stole the lizard and that's enough. If I don't get us out of here, we'll both be stuck on this lake forever. That's the way it works.'

Jason shakes his head vehemently, aims an imaginary gun at the mouthy thrush and Thettie acts shot. She is excited, can't wait to see the look in Cassie's eyes when she, Thettie, brings Jason back to his mother. Looking askance at the black veins crisscrossing Jason's face and the red welts around his neck, she hopes they make it in time. Thettie swipes away the bloody tears swimming past her eyes, and tries to stuff her own tongue back in her mouth with a mangled hand. Cassie'll know how to make her presentable again. Cassie's not as good as Thettie is with the herbs and potions, but is magic with mascara and a bit of blush. She stifles a sob, and Jason looks up in alarm at the thrushes—dancing wildly on the branch screaming, 'Seeeek-you, seeeeek-you!'

Thettie hisses at them and the birds burst from the Hemlocks, swarm and hover overhead.

'Let's go, Fucktard. Been a while since I've been out west.'

Another lie. Thettie has never been out west, never been anywhere.

But being dead doesn't mean you can defy all the laws of physics and many of the old rules still apply. So it's not being dead, but the way moment after moment plays back to her now, like a magician's deck. Minutes that she can achingly sense, smell, and hear ticking in her branching mind. The glacial burn of the lake-effect rain in the webbing between her toes. The sweet rot in the gummy trampled paddocks—she smells that with her fingers. They cross a shallow stream and she points out the branching glaucous stems of a dark plant, its joints swollen, the recurved petals of its pumpkin-colored flowers littering the dark soil.

'Jewelweed,' she says. '*Impatiens aurea*, part of the geranium family. Good for piles, bloating and some kinds of skin poisoning. Worked like a treat on Frankie's foot.'

Except that, too, was a lie. Nothing worked on Frankie's foot in the end.

'War stories,' Jason begins. 'Dutch uncles told war stories.'

She hunches beneath the shoulder-sagging heft of the sky beneath which she leads Jason at a crouch, stopping every now and then to let him catch up. Waiting for him allows her a chance to scuttle ahead on all fours toward a puddle of brackish ditchwater. She washes off the black blood that streaks her arms and her thighs, sticky and clinging. But the minute her skin is clean it comes back, slowly, like leeches from the inside.

'We all got one or two of those war stories,' she says.

What Lee said about his missing child, Vernon—except that was the wrong name—was a war story. Things she wishes she'd attended to more closely, come flooding venomously back. How the mnemonic effects of the peptide sequence, HSEGTIFTSD in the synthetic peptide Helotide, extracted from Gila venom, are evident twenty-four hours after administration, and present one week or more after a single dose. How its effect on humans is at yet untrialed. Unknown.

On rats is, Lee said, one effect of the Helotide is to carve out a new path in memory. Or to activate a compensatory one, Lee said, like a phantom limb. Like, if you lose the use of one eye, the other gets stronger, does the work of two. Like, how one sense—smell—learns the skill set of another—sight. And in remembering the new skill, forgets some of what it was. New paths flicker into being in the dendritic forest of memory, flashing signals that blind you to what you were.

You make do.

Thettie drinks deeply in of the secretive dawn as if to suck the life out of it while she still can.

'Because we're going places, Jason Dipshit. We learn by leaving behind.'

Even taking into account the fact that with the combined dose of venom and Benzedrine, which is the active ingredient in Ambien, she'd had a double or triple whammy, Thettie knows she doesn't have much time. How long before the consciousness-expanding-path-carving effect of the lizard spit diminishes? End of story.

'Seek you,' Jason Henry Harpur yells from behind a tree. 'Seek you!'

'Vernon found me,' she says, turning to the jittery kid lost in his games. 'What's it look like? But that's not my war story. Not the beginning of it anyway.'

Jason stops at her voice. Mutters something in answer to a hellish chorus of the thrushes. He picks at the pimples on his jaw. Thettie sighs. Lord knows it's a face only a mother could love. If it wasn't for the fact he was already dead, Thettie would kill him again just for stealing Vernon. Poor Lee.

'The beginning of my war story is that I was dead before I died,' she said, pointing an imaginary gun at her head. She doesn't need some freaked-out tweaker to tell her that. 'Doc would have killed me after he found Frankie. After or before, depending on what he found. He said I was the key, but what I really was, was the bait. Do you understand? Means to an end. Three different ways of saying the same thing . . . '

Jason holds up four fingers on one hand. So maybe he can hear her after all.

'Who's counting, Blondie? A mixed metaphor'll fuck you every time.' It occurs to Thettie in her altered state, that metaphors, like the Docs of this world, are inescapable—one leading to another—with no end in sight.

Frankie would say that was the beauty of language. That words were more than a means to an end. And less. She's beginning to get that now, and it fills her with wonder.

'Anyway, it didn't quite happen that way, thanks to Vernon.'

Vernon-not-Vernon had vomited into her dying

mouth the spit of undying memory. She can't help but shiver recalling the fifty outsized teeth sawing into her face. Imprinting on the speedily enfolding proteins of Thettie's DNA the milk of cacti, of flesh-pink desert dawn reflected in dank arroyo, dim burrow where another awaits to carry the seed of memory, and of light. If the lake monster was a metaphor, it grew legs to save her.

Lee—the name makes her nostrils quiver with the smell of lake water and whisky and something else that makes her hands travel south, under her nightgown and past her belly, splayed across familiar flesh, but no. Not yet.

Thettie cuts across an alfalfa field, then through fleshy corn stalks, past grazing cattle that low and dance sideways at her passing. Jason closes in. They head along Moonshine Road, keeping the meadows of wild blackberry and morning glory grown over extinct orchards, between them and the village.

He takes the lead through a wood on deGroot land, where a path leaps out at her from memory. A shortcut to the Tinker's Glen bus station. The birds stir and sing in Greek, in Senecan and in French. She could whoop Jason for trying to trip her up on the bizarre forest of his deranged recall, for interfering with her own, because there is always punishment worse than death. She knows that now. She stoops to pick up an ancient peach pit, seed of time.

'Bad metaphor,' she croaks.

'Useless,' mutters Jason ahead of her. It had made his mother cry, how his old man used to call him that.

'At stealing lizards, yes,' Thettie says. 'At that game you truly suck and blow.'

'Your ma said she hated how deGroot, your own father, called you useless. She told Frankie that she had to leave so she wouldn't kill him.'

But that's another lie. Frankie would have killed deGroot for Cassie. It was all they could do to stop him. The real reason Cassie left was so she wouldn't kill her*self*.

Thettie feels bad for teasing him, but she has no time for tweakers. Jason hitches up a non-existent backpack.

'Your backpack is what's gone—and you'll be haunting the lake for all time, looking for it, unless I get you out of here STAT,' she says, panting propulsive drops of blood. 'Because it's evidence, like the Steelers' bag they hid it in. Steeler with two 'e's. Stele with one 'e' is another word for grave marker.'

'Stealer,' Jason says, in Frankie's irritable voice, 'with an 'a."

In the end, Cassie had to leave it all behind if she was going to live, if she was going to be any good to Jason now or later. Thettie wants to say how much she missed Cassie after she left. How lost she is without her. She even dreams about her once a month, like a period. Troubled dreams of Cassie turning down an unfamiliar path, over and over again. Or naked and wearing a wig over her razor-cut punk hair, a Halloween Afro-wig that she was always in the middle of taking off, but never quite did before the dream ended. Her bare arms eternally raised and obscuring her face. A stranger to herself.

Thettie says, 'Hey, Henry Jason! At the Way that night, that was you, wasn't it? Scheming and dreaming with Doc. I didn't know it was you, I mean Cassie's little boy. All grown up and all, didn't recognize your schizoid-ass.'

'What's up Doc? What's up Doc?' Jason lopes to the rhythm of the words, a grotesque little waltz.

'Lee pointed you out. Told me about how you'd worked in the lab and how you loved your animals, thought it was up to you to save them. Me too! I'm a vegetarian, like you. Slow down.'

'Vaja-what?' Jason babbles. That angled skinny-giant lope against the scrim line of the horizon.

'Yeah, well I've probably had more pussy than you, for real. Not vagitarian, Fucktard. *Vegetarian.* Like you. Because of all those cute little mice-ies you sacrificed, right? For me it was because of Frankie. For what I did to him, leaving him behind to die. I'd already given up drugs but that was for my boys. Only thing I had left was meat. So, that had to go, for Frankie. Except that's the middle of my war story. The boys are the beginning. That time they nearly drowned.'

Jason's hands fly to his throat and claw at the imaginary noose.

'Exactly my point. You want to be doing that till the end of time? I didn't think so. Now get moving.'

The story starts, or continues, with Thettie sick from whatever cure Doc had given her.

'You know the disease I'm talking about? Not the dope itself, which is bad enough, but the self-hate it leaves behind to feed on if you let it?'

Because the thing was that Archy wanted to take the pup, Scrappy, out with them. And it was Scrappy's barking that Thettie heard in her dreams. But Doc heard it for real and it got him out on the lake when the boys went out too deep.

J.S. BREUKELAAR

Talking wearies her and she's fallen behind again. Jason veers to the tree line in an effort to stay out of the pinky wash of the dawn, and all around her a doubtful drip from the leaves beats an uneven rhythm to the early birdsong. Her nightgown drags a train of fallen leaves and her arm flaps behind her hanging by a sliver of exposed bone.

'The way my war story goes is this. I'm in the house all strung out on what? My third or three-hundredth attempt at getting clean, and Doc's been making house calls with his doctor's bag, and there isn't enough to eat. The boys decide to go out to get me some fish. To make me better.'

Her voice cracks and Jason stares in terror at the barren stalks crushed in her immaterial wake.

'There'd had been an old leak in the side of their little Jon-boat and they hadn't been able to use it for weeks. Doc finally fixed it, found them a cheap 2-stroke on Craigslist. So, that's what they went out in. It was a good size for them, twelve-footer, but too small for deep water.'

Jason pulls at his bleached hair.

'They go out in the creek with Scrappy but the fish they want, new season salmon? That's the one they want for me. Grif knows how I hate trout. Salmon's one with all the vitamins in it, I always told them. There's none of that in the creek. Their ma needs to get better, is what Grif says. So they go out for salmon, right to the mouth of the creek, where they're not allowed to go in that little boat of theirs. And that's when Scrappy starts barking.'

Jason leers at her with his blackened teeth and he says, '*Le poisson est mon plat prefere.*'

'Your favorite dish? Can you finally see me, dipshit? No, I didn't think so. Yeah, well not just any fish. *Les saumon,*' she doesn't know how she suddenly knows French, except that one of the voices in Jason's schizoid head taught her. 'Although you ever stop to think how the French word for fish, *poisson,* and the American word, poison, look almost the same?'

Jason brings his hands to his ears and starts to cry. Not just a little weep but a full-bore belly-sob. *Mamamama!* He sinks to his knees pounding the cold ground. His eyes are black bowls of despair.

'Hold up! You already told your war story. This is mine, so wait your turn. They go out too far. Out into the deep mouth of the river where it empties into the lake and that's where the salmon feed. Engine gives out, and the boat takes in water, of course, because the current kept on pushing it sideways, licking over the side and even Grif—skilled on the water as he already is—he can't handle the boat, Archy and the dog in that little boat. Scrappy's going nuts. All three of them go over. Doc hears Scrappy and takes his boat out, dives in his own self, and pulls them to safety. All except Scrappy. And all except their little Jon boat. God only knows where that washed up.'

'*Trofi gia ta psaria,*' Jason turns and begins to lope off again.

'Fish food is right,' Thettie says, not knowing how she knows Greek either, except that it's not Jason's voices teaching her. It's some Albanian ancestor of her mother's who stowed away on the *San Antiago* in 1496. 'Archy never forgave himself for losing Scrappy. Grif never forgave himself for nearly losing Archy. Frankie never forgave himself for not taking care of the boys like he promised he would. And what I never forgave myself for?'

Jason's head cocks in the direction of a host of disembodied answers. She backs off slowly from how the memories are affecting Jason's face—the black veins across his skin spreading like roots, while time-lapse tree branches push from his skull, intersecting above his head. Except they're not tree branches. His gray teeth pierce his lips, and elongate, and his eyes are roiling seas of black.

'What I couldn't forgive myself for was how I'd sold myself to Doc. Two lives, three counting my own. Three lifetimes it'd take me to pay that off, not counting interest, and don't think he didn't remind me every day. Because the price of default? My boys. If I turned against Doc, he'd get my sons, like deGroot got you. The state would award them to him in a heartbeat—decorated war medic versus whatever name they got for me—and I couldn't let that happen. But I paid the price.'

'*Faux pas,*' Jason says, coming across a pumpkin patch and proceeding to smash them one by one with his heel.

'No mistake, Blondie. You and me's going places.'

22. AX A STUPID QUESTION

THIS IS THE second time Lee has visited Jason in a week, exactly twice as many times as in the whole decade that he's lived in Little Ridge. He polishes off a third beer while steering through the lifting rain that feels like it's drilling against the inside of his eyelids. Bleached fields terminate in blackened woods and hemlocks mass along the ridge to the east. Lee doesn't want to think about Jason—abandoned by his mother, shunned by his father—invisible to everyone including Lee. The lab had been Jason's life. It had been all of their lives. But Lee hadn't followed Habib all the way from UNM, dragged his wife and child across the country back to a hometown she hated, only to find Habib entranced with a sly young head-case. Hunched Igor-like in the great Professor's shadow, fleet and watchful as a rat.

He was wrong.

Lee fishtails down the gravel driveway of the deGroot farm, gets out and slams the door. He leans his head on the door to the farmhouse, his thumb on the doorbell. There is no sound of vacuuming this time, just a rumble of machinery that Lee feels in his feet. He registers it as a subterranean grinding of gears growling up from beneath the hard winter soil.

What machine hums from deep within the earth on a rainy October weekday?

Lee knocks on the door and listens. Cartoon voices ghost their way from somewhere in the house. Lee backs off down the steps. Sponge Bob, Dora, Bugs Bunny—his son's ultimate rainy-day favorite. He weaves across the wet gravel to the rear of the house, and pounds on the garage door. Then he starts toward one of the barns. Behind it, near a spruce grove, there is a pile of old machinery and rusted drums, and beside that a barn significantly older and more decrepit than the rest. Lee peers through rain-flecked lenses. The door is ajar and he can make out men milling around.

'Hey!' His feet feel far away. The field onto which he's wandered is a minefield of fleshy shoots and he trips over something soft. He cuts a reckless diagonal across the vicious old growth. He stumbles against another soft thing and the hairs on the back of his neck stand up.

With the toe of his sneaker, he's kicked a doll's head a few feet along. Lee feels like he's going to vomit, and closes his eyes. When he opens them again, it's still there. It's a newborn baby head torn loose from its body, one of those silicon nightmares. He pivots on his heel. Behind him is a tiny leg with tiny curled up toes. To one side of him where the rubble has been crushed beneath careless boots, there is an arm with chewed-up fingers. Lee bends down to pick it up, his flesh still crawling. Someone yells. Lee drops the doll's arm into the pocket of his jacket.

'Help you?'

Lee neck burns hot, then cold. He summons the skills of the functioning alcoholic, like riding a bike. The man looks very far away and very small, as if Lee could pick him up with his dissection tweezers and drop him in a specimen dish. It's not Jason's old man, but one of the uncles maybe. A hinge-jawed farmer with a ruddy nose and a farmer's stoop, blond hair turning gray. His eyes hidden behind wraparound shades. The man's swinging an ax. Of course. That's what farmers do in the fall. They chop firewood. Lee recognizes the rumble now. It's the mulcher. Lee asks for Jason.

'Jason's not here,' the man says, looking backward toward the barn. 'What has he done?'

'Any idea when he left?' says Lee. 'Or when he'll be back?'

The man's hand gives the ax handle a jaunty twirl, majorette style. 'Couldn't say.'

'I'm Lee Montour. Jason and I worked together at the lab a long time ago. Is Piet—is his father here, by any chance?'

The man seems to be considering how to answer. 'I am his uncle. This about a job, *ja*?'

'So, it depends. Maybe. I just need to speak with him first, quite urgently.'

'You are the lizard guy?'

Lee shoves his hands in his pocket, his fingers curling around the chewed-up dolls hand. The man pauses, as if drawing from a dead reservoir of quaint phrases and clumsy modifiers of questionable use.

'It is venomous, *ja*? This Gila monster.'

'Gilas aren't aggressive,' Lee says.

'That how you say it? Gillah?'

'Heelah.'

'You could call it, like this: 'Heelah? Heelah? Where are you, leetle Heelah?' But these lizards, they don't have ears, *nee*?' The man points to his own large ears, which poke through fine strands of white-blond hair streaked with grey.

'Actually,' Lee says. 'The do. They . . . '

A cell phone goes off in the farmer's pocket. Lee has a feeling that it's from someone who is watching them. The ringtone is vaguely recognizable, but Lee can't quite place it. The rain runs into his eyes.

The DeGroot uncle—Lee tries to remember if his name is Pim, or Fie—dangles the ax and reaches into his shirt pocket take the call. 'I must take this. Do not be coming back please. Jason is very busy on the farm. Much to do.'

Lee follows the arc of the ax in the man's sweeping hand and notices a large opossum hanging upside down beneath the dripping eaves of the barn, its head swiveled toward Lee and its needle-toothed mouth smeared with red.

23. TICKET TO RIDE

JASON FORGES AHEAD, keeping one or two steps between them, sometimes more.

Thettie is not right in her body. She finds herself crawling at one moment, slithering the next, or scuttling in a cramped sideways run, or bounding after him, airborne like a virus. She keeps her attention focused on that broken-bird silhouette ahead of her. Apart from his height, Jason is not like the rest of the deGroots with their myopic Dutch features, porous skin and heavy jaws. He's more like the Harpurs. She can see that now. Dark and brooding. More like Cassie, which makes him, what? Her second cousin nth removed?

But Jason still can't see her, or not completely, so whatever the source of the new distress furrowing his brow, it can't be her. He reaches up and touches the obscenely external dendrites branching above his head. Then he tears across the field at a fearful run. Thettie scuttles after him as fast as she can on all fours, her breasts exposed above her torn nightgown. She has a question for him, but before she can ask it, his head cocks in the direction of a flock of headless answers.

Thettie stops, gasping. 'Not that one? That's not a war story. Besides I already told it.'

Jason points at her. Bingo. 'The end.'

'The beginning,' Thettie says. 'The day you were made.'

'Lalalalala,' sings Jason with his hands over his ears.

'Lizards have ears,' Thettie says. 'I bet you didn't know that.'

Jason presses his hands tighter over his ear plugs and tragus studs so he can't hear her. He starts to run but the story, spinning out of Thettie's head like a branch, hogties him and brings him to his knees on the razorous cornstalks. Thettie nearly dies again laughing.

'Your ma, Cassie . . . '

The story that begins with a stupid prank and veers off in the middle to a Motel 6 room, the blister packs of Rohypnol, Cassie crying and peeing the bed.

'Fie deGroot's telling weirdo ghost stories about hook-handed hitchers and armless nuns and exploding pus and hands under the bed and whispers in the night and blood that bursts into flame.'

Thettie turning to retch off the side onto the rug and rolling over too far and falling off onto a pile of spilt Cheese Doodles. Her vulva aflame.

'Rewind to earlier that day. Halloween pumpkins on porches. The deGroot boys driving toward me and Cassie in their F-150. Whistling out the windows. Offering us a drink. Saying why not come by the motel for a party? No harm, no foul. VISA had covered the funds from the credit card Cassie'd stolen from the Motel 6 where she worked—no big thing. They're all, like . . . ' she deepens her voice to approximate a man's ' . . . we would of done the same—finders keepers and all. They're like, it's your birthday? How old? Sweet sixteen? Damn, bitchez, let's get this party started.'

Jason howls, his externalized neural branches dragging his face in the mud. He spits black bile, like the shadowy slime swimming in the lake.

'The deGroot boys later rocking back and forward on their plastic motel chairs, swapping tricks and treats, me already drunk. The drapes drawn and the branches of a couple of twin maples scratching against the window. Cassie telling fortunes, thinking she had it all under control.'

She pauses, remembering Cassie bent over Piet deGroot's big square farmer's hand, its lifeline begrimed with dirt. When Thettie begins speaking again, it is Cassie's little-girl voice that comes out of her mouth: 'There is a dark highway, and a bend in the road you won't expect.'

Jason freezes at the sound of his mother's voice. Tears stream down his ravaged face.

Cassie's green-varnished finger nail had stopped at the point where Piet's lifeline veered off his palm. Thettie remembers the bangin' cocks of the deGroots whimpering in fear between their thighs. Some wore boxer shorts, or jeans. Thettie isn't sure how many of them were in the room at any one time. In her memory they are legion.

'Piet didn't like his fortune,' Thettie continues in her own voice. 'How's this for a bend you didn't expect?' he tells Cassie.

'Later on, after helping themselves to girl-candy, Piet's brother Fie—they'd all have been early twenties then—goes back to telling ghost stories. Piet's still pissed about his palm reading. The roofie he'd given Cassie's wearing off and she's starting to freak.'

Jason staggers up from the mud.

"Why do you care so much about those scary-ass stories?' Piet asks Fie. And Fie just looks across at his brother and says, 'Because it's all I got.' "

And what Thettie remembers is how much that seemed to cheer Piet up. How he'd looked across at the girl he'd had to drug in order to fuck, and tenderly adjusted the condom stuck to her forehead.

That's how Thettie will always see Cassie now. The moonlight slanting in through the open window on her drooling mouth and staring eyes. The branches of the twin maples babbling some scary bullshit to blow on the wind.

***

Jason swallows a sob at Thettie's sudden silence, and when she begins walking again, he takes his place quietly beside her. He stinks of that black slime that's all over his face now, dripping from his nose. And the end of the story comes back to her now. Not one of those ghost-story endings, which she listened to it while dozing on and off on the Cheese Doodles, but the real ending, which she revisits along a hidden forest path of memory that opens up before her like quicksilver impelled into the branching paths above Jason's head. How eventually the men stopping fucking and talking and said how it was late and tomorrow was another day. How eventually the motel room off the Interstate grew silent and all Thettie could hear was the sound of Cassie muttering urgently in her sleep, lit by moonlight coming in through a crack in the drapes. Thettie wanted to take the condom off Cassie's head, but she couldn't move, and eventually she must have slept, too, because the next thing she knew, a chalky dawn lurked behind the heavy drapes. Cassie lying puffy-faced on the bed with the condom still stuck to her head. Thettie brushed off the Cheese Doodles and peeled the condom off Cassie's head. Blearily opened the drapes onto a parking lot with no deGroot cars or trucks to be seen. She got to work on the room, so Cassie wouldn't lose her job, sweeping litter into garbage bags, flushing blister packs and candy wrappers and emptying gin bottles down the sink. Thettie and Cassie helped each other shower and dress. They snuck past the front desk to the parking lot and onto the highway to the gas station where they called for Frankie to come get them. Thettie sat in the back seat so Cassie could ride shotgun—Frankie had to stop frequently so they could both puke by the side of the road—and he stayed off the Interstate.

'Frankie takes us both to the place high in the woods that only us Harpurs know about, a secret pool at the source of Harpur Falls. The trees trunks have this moss on them that glows in the dark. The water in the swimming hole has these special minerals in it that burn, and glow, too. Luciferins, Frankie called them. Cleansing minerals. Frankie tells us both to wash in the falls, that even deGroot's evil seed can never stand up to the secret water's purity.'

But Thettie wasn't so sure. She rode up to the Planned Parenthood clinic at Ilium before she missed a cycle and tried to get Cassie up there, too. Cassie said she knew about all those morning-after options, and she'd get there soon enough—until it was too many mornings after and soon enough was too late. Cassie shrugged and said she would be almost seventeen, after all. A year older than her own mother when Cassie came into the world. When Frankie asked her how she was going to be a punk rocker with a kid in tow, Cassie said that lots of rock stars brought their babies on tour. 'Celebrity babies are the ultimate accessory,' she told him, as if she knew.

***

'So, the end is the beginning,' Thettie tells Jason. 'You're another dead Harpur, same as me.'

It's in the ropy musculature, telltale blue-ray eyes. Of course, Jason's teeth are on the way out, but that's just the crystal, which Thettie can smell, with its cold chemistry-set reek beneath the periodontal rot.

Jason sees her for the first time when she finally gets him to Tinker's Glen. She cannot yet materialize at will, if that's what you can call it, but she manages in a staticky way, like tuning into a dead channel on an old TV set. Jason screams and starts crawling away from her on his feet and hands like a Space Monkey. She pulls back, tries to reassure him, but he turns from her in terror and runs sobbing into the Coach USA building.

The shutters over the ticket office are still down. A vast woman in yellow shorts and a green and white blouse snoring on a bench jolts awake, glares at Thettie and takes over.

'Percha munny in deah, baby. Addie-ait terminal,' the fat woman laughs. 'Chew see a meer lately, chil'? Little gals room ober deah!'

The woman points Thettie in the direction of the restroom, and turns back to Jason, blocking him with her vast body, from Thettie's view. It's true, Thettie realizes. She should freshen up for the ride—doesn't want to see Cassie after all this time looking any worse than she has to.

Tinkers Glen feels further away than Thettie remembered—extended down the kaleidoscoping hallway of time. She swallows a bitter reflux of panic, maybe more than a little, being so far from home, but she'll adapt. She'll learn because that's what memory is for. This road, this long and winding vein that circulates being through the body of time has many blind alleys, dead ends, short cuts and through ways. The trick, she now knows, is just to keep moving.

In the restroom mirror, her hands fly to what's left of her face. One eye is squeezed shut and spinning a web of tears. The other has opened so wide that there are little hairline splits in the skin at the corners. The tongue in her once tantalizing mouth lolls like a red rag between black lips, cracked like scales. Her Victoria's Secret nightgown, the one the boys bought her for her fortieth birthday, is stiff with filth, and gapes, but not in a good way. She rages, she weeps, and she claws at her cheeks with recurved fingernails, slips and slides on her own leakages, pounding on the walls and the door. Why, she howls, could she just not die pretty?

But there is no one to tell her. Jason is already outside on the slumbering, garbage-strewn street. He leaps onto the bus and disappears inside. Thettie clutches the flap of her nightgown to her breasts and is a blur through the bus station doors. She just makes it onto the bus as the driver is closing the door, which she jams open with her dematerializing self. She peers from beneath her matted hair, down the aisle. There are no passengers on the bus except Jason. Although it is already getting light, the overhead fluorescents are blazing and the bus windows are flat black squares, like blank film, reflecting nothing.

'Uh huh,' says the driver from behind wraparound shades. 'You ain't going nowhere.'

He pulls the stick, and the bus grumbles to life. The pneumatic door opens again.

'I have to go with him, make sure he gets there.'

'He'll get there all right. That's my job. Unfinished business is yours. Now git.'

Thettie looks down at her smeared nightgown, her naked flesh beneath. She puts a hand over her landing strip. 'You see me?'

The driver chortles without mirth. 'I see an unnatural blonde, hand to God. But I smell clay, and you are rank, baby. Now gwon.'

'I don't want to stay here anymore. I don't like it here. Look at him. He gets to go.'

The driver shrugs. 'He's got a ticket to ride and you ain't. Not up to me. And I got a schedule to keep.'

Jason seems to have dozed off on a seat about halfway down the bus.

'How can you drive a bus if you're blind?'

'Blind and dead,' he says. 'Hehe.'

Instant recall scuttles like a pickpocket across the neural paths branching from Thettie's mind to the world: an IED that took out the bus driver's platoon outside of Falul, summer of '06, one quiet Monday morning. No survivors.

'We all got unfinished business. The trick is to work out what it is. You got to go back and find a purpose.'

ALETHEIA

The driver lifts his shaded eyes to the rearview. Jason sprawls on the seat touching his crown of intertwining branches, and whispering to the voices in his dreams.

'What's yours?' Thettie asks. 'To ferry the dead?'

'And the deadly, baby,' he raises his hand. 'You feel me?'

'Feel this, asshole,'

The driver waves away the floating debris of bone and blood that issues from her wound of a mouth.

'Say it, baby, don't spray it.'

'How do I find my purpose?' she whines. 'My boys were my life.'

'You're your own purpose, woman. You got to shine by your own light.'

Thettie begins to sob, lets it all flow out of her. 'Henry J. When you see Cassie, ask her why she left me alone when I needed her most? Tell her I miss her. She was the light through the window.'

Jason flinches and gibbers. Thettie sags against the door frame. The bus driver glowers and makes a ticking sound in the back of his throat. 'Act your age for once, woman, not your bra size.'

'I'm a 36B, is what I am. Same as my age.' She hiccoughs.

'36B, my eye.' Perched high on his chair, the driver grabs his white stick and jabs her in the chest, flings her backward out of the bus. The pneumatic door slams with an angry hiss that screams of rain puddles and diapers stuffed behind seats. Thettie lands on her bare ass but her dendrites have already joined with Vernon's, who calls her back to the path that winds and intersects with other roads and hungers on the stations of her want. She aches from the journey, a hurt lost to other injuries she'll yet suffer on the path. She stands in the rain watching the bus get smaller, its tail lights fading. Raindrops soak her pretty hair and burn her terrible tongue, and all the lights and wheels and noises of the world wake to rain, to light, to fading stars and the whistle of departing trains, a host of useless tangled signs.

24. BLUEBERRY CHUNKS

LEE STANDS AT the dark studio window, side-eyeing Vernon's tank and not knowing what else to do. Phone to his ear, he leans his burning forehead against the cold glass. Further down the slope, his son's rope swing jerks once or twice in the still and moonlit night. Habib, on the line, is saying something about the scale of the attack.

'Attack?' Lee says.

'Did I say attack? I mean her so-called self-inflicted wounds,' Habib clears his throat and continues. 'The scratches and cuts and so on, are mainly, or centrally, on the left side of her body.'

Lee lifts his forehead off the glass. 'I already heard you on the phone to the medical examiner.'

'Her cousin, Frankie, was a self-harmer. Broken glass, box cutters, razor blades, mirrors, the serrated cutters on kitchen wrap cartons, staples, sharpened pencils . . .'

'I saw Frankie's cuts, Sam. What's your point?'

Those careful marks in various stages of scarification—red and swollen or purple scabs or ghastly ellipses like cuneiform across his cheeks. His forearms, too, and hands, and what you could see of his feet and ankles. It starts off as a compulsion and then becomes a kind of meditation. A methodical, secretive assemblage of pain, Lee knows, like painting the lake over and over again. Each painting, each cut, carves another piece of self away. Or puts one back.

Habib says, 'So Thettie's actions are consistent with that strain, I guess you could say, of Harpur pathology. Which no one is going to question.'

'*I'm* questioning it,' Lee says. 'You're questioning it.'

'You've never thought about it?' Habib says. 'Ending it all?'

For Habib, these moments of darkness tinged with aggression have become more frequent lately—Lee doesn't know why but they remind him of his mother's Siamese cats as they aged. He tells himself that they're some kind of existential panic attack and not an attack on him. He tells himself that it doesn't make him miserable.

'You know the answer to that, Sam.'

'I know. Sorry.'

'But I still can't see her doing it. She was, too . . . too . . . '

'Angry?' Habib probes.

'Present.'

Before Lee knows it, he is weeping silently against the window. His tears streak the steamy glass.

'Family history notwithstanding,' says Habib over Lee's silent sobs. 'Her cuts are all wrong. They're not horizontal, Lee, or even diagonal as you might expect from the broken bottle or kitchen knives or what have you, that she was supposed to have done it with. Even if a left-handed person could or would want to reach the left side of their body—left buttock, left shoulder blade and so on—broken glass or blades would make gashes, or slices. These are different.'

ALETHEIA

It is a dangerous path and Lee's mind looks for another. Habib would say that the metaphor of the path is a good description not only of human thought, but into it. Humans remember by connecting one thing to another. The metaphor of the forking path, Habib said, so beloved in literature, is a pretty good way of describing how memory actually works.

Lee wipes his nose on his sleeve. Suddenly Aristotle jumps out of Lee's mnemonic path, like an ambush, toga and all. And is reflected in the tear and snot-streaked window, from which he begins *his* shtick on metaphor, pacing around in between all the piled canvases and kicking the Tonka Truck back and forth with his sandaled heel. Aristotle says that he may have been wrong about nature, which thrives on mutation and difference and not—as he claimed—on likeness. His toga falls off his shoulder and Lee gets a glimpse of blue nipples. Old Ari says he was right all along about humans making meaning by drawing similarities where there are none. A thorn in your side, for instance, is a metaphor for a small irritation that becomes a big problem until it is removed—like Jason deGroot. Human brains function by comparing unlike things and finding the room to move between them. Between a tiny thorn and the vastness of human suffering—at that old Ari pinches his thumb and forefinger together. Between a drop of blood and the treacherous depths of filial guilt—he stretches his arms out wide, hitches up his toga. Between self and other, of which we can know nothing without resorting to metaphor. *I feel your pain,* Ari says, *but only by comparing it with my own.*

But my son was my second self, Lee says, and this

is where Aristotle dissolves into the rain, holding up his hands in defeat.

Lee feels every violation inflicted on his son, every insult to his flesh as if it is his own. He can feel, unfolding in a perpetual present, his son's terror and unimaginable dread, the false hope fading. Through his son's remaining eye, Lee sees the gods' final turning away and is unable to call them back. And above all Lee knows the horror of captivity because whenever he tries to move, he feels the prick through his heart, the non-metaphorical pin that fixes him, alive and not, forever to this place.

For real, Thettie would say.

'Earth to Lee?'

The sound of the rain drilling on the metal sheeting, a truck on the highway, the faint buzz of the heating component in Vernon's tank, TV noises from Habib's living room. The phone feels hot against his ear, leaking radiation and death rays into his brain.

'Have you seen Jason?' Lee says.

'Forget Jason for a moment,' Habib pauses to sip some water. 'Focus on the cuts. They're messy, random—on her buttocks for instance—and I wouldn't call them cuts.'

'What would you call them?'

Habib's chair creaks in Lee's ear. 'I want to say gouges, in a sense. Puncture wounds. Tears.'

No. You don't want to say any of that in any sense. 'What? Like bites?'

'Did I say bites?'

Lee stares at his reflection in the mirror, his white face, swollen nose and dark eyes materialized on the rain streaked glass without him noticing. The world outside a blank, no way to tell what's in and what's out any more.

'She could have done that,' Lee murmurs. 'Get fucked up enough, start gnawing on your own self. It happens.'

'Did I say gnaw?'

The line is quiet so long that Habib may have passed out on him. Lee can hear the older man's labored breaths.

'Point being,' Habib finally says. 'Is that we never do it to ourselves. You didn't hear it from me.'

'Who would I tell?'

***

Little Ridge is a palette of wounds. Vermillion leaves suture themselves to the pavement. Bruised sycamores and oaks line Main Street like refugees from an explosion. Everywhere the stink of rot and fire. Deputy Abbes stays three cars behind him. Lee's glad he asked the brothers to meet him in a public place. He has something to tell them.

By lunch time, Maxine's Pie Kitchen on Main Street is over half-full, mainly with college administrative staff trying not to make eye contact with the stricken and unkempt Harpur men crowded into two booths against the wall. The manager glowers at the motor-bikes chained up outside like dusty horses. Waves at the Deputy and sends him out a bag of bear claws.

Lee walks toward Archy sitting at a booth hunched over a messy cup of coffee. His mouth isn't working as it should and most of the coffee has dribbled onto his beard or down the side of the cup. Across the table Grif chops into his second piece of pie, flicking cigar ash onto moraines of cream. Emilio and Dustin and some others crowd into a booth behind them. Dustin is a huge white man with horn-rimmed glasses who plays anxiously with his wedding ring, and Emilio is a lethal looking Hispanic constantly on his phone. Lee follows the waitress ferrying pie, crullers and coffee to the tables.

He waits for them to notice him.

'Sit,' it's the one-eyed girl's voice behind him. She's got her beanie pulled down over the boy-cut hair and a sweater on over a loose dress. Her parka, he sees, is on the chair beside Archy. Her good eye directs him to a space in the booth beside Grif, and she perches on the opposite seat next to Archy, who lists against her like a tree fallen against a sapling. Archy's eyelashes are greasily clumped and his ringed fingers are yellow with nicotine. Grif's unwashed reek makes Lee's eyes water.

Grif shifts in the booth, 'Why'd you bring us to this dump?'

Lee wipes his sweating hands on his jeans and orders coffee and blueberry pie. After Habib's call, he'd gone to the campground and left a message with some of the other Harpur men, but only now, surrounded by their tectonic rage and grief, does he realize what he's set in motion. A drink would level him out. The waitress brings his order, and the one-eyed girl reaches into the pocket of Archy's jacket and pulls out a small flat flask, passes it to Lee. He dumps some hooch in his coffee and the girl takes it back so quickly, he wonders if he imagined the whole thing. The welcome bite to the brew, however, tells him otherwise.

Grif sits back and jams the cigar back between his teeth. A bandage around his head from some inconsequential altercation makes him look like a Hollywood bandit, drug-store Indian. Archy raises his eyes to a buzz coming from the ceiling, and Lee hears it, too, like the whine of an insect that isn't there.

The cut across the bridge of Lee's nose from where Grif punched him is still swollen, so he has to wear his glasses above or below it. The cut is in shape of a little red eye. An eye for an eye, a punch to the nose for a canoe paddle to the ribs. A perverse kind of handshake, maybe? Better than none.

'The sheriff is on my tail,' Lee says. 'I thought a public place makes it all seem above board.'

'Over Ma?' Grif says. 'What do they care? Just another low-life OD lowering the tone of the neighborhood. Her case is closed.'

'Maybe,' Lee picks at a thread on his jeans. 'But Boyle doesn't need much of an excuse to try and get rid of both of us.'

Grif throws a mocking grin at his brother but gets no response, so he tries the girl. But she's staring in confusion at a huge vanilla milkshake. 'Wait. You're saying they want to run some *artist* out of Dodge? Why you?'

'Yeah, why you?' Archy says thickly, turns to stare at the wall like an old blind dog, following a deceptive scent.

The girl slurps her milkshake uncertainly, her good eye downcast, but the other looking who knows where. Lee feels it on him, insinuating itself from behind the patch into his mind, snaking slender and incorporeal towards some kind of understanding. A question forming.

'Boyle mishandled the investigation into my son's disappearance. His ineptitude may or may not have cost the child's life. But it cost something.'

Archy swats in slow motion at the source of the buzzing around his head. 'So?'

'I accused him of more than ineptitude. I alleged it was because of a conflict of interest. That the deGroots warned him off the kidnapper, Bud Wallace . . . '

'The guy who was in the army with Doc?'

'Yes. But Wallace had a prior connection to them through their . . . crops. I got a lawyer, contacted the press, the DA, the Mayor's office, the Feds. None of which was any match for the deGroot lawyers, or their coffers—but that didn't stop them from trying to run me out of town. And making sure no decent college or research facility in the state would ever hire me again.'

'You were a thorn in their side,' the one-eyed girl says with her mouth full of milkshake. And the buzzing abruptly stops, as if someone swatted a fly.

At a nod from Grif, Emilio reaches across the booth and passes over the Polaroid that Thettie left in Lee's studio. Both the brothers look away, as if to give Lee some privacy.

The table begins to spin in space. Everything around it has gone dark. Lee can hear the steady suck of the lake lapping on the rocks, the sounds of Thettie's sighs, the sound of the Harpurs returning drunkenly to their cabins. He can see the flickering patterns made by the candle on the walls of the trailer, and above him and Thettie, the misty skylight framing the stars.

'That's where it went to,' he finally said. 'I wondered.'

'Why did you take that picture?'

Grif concentrates on staring at the waitress's chest. Archy's eyes drill holes into his brother's from behind his veil of hair. Lee looks at the face in the Polaroid, low forehead, wheaten hair and grave mouth. Electric eyes a little surprised at herself.

'She took that herself when she came by the studio on Monday. I was detained by Boyle. We missed each other by seconds.'

'Why'd she take the picture?'

Lee pushes his glasses back onto his smashed nose and winces. 'I don't know. I wish I did. Thank you for returning it.'

The minders in the neighboring booth grumble and fidget.

'Tell us what you want to tell us,' Archy says. 'And let's get this over with.'

Lee looks around the steamy café. He lowers his voice. 'The sheriff is saying it's suicide, right? That she cut herself.'

'Maybe she did,' Grif said. 'Maybe you broke her heart, Lizard Man. Maybe you broke a date—how come you never turned up at the Way? Maybe she was expecting you, ever think of that? And what's with the disappearing lizard trick?'

'Shut up, Grif.' Archy's voice is dangerous.

A freight train roars in Lee's ears. 'What *is* with the disappearing lizard trick? The one where he goes missing on the first night I'm not in my studio for five years. You tell me.'

Emilio and Dustin are on their feet, but Grif just gapes at him. 'You saying it's been five years since you went with a woman? Seriously? No wonder Ma looked fried.'

A few mouths twitch in weak smiles, but the effect is to break the fuse. Emilio and Dustin sit back down.

'You don't really think we stole your lizard?' Archy says, blinking. 'Last time I brought a lizard home to Ma, she freaked.'

Grif cracks his knuckles.

'You don't really think I killed your mother?' Lee says. 'I was on the lake, looking for her.'

'Jeez. Why the lake?'

Lee swallows his pie and wipes the sweat off his forehead with a gloppy napkin. 'I felt, when she didn't come back, which is what I took the meaning of the Polaroid to be—I felt that someone, or something had suddenly changed on the lake. That with Vernon's disappearance on the same day as my son's, five years later to the day, that a door had been opened out there. A door I'd been waiting to open in order to go through it to find my son. But Thettie made me think again. I don't know. It's confusing. But I think I realized that she was in danger from whatever was out there, and I tried to go out there to try and maybe close the door, or maybe try and send whatever crawled through back to where it belonged. Whatever the cost. I wasn't ready to do that until I met her. To close the door.'

He looks from Archy to Grif. Blue eyes floating on feral faces.

'The lake is full of hurt and harm, Ma always said,' Archy says. 'Like every time you try and save your own self, lake's there to tell you forget that shit.'

Grif stares at his brother with a naked jealousy that makes tears needle the back of Lee's throat. 'She say that to you?'

The one-eyed girl gently pushes Archy off her

shoulder. 'This thing you're talking about. This thing in the lake. That why you brung us here? Because of Seek You?'

Grif jerks like a fish fighting a line and Archy stares at the girl like a new pet they're maybe wanting to exchange for something more manageable. 'Seek You? What's that?'

'Never mind,' Lee says quickly, feeling suddenly fearful for the childlike creature blowing milk bubbles. The place will be closing soon. He's running out of time. He struggles to get control of the meeting. 'The Sheriff, for whatever reason, prejudice or laziness . . . '

'Or a deGroot paycheck,' Emilio says from the next booth.

Lee sighs. 'Or maybe so as not to attract a media circus—for whatever reason, the Sheriff is saying that she did it to herself right?'

'She was upset over Sarey,' says Grif, tracing patterns in his ice cream with his spoon. 'Saying she was trapped just a means to an end. Which we could have told her years ago.'

The girl leans forward. 'Let him talk. It's getting dark outside.'

Lee says, 'So why I brought you here, is just to pass on some information from a, um, reliable source, who seems to think that her injuries are possibly *not* consistent with self-harm. Maybe. I thought you should know.'

Archy's leather jacket creaks. 'They found a used meth pipe on the floor. We didn't see it, but Doc said the Sheriff found it.'

'Maybe someone put it there,' The girl angles her eye patch to Lee, the golden fleck in her good eye dancing like a flame. 'And all the knives and broken glass, too.'

Lee's glasses begin to slide down his nose, but he doesn't trust himself to push them up.

'This reliable source wouldn't be that Arab guy that lives outside of town?'

And Lee doesn't ask how they know. Nor does he tell them he knows they've been tailing him.

'What does he know about wounds?' Grif asks.

'Plenty,' Lee said. 'He trained as a psychiatrist—that involves a medical degree for a start.'

'No one kills their own self,' Archy says, softly.

There is a subtle shift in the body language of Emilio and Dustin at the next booth.

'Well, Habib would agree with Archy that the very word 'self-harm,' is a contradiction in terms.'

'You'll be a contradiction in terms,' Grif spews cigar smoke. 'If you don't get the fuck on with it.'

Lee says, 'Okay, so, the coroner mentioned cuts, slashes. That kind of thing. Sheriff's report says sleeping pills and alcohol, plus drug paraphernalia.'

The brothers' eyes glitter.

'But the cuts are the problem, even if it does run in the family.'

The girl serenely burps. Another Harpur man twists around the edge of his booth to face them. 'She wasn't a cutter, and you don't know shit about the family.'

Dustin and Emilio get to their feet.

Maxine's Pie Kitchen is all but empty now, the sky low and grim behind the windows.

Lee places his hands palms-up on the table in a kind of surrender. 'In any case. Thettie's cuts indicate violence of a nature . . . '

'Of a nature?'

Sweat trickles down Lee's ribs under his shirt. Maxine comes up and puts a large pastry box down on the table.

'Condolences,' she says, wiping her hands on her black apron. 'I knew your ma, she was a fine woman, and it's terrible what happened to her, but we're closed.'

'What happened to her?' says Grif, smiling ferociously up at the waitress's breasts while reaching for the Sweet 'n' Low. 'Can we have some more coffee please?'

'We're closed,' says Maxine and puts the check in front of Lee and stalks off. Lee's heart booms like a bomb about to blow. Boom, boom.

'Violence of a nature?'

Emilio puts his bulk between Lee and the door.

'There were signs on her body of violence not necessarily—of wounds that it would be difficult or impossible for her, even *if* she was predisposed, to have actually self-inflicted. They were messy.'

'No shit.'

'And they were on the wrong side.'

Archy giggles with mounting hysteria. 'Why are you telling us all this and not Boyle?'

'My son's killer was right-handed,' Lee says, avoiding the girl's lopsided gaze. 'When evidence started to accumulate that proved inconvenient for Boyle because it implicated someone with past connections to the deGroots, they shut it down. They tried to pin it on a local farmer who was left-handed and who would be unlikely to have inflicted some of the injuries as they presented on my son. According to photographic evidence.'

Grif has frozen with a crooked branch of cigar ash clinging to its tip. Tears running down his face. 'Holy shit,' he says.

The space beside Archy is vacant, the one-eyed girl abruptly gone.

'So what you're trying to say is that,' Archy says, 'Ma didn't do it to herself.'

Lee briefly tells them how he saw Jason talking to Doc's men at the Way, and how Jason seems to have disappeared, too. 'I don't know who or what did this to her, but no. She had help.'

'End of story?'

'You tell me,' Lee says, sinking back into his chair.

The girl comes back from wherever she went. Grif tears open a sachet of Sweet 'n Low and pours it into his coffee. He brings the empty sachet under the table, does something to it.

'We found what's inside this sachet, on the floor of the trailer where Ma—where what happened to her happened. You look inside. Don't say anything at all. Don't do anything. Don't touch anything. My man Emilio is here to help you do what you're told. Keep the Arab out of it. Don't tell him what you see, or Emilio might be able to show him a few wounds he hasn't heard of.'

Emilio stands over Lee. Like the others, he reeks of BO. He folds his arms over his chest. Lee does what he's told. He looks in the emptied pink sachet of Sweet 'n Low. He doesn't empty what he sees in there onto the table. He doesn't take it out. He looks at the recurved reptilian tooth bristling with tiny crystals of cyclamate saccharine, and then he passes it back.

Archy sits back, still giggling helplessly. Snot

speckles his moustache. Grif drops his cigar butt into his mug. It sinks and then surfaces, a bobbing hissing turd on the surface of the falsely sweetened brew. That's when Lee throws up on Emilio's boots, on Maxine's reproduction checkered drug store tiles and over the base of the old-style booth, chunks of blueberry pie all over the shiny new chrome.

25. BALLS

THETTIE'S CONCENTRIC CIRCLES paced around Lee's studio get smaller and smaller, but never small enough to get her to the heart. Her bare feet crush the tiny markers of the pet cemetery. She trips on a home-made cross and it catches in the hem of her nightgown. Bones of a lab rat rattle in a shoe box. She cradles the skeleton in her mud-streaked hands, strokes the strange boney studs growing on its skull, rocks it back and forth in her arms. 'Here kitty,' she weeps. 'Here kitty-kitty.'

She wants to get to the studio. She needs to get back to that warm place, huddled on the hill in the dark, the reflections of the lake on its windows. Something or someone is stopping her. But she can see the island now, of course, from the headland. It's bathed in moonlight, so close she can almost touch it. She reaches out to Frankie, her shadow magnified across the lake.

'Frankie, it's me. Thettie. Come home.'

***

'All my life, I've felt like everything I am is just what other people have put in me or taken out. I can't see myself without looking through them.'

'I see you,' Lee said. They are still in the Winnebago, the night that keeps happening.

'What do you see? There I go again, see?'

Thettie laughed. That such a fine man could fill her with an alien joy. So much waiting in his eyes.

'So, it doesn't matter what I see,' he said. 'What do you see? In yourself?'

He was getting hard again, which also made her laugh. He hadn't had a proper lay in a coons age. He made her feel nineteen again and in a good way—it had been so long since sex had been funny-haha and not funny-strange. He laughed back. The trailer was chilly, but the bed was warm. The scratched skylight blurred and distorted the stars—but she could see Libra on the rise. Her and this fine man bubbled in the grimy dome of night and forever coupled in its floating fragile truths.

'Tell me,' he said a little thickly. 'What's alone inside you?'

'Nothing,' she said. 'Everything.'

'Before you had Archy and Grif?' he said, passing her the beer, and watching her face. 'Before you got all messed up in this?'

'You mean Doc?'

'Yes. And before that too. Before your sons.'

'I don't know.' She got that he was asking her, but also asking himself. 'I don't know if I want to remember that person. I was a piece of work, I guess. Ran wild. Me and my cousin Cassie used to give hand jobs up at the Motel 6 at the highway, where she worked. Salesmen, farm boys, professors from the college. Then we had a scare, some jerks spiked our drinks at a party in one of the rooms, and I stopped. Me and Cassie didn't see so much of each other after that. And then she went to LA. For a while I went even wilder, then I went straight more or less.'

Lee said. 'Did you miss her?'

'I couldn't forgive her for leaving me. I tried to punish her by not taking care of her child, Henry Jason, like I promised I would. My mother used to say Cassie and me were no good for each other. Blind leading the blind, she said.'

'The blind make great leaders. Harriet Tubman, Teddy Roosevelt.'

She looked at him without smiling. 'That's what Frankie said. You remind me of him sometimes.'

'What do you think you'll do when you see him again?'

The lump in the back of Thettie's throat made it hard to answer right away. 'I'll tell him I've come home. If I can. If he'll have me.'

'Do you think he's dead?' Lee shifted on the pillows, the flickering candle-light playing across his chest.

'I don't know. Somehow he sent for me. Somehow. Through Bryce, maybe, or maybe I just knew it was time. He always said a person had to face their demons.'

'What do you think are his demons?' Lee was a good listener and the sweetest fuck anyone's thrown at her forever, but Thettie squirmed a little, and didn't at first know how to put it into words, or even if she should try. What place was it of hers, or anyone's, to measure a person's life by what they spend it running from? She reached under the sheets for Lee's balls. Maybe that'd keep him quiet while she tried to find the right words to say that whatever Frankie's demons were, he stirred them up by going to the island in the first place. Maybe it wasn't their time. Demons like to call the shots.

'That time he went over there, where he shouldn't? Had a look around, got back in the boat and rowed home? He only thought he had got away. It's like Afghanistan. Some places, they don't want you there in the first place, and if you come anyway, they punish you by never letting you leave. For the whatever of thinking you can come and go as you please.'

'Hubris,' Lee said. 'False pride. Oh.'

She gave his jewels another squeeze for luck, and so he'd keep his eyes closed, wouldn't see her face wet with tears. 'I visited Frankie in jail before we left. I never told Doc. I never told anyone. I snuck off at night, paid the guard in the usual way. Got ten minutes with him outside regular visiting hours. I told him I had to go but I'd be back. He said it was okay. He understood. He said he found out the hard way, and I said, what, Frankie? What did you find out? You know what he said to me? 'We think we make our monsters, Thet,' he said. 'But it's them who make us.''

She swiped at her tears with her free hand. Lee then told her that it was the same false pride that made him think he could leave New Mexico and still come back one day, drag his family with him against everything he knew was right. Just because he was afraid to fail as a husband and father. Just because he couldn't stand the thought of Habib—the father he never had—leaving him behind.

'But that's different,' she said. 'I would have gone to jail if I'd stayed.'

'You ended up in a different kind of jail where you went.'

***

She gets the thing about jails now. Circling around and

around the studio, trampling the pet graves and trying to fix her face in a reflected puddle—lick the blood off her wounds. So lonely, so dark in the woods. She peeks in on Lee's son in the little cubby house, all but camouflaged beneath a soft carpet of fallen leaves.

The heart is a mouth. She wants to show Lee she gets that now, to lay it all at his feet. But also to tell him something else. Running rings around him without getting closer, because the cage is locked and she can't find the key.

'Wake-up,' she says to the sleeping child. 'I need to get in. I need to tell him. That it's okay to forget. It's okay. Plenty of time to remember when you're dead.'

26. UMBER

T-*TAP*. *T-TAP*.

Lee draws his best sable brush across the umber. If he stands with his back to the door, it's easier to ignore the beat of soft knuckles. The chewed-up doll's arm, that he'd found at Jason's farm, lies on the work table.

Tap-tap. T-tap.

He can't really get his head around the doll's arm. It's like the tooth. Not so much a metaphor as a metonym. Not a figure of resemblance, but rather a figure of association. A part of something that stands for the whole. Lee shakes his head, not wanting Aristotle to turn up again. Grif could have found that tooth anywhere. At the studio, maybe when they ransacked it. Granted it was a Gila's (Lee would have recognized it anywhere), sharply recurved with longitudinal grooves for applying venom. But there was even less reason now for Lee to believe what Grif said—that he found it in her room—because of what Habib said about Thettie's wounds.

No kind of Gila Monster on earth could have inflicted that kind of damage.

'Go away!' he yells at the tapping on the door. 'Go away!'

On the easel is the new painting of Thettie, her back turned to him in denial. Lee rummages among the sketches and Polaroids of the lake on the table for a charcoal sketch of Vernon he made last year. A miniature. He finds it beneath a painting of an icy inlet in a willow grove, and rests it on the easel in front of Thettie. Gilas have a sausage-like tail that stores fat and water like a camel's hump. Their lumbering yet surprisingly athletic wrestler's body is well adapted to trudge long distances for food and water. As a grad student at UNM, Lee tracked their circuitous yet oddly south-bound routes via radio telemetry. The Gila's blunt skull is unchanged over millions of years. Its black snout and low center of gravity adapted, like the bulldog's, to a prolonged bite into soft underbellies. Lee stands back from his charcoal drawing. It captures the basketball-like texture but not the color of Vernon's beautifully banded body. In life, the color is the dusty orange-pink of the Sonoran sunset. But even with the charcoal he's managed to convey the disproportionate size of the claws, and strong segmented fingers designed for climbing and fighting his own kind—dueling with, but not killing males over mates.

Tap-Tap. Lee can't tell if the knocking is getting weaker or stronger. Or what it means.

Lee's drawing details Vernon's mottled dorsal armor or Heloderma—*helos* from the Greek word for nail stud, and *derma* for skin. Vernon's wide extendible throat is open in the drawing to show how he hisses in the advent of a predator—especially one larger than him.

The deep blue tongue of the Gila Monster, or

Heloderma Suspectum, is forked for drinking and for ferrying food into the throat. It is ideally adapted for scooping the yoke from eggs, for instance. But the most important function of a forked tongue in any lizard, is for receiving information about the world—capturing odor particles—which it then transmits to two little holes in the roof of the mouth. From these the information goes to the Jacobson organ, where the chemical olfactory compounds bind to receptor molecules, sending important messages to the lizard brain.

It was his wife who saw in Lee's scientific drawings something beyond the scientific. She suggested art classes back in Albuquerque but it wasn't until they moved to Little Ridge, and it wasn't until the lab closed down that Lee took her seriously. Too late, in other words.

The tapping at the door seems to have stopped. Lee takes a slug of lukewarm coffee laced with whisky. He smudges a shadow over Vernon's throat. During the course of his research, he'd drawn the Heloderma hundreds of times—his son would say gazillions—inside and out. He has drawn them whole, but also in pieces. Split open on the dissection table, its organs sorted in pans—osteodermia chain, venom globes. Ovum if female or, in males, the twin retractable penises. He has removed and observed and described their individual venom ducts, which are basically lobes on repurposed saliva glands in the lower jaw. In the Heloderma Suspectum, venom ducts deliver venom uphill along the grooves of the teeth for protection against an attacker yet not, in most cases, for disabling prey.

Which was Vernon—prey or predator, or something else again?

J.S. BREUKELAAR

Tap. T-tap.

Lee can't remember how many verifiable Gila Monster bites there have been in the last sixty years. He opens his laptop and Googles 'Gila Monster attacks.' A hundred or so, mostly bites on the finger or hand, delivered by a pet usually, or a wild Gila avoiding capture. Other bites occur in demonstrations—lectures at zoos or in classrooms. The longer the duration of the bite, the more venom enters the body of the prey. Like the bull dog—whose jaw is purpose-built for causing the maximum amount of damage, when, for example, they were unequally pitted against chained bears back in Elizabethan times—once the Gila gets a grip, it holds on, and can chew, steadily envenoming, for fifteen minutes or more, the grinding of the lower jaws pumping the poison upward via capillary action.

In nature, with Gila bites, there is a minimum of blood. And rarely, in nature, gouges, rending, or dismemberments.

What possessed him?

Tap-tap. Tap-tap.

Because there's another thing. Gila Monsters rarely leave their teeth behind. Victims are advised to light a flame under the attacking Gila's jaw or immersing the lizard in water while attached. Victims are advised against the almost impossible task of prying the lizard off for the very reason that leaving a tooth left behind in the wound can cause infection, septicemia, and subdural hematomas—which is when the poison travels to and infects the brain as with Frankie's shrapnel. In the rare occurrence of bites, it is essential to make sure there are no the teeth left behind.

Lee tried to close the door that night out on the

lake, but who prized it open, and what crawled through?

Tap. Tap.

The pain of the bite is excruciating. Like hot nails driven into the flesh, is the way one victim described it. But the pain isn't what kills. The two most dangerous effects of the Gila Monster bite are swelling, including that of the throat, and a critical drop in blood pressure. The blood pressure dip is made worse when, as is the case in the majority of reported Gila bites, intoxication is involved.

He freezes with the chipped mug half way to his mouth. How drunk was she? He wipes the whisky off his sleeve and shakily resumes painting.

The last reported fatality occurred in a pool hall in Arizona in 1930 when a man called Reap walked into the bar where the patrons and the barman, were standing around gawking at a captured lizard. To get the barman's attention and get himself served the whisky for which he thirsted, Reap lowered himself to a wobbly squat, and started tapping the Gila Monster on the nose.

Tap-tap. Tap-tap.

Reap died on the floor of that Arizona pool hall, up to his elbow in lizard spit.

Rain has turned the MISSING fliers around the Village into pulp. Lee will have to make more. He pencils the word 'MISSING' onto a Post-It so he doesn't forget.

Research into fear has shown that it is the most powerful emotion of all. Fear of pain or death is stronger than desire for life. Male Gila Monsters, for instance are more induced to copulate with females who come into their own turf—even if they come across a willing female on foreign turf, they will waste so much time on marking their new environment against the fear of intruders that they might forget about sex. 'When push comes to shove, *Thanatos*,' Habib said, 'wins over *Eros* every time.'

Thettie's face, accustomed for the most part to meeting the world on its own terms, had simply drained of color when Lee showed her the picture on his phone of Vernon. Strobed by candle-light in the little trailer, she turned as white as the sheets that fell from her breasts. Lee had quickly put his phone away, sorry for showing her the picture, for making her see what could not be unseen.

***

Lee gets up and walks to the window of the studio and peers out into the rain and across to the middle of the lake, to where it lashes the uncertain outlines of the island. On the night he went out to meet his monster, the island loomed larger than life, larger than physically possible and closer than it could be, just as the shore looked much further away than it was.

The soft taps on the door persist, as coded as the beat of a heart.

27. MEMENTOMORIUM

LEE WASN'T A talker, so sometimes Thettie forgot to listen, forgot to hang onto the things he *did* say to keep them for later. Lucky for her some of these things remembered their own selves.

'Genes,' Lee said.

It was during a break in lovemaking and when she asked about the Helotide, which was named, he said, after the Gila Monster AKA Heloderma Suspectum. 'So, genes are important in reproduction, and also in replication—two separate things. In reproduction, like hungers for difference. It wants to create others. In replication, like thirsts for like. It only wants to recreate itself.'

He was lying flat and partly diagonal across the little bed at one end of the trailer. His speech was soft, and his chest moving up and down with his breath. That's what she liked best about him—how he took his time.

'Like memories,' Thettie said, reaching carelessly for the lighter and the crushed pack beside the bed.

'Exactly. Yes. Like memories,' Lee said, taking his arm away from his eyes and staring up at the Milky Way through the sky light. 'Except what the Helotide does, what we saw when we realized that we'd discovered a new neural pathway . . .'

'In the brain. Those branchy things.'

'Right. In those branchy things, the peptides in Gila Monster venom *do* activate the genes responsible for replicating short-term memories, but they change the gene function specifically to make something different—not just long-term memories but long-term *learning*. Not instant recall, but total, cumulative, recollection.'

Total because it is always present.

Total because it is bigger than the sum of its parts.

'Total because it sees the forest *and* the trees,' she'd said.

And Lee had laughed and looked at her with her unlit cigarette held between her lips and pulled himself up so he could kiss one of her eyes and then the other. 'So many metaphors, so little time,' he'd laughed, and fell back down on the sheets like he was finally free.

***

Thettie's recall is total meat blanket. Song bottle. Always present, her memory now is a dump tree, extending and forking, each blindingly parti-colored leaf on every branch experienced in full. Each flash of leaf-light distinct from the next, even as it unfurls, or falls, or is blown on the wind, or ravaged by mold or pest, or webbed in silk, or rain, tongued by doe, or encased in ice—leaf-light different not only in itself, but also between every instance of it either in her thinking or her fear or her self-consuming want.

The sensation from the stone in her left Converse high-top at twelve years old wandering through the empty summer campus after raiding the vending machine easily contrasted to the stick in her right-foot pre-loved Ked at nine years old following Frankie home from Harpur Falls in resentful silence after he refused to explain, even in theory, what a wet dream was.

Bigger than the sum of his broken parts. Grif, in the sixth grade, while they were still at Little Ridge, had saved up for some pumpkin seeds in order to grow pumpkins to sell for Halloween. But the sloping dirt patch behind the float home in Triangle Gully was too small. After Grif sowed the seeds, the back yard became a pumpkin patch from hell. It grew into a pumpkin forest, a tangled brood of blighted fruit, rotten from within, the pale furry flesh ulcerated and leaking black sticky seeds down the slope to pile and ferment at the base of the house. The buzz of flies droned from the rotting fruit and vicious little midges attacked her every time she went outside. Archy would not go near it. Defeated, as she often was in those days, Thettie lay in bed at noon, bleary from one too many Ambien, listening to the sodden whimper of the rot, the whine of the flies. Finally, Grif went back out with his hoe and hacked at the writhing stalks and seeping meat until he was spattered head to heel with pulp and there was nothing left to feed even the fish.

Thettie lies forever in the moment of that endless noon, a moment protracted over hours yet shrunk to the blink of an eye, the *huck-huck* of Grif's hoe drifting in and Archy sobbing from the bedroom. She'd wondered, lying in bed at noon, if she had anything left in her to die. Until Aunt Sarey arrived and in the doorway with a bunch of cornflowers—Thettie recalls seventeen florets on each flower. Sarey carried a fish pie under a yellow dish cloth, and a couple of the other girls milled behind her, looking all businesslike, told her it was time to

J.S. BREUKELAAR

W-w-wake up. Wake up.

***

The wake! Because of circling around Lee's studio, trying, and failing to get in, she is late for her own wake. There will be no funeral. Harpurs don't do the whole funeral thing, a superstitious aversion which Doc either forgets about or never knew. As a show of what he calls good faith—and that makes Thettie laugh until she almost dies all over again—Doc has forked out for her meat blanket to be kept on ice at the morgue. Having lost his means to an end, he thinks he can bribe Archy and Grif with a proper burial for their ma if they help him get to the island, to Frankie. Archy and Grif make like they'll think about it. They pretend to be grateful. Doc would know they were faking it if he was really one of them. Which he isn't. Harpurs have nothing to be grateful for, nor anyone to be grateful, too. Never did.

What did Lee call Doc's blind spot? Hoob something. False pride.

Thettie leaves off circling Lee's studio and heads to the Way Out tavern for her own wake. The closer she gets to the trailer in which she died, the stronger she feels its pull, like a bear escaped its chain and drawn inexplicably back to captivity. In previous times the wake would have been a lost and drunken afternoon in someone's living room in Triangle Gully but there are no relations left except for S-S-Sarey, gone to ground. A few of the girls bring pies and casseroles to the back room which Avery has set up for them. Avery must have had Harpur blood in him at some time, because whatever the Harpurs want is okay by him.

Her girls have worked so hard to look correct. Liz

296

in her bootylicious pants, the white ones she wore to that job interview on the way up through Bucksport. Shellie in a black straw hat. They covered the pool table with boards and a checked cloth and laid out sandwiches and cakes. Liz brings her famous cranberry and white chocolate brownies and Joanie her rice salad. Amazing what you can do on a camp stove, a barbecue grill, or a trailer microwave. Shellie makes chicken and pecan sandwiches, and Randall's wife Rianne mixes two different punches. The twins catch some flounder and Granny V. sets to frying it on a barbecue grill set up beneath the sycamore tree. The one-eyed girl, Bryce, is not here of course, just Thettie's real girls or what's left of them—puffy eyed and sniffling. The men will come later, but this is girl time.

Thettie sashays around the tables. She loves her girl-time, with no men to tell them what to do or be. She drifts among them maimed and stinking, and they raise their noses as she passes and they speak of times that make them laugh or cry. Grif's monster pumpkin patch, Shellie's miscarriage, Brianne's second wedding, the birth of the twins. They are transported to Aunt Sarey's Wednesday bottling nights back at the Harpur compound. Preparing salves and serums for sale at fairs and markets, the taste of Sarey's apple wine on their tongues. The memories are too much for Liz. She falls stricken and her knees buckle, and she gets her second period for the month all over her white pants. Rianne looks as beautiful as ever in black lace, but she has put her dress on backwards, and her nipples poke out above the scooped back. The teenage twins are asthmatic, sucking on their puffers, purple blotches on their cheeks. Thettie has babysat them countless times, took them berry picking and watched *New Girl* with them and kept it a secret from their dad. She bleeds for them, her tears flow for them all.

'It's me! Thettie!' she cries out, waving her hand and swirling her bloody nightgown. 'I'm not there!'

She whirls up to the table and dips the ladle in first one punchbowl—lemon-yellow for remembrance—and then the other, berry-blue for forgetting. Each time, she lifts the ladle to her lips and drinks, and each time, a spider-web of blood unspools back into the ladle, blossoms back into the punch, and changes it. A chain of proteins and amino acids, in one bowl blood and in the other venom, in one a potion, in the other poison. One to remember and one to forget.

The girls say that her sons will refuse to come, furious at her for killing herself, and Thettie wants to applaud the pretense. She is truly proud of them for swallowing their hoob-whatsit, their false pride. She can imagine how hard it is for them not to yell at everyone how their ma didn't kill herself, how she's not there! It must be hard for Archy the heart and Grif the soul, not to shout out from the tree-tops: *Our ma is no cutter! She did not die in that way.*

She may have thought it. She may even have wanted to. To throw away the damn key that she'd been to men's doors all of her sorry life. But she didn't. She lacked the certainty, saw only the forking path, could not make up her mind to stay or go. Archy and Grif must know in their hearts, that what she did was she looked at the key. She saw the door. And then she saw another.

The tooth.

'A cunning stunt,' she smiles. But it hurt. It hurt to pull that tooth out. To yank it right out of her own mouth from where the monster had bitten her, and left it on the floor for her sons to find.

The truth.

But that's not what Doc is saying. Not what the girls are saying, a little enviously. Not a stunner among them who hasn't thought it, at least, wondered what it would be like, the letting go of want. Just a cut, pill, or shot away. To watch that door open up in yourself, your life pooled in cupped and chaliced hands.

'You should have seen her,' the girls whisper in awe. 'You wouldn't wish that on anyone, seeing your own mama naked and befouled like that, and by her own hands.'

It still hurts where she pulled out the monster tooth. And even though it's gone, she can still feel it biting her from the inside. The grooved and venomous tooth of time.

Doc, makes what he calls 'An Appearance,' like Donald Trump. He and his tools pull up in that shitty red Ford Lyle boosted from Ilium. Homer oozing out, splay-thighed, from behind the wheel and Lyle all buck-shot in his heiney—his failing heart aflame. Those tools, Thettie allows herself a hollow laugh. Ears cock in the direction of what sounds to them like a chained animal. More fool Doc for thinking they give him added strength or special powers—like one of those monsters in a video game.

Sarey would say, 'S-s-some lesser monsters make humans their familiars, their guides or guardians, what have you, th-through the earthly r-r-realm, not because they should but because they can. Because it's easy.' Sarey always said how Doc's all for the easy road. Quickest way from point A to point B.

You knew, Sarey. You always knew.

Homer's gimlet eyes undress the Harpur girls. Lyle's mouth is a grim slot. Together, they are a force field of hurt and harm behind which Doc struts like an evil Oz behind a sick curtain of fear. Thettie jumps up on the punch table, scoops blue and yellow punch into her mouth by the handful, remembering with the one hand, forgetting with the other.

Granny V. in her wheelchair tut-tuts at the spilled punch and rolls away for a dish cloth. Thettie slinks shamefully off the table to crawl under it. Doc is flanked by his minders. His one remaining nipple is erect beneath his shirt at the sight of the Harpur world he has claimed to rule. Oh, at first Thettie's death was a terrible inconvenience but they don't call him the Cleaner for nothing, and Doc is nothing if not adaptive.

Thettie crouches beneath the table and puts her clawed hands to her head, Doc's memories flitting like fire-flies along the self-organizing path of the forest. Paddy the Hook, for instance. How Patrick Horkowitz told Doc he was the best Cleaner in the business. 'I've never seen anything like it,' Paddy said. 'Why you can clean the bark off the trees.'

Paddy, a horror fan, would say that Doc was like a vampire. Until Paddy removed Doc's fangs.

'You'll adapt,' Paddy had said. 'Smart lad like you. Blades and finger claws and such.'

Homer and Lyle are Doc's fake fangs and finger blades—but fake doesn't mean harmless, and Thettie begins to fear for her sons. She clenches her fists and her own claws pierce her flesh, for real. Thettie calms herself by unleashing a fart as silent as it is deadly.

At the smell, Homer lifts his nose to the air and adjusts the crotch of his jeans, his mind going to a part of his anatomy he can only see in the mirror these days. Lyle licks his lips, and recalls a dead teacher's high hard titties. And there is Doc momentarily unconcealed in his monstrous lack before they shield him once more behind the hunger in their eyes.

Her eyes fill with tears of gratitude to the blind bus driver for not letting her leave. He was right. She has unfinished business here and she needs to find her purpose, or spend eternity licking blood from her hands. She rocks back and forth beneath the table and sniffs her fingers, allowing herself to mourn her good hands and nice feet. Allowing tears to flow over a once-lovely face that must learn to meet this world, as it had the last, on its own terms.

28. SEA HORSE

SCIENTIFIC RESEARCH OPERATES on the questionable assumption that aversion training has more effect on memory than positive reinforcement. The received wisdom, if you can call it that, is that test animals learn through punishment—like a shock to the bottom of the foot—faster, and remember it for longer, than a reward—like a chocolate chip. It wasn't just the struggle between *Eros* and *Thanatos*, Habib liked to tell his students, but more that the distinction between these categories—fear and desire—is not as clear as one would think.

'Aristotle for example,' Habib was not, in his lectures, one for sticking to the script, 'Aristotle categorized the real world in terms of similarity and difference. Fear creates fear. Desire feeds desire. Aristotle figured anything that lies between—a composite of fear and desire—was dangerous, if not impossible. And quite frankly monstrous.'

Lee brings paint-smeared fingers to his nose. He can smell Thettie. He can taste her. Vernon's tank looms empty, a plastic desert. He pulls out his phone and stares at it, willing someone to tell him how he can get past the crime scene tape at the campground to search for Vernon. He takes a step back, hitting his heel on the Tonka truck and sending it crashing into the wall where it flips on its side, its wheels spinning.

One of Habib's students had raised her hand. 'What does reproduction—the desire of like for unlike—have to do with memory?'

Never one for directly answering the question, Habib had said, 'We desire difference because our future depends upon it.'

The tapping on the door has become frantic. A non-stopping tap-tap-t-tapping, the same rhythm with no respite. Thunder growls from the west. It is a Sunday midway through October and it is almost four o'clock. Too early for Netflix. In the watercolor painting of Thettie, Lee has placed her on the headland with her back to him. She is naked. The island is in the distance, and if you look closely there is a figure there, but Lee has rendered that uncertain, its outlines vague. He has a better understanding of the geography of the island now that he has seen it through the door opened up by the lake monster. Congregated silhouettes of ruin. Crumbled walls and old stone stairs chiseled by cold moonlight. It was as if the surface of the water parted like a curtain, and there it was.

In his confessions, Bud Wallace, who is neither a Harpur or a deGroot but something else entirely, spoke of how he'd tried to silence Lee's boy. Fed him roofies—Rhino, or flunitrazepan, a benzoate derivate— mashed in ice-cream, *shhhh*. The eyes of his son stared out at Lee from the pictures they found in Bud's basement, one eye blackened and swollen and the other open forever.

The brush falls from Lee's hands. He sniffs his pits.

It is late in the day but he decides to let her in after all, because there is still too much left of Sunday.

Enough to drown in.

She stands poised at the threshold with her knuckles red-raw and ready to strike, tap-tap.

'Wake-up,' she says.

When he figures out that she wants him to go to Thettie's wake, he tells her, 'I don't do those. I didn't even go to my wife's funeral. *Nada, nyet*, no.'

But he lets her in anyway, because she looks like she's been waiting for a long time. Her knuckles are red from pounding on the door. Her eyelashes on her one eye are gunked with tears and her boy-hair sticks out in greasy tufts around her eye-patch. First thing she does is go over to one of the steamed-up windows and, with her finger, slowly mark some crude scrawl in the condensation. It takes an effort and when she is done she puts her good eye up against the marks to look through.

The wood burner has been pumping all afternoon but she shivers in her puffy parka, refuses at first to take it off. He makes her a cup of cocoa and after a few sips, she stops shivering. In one smooth reckless motion she pulls off the parka and lets it drop to the floor. She is wearing a too-small pink T-shirt and her usual camouflage pants. Lee's heart skids at the sight of a crescent-shaped scar on her left collarbone.

She cradles her cocoa and angles her eye to peer into Vernon's tank. 'So you think he was stole?'

'Maybe.'

She leans over the edge of the tank to touch the dwarf Mesquite. The T-shirt rides up on her back and Lee bites off a moan. There are stale bruises on her narrow hips.

'You used him in your experiments? Vernon?'

'Not him. His venom. It contains these peptides. We extracted them, copied them, gave them a name. Administered it to rats and mice and they remembered more. Learned faster.'

'Vernon's venom makes you learn faster?' Her tongue flicks at the frothy surface of the cocoa. She picks up the gnawed doll's arm and puts it down again.

Lee turns to the easel, and regards Thettie's too-yellow flesh tones. 'Helotide. The peptides are in all Gila Monsters, not just Vernon's.'

'But his were special?'

Lee runs a tongue over mossy teeth. 'Maybe. We made some modifications to his DNA, fed him dietary supplements, honed his natural skills and instincts in an enriched environment using programmed stimuli. So, yeah. Maybe his venom was special.'

'How does it work?' She drifts to the shelf, picks up the snow dome of Monument Valley, makes a sandstorm.

'So, cells in a part of the brain called the hippocampus,' he points to the back of his head, 'which is basically a forest of nerve connections called dendrites—when messenger proteins move along this forest, they create a path . . .'

'How do you know?'

'The dendrites light up—in fMRIs . . .'

'What's the message? In the proteins.'

He looks at her to see if she's bored, or making fun of him, and he can't make up his mind, so he decides to continue anyway. 'The proteins tell the brain to remember.'

'What's their name?'

'So these messenger proteins are called cAMPs, but they bind to gene activation proteins called CREBs.'

'Crebs? With a 'c' or a 'k'?' Her parka, slung over the chair, slides to the floor, and lies there, sighing and rustling like an animal.

'A 'c'. CREB stands for 'cAMP Response Element Binding Protein."

She moves around the studio with a kind of dogged purpose, stopping to pick up a book, or a cattail from a bunch he kept in a paint can, like she's looking for something. Lee's discomfort mounts. He moistens his lips. He doesn't want her to stay, but he doesn't want her to go, either.

'What does the Helo thing do to the CREB?'

'The Helotide changes the messengers, and by doing so it changes the message. So it basically changes the binding proteins, cAMPs, making them more powerful.

'Power to do what?'

His brush hovers above Thettie on the painted headland. 'They remember more because they learn more efficiently. Like if you do an exercise in the right way, you get stronger. Kind of. The Helotide helps the CREB help the binding proteins to activate genes that in turn produce new proteins, proteins that cause nerve cells to learn in different ways. Hey, be careful of that camera. My wife bought it for me in Japan.'

She aims the camera at him and presses the shutter. Her pink sleeves slide up on rope burns on both wrists. 'What different ways do they learn in?'

She waits and then passes the picture across to Lee. In the Polaroid, he's lurching toward her with one hand reaching out, as if to catch his own fall. A blurred figure moves across the painting behind him. Lee stares at it, wondering if it's an after-image, and knowing that it is not. He carefully puts the Polaroid down.

'So,' his voice falters. 'So, basically the Helotide causes some of these cells to carve new neural paths that weren't previously thought to be related to making memories. Are you looking for something? Wait, I'll get a rag for that cocoa. No it's okay. I was going to trash that sketch anyway.'

'Paths? How?' She finds the Tonka Truck and squats down before it, her pale face rapt.

Lee remembers the Forest Path metaphor Habib gave him long ago to try and convince Lee to change his PhD from biology to neuroscience. He puts the brush down and goes to sit cross-legged on the floor next to the girl, passing the Tonka Truck between them, forward and reverse, forward and reverse. Outside the studio, the wind rises.

'Say you live in the woods. Every day you take the same paths from your cabin to the stream or whatever. Back and forth. You never stray from the path.' Lee walks his fingers along the floor beside the reversing yellow truck. 'The path has everything on it you need. Water at one end, shelter at the other, food along the way. Except one day, as you walk down your normal path, maybe coming back to the cabin, you catch sight of another hut, some other cabin further in the woods. So, you decide to check it out.'

'Is there a path to it?' Her good eye is skeptical.

'No,' Lee says. 'There's no path to the hut. You have to make one.'

She gets up on all fours and pushes the Tonka

Truck along the floor around the small coffee table beside the day-bed.

'Yes. It's hard to carve out new paths. But you don't have to. You can just stay on the good old path that you know. But the problem with doing that is you're not going anywhere. You're just staying in place.'

'I don't want to go anywhere.'

'I know,' Lee says gently. 'But sometimes you have to.'

She abruptly gets up and goes to the painting, peers at the island behind too-yellow Thettie.

'I mean what if the water dries up? Or what if, one day, you're looking for food on your usual path, and the berries are all eaten by birds, or what if you get lonely? Or scared,' Lee says. 'That other way could come in handy.'

'But what if there are bad things there?' She jumps back from the painting and bangs against the table, spilling water jars and upending her cocoa onto Polaroids and sketches of the lake. 'Things you don't want to remember?'

Lee's vision goes dark. He pushes himself to his feet, turns toward the easel. The air in the studio is electric. There is a figure on the island that he didn't paint. It is blurred and indistinct like the blurred figure in the Polaroid, as if it moved from one medium to the other. He points to it with a shaking hand, but the girl isn't looking.

'You have a choice,' he finally manages to say. 'You don't go back to the scary place. You try to forget about it, pretend it isn't there.'

'But it is there,' she says. 'It's hard to forget.'

He mops up the water and the cocoa, keeping an

eye on the figure in the painting. 'Yes, it is there. And sometimes the memory hurts.'

Maybe he should try and 'science it up,' as his wife used to say when his sketches got too lyrical, or too fantastical—Joshua trees sprouting legs, or Gila Monsters looking like dragons, or their son's smile frozen in time.

'The point is that if it's good—if it's beneficial somehow for you to go back to that scary, hurtful place that's off the path, you do. The second time the trail seems less difficult, the third time even less so, until it becomes a well-worn path that you don't really have to look for any more, or think about. The more you go back and forth along the new path, the more familiar it becomes. And less scary. It's the same with the messages from your brain.'

She looks confused. 'What about the first path?'

'It's still there if you need it. Sometimes you don't need it for a while, and it goes dark, gets a little overgrown maybe. But it's always there when you need it. Just a matter of lighting it up again.'

'Like, with electricity?'

'Yes. With actual electrical impulses called synapses.'

'The venom does that?' She's back by the window now—he didn't see her move—peering through the writing in the steam. 'Lights up the path?'

'In animals the venom does that, yes. We don't know exactly what it does in humans.'

'I need to pee.'

He shows her where the bathroom is, tries not to listen.

He regards the painting of Thettie. It is perfect now

with the blurred lonely figure on the island in the background. He turns on the faucet to clean his brushes. He hears her from behind the closed door saying, 'CQ. CQ.'

When he turns around, she looks so small in the open bathroom door, like someone in one of those surreal German films he and his wife went to in Albuquerque.

'What did you say?' he said.

'CQ. It's Norse Code.'

'Morse Code,' Lee whispers over the running water.

'The lights on the path,' she says. 'The dendrites to help you find what you're looking for. What you're seeking. CQ. CQ.'

Her good eye turns muddy.

'How did you learn Morse code?' Lee says carefully.

She is suddenly beside him, pulling the brushes out of the sink and stacking them in the drying rack. Their arms touch and the tiny bones of her wrist rub against his sleeve, her slender fingers brush against his as they tease the paint out of the sable. He keeps his head down so she can't see the blood from his bitten cheeks running into the sink and swirling down the drain with all the self-annihilating colors. She swivels around to look into his face, her head twisted so far to the left that it's as if it's on backwards.

'Why do you have a girl's name?' she says.

'My mother wanted a girl,' he spits blood into a paper towel and throws it away. 'L-e-i-g-h. Or L-e-a-h. So I have a girl's name and you have a boy's name. Is that the way you've always spelled it?'

'Archy told me,' her breath smells like cocoa and some kind of vegetable that Lee can't place. 'Archy said it was with a 'y' because it was Bryce for a girl. If I was a boy he said it would have been an 'i.'"

'Archy told you how to spell your name? You didn't know?'

She places a brush on the rack, picks a scab just below her ear. 'I forgot.'

'Can you read and write?' asked Lee, peering at the words she scrawled on the window, but the glass has cleared so he can't make them out. 'Did you go to school?'

'Some.' The band of the eye patch buckles over her creased brow. 'Why do they call the forest a hippocampus?'

'Hippocampus means seahorse in ancient Greek. Kind of. Horse Sea Monster is a closer translation. I guess they thought that it kind of looked like one.'

She takes a Sharpie from the table and draws a seahorse on her arm. 'Does it?'

He smiles. 'Pretty close.'

'If a real person takes the memory venom, will they remember how to spell their name?'

'We don't really know what it will do to humans.' He stares at the hippocampus on her arm. Rats got faster at finding a platform submerged in in water.'

'Like an island,' she touches her own nose. 'In the storm.'

Lee waits.

'I know where to find it, too,' she says.

'Find what?' He licks blood off his lips.

'The island. I know where it is.'

Lee says. 'You found me there the night Thettie . . .'

'I knew what you wanted.'

'You can get me back?' He pulls one of the fake

bone buttons off his shirt, hears it roll along the floor. 'To see my son?'

She wiggles her arm and makes the seahorse swim. 'What if it's not him anymore?'

'It will always be him.'

The girl's arm flops to her side and her good eye rolls up and disappears in her head. Froth foams from her mouth.

'Seekyouseekyouseekyouseek,' Her voice is a staticky growl and he doesn't know what to do.

29. MILKY WAY

IT WAS THE end of the world, and they were in the Winnebago, and they were always fucking because that's what you do when it's the end of the world.

Except she is also under the punch table at her own wake. The underside of the table is speckled with boogers and spitballs and gumwads, and some of the gum is hanging by threads like shooting stars. A gravitational force of ancient spittle holds meteor showers of old filth in place, in a solar system of gum planets and moons. And she *can* be in two places at once, because when you're dead, the laws of physics can be a little bent. So she is *both* under the table at her own wake beneath a cosmos of spitballs, trying to out-pheromone two sadistic body guards—not an easy proposition when her skin is beginning to take on the quality of pulped aspen leaves—*and* she is also in bed with Lee in the little Winnebago. They are looking up at the Milky Way through the weathered skylight between endless rounds of coupling.

***

'How many stars in the Milky Way?' she asked. The spangled grin of the firmament wheeled above like the crack in the sidewalk, the one Frankie always said was laughing at their sorrows—and Sunny Weeks and her

Progress Association could cover it up all they wanted, Thettie knew. It was still there and always would be.

'So in the Milky Way—about two, three hundred billion stars,' he said. 'They used to think the stars in the sky and the neurons in the brain were roughly the same, but that was before they knew how many galaxies were out there—millions, actually. And about eighty-six billion neurons in the brain.'

His hair was the color of shady sand and it stuck out around his head. On his right shoulder was a small tattoo of New Mexico, a blue square with a crimson river bisecting it like a vein. She liked to have a cigarette after sex, but that habit could go the way of so many others in this whistle-stop tour of her life that has slowed to a stretched-out pause.

A light flared overhead through the skylight, like an eye opening wide, or a switch being thrown.

'Still,' she said. 'Almost a whole galaxy in the brain.'

'At least.' He entwined a strand of her hair in faintly olive-skinned fingers. 'Because we've also got about a hundred trillion dendritic spines.'

'A hundred followed by twelve zeros.' She'd always been good with numbers and was top of her class in science. Ones and zeros . . . she snuggled closer to him, moved her hand lower on his belly. 'Dendritic spines are those branchy things?'

She rested her head on his chest. The stars winked open and shut, ones and zeros, his heart beating in time to their exchange of light. On and off. Between some of the winking lights were dark spaces, like gaps or breaks in the signal. There was a sudden crash outside the trailer, and they both sat up and looked at each other, his eyes a pale fire. Thettie went to the window and looked out but could see nothing except the dark void of lake and above it the freewheeling mirth of the cosmos.

'There is something out there,' she said. 'I feel it, getting closer.'

'Me, too,' he said, and when she turned around to him he was pale and his hair was wild, and she knew that he wasn't seeing her any more, but the man who took his son and who, despite being in jail, was still out there and would be until his son's remains were found.

'Come back,' he said. And so she did.

And then they talked about Dark Matter.

She and Frankie and Cassie had also talked about Dark Matter—how something as complex as the universe sometime breaks, leaving black holes, a kind of ghost framework, as Frankie put it—a dark gravitational skeleton keeping it all together. Cassie loved talking about the universe. It made her feel small, she said, and she'd shivered, all cheekbone and red-tipped bangs. Frankie was doing physics and was just trying to explain what a 'self-organizing' system was. He said it just meant a system that could learn.

When Thettie asked Lee what all that had to do with memory, he said, 'Self-organizing systems have the capacity to learn, through memory, how to be themselves.'

Thettie looked at the window. 'It's still out there,' she said. It seemed to be trying to crawl up the outside of the trailer, as if trying to find a way in. They listened to it scuttling up the outside walls. Gooseflesh rippled up Thettie's arms.

Lee said, 'Self-organizing systems make mistakes, though. Planets collapse under their own weight. Stars nuke themselves and everything around them. But the system works as a whole to keep itself alive. The brain and the galaxy are both infinitely complex, self-organizing systems. An unending exchange of light.'

'Like a giant brain?' she asked, her voice suddenly reverberant in the descending silence. At the sound of her voice, the thing that was half-way up the trailer stopped moving. Lee extended both arms, the free arm and the one around her, pressing her closer to him, and he framed the stars through the skylight with his thumbs, a frame within a frame, world within worlds.

'A universe of brains,' Lee said.

It happened slowly. The wind tore a branch off the pine, which disengaged with a prolonged screech and fell on the trailer roof with a crash. They looked at each other and smiled. She reached for his hand and peered through the frame at the fallen branch across the skylight obscuring the view of the leering Milky Way. He brought down his hand and passed his thumb across her lips lightly and then harder and then her face was in his hands and she would have let him reach right in and pull out her heart if he'd wanted to.

There was a part of her that wished he did.

30. BUST

BEHIND THE WHEEL with the one-eyed girl riding shotgun, Lee says, 'I loved my wife. But I don't think I was very good at it.'

'What was your son's name?' she leans against the window, her eye patch smeared with paint.

'I was down at the shore, getting the supper barbecue ready. The sky was the softest of pinks, I remember that. But the clouds—I remember them too—were smoky, dirty against all that pure pink. My wife was packing plates and salad and picnic things into a basket. He was on the swing set. And then he wasn't.'

She doesn't reply, just keeps her good eye fixed on the window, but the exchange between them is now complete, and they ride the rest of the way without the need for words. Half-way through the Village, Lee has forgotten she is there, and is instead wondering how he will get out of staying any longer at Thettie's wake than he has to.

He has an idea. He swerves into the campground parking lot. The girl seems to have fallen asleep against the window. Lee gets out and grabs the pheromone spray from the trunk and hurries down to the campground. With the Harpurs at the Way, the trailers and cabins are mostly in darkness although there is a dim light burning in Archy and Grif's window. Crime scene tape flaps around the cabin Thettie died in and Lee avoids that, instead heading straight to the Winnebago. It is empty but locked, as he expects. He sinks to his knees and crawls under it whispering Vernon's name and squirting pheromone spray. Worms wind their way around his fingers and he kneels in scat and butts and pushes aside an old diaper, but there is no sign of the Gila. Lee crawls out, brushes himself off as best he can. He heads to the double wide behind the yellow tape but at that moment Doc's bodyguards appear over the crest of the parking lot, followed by Doc on his phone. Lee quickly splashes the rest of the spray beneath the flapping tape. Then he melts into the darkness of the trees and heads back to the car.

***

At the door of the tavern Lee opens his mouth to say he's changed his mind, but the girl's lips quiver at him over her shoulder like a snarling dog, so he lets her lead him through. They walk past a few regular customers in the front bar, but Avery has reserved the back room and garden for the Harpur wake. There are no Harpur men yet. The women look so pure in their grief, their blue eyes like stained glass in the black leadlight of their heavy make-up. They stand in groups, cousins and aunts—a set of teenage twins in matching fake leather jackets, puffing on inhalers. Avery pours Lee a beer and Bryce a cider. She's recovered from her fit, or whatever it was, and if it wasn't for the paint on her eye patch— Lee had tried to catch her fall—he could tell himself that he imagined the whole thing.

ALETHEIA

Doc, in neatly laundered and pressed fatigues, his medals rattling, greets guest flanked by his security detail. His crew-cut is as crisp as ever but his skin grafts look more pronounced, like fragments of bone detached from his skull and pushing to the surface of his face. His close-set eyes flick to the girl beside Lee, flick away, and ignore them. Homer and Lyle look more dangerous than they should, like they've waited long enough to do what they came to do, and the Laurel and Hardy act has run its course. It occurs to Lee that whatever they're here to do, it might involve Thettie's sons—compensation for completing Doc. Or maybe just a debt they are anxious to pay and be gone from this place.

In any case, the monster that killed Lee's son had no such complications. His son's killer was pure interior, a want so totalizing that he had no need to see himself in another.

Harpur men begin to arrive, but not Archy and Grif. Lee finds the punch table and stays there. The edge of the table digs into the back of legs and he can feel wads of chewing gum stuck to the table's underside. A piece of paper, a gum wrapper maybe, comes off in his hands and he doesn't know what to do with it. The mourners look naked in their grief, mascara running and tattooed arms entwined—many of them already drunk—and all this naked reality is too much theatre for Lee. There are two kinds of punch, a watery blue one and a dirty yellow one. Furry ice cubes swim on the surface along with slices of orange and watermelon, some of which look partially eaten.

Archy and Grif push through into the tavern in a gust of cold air. Lee gathers that this is unexpected.

The women fuss over them and the men pass them drinks, but they just stand at the door and keep their sunglasses on and don't accept any offering of food from the women or drinks from the men.

Lee stinks from crawling around beneath the trailer. He has scat and squashed bugs on his pants, and pulls what looks like half a worm out of his hair. Archy and Grif move to a booth, and there is a sharp blue flicker at the edge of his eye.

After they showed him the reptile tooth and he threw up all over Maxine's fake marble tiles, he asked them if anyone had searched the trailer. Archy said, 'A hundred times. We searched the big trailer *and* the Winnebago when we could. No lizard. Nothing.' And then Lee asked how they could think what he thought they were thinking? Lee had looked around at all the tear-streaked stubble and glittering Harpur eyes and whispered—he'd wanted to yell, to hit someone, to throw something. But the girl had put a finger across her mouth, *shhhh,* so his screamed whisper came out like a rasp—how they could imagine that Vernon, an eighteen-inch lizard in his twilight years, exhausted from a lifetime of sacrifice and homesick for the buttes, could have been capable of such ungodly carnage. Vernon never could have done this, Lee hissed at the Harpurs, in a hundred trillion years.

And Grif was all, well what the hell did?

31. TEAR

AT THE WAKE Thettie tries to get close enough to Doc and his two-faced familiar, Homer and Lyle, to listen to their plot against her family, but the other Harpurs block her path, and she catches words like 'OD,' 'sleeping pills', 'depressed.' About Lee rejecting her and her not being able to take it. About how she pulled out all the kitchen drawers and hacked into her flesh, and how she even screwed that up, turned herself into a monster. Unspeakable, yet it is all they can speak of. About how she is a victim instead of a hot mama who never took any shit from anyone. All the usual things they say about women who die bad deaths.

Thettie she wants to tell them that she always knew she'd die hard. Because death is a self-organizing system into which failure equals feedback. Some paths are dead ends but the system can't always know that in advance and that is where its self-correcting mechanisms kick in. So it wasn't how it looked, she wants to tell them, but even her girls aren't listening. One thing she knows is that it is time for her to leave. There is something unnatural, unlawful about attending your own wake, and Thettie decides that she doesn't recommend it.

J.S. BREUKELAAR

Lee will listen to her theory of entanglement. She wants to go to him, but she is afraid that the same field of possibility that is repelling her, will attract her to a point of no return. It is a strange side-effect of this new condition—quantum logic has gone all tangled over her sorry ass and Lee-the-scientist might have some insights.

Or he might fuck her breathless. She'd take that.

She pushes out the door of the tavern, letting in a gust of frigid air and Avery yells about the heating costs. Thettie is glad to be gone from that place.

She scuttles back to Lee's place on all fours, a pale apparition along the empty highway, across a sidewalk that re-cracks in her wake. Scents of rotting jewel-weed claw at her throat and she rears on two legs to paw at the meteor showers. She smashes Jack o' Lanterns on porches, leaves a smear of black goo on plastic tombstones in front yards, and becomes, in her rage, ensnared in fake spider-web.

But by the time she gets back to Lee's studio, the force-field that has been keeping her away has lifted. She is able to get right up to the fogged-up window, where she sees some marks crudely scrawled and all but unreadable. Damn mooncalf! But she must have written them backwards from the inside—no easy task—because from the outside, squinting with her tongue hanging out and her neck grotesquely angled, Thettie can finally make out the two words she's been waiting for.

'Come home.'

The door swings open and she stands in the narrow entrance between the crammed shelves. The small space is empty and dark apart from the glow of

Vernon's empty tank. It illuminates a painting on the easel of her naked on the headland, facing out to the island where a blurry figure walks, neither man nor woman nor beast.

She looks around at all the lakes, and is instantly wet with want. One broken hand gropes between her legs, and with the other she rifles through the papers on Lee's desk. Her powers of interacting with the physical world come and go with her fluctuating materiality. It's all in the timing, and she has a lot to learn about this new life. Frankie used to say she was a quick study but had no patience. The heat builds in her belly. The papers awkwardly slip from her hand and spill across the desk. Some float up in the air, some down to the floor. It's a mess. A paragraph on a Xeroxed article catches her eye because it is highlighted in pink.

The primary function of memory, she reads, *is to mesh the embodied conception of the projectable properties of the environment—the forest—with the embodied experiences that provide non-projectable properties of the path. Thus, through memory, the path through the forest becomes the path home.*

Thettie's fingers slide into her cleft. Waves of heat pulse up her thighs. She lifts her nose and sniffs. There is a new smell in the studio, one that was not there before but which she recognizes. Chocolate and something else. A mug of spilled cocoa sits on the desk. She wheels around, stumbles. A dirty parka hangs over a chair.

Bryce.

Thettie has to admit. She feels jealous, possibly.

Bryce.

Sidelined, probably.

Bryce.

Dead, indefinitely.

Thettie lifts up her head and howls the unspeakable name. Rainwater from a leak in the roof falls onto her distended tongue and puddles on the floor.

32. HOLE

LEE FINALLY SLIPS away from the wake. He lowers himself behind the wheel and is about to toss the foil gum wrapper into the cup holder. It's stained and torn and there is writing on the non-foil side. He turns on the glovebox light and flattens the wrapper on his knee. There are some letters written in cheap blue pen, faded and patchy, and Lee has to stare at them for a few moments before he can be totally sure of what it says.

'*Midnight HF*'

He carefully puts it in the glove box because he doesn't know what else to do with it. The darkness presses in around the car. He balks, his mind emptied, unable even to remember what to do to get the car in motion. His lizard brain kicks in and he pulls out of the unlit parking lot and halfway down the highway into the starless maw of another Sunday. Another set of headlights keeps well back. At first he is sure it is Deputy Abbes again. The sky is as dark as tar-paper and the road ahead is runny in the rain. A loon shrieks. Lee, feeling drunker than he should, rolls down the window, sticks his head out to find some stars and the car veers across the lane. The headlights behind him pull back even more until he's not even sure they are there until they emerge again out of the darkness. It has to be Harpurs—maybe some men Doc thinks he can spare. Lee's laugh drowns out the loon. He steps on the gas, sprays gravel swinging left into his driveway and watches the car pass him and disappear on the highway, wondering how long he'd have to wait before it doubles back.

'Fucktards.'

He parks in the garage, weaves down the path past the empty house and into the studio. He shivers but something stops him adding another log to the stove. He takes the girl's parka and folds it carefully onto the shelf by the door. He wipes her spilled cocoa. Turns back to his easel, but slips on a dark puddle that has formed on the floor. His back twinges as he loses his footing and regains his balance. He inspects the puddle. There is a muddiness to it, a musky, sappy smell which fills the studio, makes his eyes water like walking in aspen woods. He looks for a crack in the sheeting but can't see one, gets out his silicon gun anyway and stands on a step ladder to squish the filler along the steel frame just over the puddle.

When he's finished, he lies down and watches the clouds wheel past the window, and when he dreams, it is of how in grad school he came upon a lizard burrow in the desert and soundlessly crept up to it, then shone his flashlight inside onto a couple of Gila Monsters entwined in the mouth of the burrow. The male was on top, his tail hooked under hers. Except in the dream, it is Thettie he tastes. Her sap and her musk taste like tears and when he wakes up his boxer shorts are sticky, and the pillowcase, too.

33. REFLECTION

SHE IS BACK in the trailer, unsure of her next move. The days are hell. By day she can only venture out clumsily, like a beast on a chain. She moves with an effort across the hairy crack in the sidewalk, and its dippy grin trips her up each time. She slithers through the unremembered town and cowers in the gutter, skitters behind a hollow tree. It's not that the townies can't see her that's the problem. It's that she can't see herself.

She hoped the tooth would set her free. She figured that by pulling it out of where it had lodged in her own mouth, and offering it to Archy and Grif, they would see her for what she always was and how she came home like she said she would.

But they can't. They can't handle the tooth.

She claps her hand to her face, and her tongue splits and slithers through her fingers. Her giggles turn to scummy tears. How can she break the chain that keeps her between worlds—a creature of the night, and a horror at that?

Shoppers select bunches of snap dragons from reproduction tin pails in front of the Village Market.

A shadow follows her, a beast-master who moves between her and the world, keeping her out. Her jailer, childhood apparition. Bald witch, demon with a broken yellow eye like a smashed pumpkin. It'd chase her and Cassie on their Costco bikes, Cassie surging ahead, a Kool dangling from her mouth. 'Run!' Cassie would yell. 'Run!'

But you can't outrun the monster.

***

Thettie cannot stay out long in the day. She slithers back to her trailer, clutching a sweaty gum wrapper from Frankie in her hand, telling her for the last time to meet him at midnight at Harpur Falls—*Midnight. HF*—where he'll be waiting forever, because she never turned up. And when she gets to the trailer, the note is gone, and her hand is empty, gnawed down to the bone by fifty lizard teeth, forever pointed and grooved to enable the flow of venom. The memory of Vernon's muscular jaw and prolonged bite burned onto her immaterial flesh, his throat extended and throbbing for the tongue-kiss of death.

Mamama

She listens for answers, for direction from the needles of the fir tree tapping messages on the roof of the trailer. *Tap t-tap t-tap tap t-tap*. The needles are white tipped, like the spikes of broken bone Doc told her about that poke through the sand in the desert. Doc told her about Moloch in the desert, this Jew God, he said, who demanded child sacrifice in return for his endless love.

Leaf peepers in puffy vests stroll past Thettie's trailer window, checking their watches so as not to miss today's special at the Village Inn—grilled char on wilted zucchini and celeriac stacks with blood orange *jus*.

ALETHEIA

Thettie watches a movie—a film—to pass the time. It's a silent film of a desert war. It runs in a loop on the little TV in the living room. Medic Doc 'What's Up' Murphy is playing Hero. The film shows him carrying the Victim, Private Frances Washington Harpur from a burning building. The building is a new school outside of Bagram base, which luckily doesn't have any children in it yet. The Hero is charred and smoking like something pulled off a barbecue, because he was off-duty and just wearing a T-shirt and his regulation chinos. Frances Washington Harpur, the man in the hero's muscular arms, is an engineer, and had been called to the school in response to a bomb threat. Luckily he is wearing his fire-retardant combat kit, although he is bloody and broken from the blast, with a hunk of rusty rebar sticking out of his foot.

The film on the TV in Thettie's half-lit cave replays endlessly. It cuts to a little yellow car melted and twisted beyond recognition on the street outside the exploded school in Afghanistan. Around the corner a man called Bud 'Ham' Wallace walks away from the yellow car, pocketing a Nokia burner-phone and a wad of cash in a folded newspaper he retrieved from under a designated door. Although he has his back turned to the camera, Thettie's mind extends over the sandy dunes of years to the four digits he dialed to set off the blast. 2727.

CQCQ

In army speak CQ stands for 'Charge of Quarters,' which is basic guard duty including monitoring the radio and even cleaning the barracks. But Wallace is already a ham radio nut, and in ham radio, CQ means something else entirely.

J.S. BREUKELAAR

***

One May afternoon back around 1986, at Clinton High, they had to watch a mixed-grade viewing of a movie, or a 'film,' as Cassie would say. It was *Hamlet*, a boring black and white blur on the dirty screen hanging between a map of America and the Periodic Tables. The blinds were drawn but not enough, and Thettie tried to make out the sooty shapes and none of them could understand a word of whatever language it was in, except Frankie.

But there was a scene in the movie that stuck in Thettie's mind, in her memory. It was the scene where Hamlet, the doomed prince, who looked as old and boring as she imagined princes to be, picks up a skull from the graveyard and stares at it.

And the skull stares back.

And smiles its lizard smile.

And says, 'Remember me.'

Remember, the teacher wrote afterward on the blackboard. *Remember you too will die.* That's what the skull symbolizes, the teacher said, reminding them to always talk about books or plays in the present tense.

'Why?' someone asked.

'Because story worlds are not the same as our world,' the teacher said. 'What happens in a story cannot be in the past because it never really happened. It's all speculative—what if. Fiction is always in narrative time, which is always out of real time. Every time you open the book the story starts all over again from wherever you open it.'

'What about when a character dies?'

'The characters might die on the page, but they're not really dead. They're just alive in a different way.'

ALETHEIA

'Like Permadeath,' Frankie whispered loudly, and Rogue was all the rage that year, so they understood.

Thettie decided to ask him later about the skull. Cassie was a junior and Frankie was a senior at Clinton High. He'd skipped a year on account of being so smart. Frankie was smarter than anyone she'd ever know. He just had a hard time expressing it, except to her and Cassie. Much later, Doc would call Frankie a polymath, like it was a good thing.

'*Memento mori,*' Frankie explained. They were at Harpur Falls, having agreed via a series of notes passed on gum wrappers, to cut the afternoon classes. 'Remember to die, is what the skull is saying, or not to die, and Hamlet can't make up his mind which it is.'

(Was that what Sarey was trying to tell her? To make up her mind?)

'Whose skull was it?' she'd asked Frankie, confused. 'Who the hell was Yorrick? I mean, 'is' Yorrick?'

'Yorrick was dead already in the actual play,' Frankie sighed, 'so you can talk about him in the past tense. It's complicated, see? Anyways, he was probably just some old pedo.' Frankie was seventeen. She was fifteen, three years away from being a mother. Cassie was sixteen, already carrying deGroot's rape-baby. Frankie's ribs protruded and he'd already begun to cut himself. Tiny flesh wounds, inched up his arms like pale worms. Water streamed from his coarse dark hair—Haudenosaunee hair from Sarey's side of the family—into his bloodshot eyes, like broken blue glass at the bottom of a lake.

Frankie, half out of breath, tried to explain. 'It doesn't matter who Yorrick was, see? He was a minor character, from Hamlet's past. That makes him, what, a metaphor for time. Yorrick reminds Hamlet how the choice to be or not to be is just an illusion. Choice is a fiction, see? Time plus choice equals death. Do the math.'

It's taken me forty-two years Frankie, but I worked it out. Better late than . . .

Frankie?

Even before he went to actual war, there was a war going on in Frankie's head that he didn't like to talk about, but which wore him out. Rings of red beneath his eyes and deep painful zits on his jaw. Voices that told him to do things. Only way to shut them up was to cut them out. Sarey went through tubs of MiraKil salve over those cuts, but the only one who could get through to the voices was Thettie. When she saw the voices crowding in his head (she couldn't hear them like she can now, but she could see them moving behind his waterfall eyes), a greasy bloom of sweat across his nose, Thettie'd yell in his ear, 'Shuddup!' and they'd go away. She was the only one the voices would listen to.

'If you weren't there,' he said, 'to shut the voices up? What then?'

'I'm not going anywhere,' she said.

***

'Frankie?'

They are almost at the island. In the last of the sun, she can see it ahead of her, with its nostril of stone and above that the nose-hair foliage. Frankie kills the engine and they drift toward the little bay.

'*Mori* is the present infinitive form of the verb, 'die'.' She can hear him but she can't see him anymore.

They are on his little silver speed boat, and he hasn't left for Afghanistan yet, but he will soon. She wants to stop him. She doesn't want him to leave her here all alone. His voice is hoarse and soft, and when he sings, he has perfect pitch.

'Sing to me, Frankie.'

But Frankie isn't singing now. 'See, *memento mori* actually means 'remember *to* die,' or even, 'remember *how* to die.'

'How can you remember how to die if you have forgotten how to live?'

All she can see is the outline of his skinny shoulders over his quivering pole, the line slicing the setting sun in two. 'That's the key, Thettie. The tooth. The tooth will set you free.'

His silhouette on the bow is dark and ringed in fire. 'Frankie?'

Thettie cocks her head and listens for his answer. She hears nothing but the lap of water against the shore, and realizes that he's not there anymore. She shields her eyes from the dying sun to peer toward the island, but there is nothing behind the warning beacon. Just dark restless water streaked with red.

'Frankie? It's me, Thettie. Come home,' she is crying again, tears of blood running between her teeth.

But he never does.

34. KILLER MIX

LEE 0: LONELINESS 1.

Habib sends a text saying that Jason seems to have disappeared—last seen by his kid brother on Sunday night in the bunk beds they shared in a single room, and the next day, by a passerby who said that he saw Jason's truck heading south down the highway away from the family farm, a little red Ford Focus in hot pursuit.

Lee doesn't text back.

Partly because Lee doesn't want to know how Habib's radar has picked all this up—the red Ford, for example, which Lee saw parked outside the Way and is Doc Murphy's unlikely ride. But also because of what Habib is possibly saying. That Jason is plausibly dead. That Jason's combat boots were most likely responsible for the crushed markers in the pet cemetery. That whoever was mulching wood behind the barn at the deGroot farm may not have been mulching just wood.

But why?

If Jason was with his brother on the night Thettie died, and Doc and his men were at the Way at midnight, as were Archy and Grif, and if Lee was on the lake, then the only one not accounted for was Vernon. A Gila Monster, not a real monster.

ALETHEIA

The days are hard. The Harpurs have gone to ground, including the girl. He watches them out on the lake, fishing, Jet Skis following Doc's yacht out to the island and returning with it in the storms. He hears the distant rumble of their bikes. But no one comes to see him. He is once again alone.

The nights are better. He lies on in the dark and waits for her to come to him in his dreams. *Wake up*, she says. But he is never asleep.

A few unslept nights after her wake, he burns the lakes, like he burned the drawings of his son. He throws the paintings into the stove one by one, drinking Amstel while he watches them burn. In the end the smell drives him out. He deletes Habib's texts.

The Harpurs keep to themselves as always, but without their old compound to take refuge in, they have no choice but to haunt the streets of Little Ridge. Lee drives slowly, his arms on the steering wheel, behind a convoy of preloved Honda Shadows and Kawasakis. This whole mess is exactly what the folks of Little Ridge feared would happen if the Harpurs ever rolled back to shore in their Army surplus pontoons and junkyard trollers. They've trashed the beach, and the park beside the Village dock is now littered with wrappers and paper cups. The Harpurs re-ignite the feuds between the deGroots and the college townies. The Harpurs have cracked open the veneer of smug, cultured superiority. They've torn the collective reality asunder—exposing its movable parts, its fears and prejudices—so that in the larger-than-life immediacy of the Harpurs' hungry presence, everyone puts aside pretense and reverts to their realer, forgotten selves. Everyone from storekeepers to

Faculty Deans spouts vitriol and counts the days until Halloween when the managers can throw the Harpurs out, and life can return to their self-congratulatory bubble of social conscience and sustainable inclusivity—without the reality of the Harpurs' actual presence to test it. The Progress Association fast-tracks their Halloween Parade plans. Truckloads of pumpkins arrive at the Village Inn for carving.

Lee chuckles a little hysterically. Those Harpurs!

Feeling even more invisible, and doubly-sidelined now, he manoeuvers out of the Village. He pulls in at the Rod 'n' Reel. He tells himself it is to buy some more pheromone spray. But the real reason is that he might see the brothers there. Archy and Grif. He wants to ask them to get him into Doc's trailer so that he can look for Vernon himself. Not because Lee thinks that Vernon did it, but because he wants to save him. To get him back, if possible, while there is still a 'him' to get.

The walls of the store are covered with angler-porn like the inside of an aquarium gift shop, and the air is heavy with the smell of scented candles. TV monitors play YouTube videos of the ones that got away—salmon the size of dogs and steelhead the size of cats—blinking white men pulling on their Moby Dicks.

On his way through the aisles, Lee almost collides with Piet deGroot. Lee veers away toward the door but his basket is filled with merchandise he's picked up without realizing it. He goes to wait in the line. DeGroot comes up behind him, and, Lee, in a sudden rage, turns to confront him about Jason, but someone else is suddenly there between them—the girl. Her eye-patch is still paint-smeared. She winks at Lee with her good eye.

Lee could fall at her feet, but his throat is too raw to say anything. She is shopping for supplies to make lures. She carries a list. Her basket is filled with bright beads and feathers, packets of rubber minnows and hooks. She points to the inflatable flamingo water wings in Lee's basket and her good eye widens.

'No cut-in,' Piet deGroot says. 'End of the line's that way.'

What happens then is that it looks like the old man has a stroke. His jaw drops open and drool spills out and his pale eyes turn white and he points with a shaking finger at the sliding glass doors to the parking lot. But when Lee turns to look there is only Archy and Grif idling outside on their motor bikes.

DeGroot pulls at his throat and staggers and when a clerk goes across to help, deGroot shoves him away, tries to look over his shoulder at something outside the window. Lee and the girl move along the line. After she pays, she tells Lee she might see him around, but when he opens his mouth to ask 'when,' she waves and is gone. And all that is left is a ringing in Lee's ears from the roar of the bikes, and a stink in the store from how old man deGroot soiled himself that even the scented candles can't mask.

***

Habib's door is open. Lee has decided to see him again after all, in case Habib can suggest a way past the crime scene tape for Lee to search for Vernon himself. The overcast sky above the lake darkens the window at the end of the hall. Lee wanders into the study where the Professor is at his desk watching footage of Vernon that Lee made in the early days of his research. It was when the Gila was in the wild, before he was captured and taken to the lab. The footage shows Vernon engaged in a dominance ritual with another male they'd been tracking, and who they called Meatloaf. It looks very much like Olympic wrestling—the lizards circle each other, hissing. They charge, grapple and flip their opponent using powerful forearms and outsized claws, their bodies stabilized by fat tails and lumbering hind legs. The endless scuffle in the sand, the terminal face-off replete with rasped exhalations, clicks and grunts fills the room while Lee and Habib watch for a while in silence.

Habib is shirtless and smoking.

'I thought you quit.' Lee takes a seat on the other side of the big Italian desk. A new telescope, he notices, has replaced the broken one. But this one is modern. All white enamel and brushed steel, and angled toward the island.

'I'd forgotten how good it was.'

'Looks like you also forgot to take the strap from around your arm, but what are a few track marks between friends?'

'Is that what we are?' Habib's voice is hoarse. His coaching whistle lies in a pool of spit on the desk. Beside it is the syringe and an engraved silver lighter, a gift from Lee and his wife.

'What is it?'

'Painkillers, Lee. Opiates. For an old war horse.' Habib runs swollen fingers through his wiry hair, makes it stick up like in the David Lynch film, *Eraserhead*, that Habib and Lee and his wife all went to see together in Albuquerque. 'I scored them from Frankie years ago. Haven't needed them until now.'

Lee listens to the hiss and scuffle of Vernon and

Meatloaf on the sand. He goes to the kitchen, pours them both a coffee and sits back down.

'I need to find Vernon—if he's still here, if whoever took him has him, I need to find him. I've been to the deGroots, no Jason. I need someone with a search warrant for either there or the campground. Or both.'

Habib doesn't answer.

'I saw Piet deGroot at the fishing store,' says Lee. 'Looks a little worse for wear.'

'Don't we all?'

Lee can see himself, with red moons under his eyes and a bloody mouth from chewing his cheeks, reflected in the telescope's large oval eye. Outside, dark branches fling themselves on the wind.

'Fall came too soon this year,' Habib says.

'I wasn't aware you and Frankie were drug buddies.'

'Don't be a pain in the ass.'

'So, because I don't approve of you scoring opiates for your personal use under the auspices of experimental protocol, I'm a pain in the ass?'

Habib chews on his lip, gazes out the window.

'You scored black market Oxy from Frankie in return for him mixing Cheracol-flavored Helotide to offload in bulk at raves, Sam? Seriously?'

'If it pleases the jury,' Habib tries to clear his throat, gives up. 'A precise mix of enzymes and vitamins, Guarana, caffeine and the venom peptides. The thinking person's party drug.'

'So, Frankie came up with the mix? What's so killer about it?'

'It could have been,' Habib squints out at the lake, gently bumps his bare chest with his fist. 'In the right hands.'

'Or the wrong ones.' Lee watches the Gilas crash around in the pink sand, their tails turgid and eternally seeking. Vernon's open throated hisses sound like something between the snickers of a creepy old man and a young girl's sigh.

'Forest Path. Patent Pending,' Habib gives a sideways lurch. 'A drug that blurs the line between consciousness and neuronal effect.'

The soundtrack to the footage of the wrestling monsters is 'Bat out of Hell.' Habib plucks the strap around his arm like a banjo. He smiles at Lee.

Lee smiles back and taps out the piano intro on his knee. 'What about a drug to blur the line between life and death?'

'If you took enough pure Helotide—not the Killer Mix, but the unadulterated analogue—you might forget the difference. I mean you'd remember everything all at once from your birth to your death.'

'So, by 'you,' you mean a human being? And by 'remember your death,' you mean a paradox, right? Like time travel.'

Lee has brewed Habib's artisan coffee too strong. He feels jittery, the 'Bat Out of Hell' intro still born on the keys of his air-piano.

Habib—or one of the Gilas—makes a papery click in the back of his throat. 'The memory of our own death is there in all of us, Lee. The Greeks knew it from Day One. The river of *Lethe* runs deep in our veins and is the path we open up in ourselves to get to the other side. In order to live again, we firstly need to forget what we were—or thought we were—to learn once more how to be ourselves. In a sense, I guess we must forget how we died, even if it hasn't happened yet.'

ALETHEIA

'So *Groundhog Day* was a horror movie.'

Habib starts to laugh but is instead gripped in a coughing fit and can't stop. His face reddens and then pales. Lee stands up, pours some water from a carafe and puts it in front of his friend.

Between sips and coughs, Habib tells him: '*Lethe* (cough cough) comes from the Greek word meaning oblivion or concealment, and is in fact related to the word, *A-letheia* (cough) via the privative alpha, a prefix that expresses negation or absence—literally un-concealment, or un-forgetfulness, or more accurately, 'not a lie.'

'*Aletheia*?'

'*Veritas* in Latin. The Goddess of Truth.' Habib dribbles water down his chin, which runs onto his chest and pools in the wiry hairs. 'The Greek form contains more room to move, though. *A-letheia* implies that the truth is always in a sense not disclosed. Am I making sense? I can't tell anymore.'

'So *Aletheia* is not so much the truth, but how you find it.' Lee's heart lurches at a sudden memory—Thettie telling him about this black thing crawling beneath the surface of the lake, leaving the stink of memory in its wake.

'Or lose it,' Habib says. 'The concern is that pure Helotide—not the souped-up Cheracol I was planning to retire on for my sins, but the real deal mainlined directly from Gila venom glands to humans—would block forgetfulness in the process of enhancing memory. In humans, what Helotide could theoretically do, is arrest necessary oblivion in favor of totalizing recall, even to the point of remembering past lives.'

'Necessary oblivion?' Lee shivers despite the

roaring furnace in his blood. 'Past lives? Give me a break.'

'Unending truth is a contradiction in terms, my friend. Everything unconcealed is a chimera. Why should death be the end of memory?' Aristotle's voice cuts in and speaks through Habib's spit-flecked mouth. 'What if the crossing of Lethe gets interrupted somehow? What for example, if there's a sudden storm, and you go out too deep, and you are arrested in some mysterious way in the incomplete process of forgetting?'

Habib's ravaged face shrinks to a pinprick on the other side of the desk. The monsters tangle on the screen.

'We need to forget, Lee,' Habib says back in his own voice. 'Living is forgetting. We've both done work with hyperthymesiacs and eidetics. Total recall is not life. It's a living death.'

Some wag in the lab made a gif of the fMRI of an eidetic subject's brain because it looked like the bridge of the Starship Enterprise under attack from aliens. Everything lit up, with little mushroom clouds of yellow and blue interspersed among a catastrophic exchange of light.

'So, what you're saying is that if Helotide . . . '

'The waters of *Mnemosyne*, say, or memory . . . '

'If *Mnemosyne* contaminates forgetfulness . . . '

'*Lethe*.'

'That, in effect, leaves you stranded on the other side. How do you get back?'

Habib laughs uncertainly. 'As Hendrix said, my friend, it's not the trip, it's what you do with it.' He sits back hard on his zero-gravity chair so that it rattles the framed picture of his dead family. 'Who knows, with humans, what it would actually do?'

'But you did trial Forest Path, I mean the Cheracol thing, on yourselves, right? You and Frankie?'

Again, that tight stab of jealousy. Why was he not invited to one of Habib and Frankie's nootropic sessions? Munchies in a bowl. Radiohead albums on rotation. 'That protein-enriched Adderall? I didn't think you'd be interested. Augmented perception, Lee. It was fun but nothing to write home about.'

Lee walks over to the window. Down at the jetty, some men are boarding Doc's cruising yacht. Lee can't be sure from here, but he suspects it is Doc and the fat and thin bodyguards.

'So, but a dealer, Sam? I can't see you . . .'

The monsters sigh. Their worn-out panting fills the room. 'Not drugs, and not a dealer, Lee. A designer, if you please, of high performance life sciences reagents.'

'With Frankie Harper.'

Habib looks up at Lee and then points to the island.

'Frankie approached me, initially. He already had—years ago, while he was still around—the formula for the peptide analogue. It was just a matter of tweaking it, he said. A few amino acids here and there. Glutamates. Taurine. Methylenedioxies. Frankie had more contacts in the art, friends in peptide libraries and so on, than I do. The idea was that the chemicals get shipped to me, I send them across to him with one of his men.'

'What about me?'

'You Lee, yes, and I love you, kid. I do. But after your son died. You went away,' Habib doesn't look at the island. 'Of course. But I couldn't follow you. Out there. And I couldn't save you either. It was your trip.'

The lizards draw breath, rush at each other.

'He was my child.'

'Always will be. Wherever you are.'

There is a sudden downpour, and lightning bleaches the horizon. The telescope does a little jig on its squat legs.

Habib's bare shoulders rise and fall, each crowned by an epaulette of silver fuzz. 'There's subsidence. And even its original size is a matter of dispute, yes? Even on the maps, you can barely describe it as an island, just some hunk of rock, and now the lake is trying to take it back. *Lethe* at war with *Mnemosyne*. It's not natural.'

'Nothing's natural about an island in plain sight that no one has been to,' Lee says.

'Liar, liar pants on fire.'

The pause that follows is filled by the grunts of the lizards and the roll of thunder

'Don't you have a friend in Ilium? A detective or something. Maybe she can help you get a warrant to look for Vernon. Although I wouldn't hold out any false hope, my friend.'

35. ROD 'N' REEL

BRYCE IS THE key to the door. Thettie doesn't know exactly why, but when Bryce is around, there is more chance of Thettie being seen and of seeing herself. For what she now is.

She is unsettled by being in the trailer day after endless day. So, one morning in the third week of October, she rushes out at the sound of her sons' bikes in the parking lot. The bear chain around her neck that keeps her between worlds yanks her back. But she wills a link in the chain to pull apart, just for long enough for her to drag it onto the back of Archy's bike. She can see by his sudden pallor and a shadow across his eyes that he knows she is there, too.

They drive to the Rod 'n' Reel to get Bryce. They dropped her off earlier to buy some fishing supplies from the proceeds of the catch they offloaded at the Village Inn. Thettie clings to the pillion of the idling bike, but her hand flies to her heart when she sees Lee in the store, too, standing in the line. Bryce swings a basket full of lures behind him, and Thettie gnashes her teeth at how the girl simpers and dimples at Lee. Sluzza!

'Get back to the frozen hell where you came from, water-rat!' Thettie hoots, but Bryce just winks at her with her good eye. Thettie is horrified to see paint stains on her eye patch. Paint stains! Lee!

Behind the girl is Jason's old man, Piet deGroot, looking pissed. Thettie jumps off the pillion, fleet in her changing body. She rushes to the store entrance with her white nightgown flapping, coal-black matter leaking through the holes in her face. With the palms of her broken hand, she pounds on the sliding glass doors which remain closed at her approach.

Lee looks terrible. His eyes are puffy and his clothes are crumpled, with garbagy stains at the elbow and knee. In his basket, he bears water-wings for a child already flown. Thettie forgets about deGroot and spreads her good arm out to Lee, the sleeves of the nightgown like angel's wings. She presses her breasts, her thighs against the window. But Lee can't see her. DeGroot says something to Bryce and Lee turns around, his back turned to Thettie. DeGroot says something else, pointing to Bryce. Lee raises two hands in the air in mock surrender.

Thettie has to stop herself from smashing the glass, scrabbling over to Lee on all fours and slavering at his feet. She feels the weight of the bear chain and pulls against it. The crimson leaves swirl at her feet.

Because Lee. The way he looks at Bryce. Horrible. With such fear and such longing. Such a terrible, terminal need.

Terminal. Did she say that? No. She'd never hurt Lee. Never.

Bryce! She spits out a venomous loogie. It lands on the window and runs darkly down the glass. Lee is still turned away but Bryce and DeGroot face the window. So Thettie, with time on her hands and Bryce egging her on, forces herself to materialize, like static, to the man who violated her and Cassie in that Motel 6. He gapes at the apparition in its terrible beauty—a warning or a promise, a summoned gust of ruby leaves bright against her white gown, with her voluptuous gash of a mouth and her halo of wheaten hair.

His jaw drops like a stroke victim's and her son revs the engines, and Thettie is gun-gun.

***

Patti Smith was Cassie's idol. To please her, Frankie would play the chords to any Patti Smith song Cassie wanted. And Cassie wanted them all, no end to her want.

'Fate is a paradox, get it?' Frankie said, softly strumming cords that were never meant to be strummed softly. Cassie swayed precariously from the railing of Triangle Bridge, humming the words across a sea of possibility. 'The only way we can know what death is, is when we're not us to know it. It's like time travel. There's a law of logic against it.'

'Oh the irony!' Cassie drawled through a cloud of weed. There one minute, gun-gun the next.

***

A few days after the wake, Fie and Piet deGroot come to visit Doc to pay their respects. Conveniently for the deGroots, Archy and Grif, along with their Harpur protection, are away. But Thettie is there, and Thettie will be her sons' eyes and ears, and she will be their life, because even after you're dead, you never stop being a mother.

And because, Doc. Because I am in your crawlspace, Doc. Because you didn't see that coming.

Thettie snakes from her trailer back to the 'Bago on

bleeding elbows, dragging her gnawed ass beneath the weight of the chain. The chain around her neck is existential in one sense, and metaphorical in another, but a bitch all the same. Homer and Lyle are on CQ duty outside the Winnebago, and she puts one hand between Homer's fat leg and squeezes experimentally. The response is immediate. Homer's eyes get distant and his fat tongue moistens his belly-button lips, and where her hand is between his legs leaves a bloody smear that he will wonder about later. Lyle is looking sadly at the parking lot wishing to be gone from this place. It's giving him the skeevies, all this lizard business with no end in sight. He reaches into his pocket for his heart pills and Thettie drops her hand from Homer's crotch and sidles over to the other side of Lyle. She whispers, 'See you,' and she dribbles some spit in his ear, leaving a black goo that will leak from it for a week. While Homer and Lyle are busy with their crotches and their ears, Thettie drops under the trailer to listen to what Doc and the deGroots have to say.

She can't hear much. The moorings rattle in the rain, and there is traffic from out on the highway. It's dark and wet underneath the trailer, and crawling with pill bugs and slugs pushed to the surface in the wet. Doc is spouting the company line about Thettie being an accident waiting to happen. And Doc now saddled with a grown family to keep, but the deGroots don't seem interested in anything but Frankie and the Killer Mix.

'Leave him to me, boss,' Doc says. 'I told you that back in PA. Frankie's the forgiving type, always was.'

'Strange he wasn't at his own cousin's funeral, *ja*?' Fie says.

'To be sure, that wasn't a funeral as such, more like a wake.'

'Who has a wake before the funeral?'

'Ah, you know them Harpurs. Ass about face, and all. The funeral won't be until we get Frankie off the island,' Doc's laying the Irish badass on thick enough to make Thettie barf.

'How are you planning to do that?' one of the deGroots says. 'Without her? You told us she was the key. Now the key's gone, you got jack.'

'I still got them boys,' Doc says, sounding aggrieved, 'Why, I'm like a father to them. Raised them like my own bairns. They'll talk Frankie around.' He lowers his voice in an attempt at ambiguous menace. 'Worse comes to worse, I've got those two hard cases from the Hill.'

The deGroots bristle, and Thettie flings a slug off her finger in disgust. 'Bairns is a Scottish word, you old ham. Even you've forgotten what you are!

One of the deGroots scoffs. 'Laurel and Hardy, are you serious? They are your back up?'

Doc gives his best leprechaun chuckle, and Thettie does bring up some black bile at that. 'Homer and Lyle can be mighty persuasive in a pinch. I've seen them persuade many a healthy young man to give up living—truth be told, I've promised them Frankie's nephews when all is said and done. There you go. I knew that'd bring a smile to your dials and all. Stress'll kill ye, gentlemen. Trust me, I'm a doctor.'

Thettie rolls over onto her back and bangs her bleeding feet on the underside of the trailer. She scuttles out from under the crawlspace and tries to climb into a window or onto the skylight, willing herself to materialize. But her time's up. The chain yanks Thettie out from the crawl space and over to her trailer to watch TV.

***

On the little screen in saturated blues and yellows she watches Piet and Fie, of course much younger then, rock in their truck down the switchback into the Gully to meet Doc at the shack where Frankie cooked and brewed. Doc thought he was alone, but didn't realize that Sarey was on the prowl for some late-season cow parsley for her stomach complaint. Later she tried to tell Thettie what she saw. But Thettie didn't pay it much mind. Doc had been playing ambassador between the feuding families ever since his arrival in Little Ridge—another thing the Harpurs owed him. So Thettie figured that the meeting was just something to do with that—getting Doc to run interference between the younger deGroots and Frankie's team of Harpur boys over a saturated market unable to pick its poisons. But Sarey said that the meeting got out of hand. That the hostile handshakes at its closing, and Doc's skulking away looking like a whipped dog, may have had something to do with Boyle raiding Frankie's secret operation in the woods, and Frankie going to jail and the rest of them gun-gun.

***

Thettie's body stiffens in the Ilium morgue. There is no money for an undertaker, no money to make her pretty again. Those of the clan who remain are restless. They avoid the three-headed Moloch of Doc-Homer-Lyle which looms over their lives, demanding sacrifices they can no long stomach. Emilio and Dustin remain staunch, ever vigilant. Others confront Archy and Grif for some explanation, some guidance, a loan. Archy and Grif have nothing to give, and one by one the Harpurs drift away.

Thettie listens to Grif and Archy in private. Even though she knows it's wrong, she also knows it's for the right reason, and mothers must make these judgement calls, alive or dead.

Archy keeps wanting to take off in the night, grab Sarey and take their chances.

'What about Frankie?' Grif says.

And Archy says that Uncle Frankie can probably take care of himself better than anyone against Doc, and besides that, he says, 'Frankie has Ma.'

And Grif asks him if he honestly thinks that either of them could leave, could live, without seeing justice done for what happened to her, and Archy doesn't answer because Grif isn't asking.

'We need Doc to think that we're on side,' Grif says. 'That he's got us where he wants us.'

'What about them bitches of his?' Archy says.

'Homer and Lyle? Leave them to me, boys,' Thettie says, the force of her intent rattling the cups on the table. And they look at each other and smile.

Doc tries to negotiate an extension on their trailer rentals, but management says no on account of not having insurance for after October 31. Doc says he'll get his own, like the permanent renters, and pay for Archy's and Grif's, long as they help to persuade Frankie to come home. Archy and Grif agree to go out on the lake as soon as the weather clears and try and get to Frankie, but Thettie knows that they are just stalling for time while they try and figure out what to do. How Vernon got into her trailer, and what possessed him to attack her. And what happened then. That last one's the key, boys.

She wills them to see her. But men are blind. You can tell them the ketchup's in the refrigerator until you're blue in the face, but all they'll ever see is the refrigerator, not what's inside it. That's the problem. Men don't see the forest for the trees. The possibility in the sea.

Of course, not all men are the same. Take Lee, for example, the scientist. Science is in the details. Look at those drawings of his. Not just the lake, which Lee sees in ways that open up enough possibility to drown in—each painting of the lake looking entirely different from the next not only due to a stand of rain-heavy cattails here, wildflowers in an eddy there, a whorl of mist or a smear of moonlight. But also, depending on the oils used, or watercolors, and which brush or palette, or if he used his thumb to blur an outline, or a rag, or if he hurled the paint on with a coffee-cup, or used charcoal, or pastels. And the Vernons, ditto. Rearing up from the tank, or burrowed with a female, or lying split open in a dissection dish, the armored flaps of the scalp peeled back to reveal his reptile brain. The Gila's heart exposed and still, his venom glands excised for further study.

So Thettie knows that there is an infinite variety of men and that the devil *is* in the detail. Tell Lee the ketchup's in the refrigerator and the last thing he'll see is the refrigerator, but instead a universe of dread possibility within that nails him in place.

She'd still have to come over and get the ketchup herself.

If only she could show them how alive she is! Her

head is popping like the inside of a starship. She's really going places, now, she wants to say. She is changing—look at me now! She jumps up and down in the trailer, runs in circles, leaving a bloody smear.

***

After the meeting with the deGroots, she watches Doc saunter down to the barbecue pit to join Archy and Grif, the Ham (a word she now knows comes from that old drama queen, Hamlet). He's gabbing about the Black Dog or some such nonsense, trying to tell everyone what she is, when she's perfectly capable of showing them herself. All she needs is a little time. 'It can spring from nowhere,' Doc says, taking a reflective bite of the soft meatball sandwich Homer has bought from the Market. 'You let the Black Dog off its leash,' he says, 'thinking it to have learnt its lesson, only to have it bite off the hand that feeds it.'

Because, the wonder of it all, Doc! I've found a way. A way to be neither the means, nor ends. But something for herself. I am the forest and the trees.

But she weeps anyway for the effect Doc's words have on her sons. Because there is no comeback for them yet. Because the lie is their path to the truth. Archy's eyes brim. Grif sniffs and rakes both hands down his cheeks.

Archy's pupils disappear in the wide blue seas of his eyes. The blue is pure and glacial, no island in sight. Just twin liquid orbs of glittering rage. Grif shrugs his hood over his greasy hair, and they part to make more space for her.

Doc likes to tell other people what they are, to avoid being seen himself, but Thettie, standing between her two boys, like always, sees him now. Doc

353

hiding behind his vampire teeth, Homer and Lyle, but there's a rotten gum in that metaphor now. Fat, slow, horny Homer with his necklace of sutures, and cutter-killer Lyle with the dicky ticker. Thettie puts two clawed fingers to her eyes and points at him, and he blanches at a sudden rushing in his ear. Sticks his finger in and looks in horror at the black slime it pulls out. I know you had a heart attack, Wiley-Lyley, not just because of the statins you eat like candy, but also because of those three months in the prison hospital, sent back to solitary with a six-inch scar down your sternum. Her mouth waters at the thought.

Lyle and Homer have been each other's family since meeting on the streets in Manilla in 1998. After a late-night fracas, Lyle found Homer tied up in the back of a fabric warehouse in Manila, with his head in the process of being hacked off by a Burgos Street gangster who caught Homer trying to sell DMA to underage girls in his dance clubs. Lyle shot the gangster, a kid of nineteen, in the back with his nine, then drove Homer to an abortionist with a strange accent, called D. 'Whatsup' Murphy, holed up in Bagoong Silangar. Whatsup sewed Homer's neck closed and returned him alive to his grateful soul-mate. It would be a decade and a half before the good doctor called in the favor.

When Homer was better, Lyle, who'd been a merchant seaman for years and had sailed all around the Pacific, bought him a *Karambit*, a curved Philippine fighting knife, and taught him how to use it.

Thettie doesn't know how she remembers the warehouse but she does. The fabric bolts stacked in vertical rows. The loading dock where the trucks come in with ecstasy pills stuffed into the slots of the corrugated cardboard filling of the bolts. She runs a clawed finger around the circumference of her own neck, opening up a necklace of black blood.

***

Doc wants to confer with Archy and Grif about the island. Thettie elbows them in the ribs. They listen to him talking about weather charts and the price of Armorflate Zodiacs on Craiglist. He says that he might be able to get his hands on some amphibious equipment from the deGroots, who are still Reservists, but he doesn't say why the deGroots would agree to that and Archy and Grif don't bother to ask why the old Harpur enemies are suddenly their friends, because they don't have to. Archy cracks his knuckles, a habit he's acquired since their return to Little Ridge.

Thettie claps her hands together, spraying bone, and tells them how proud she is, what good boys they are. Smart as whips. Wait for night, she whispers. Then you'll see Doc as he is. The soft minced meat perfect for a man with half a mouth. What Thettie wouldn't do for a slice of pizza right now. Lee has pizza. He keeps it frozen in his little refrigerator where the hamburger used to be. He keeps it for Vernon, for when he comes home.

Doc is so proud of the way he arranged the trailer afterward to cover his tracks, make it look like she hacked herself with this broken bottle, that steak knife—that he can barely stop himself from telling the whole world what a cutter she was. Oh, the irony! Oh, the *faux pas*.

Homer and Lyle flank Doc. Thettie leans in

between the boys and hisses: 'Why would I need to be a cutter, Doc? How could you make such a *faux pas*? Why, if you were a real Harpur, you know that I had as much jimsonweed, water hemlock and what have you in Sarey's greenhouse to kill myself ten times over, and don't think I didn't think about it, you prick. Don't think I didn't sometimes ask myself if it would be the right thing to do, especially after you came along. The unselfish thing to do for my boys. Set them free once and for all.'

And Thettie remembers how it was the slipperiness of the question that in the end made her stop trying to find the answer. And that's the truth, Doc. She crawls back to her trailer, alone and unheard, slinks up onto the roof. She can smell Doc's hubris from here, can feel it in her entangled network, and measure the possibilities it opens up.

Because the truth is even stranger than Doc's fiction. What crawled out of the misplaced Steelers' bag was Vernon *and* it wasn't. When Vernon crawled out, another crawled out to meet him through a door opened in the sea of possibility.

And in forgetting how to live, it made her forget how to die.

36. HABIB, INTERRUPTED

'**So it was** Ginsberg, by the way, not Hendrix who said that thing about the trip.'

The Professor's eyes droop at the corners, and Lee thinks he should probably go home now.

'Doc Murphy might come looking for you, Sam, if word gets out that you have any Helotide. Get rid of it is my advice, and go on a long vacation.'

Habib laughs weakly. 'I hope he does. I'd swap some of that lizard spit I've got in the freezer downstairs for some good old fashioned morphine any day.'

'Is the pain that bad?'

'It's what it is, my friend.'

Habib asks him again about seeing Doc and Jason talking at the Way on that first Sunday. The three of them—Doc and his boys. Lee is in the process of repeating it when he stops.

'Her sons found a tooth on the floor, Sam. Vernon's . . .'

Habib nods with eyes half closed. 'I didn't hear it from you.'

'I promised I wouldn't tell anyone. I think Jason's behind it somehow. I know you're fond . . .'

That hairy shoulder-shrug again. 'My immediate guess would be that Doc—I can't imagine who else— talked or threatened him into doing it and then the boy got scared and ran off.'

Again, Lee recalls the mulcher and the cleanly wiped-down ax dancing in Uncle Fie's hand, but decides that Habib is hurting enough without these speculations to add to his suffering. 'Doc? For the Helotide?'

'Why else?' Habib coughs weakly. 'As leverage over the deGroots and in case Frankie proved problematic. Or the island did.'

'It wouldn't be the first time.'

Habib reaches for a T-shirt slung over the telescope and puts it on without undoing the strap around his arm.

'But even if Vernon . . . I mean those injuries you were telling me about, Sam. Even with Thettie passed out on booze and sleeping pills, and even if she couldn't have inflicted them on herself, Vernon isn't . . . wasn't . . . none of it makes any sense.'

Habib kicks at a knot in the rug. 'Just because it seems unlikely, an attack of some kind isn't out of the question. Sense or not, you're the expert. All that stuff about the left side of her body and the lacerations and so on. We both know that provoked, the Gila *will* attack, especially a genetically modified lab animal. Vernon is bigger than a Gila in the wild, stronger, and smarter, too. If she was high enough, or scared enough, she could have reacted violently. Causing him to attack in self-defense. Just look at these bad boys.'

They both stare at the footage of Vernon and Meatloaf, wrestling each other to death. 'Or someone could have, I don't know. Sicced him on her, perhaps Some kind of torture or ritual, god forbid. He wouldn't be able to let go. He wouldn't know how.'

'Sam. Genetically modified or not, we're talking about an eighteen-inch lizard on borrowed time. He may have hurt her badly, but not enough to kill her without giving her a fighting chance of getting off the bed and calling for help. That's not what did it. Not on its own.'

'What if he scared her to death?' Habib's Brillo-pad hair crackles and his gaze is unwavering and alert again. 'You can't always defend the ones you love, Lee. Vernon was . . . is . . . a wild animal, whatever you may want, or not want, to imagine.'

'Imagine,' Lee's tongue feels thick, his brain vertiginously blank. 'Imagine some kind of hybridization with the exchange of fluids, some kind of symbiosis between Thettie and Vernon—fueled maybe, by fear, maybe by something else. But something that changed him as much as it changed her. Some kind of killer mix?'

There was a sudden silence, like even the lizards were holding their breath.

'You're talking about a chimera?'

Lee's son loved to draw monsters. He could have been an artist. Lee would have tried to dissuade him from science. He could have met a girl. Or a boy. Could have had children of his own. Taught them to be kind to animals.

Habib fiddles with the syringe, rolling it back and forth. 'Where is she now?' he says gently. 'Your false hope.'

In the video, Vernon and Meatloaf resume their

battle. The Gilas would not deliberately kill each other, but they wouldn't stop until one was rendered too exhausted to continue. The ritual could last hours, even days. The female waited alone in her burrow in the dark to receive the winner. Often she waited in vain.

Lee feels Habib's on him gaze sharpen, like the scope of a gun. The older man gets up stiffly and goes to the filing cabinet and takes out a folder, rummages through it and passes Lee a clipping, tells him to read it later. Soot-colored circles ring Habib's eyes.

The doorbell rings.

'That'll be the pizza,' Habib says. 'They make a thin crust over at Henksville Napoli that's to die for.'

Lee pockets the clipping turns back to the footage where Vernon finally pants alone on a desert rock, his heart pushing against his sunset colored hide, bloody gashes across his snout. Meatloaf sprawled motionless in the sand.

And even if Habib were to ask, which he doesn't, Lee is not at all in the mood for pizza. He raises his hand in salute to the Gila Monsters.

Vernon: 1. Meatloaf: 0

37. LAKE MONSTER

ONE THING ABOUT Homer and Lyle. They seem haunted and skittish, all dressed up with no one to kill. They grumble and whisper to each other, shoot gastric looks at Archy and Grif. Like maybe what's left of their shrunken souls has had enough of making Doc look bigger than he really is. Thettie lunges at them from the low roof of the Bago, 'Remember Manila?' she whispers to Lyle. 'Those tropical nights? Those little girls?'

'You say something?' Lyle says.

Homer says, 'Did you?'

And then Homer has to get up and waddle into the trailer to jack off, remembering those Manila nights.

In life, she could bait anything that bit, and switch it, too.

Bait and switch. She will.

It's not easy to think clearly with nothing but the scream of memories in her head, and she knows she's running out of head space, but who knows how long she has? She shuffles back to the double-wide trailer that once seemed too big for her and is now a cage, getting smaller.

The bad weather keeps up for days. Doc paces up and down the shore, hatless in the rain. He sits under a tarp slung outside the Winnebago, consulting soggy maps. Once or twice he and his boys load up the Sundeck with their villainous pistols, head out to fire blindly at the island until the winds turn it around and they come back empty-handed yet again. Thettie watches Doc drink the green protein shakes Homer makes him, a little bit of that, a little bit of this. His own special mix of vitamins and powders. And that's when it hits her.

It takes a killer to make a killer mix.

She backs away from the cracked window of the trailer, gasping. How could she not have seen the sea of possibility? She brings a finger to her missing tooth, the gum slick with venom. Her finger comes away dripping thick black matter and Thettie can barely contain herself. She howls with laughter, has to slap a clawed hand to her mouth.

'Shuddup,' she gurgles. 'Shuddup, shuddup.'

The laugh cuts off at the sound of Grif and Archy heading off again on their rumbling rides. She dashes across and peers out between the net curtains of the kitchen window across the parking lot. The rest of the Harpurs have bought, borrowed or stolen rides, too—Clay and Joanie get a rusted-out Kawasaki. Randall gets himself a Nighthawk and a scooter for Granny V. Dirt bikes and ATVs give the parking lot the appearance of a State Fair, or a monster rally. Not a decent muffler amongst them. Sounding like lake farts. She blows a venomous raspberry in reply.

So, the days. Better to keep indoors by day, trapped in a rage of her own making, than to haunt the Village—hobbled and slavering like a dancing bear— asking questions no one can answer or even hear. She blows a phantom spit-bubble of time on her tongue and waits for night.

Because the night! By windblown starlight, Thettie is free to float across the rolling lawns of the campus, through restaurant kitchens and backyard swing sets. Down to the lakeshore, where she kneels in the shallows in an attempt to get clean, to wash the blood and the poison from her scales. To fix her face, her hair, and is able, with a mighty will, to at least push her tongue back behind the teeth exposed through black lips, and to pull her awkwardly dislocated arm back into place so that it's not so grotesquely out of true.

She halts, the blue water around her thighs webbed with squirmy black threads. Water and blood run from her nose, between her thighs. She slithers around on all fours. The light from Archy and Grif's trailer burns, maybe to ward something off. Are the boys watching? What do they see? The island behind her with its wordless secrets? Or something else? Something closer to home that should never be seen? Something unburied, washed up in the current or a tangle or mass of filth that's neither dead nor alive, lost or found?

Two figures emerge from Doc's little trailer at the end of the line—Homer and Lyle on permanent Charge of Quarters. Homer's bulk and Lyle's twisted prissy frame. She sniffs the cold steel of the curved blades they conceal in their ankle belts and the oil from the guns stuck in their ass cracks. She inhales deeply and squats in the dirty water, her bloody torn nightgown swirling around her. They're Doc's ears and eyes but they don't see her.

One of the Grif's favorite books was *The Cat in the*

Hat. There is a scene where the Cat, in a desperate bid for attention, tries to balance all these crazy things on his head and shoulders—a fishbowl, an umbrella, a toy boat, a book, a cake—while running in place on a spinning rubber ball.

'Look at me, look at me, look at me, now!' crows the Cat in the Hat.

He stacks up more and more junk, spinning faster and faster in place on the rubber ball. And in the end, the juggle is too complicated and the burden unmanageable for the false pride of the Cat—causing him to overbalance and fall.

But before his fall, the Cat was the shit.

So Doc's false eyes don't see her yet for looking, but they will.

For it occurs to Thettie that she is the lake monster now. There has never been another.

38. DARK MATTER

ON **THE WAY** home from Habib's villa, Lee sees Archy and Grif buying Halloween costumes at the drug store—a sheriff's hat and star for Archy, and a farmer's pitchfork and dungarees for Grif. A child's Spiderman suit hangs in the window. Sometime later, Lee wakes up on the floor of the studio. He pushes himself to a sitting position beside the yellow Tonka truck and gets out the clipping Habib gave him:

> *November 3, 1986.*
>
> *A farmer is in the hospital after having been run off the road by a man driving a blue 1978 Pontiac. Piet DeGroot of Little Ridge suffered minor injuries after Frances George Washington Harpur allegedly tried to run his Ford truck off the Interstate. Earlier in the month Mr. Harpur filed a report to the Sheriff's office about an alleged assault on his cousins, Thetis Harpur and Cassandra Tully, in a room at the Motel 6 on the south end of Main Street. Mr. Harpur alleged that the girls were drugged and repeatedly assaulted in a motel room rented out in Mr. deGroot's brother's name, after the girls were allegedly*

caught attempting to use a credit card belonging to the brother, Fie deGroot, to purchase groceries and alcohol. No charges were laid.

Lee crumples the clipping onto the floor. He steps outside the studio and slips on a puddle of black goo at the threshold. There is more ahead, on the path down to the lake. He bends down and touches it, inhales its musk. He lowers himself into a crouch and for some reason, he peers up at the sky. More of the slime is spattered on a leaf, and quivers on the tips of the long grass. Further along it, the same matter quivers, tar-colored but with the consistency of mercury, between the roots of the big maple, and drips off a corner of the rope swing. He haltingly follows the trail of the black matter down to the shore. It is smeared over every inch of the rocky beach, like an oil slick. It smells aquatic but half-digested too—feels velvety between his fingers, and gritty. There is something voluptuous about it, both liquid and metallic, unseemly and comforting. His heart pounds. He feels nauseous and aroused. He pulls off his shirt. Struggles out of his jeans. He sinks to his knees, naked on the freezing shore, and draws his hands across the sticky, scaly slime. He uncoils like a serpent, drags himself along the black slick. He rolls on his back, feels the slime in his ass crack. Rubs the shadowy ooze through his hair and on his face and then his neck, all up his arms and ankles, too, covering himself with the goo of his chimera, all that is left of his false hope.

He goes back up the slope, pulling on his glasses and his clothes, and gets in the car, his face still smeared with black. He drives slowly down Main Street, stopping frequently to take down all the Xeroxed pictures of Vernon from power poles and mailboxes. The colors on the fliers have bled and faded beyond salvaging, so that Vernon looks fraudulent and obscene. Lee takes down the fliers because if Lee no longer recognizes Vernon in them, then neither could anyone, including Vernon himself.

Lee goes into the post office and people stare at him removing the fliers from the community notice board with his black-smeared fingers. The whites of his eyes stare back at him from store windows. He goes to the college and the co-eds smirk at what they think is an old Goth with black make-up, ripping down posters. He goes to the campground and pushes past what's left of the surly Harpur teens to take down the picture the girl put up at the rental office. In the reflection of the rental notice board, his glasses seem to float on a faceless mask of dark matter.

For the flier, he'd used the picture he had on his phone, the one he tried to show Thettie, of Vernon eating pizza. He'd meant to thank her for telling him about pizza being a cure for everything, because it certainly seemed to have cured Vernon. He'd used the picture because it was the most recent one. Lee had figured that would be the easiest way for people to recognize the Gila monster, because the thing with the missing is that people don't always know what they're looking for.

39. DAMAGE

'**F**RANKIE WAS THE key to her heart, lads, and she to his. I knew that from Day One. The minute I saw her face on Frankie's computer Over There, the first thing I says, says I no matter what, I was going to bring that boy back to her alive . . .' He holds a hammy hand to his heart.

Inside her double-wide cage, which functions at times like a giant amplifier, Thettie claps two hands over her lizard ears and flicks her tongue at the ferrous air. *What's up, Doc?*

'Strange,' Grif says. 'How a trained engineer like Uncle Frankie gets called to a bomb threat just so he could be the one blown to kingdom come.'

'Ironic,' Archy's pupils are pinpricks. Grif spits tobacco juice onto the planks of the jetty and continues to work on a broken spinner.

'I was a mite unprepared, even so,' Doc goes on, 'for how she and Frankie were so tight. Trotting off into the woods together like a couple of fairies to collect their damn flowers and herbs. Frankie strumming on that damn guitar. All that caterwauling.'

Unfair, Thettie thinks. Frankie had perfect pitch.

'And when she wasn't with him—she was fussin' over you two.' The strain is showing in Doc's rising registers, the slippery brogue betraying the undecidability of his origins. Homer and Lyle stand a way behind him, blocking Thettie from her boys. 'Except where was she, or Frankie, when you two went down into the drink? That was me, lads, Johnny on the spot as usual. If it weren't for me . . . well, we're family now. A life for a life.'

'I don't remember much about that,' Archy says with a shrug. 'Ma never talked about it.'

Doc smacks his half-lips. 'Well she wouldn't, would she? Blames herself, poor lamb? Even though I told her it coulda happened to anyone. That old cow Sarey has a lot to answer for, you ask me.'

But no one is.

Doc frowns. 'You'd think it was your own sister the way you cried over that mutt, Scrap.'

'Scrappy,' Archy says coldly, his rage honed on grief. 'Those pills you gave Ma when she decided to go clean—what were they? They made her like a vegetable, is what I remember. We thought salmon was the answer, remember, Grif?'

'Shhhhh,' Thettie hisses. Archy looks over to the trailer. Grif tries to warn his brother into silence with his eyes. They've come too far to show their hand now.

'Ah. You're going back a while though,' Doc grows thoughtful. 'Coulda been Haloperidol, carried around from my Psych. ward days before the army. A good anti-psychotic in a pinch. And your ma, she was in quite a pinch. It's one thing to want to go clean, I says, but baby steps for a baby, says I. She wasn't cut out for the whole cold-turkey hijinks. Some are and some aren't. No point getting yourself all strung out—you'll be no good to anyone, I says. Know your limitations, says I. Back in Dublin, we always used to call Haldol, 'mothers little helper."

'I thought that was gin.' Archy lowers sunglasses over his eyes. 'And I thought it was Liverpool.'

'Enough, Arch,' Grif says.

'You two are all I have now,' Doc blinks tears from his twin-cam eyes. 'Until we can get to Frankie. Least we can do is bring him home for Sarey.'

'What about them? Thing 1 and Thing 2?' Archy wipes his nose on his sleeve. 'They family, too, now?'

Lyle bares what's left of his teeth, and Homer picks his nose. From the trailer, where she waits for night, Thettie vomits black feathers, and bangs at the door locked from the outside. She wishes she knew what her purpose was, like the blind bus driver said. Her boys seem to have found theirs—to discover the truth about her death, but Thettie wonders if they're asking the right questions. It's not the truth behind her death they need to know, it's the lies about her life.

Frankie and Cassie had to read this book in junior high called, *Metamorphosis*. All Frankie kept saying all summer long, was, 'You think you're a cockroach, you're a cockroach,' until Cassie said that if he didn't stop talking about cockroaches she'd exterminate him herself. Frankie laughed but Thettie didn't, not because it wasn't funny but because she took Frankie to mean that choice was an illusion and self-defense nothing but a lie.

***

From the crypt where she waits alone and self-forgotten, Thettie watches her sons go through the rituals of remembering her, and in the process, she begins to forget herself. She bangs around the trailer looking for a key to the door, hidden beneath the black smear of scales on the mattress and the smell of venom in her hair. Doc had the trailer cleaned, of course, because that's what he is, a Cleaner. She titters, which comes out like a hiss, at how he whined about having to return to petty gangstering when they moved down to Pennsy—nothing but pit-men and pimps, complained Daylin 'What's Up' Murphy, Cleaner to the Fallen Stars.

Over and over again, from her hiding place in a dark cupboard, she replays the clean-up, the scattering of false evidence. She watches her body, lifeless in its bare-assed humiliation and feels hands over her, hands where the sun don't shine. Arranging and rearranging her meat blanket, Homer copping a feel while no one's looking, surprise surprise, that ain't your finger, Homer.

Doc, shocked that the lizard he stole for its venom could pack such a punch, dispatches Lyle off to find it, while Homer makes a mess of the kitchen drawers to look like messed-up Thettie was looking for something to cut herself with. Because if anyone suspects her death was from a razor-toothed lizard, then questions will be asked that lead back to Doc. Thettie screeches with delight at Doc's *faux pas*, what Frankie would have called a comedy of errors.

'It was you Frankie, wasn't it? I hope you didn't hurt that damn lizard.'

Because if this is a comedy, then Doc is the joke and all that is needed is the wascally wabbit. But Frankie was always kind to animals, and they were kind to him in return.

***

'What's up, Doc?' Thettie laughs her ass off at Doc and his bodyguards talking about how they must have underestimated the lizard's strength.

'Do you think it had superpowers Doc? From what they did to it in the lab?'

'What? Like Godzilla? The Creature from the Black Lagoon? Don't be daft, fatso.'

But Homer's not being daft at all, and Lyle doesn't like it when Doc calls Homer fat.

Thettie laughs till she cries. Oh, the irony!

Doc explains how he prefers to think of Vernon as a cute witty bitty wizard genetically modified to be a killer in its own right—imagine the possibilities! He sends Homer and Lyle out repeatedly to search for the runaway monster. Thettie flips over on her back and waves her clawed feet in hysterical hissing mirth. She freezes at the sound of a guitar, her nightgown up over her head.

'Frankie?'

Management says the trailer is haunted. Thettie tears a curtain from a window and drapes it over her head, hurls a chair against the glass but it just bounces off. Management say they'll never be able to rent it again, not some trailer someone's killed themselves in. They contact HauntedNY.com to arrange tours in the off-season.

'Tour *this*,' Thettie exhales a gritty plume that shreds her throat on exit.

The lake effect squalls continue and she rushes down to the shore to look for something she can use to lure Homer and Lyle away from Doc. Give him a taste of his own medicine. Constrained as ever by the weight of her bear chain, she lumbers out to Doc's boat and empties the tank, slashes the rubber on someone's inflatables, jams the motors of a couple of trollers. She leaves Archy and Grif's boats untouched, and Doc seethes. He duly sends Homer and Lyle to take it up with them, which results in a scuffle, causing another visit from Sheriff Boyle. It's a start but doesn't buy her enough time. Halloween any day now. Whole thing's over in a week. Not enough time for her sons to see the undisclosed truth before Thettie herself runs out of memory, because as much as Vernon gave her—too much is never enough.

It hits her then, what her purpose is, and she sinks to her bleeding knees, weeping to have found it. Her purpose is to re-member a new path into the forest, a way to enter it on a whole new footing.

One night, the rain lifts on the lake like a curtain. She can see Frankie going back and forth on his tracks in and out of the small but dense woods over on the island. Lee and Bryce are out on the lake, too. Bryce points to Frankie, but Lee can't see him yet. All Lee can see is some other shade that walks those paths. Unforgotten and alone.

***

Doc has a word with Homer and Lyle, tells them to play nice until he can get Archy and Grif to lure Frankie from the island. Then the boys are theirs. He brings her sons favors. Women for Grif one day, whisky for Archy the next. He buys Archy a cheap cell phone and a new set of ear buds. The brothers argue about it. About whether to take Doc's favors or whether to throw them back in his face. About which would be more believable to him, and if it matters.

No one but Thettie can see Grif wipe the rough

tears from his eyes. 'Well we better get to work. These muskies ain't going to fish themselves, and Avery's offering five bucks a pound.'

Archy cracks his knuckles. Frankie's got the killer mix, he tells Grif. The new drug that's going to make them all rich. Just need to get to the island, Doc or no Doc. Frankie'll be wondering what's keeping them.

'Them dogs are a problem for Doc,' Archy says. 'Until he can shoot them or poison them or both, and I can't see that big old Indian letting that happen. He promised to take us to Frankie.'

Thettie watches and listens from her window, chewing on her hand. Archy and Grif know time is running thin before Doc stops playing nice, and forces them to choose between Frankie and Sarey.

'Keg, Crab?' Grif's eyes glitter, the color of hell at its coldest. 'That big motherfucker we saw the first day?'

'Kreb,' Thettie hisses.

'There has to be a way past Homer and Lyle,' Archy says. 'We get to Frankie, we're set for life. Doc says everything Frankie has, or had, if he's dead, will go to us now.'

Grif, 6 foot 5, takes his brother, 6 foot 6, by the throat, lifts him up over the edge of the jetty and swings him above the water. Emilio and Dustin step out from the shadows of the cabins by the shore and inch forward, stop at a discrete distance. 'You dicking fucktard! You think Doc doesn't know how to find a way around that? Everything that's ours, including our own ma, he's taken. Everything! You think he'll stop now?'

Grif swings his brother back onto the jetty, takes

him into his arms and the two men hold onto each other, swaying and crying.

'I don't care anymore,' Archy sobs. 'I just want it to be over.'

'Shhhh,' Grif whispers into Archy's filthy hair, so only Thettie can hear. 'We can't make a move without risking Sarey.'

Sarey!

In her worry over her sons, Thettie has forgotten Sarey.

***

She waits for night. Under cover of the lake's pale phosphorescence, Thettie heads down the rocky shore. After half a mile, she turns up into the dark mouth of the creek. She goes up a way, leaving a trail of obsidian scales to light her way back, and throws herself onto a floating branch to take her across to the other side. She crawls up the bank commando-style, dripping, and approaches the old settlement. There is a car parked on the switchback that she doesn't recognize— someone Doc instructed Lyle to hire to keep guard over Sarey.

Sarey's house is unlit and two of Sarey's dogs—a Shepherd descendent of Scraps and the white mastiff who chased them off the property—lie in dark puddles of blood in the yard. The Shepherd lies in a spray of his own innards, and the mastiff's head hangs by a knot of messily severed tendons. Thettie inches closer. Sarey digs in the dirt, with her one remaining dog, a liver-colored bitch on point. The dirt flies as she makes a grave for the shepherd and the mastiff. Thettie sniffs. The liver bitch is pregnant. She inches closer. The pointer pulls her lip back at Thettie and growls low in her throat.

Thettie's claws grip into the soft riverbank. She nears the dead albino. Sarey's shovel scraps and sprays the cold black earth all way over to Thettie. Dirt rains down on her hair and into her eyes. She inches closer.

The dead dog opens her eye. It's a human eye. It blinks at Thettie and Thettie stares back. Someone took to the dog's head—while another hogtied her to a tree, must have—with a rough blade, severing her esophagus and trachea, stopping just before they got to her spinal column. Thettie strokes the already cooling white head. She puts a finger to the breathless muzzle, sees that the blood oozing from the yellow fangs has stilled. The dog will never bark again, but Thettie checks to make sure the spinal column is untouched, and when she is satisfied, she leans across and whispers into the blood-caked ear, 'Wake up, bitch.'

And then Thettie bites. Not hard, but a good sharp nip right on the dog's pink muzzle, more like a kiss than a bite. She doesn't hang around long enough to find out what she made.

***

Back in the cabin, time passes strangely, like the dreams of the living. Hours pass in the blink of an eye or stretch over days, made endless by panic. She could use a Xanax, like the old days. But Xanax is the wrong poison now. Time shrinks to seconds in paranoia. She could use a drink. In a cold sweat in the dark on the funky mattress on which she died, she feels the walls cut away, float off like shards of glass in a wreck, then come flying back in and cut like shrapnel.

The poison is the key. It's inside her now, makes her relive the monster's attack again and again. The horror of it frozen forever in a drop of blood that will never fall. She is trapped in a snow globe except the snow is black and the sky is red. Her materiality comes and goes with the tide, her movements shunt ahead in fast forward, or drag in slo-mo depending on the current of time. There is, before her death, the fact of the lizard, who Doc paid Jason-the-lizard-rescuer to steal and stow in his backpack. Vernon was to be insurance, should Frankie be uncooperative or already dead, instead of about to be. But anyway, there is the lizard who Doc paid Homer and Lyle to steal back from Jason who in turn they killed as a freebie to win over the deGroots. The lizard-in-a-backpack ends up in Doc's original trailer but has already crawled out and under the bed by the time she and Doc switch trailers. What did it want? For what was it unnaturally impelled to wait?

Or who?

The night. Because what came out of the lake was bigger than night. Bigger than a Gila Monster, meaner than false pride and hungrier than false hope. It came through the door unlocked by the Harpur return, and opened by the return of another.

Because want is the key.

After dark, she is finally free to roam. She drifts down to the dock and peers out across the hidden currents to look for the island. Sometimes it is nothing but a null space in the water, like those dark patches in the night sky from where even the stars themselves flee—dark matter where nothing can grow. Other times she can see it clearly, a luminous hunk of rock and scrub that sits like a scar on the dream of night. Frankie limps from the canal-era lighthouse where he sleeps, to his poles off the reef and then to his traps at the end of the path in the woods. There is a small shack off another path, lined with shelves from which she catches the gleam of bottle and beaker, the flap of scrawled note books. But she can't make out what is on the shelves, because when he goes in, he closes the door behind him.

Ghost dogs skulk. They dig black holes through which meaning has fallen. When Frankie comes out of the shack, they follow him again. And there are others. Stony old-timers, mixed bloods and moonshiners, who pass him on the path, and another, too. A familiar figure who, because it is night, is barely discernible, and its name is on the tip of Thettie's tongue, if only she could remember. Small and broken, it follows Frankie, holding a lantern, or sometimes meanders ahead, maybe looking for something. Thettie sees what the lantern-bearer sees, how Frankie uses a rusty hospital crutch to help him walk. When the lantern-bearer gets near enough to him, Thettie can see that Frankie is emaciated, just skin and bone with his bald scalp all crawling with critters. His teeth are black, many of them missing. He knows where all the traps are, even those that aren't his, and all the lines and can find them in the dark. He has mapped out their location using mnemonic tricks he taught himself from drinking from the springs that flow on the island, a spring to remember, and another to forget. Where he has not visited a trap for some time, scrub grows over the path, and he must hack through it. Where water has risen in a black pool where he has left a pole, he must wade through the ooze, up to his neck in it before he can return to the path.

He always returns to the path.

40. SEE-SAW

SHE SITS ON the see-saw beside the house. At first, and in this context, she looks like his son. His heart gives a sickening jolt, and he is filled with false hope.

He starts to say her name but stops himself, shocked at her appearance. In a strange way, she looks even more altered by Thettie's death than either Archy or Grif, and it's not just that she has attached herself to him, that they have become friends, at least by day. The bruises under her eyes are stark against her pale face. Her cinnamon colored hair tangles around the paint-smeared elastic of the eye patch. It's hard to believe that she is the same person, now, as the smokin' jailbait who burst into town with the Harpurs almost a month ago. But even more than her appearance, it is her manner that has changed. Moody and secretive one moment, willful and infantile the next.

There is an old blue jay who remained on the property after the Classics family moved away—partly because of a bird-feeder Habib helped Lee's son to build. The feeder blew down in a storm, but the blue jay stayed and has taken a shine to the girl. It waits for her to come, and follows her around when she does, hopping from branch to branch. It waits anxiously on the grass when she's inside the studio, flapping right up to the windows to check on her. Perched now on the rusted play set, the jay looks down on Lee with suspicion.

The girl pushes herself back and forth on the groaning swings. 'Sounds like a mule,' she says. 'See saw, see saw.'

The blue jay ruffles his wings.

'I guess I should sell it,' Lee says. 'No one plays on it anymore.'

He takes his hand away and it's covered with rust. He wipes it on his jeans and pulls down on the high side of the see-saw and she rises in the air, her long legs dangling. Her Goodwill jeans flap and he can see bruises on her skinny white ankles.

'I do.' She kicks her legs back and forth, suspended high on the see-saw against a background of black branches.

The old-fashioned metal swing set and teeter-totter had come with the property and his wife didn't like their son playing on it. It was almost rusted through, an eyesore that Lee had promised to replace with a bright plastic backboard and a hoop they picked out of a catalogue. She told the police that she'd been packing the picnic basket, when she heard the squeak of the rusted swing. She had peered out the kitchen window to see the child on it, and tapped on the glass to get him down. When he didn't seem to hear, she quickly dropped the thermos in the basket, buckled it closed and went around the back of the house to call him for supper. But he was gone.

Lee lets the girl down slowly. She scrambles off and

does a little vertical jump about two feet in front of his face. He blinks awkwardly at her through his smeared glasses. She laughs. They skirt the pet cemetery, which Lee has not had time to repair since Jason DeGroot (probably) trampled it to get to Vernon.

They enter the sparse woods. She seems shorter and walks with an uneven gait, sometimes colliding with his arm or coming up against his heels. The old schoolhouse is indistinct through the dark branches that spread as if to shield it from intruders. She asks him about it.

'Peachtree Public School.'

'Peachtree?'

She repeats the word, collecting it—or retrieving it maybe—from another conversation.

'Like peach trees,' he says. 'The fruit. So, revolutionary soldiers burnt all the indigenous orchards to the ground when they destroyed the villages across the state.'

'Peach trees.' She stops to take in the pitched roof, the gothic revival gables. Her chafed wrists, between her too-short sleeves and her fingerless gloves, are encircled with bruises, not new but not quite faded. Lee silently mouths her name and extends a finger to touch the inside of one wrist, and she jumps as if bitten.

'So, all this land belonged to the Six Nations people,' he says quickly. 'After the war, George Washington divided it up into tracts for the soldiers as compensation.'

'Huh?'

'Payment for helping him win the war.'

'And the island?' She points to a spot just behind the headland.

'Supposedly it's an ancient burial ground. There used to be a lighthouse there. Old timers described its faint blue light. The army, and the settlers used it as a potter's field. Veterans, Dutch orphans, suicides, infanticides, drowned runaways and fisherman, slaves, Spanish Flu deaths, gangsters. Anyone without a marker.'

She bends down to pick up a yellow elm leaf. Watches a small spider creep across it. Because of the rains and their exposed position on the headland, most of the trees in the little woods have already lost their leaves and the black branches are a tangle across the sunless sky.

'What's a marker?'

They stop at the point where it is possible to see the currents swirl around the warning beacons, the island itself hidden as always in fog. Lee begins to hanker for a beer at lunchtime, sometimes earlier. It's almost four o'clock in the afternoon now, and he is as spaced-out as a monkey. They turn around and continue their dance, he and the girl, down the path toward the warmth of the studio.

'A marker is something to place over a grave, like a stone. It usually has the person's name on it.'

'Oh that. Frankie says it's called a stele.'

Lee stops in the path and turns to her, his legs going cold. 'Frankie said that?'

She keeps walking. 'He says grave stones need a grave and graves need remains. He says the island is for lost remains who don't know what they are.' She seems to think about that for a moment. 'Some of them live in the caves. There are a gazillion caves.'

'Under the water?' Lee begins to shake. He knows

about these—the island itself caused by a ragged eruption from the original glacial flow, riddled with air-bubbles that solidified into a porous subterranean base.

She adjusts her eye patch. 'Franke says that under the water is something else.'

The path narrows, squeezing him into single file far behind the girl, and Lee thinks he might vomit.

'If Frankie knows so much,' he yells. 'Does he know they're back? Have you told him?'

Her voice rises. 'I don't want to go back there.'

'Okay, okay. But Frankie—is he sick? I mean that's his goddam manor over there. His own family are sleeping in trailers with winter around the corner and there's twenty-six rooms sitting empty.'

Lee knows these questions are useless. He tries to picture Frankie out on the island with the dogs that never to die, an unending supply of bones from the hunt.

'Why doesn't Frankie come home? His family need him. You need to tell him.'

'I don't want to. I want to stay with you.'

He feels out of breath, can smell the booze in his sweat. 'Me? Why me?'

She turns to let him catch up and a grimy tear snakes from beneath her patch.

***

It is another day or another hour and they are on a different path in the woods. She points down the slope to the Frankie's manor and asks him about the Zabriskies.

'So when we first got to Little Ridge, we went to a lot of faculty parties, seminars, book launches and the like.

But the Zabriskies had an exclusive cocktail party every Christmas, invitation only. The Christmas before our son was taken, the Zabriskies invited us. We didn't really want to go. It wasn't really our scene. But Habib insisted. Said it would be good for us. He even came up with a babysitter, some student of his. So off we went. The party was famous partly for being a drag, and partly for Mrs. Z's fruitcake. She spent half the year baking them for local organizations, fund raisers, charities, and so on. Each baked with one silver dollar inside. But she saved a special cake for this annual party.'

'What made it special?'

She may not have gone to high-school, but Lee admires the girl's hunger for detail. 'I don't exactly know what made it special—maybe it was a more expensive rum than she used in the other cakes. You could smell it the moment you walked in, or I could. She brought it out for dessert, served with special clotted cream from her very own cow—the cow's name was Eleanor, by the way—and some lucky guest would always get the dollar.'

'They could keep it?'

'Well,' Lee's face grows hot—he hasn't spoken about these things to anyone. 'They had to earn it. Sing a song or recite a poem or even do a dance—Sam Habib did a belly-dance one year, I believe. So anyway, I spent most of the evening in a sweat that neither of us would get the dollar.'

'But *you* did.'

'Right.'

'And you didn't have anything to sing?'

'Actually, I did,' Lee says. 'My wife helped me on the Zabriskie's baby grand. We sang 'Bat Out of Hell.''

Lee pounds out the chords on an air-piano. 'She was a hell of a musician, for a biochemist, I mean.'

'I love that song,' the girl says.

'Really? That song is older than you are.'

She laughs and plays her air-guitar and they sing the chorus, but Lee stops so that he won't cry. At AA, someone always blubbed.

'My wife and I were in a band at college with some other guys. Science nerds. They were all in love with her.'

'But you married her.'

Lee sniffs and pushes his glasses back on.

'And did you give her a marker when she died?'

Behind the hard tangle of branches, the sun looks to have soiled itself on its descent. Half of the girl's face as she turns to him is fire, half is ice.

'I wanted to bury her in the woods. That was her favorite place. But her family wanted her in the Catholic cemetery. They chose the marker.'

'What did you do with the silver dollar?'

'I gave it to my kid. He kept it in his pocket but they never found it.'

'Did you give him a marker?'

Lee shakes his head. 'Not yet. I have to find him first.'

'I'm cold,' her mouth is blue around the edges.

They have strayed from the path and are now up against a fallen tree, black and shroomy with time. The wild flowers mass hip high around the giant trunk and slender new saplings are already growing up around it. She stops to rest but Lee steps back onto the path that leads out of the woods.

He hears her footsteps following him but when he gets to the studio she is already there. She was always already there.

41. CRYSTAL

LEE STOOD AT the window. From the bed, he looked to Thettie carved from marble or ice, like a statue.

'Why don't you say his name?' she whispered. 'It could help.'

Lee's breath steamed up the window. He didn't turn his head. 'I haven't spoken his name in five years.'

'Does he say yours?'

'I hear him, sometimes. I used to go running to where the sound was, like the bathroom, or his bedroom—that's why I moved out of the house. Or I'd turn in the cereal aisle at the supermarket, hear him saying that was the one he wanted, or stop in the woods when I heard him wanting to show me something. One of those red spiders on a leaf, or a double acorn or a snake ball or arrowhead—we found a couple in one of the streams behind the schoolhouse. Or . . . or he'd call me from the club house, hey! Hey dad! But when I'd get to wherever I went running when he called, there was no one there.'

'So now? When he calls, what do you do?'

'I just keep walking.'

***

From the edges of the windows, in the crawlspace and

on the branch-swept roof above the trailer, Thettie watches Doc as he steps out of the little 'Bago and snaps the door shut behind him. His close-set eyes are as wary as ever but now sunk into deep pouches. Instead of a war hero, he looks like what he really is— back-room abortionist with his jailhouse stink and the shiny patchwork scars across his body where the burns sizzled hottest. He checks the sky and confers with Homer and Lyle, checks the provisions to lug out onto the Sundeck rocking on the lake. Yells for Archy and Grif. Homer and Lyle face outward, always at his flank, or front-and-follow. One ahead and the other behind. They can't see her, but they can sense her tapping at the wall of fear they've erected around Doc. One she can't break through until there is another transmission. Another signal along the forest path. Something more than the tooth. Something neither particle nor wave.

So, she rocks and she waits. And on the horizon, silently counting down the days that remain of this bitter contest over her soul and that of her family, the island blinks in and out of focus, on and off. Her disfigurements heal and she shifts into more of herself. Less broken and leaking. Sleeker and harder and lower to the ground. But how long before the mnemonic effects of the Helotide wear off also, and leave her lost and alone with nothing and no one but her own unfinished business?

The weather changes, too, and earlier than predicted. Today's expedition to the island returns barely ahead of the storm and Homer and Lyle stand at a distance while Archy and Doc and Grif debrief. They talk about the dogs they hear baying from the island's inaccessible shores. There were the usual gun shots and a charge that exploded in the water not fifty yards in front of them. After a while Doc and his men walk away and Archy takes his brother's arm. 'We need to tell Frankie about Ma,' he stops and starts again. 'Doc or no Doc, he needs to know.'

'How?' says Grif, taking Archy's other arm so that they are dancing like two broken bears. 'Even if we could get there without Doc, even if every time we get near it the winds didn't blow us off course—Dustin fell overboard yesterday. Water's near freezing. I'm telling you. Even if we could get there, which Doc won't let us, something's stopping us. It's like the lake doesn't want us there.'

'Or maybe Frankie doesn't want us there. Ever think of that?'

Grif's mouth is so close to Archy's ear that it's practically touching, but Archy isn't listening. He's staring out across the lake over his brother's shoulder.

'Goddammit?' he says. 'Where's it gone?'

It's then that Bryce steps out of her tiny trailer to greet Thettie's sons with a thermos. Thettie gnashes her teeth.

Grif drops his arm. 'Curvature of the earth or something, brother. Glacial-effect optics—I was reading about it. There are these lakes in New Zealand's South Island, glacial lakes as blue as the Aegean Sea, prehistoric ice particles or something suspended in them. You look across, you can't see the other side, even though it's just a couple miles away. All you can see is flat blue water goes on for miles.'

They both stand drinking coffee and staring across the lake. The breeze rifles the fuzz on Grif's long matted hair, and wafts the smell of Archy's unwashed pits to Thettie behind her veil.

A day later Doc's Sundeck pulls out again. Doc and his men arm themselves with rifles and hamburger meat laced with rat poison to catapult onto the island. Thettie shakes her head. The deGroots lend them devices to disarm the grenades and satchel charges. Thettie gnashes her teeth, spits out bone and gristle. The boat gets smaller as it rounds the bend and disappears.

They come back empty-handed, as usual. Doc, flanked by Homer and Lyle, explains the next day's plan to Archy and Grif. And the next. Long as it takes, boys. Doc's eyes are glassy. His brogue sounds shriller every day, so that it carries across the lake and toward the dark horizon, where the fleeing geese strain and pump against the weather. Raindrops quiver on the ridged leather shoulders of Grif's biker jacket, and he has one tattooed hand on his stomach, the other on Archy's shoulder, and Thettie can't tell, from her cage, who is leaning on who.

Thettie counts the tears that brim from Archy's eyes as he turns back to his chores. She numbers and categorizes them according to volume, to how fast they fall and how far. And when Archy turns to look over Grif's lethal shoulder, just as he did as a boy, to make sure his ma is still there, she smiles and she waves from behind the prison of another's making.

***

Bryce sleeps in a trailer further down the line, a tiny York, small as a kid's cubby-house. After dark, the little trailer glows. Thettie rocks and waits and counts the hours until night when she can see the glow, and can watch the watcher. Bryce, asleep, dreams in black and tangled memories, impossible to see the woods for the dark trees.

And unlike Thettie, the dreamer, Bryce, *can* roam by day, and by night, too. But after her shift at the Way, she is often just trapped dreamless in an endless night, or a dream of night. Her eye patch lies on the table beside her, because only her good eye can close in sleep. The other stares lidless and cursed for all time to light up the forest where it is always night. In the tangled, branching dark, a bulky shadow moves smelling of excrement and cum. Moving through the ubiquitous static (CQ, CQ, 6KSZ, you are 59, QSU), this bulky shadow, this materialized stink, approaches the mattress and insinuates itself into the watcher's memory. The watcher puts up a feeble struggle, but the stink works its way into her body and its memory, over and over again like a knife into a gash of its own making.

A noise from the jetty arrests Thettie in her midnight watch. Archy pulls out slowly in the Black Crown. She can see him in detail, although he is too far away for human perception. His once beautiful hair is unevenly hacked, his beard no longer patchy, but bushy and untrimmed. He pulls out slowly and quietly and Thettie, roused from her agitations, steps outside her trailer and watches from the jetty. He looks back once and waves and she waves with both hands. Look at me now!

The stars are shrouded in cloud, although it isn't raining quite yet, and the surface of the lake has the hard sheen of new coal. The little lights on Archy's boat, red and green, intermittently wink through the darkness, left and right—an exchange of information along the path. The lights dim as they approach the vicinity of island and she watches the boat toss in the currents, getting closer and closer to what appears to be a dark wrinkle on the fold of the night. The boat lurches and she extends a hand. It pulls to starboard and instead of approaching the island head-on, it circles it clockwise and then turns around and circles it again anti-clockwise. As it does the slow turn either in front or behind the dark slit of light, the green light of starboard is exchanged for the red light of port. He circles the island, around and around until an early rain begins to fall from the lightening sky.

Thettie scuttles off the jetty and crouches on the shore, her black claws glittering in the glacial night. She keeps one eye on the row of smaller trailers in which Bryce's York strobes on and off in the moonlight, and looks so small, like a clubhouse, or a kid's secret hideout. Thettie's other eye fixes on the clear horizon. Her nightgown drags in the shallows and crackles with dirty scales.

Archy returns mid-morning in the rain, his catch sloshing in pails. She rushes along the deck to greet him, only to find that Doc has beaten her to it and is waiting with whisky. Thettie knocks it out of his hand. Doc looks at his empty hand in disbelief. His face drains of color, his carefully manicured fingernails rank with dark and metallic-looking rot. She expands into this small success. Lyle and Homer mustn't have been concentrating. But they are now. They attribute the spilled whisky to Doc's nerves and their confidence in the whole enterprise takes another knock. Lyle taps his tattooed wrist—clocks a-ticking!

Thettie backs off, cringing and diminished once more.

***

'I couldn't get to it,' Archy says, clapping his hands together to warm them. 'I went up to where I saw it from the shore and I could see it ahead of me the whole time and then the current picked up and it was gone. I pulled out to circle the pylons and I could see it again, like it had been hiding behind the beacon or something—it's too bright when you get up to it, glares so you can't see anything.'

'The fog, lad,' Doc's voice is high and strained. 'And the glare. Here's a thought. Let's just satchel charge the whole damn rock. That'd serve the bastard right.'

But Bryce comes up behind them, makes them both start. Her eye patch is askew, she wields Thettie's thermos full of whisky-laced coffee.

'Frankie'd be mad,' she says casually. 'You don't want to make Frankie mad.'

Archy turns to her, his eyes filled with rage. 'Shut up, Bryce. Ma was right about you!'

'No!' Thettie bawls. 'I wasn't. I was wrong, all wrong!'

'There,' Bryce says, gamely pointing to the rain-pelted shores rising up like an atoll from the middle of the lake. 'Listen.'

Above them is an uninterrupted arrow of geese, and carried clear across the water, they can hear Frankie's rifle taking aim at the shore, the ferocious yelp of the dogs. Archy turns back to Bryce and pulls the thermos out of her hand.

'That's Ma's,' he says, turning away in shame. 'Five dollars from a garage sale in Bucksport. You can't brew joe for shit.'

She yells after him, 'I hate coffee! I want a Jamba Juice! Coffee tastes like barf!'

Thettie applauds Bryce's theatrics. But has Doc bought it?

Doc buttons his field jacket, and advances on Bryce in that puff-chested way he has. Like a leprechaun with a vacuum cleaner hose up his ass, Grif once said when he turned sixteen and thought Doc couldn't hurt him anymore. Homer and Lyle follow behind. He waves them back but just the sight of them strangles her anew in her own invisibility. A soggy moan burbles from her lips. Bryce's head swivels slowly in the direction of the sound.

'Bait,' she whispers.

'And switch,' Thettie whispers back, taking her place on Doc's blind side.

Doc drapes an arm around the girl.

'You losing weight, Shortie?'

It's true. Bryce seems to be shrinking.

'I've been thinking,' he says. 'Time running thin and all. Those boys at the end of their tether. Could be it's up to you and me, Shortie. Future belongs to the brave.'

'Archy and Griff will be mad,' Bryce and Thettie say it at the same time, and Doc looks up at the doubled sound of it, the familiar voice in the unfamiliar mouth, but his needs outweigh his doubt. Thettie and Bryce's fingers meet behind Doc. The exchange holding them together for a blink of an eye is enough for all time.

'I ever tell you what I was before I enlisted?' Doc begins. 'I was born in Dublin to a Baltimore whore and a bag man who worked for a numbers boss called Patrick Goldberg. Had a nose on him like a hook, so they called him Paddy the Hook. It sounded better than Paddy the Jew, which you could call him if you wanted to die. Our own da was a fool of a man. Thought he could bite the hand that fed him. One day Paddy invited him into a Bingo hall after hours to meet with a man called Haha, and our da never came out. Me waiting in the car. 'Look after your ma,' was the last thing he said. 'I'll be back in a jiff.'

Bryce rubs her nose raw and watches the rain falling on the spilled coffee.

'Anyways, Da never came out, but Paddy did and all, took me in like I was his own, put me through medical school, he did. I made something of myself in the firm. Started off as a saw bones. Then Cleaner—wondrous what a hacksaw and some hydrofluoric acid can do. In five years Paddy went from numbers to whores to smack, thanks to yours truly. We had half of the Merseyside bosses in our pockets, Paddy with a big spread in Woolton—me set up pretty as you please in the gatekeeper's cottage. Those were the days.'

'Hell yeah,' Homer says dully. He and Lyle have heard these lies a hundred times. Thettie leaves a swirl of ink in her wake and the black lake sucks at Doc's Oakleys. He points to the Island, drags his finger stump across the horizon and over to Frankie's big yellow mansion in the distance, with its pagoda ringed with weeds and its boathouses in need of a paint.

'That should have been me,' he said. 'That could have been me except I got saddled with Frankie's family. What could I do? With Frankie in jail it fell to me to take care of his kin. We were in the war together, you know that. That binds a man. *Semper Fi* blah-de-blah-blah. What kind of a mother's son would I be to let his people starve? And look where it got me.' He waves a patchwork hand at the sad flotilla, the few remaining Harpurs frying bread on the grilles behind the trailers. 'A long fucken way from Merseyside.'

'I'm lost, too, Doc.'

He turns and presses himself against her. Thettie kicks him in the back of the knee, makes him lurch and stumble in the black tideline. Homer and Lyle exchange looks, and Lyle jerks off the air.

'How's this for a plan, Shortie? You and me. We go in and get Frankie together. I'll make like it won't go easy on you if he doesn't. He'll fall for it. And then we split the profits. I take the manor house and island, you take the money.'

'You'll hurt me?'

'Course I won't hurt you. Do I look like I want to hurt you?' he wheedles.

Thettie's snicker turns into a howl of glee. She didn't see that coming, but she should have. Bait and switch, Frankie? *You* saw it. You were always too smart to live. Because men like Doc don't see what's in plain sight. They only see what they can do with it. They only see themselves. Frankie got that from day one.

Bryce digs a finger under her eye patch and scratches. 'What money?'

'You leave that to me, Shortie. Ain't I taken care of everything before? You'll see.'

'I don't know, Doc. Archy and Grif'll be mad.'

'You leave Archy and Grif to them,' Doc cocks his head and Homer and Lyle. 'What'll it take? Name your price, Shortie.'

'I want a new boat,' she says and Thettie dances up

and down the shore, around and around, clapping and laughing, and unfurling her forked tongue.

'All business now, aren't we? What's your pleasure, a wily young water-rat such as yourself? A nice new runabout, or bow rider with a little hold. A roof over your head, somewhere to drift safe and dry of a moonlit night on the water. Whadya say I throw in some fishing poles, brand new from Craigslist?

Bryce says, 'I want *your* boat, Doc.'

Doc steps carefully away from a slithering black tongue of water. Thettie jumps up and down to see over Lyle and Homer who have moved between her now, and all but shield Doc from her view.

'What's a little thing like you want with a boat the size of mine?' Doc spits the falsetto brogue out of his twisted mouth. 'You couldn't handle it. Pick another. Lyle has a great runabout. Something like Grif's? I could get you a nice little . . . '

'I like your boat. I want to live on it.'

'Christ on a crutch, Shortie. What the hell am I going to live on?'

Bryce looks confused. 'On the island, Doc. Isn't that what you want?'

***

Bryce has so completely distracted Doc that Archy and Grif manage to get away without some lower-echelon tail enlisted by Lyle. Archy turns back once and Thettie gimps awkwardly up and down on her toes. But he only has eyes for Bryce, who appears to be attending to some new bullshit plan of Doc's that involves getting Bryce through the dangerous water zone, then switching to a kayak to maneuver the currents at the rock walls.

ALETHEIA

Doc just loves the sound of his own voice, and always will. Give him a chance, Paddy would say, and Doc could spin the bark off the trees.

Doc's war story was this. The first time he met Frankie Harpur was April 1, 2002. He and another engineer called Bud Wallace were on the road from Kabul to Bagram where insurgents threatened to dismantle the rebuilding project.

Doc loves to describe Frankie emerging from the spiraling dust at the base at Bagram. Frankie offers them both a drink from a canteen that was always cold, Doc said, and the water tasted like heaven. Like liquid crystals.

Bud Wallace was also from Little Ridge in that first deployment to Afghanistan after 9/11, another one from the 443rd Engineer company out of Fort Drum. Doc considered Bud Wallace for a minder for when they returned to civilian life but Wallace's preference for children was an off-putting complication and would eventually lead to him being sent home.

'But hey,' Doc reminded Thettie, 'what goes down Over There stays Over There.'

Doc told Thettie that unlike Wallace, he could see that Frankie was a family man. He kept pictures of his nephews and his two cousins—Thettie and Cassie—on his computer. The girls could have been twins with their matching blue eyes and sensual mouths, but Cassie came with too much attitude for Doc— something about the red-tipped hair and black lipstick that was, to Doc at least, unsettlingly animalistic.

'Frankie talked to me about you all the time, girl, so that by the end of the tour, I almost felt I knew you.'

When Frankie was away from the base, Doc would

log onto Frankie's computer and just stare at Thettie with her Kool-Aid blue eyes and mouth neither smiling nor frowning. He'd stare and stare and the picture never stared back, but seemed to find something much more interesting at a point just behind him. 'You never looked at me, hard as I'd try and make you. You never saw me. Made me sick.'

Outside of Bagram, where they were stationed to rebuild the school, and where Frankie collapsed in one of his many panic attacks, Doc gave Frankie a shot of Benzedrine mixed with opiates, and listened to Frankie explain how chemistry is poetry in spirit if not in form . . . Fragments of a Dionysian song . . . The periodic table a delicate Apollonian dance.

'I had no idea what he was jabbering about,' Doc would tell Thettie later. 'A delicate what-the-fuck? Are you looking at me, girl?'

'Sure Doc. I'm right here.'

'Well, stop petting that cat for a minute, will you, and look at me when I'm talking to you. Is that so much to ask?'

She smiled. 'I'm looking at you, Doc. I promise.'

Doc pretended to know who Dionysius was. The shot Doc gave Frankie, not the first nor the last, filled Frankie with love for his savior, whose ginger jarhead was a tower of fire against the white desert sky. Doc pretended to agree with Frankie's rant, *yes, yes.* Apollo, why the fuck not?

'But then you'll never guess. He took up a handful of desert dust and told me to hold it up to my ear.'

'Can you hear it?' Frankie said. He explained how the main component of sand is silica, SiO, bound together with four oxygen atoms in a continuous tetrahedral framework of quartz crystal— SiO_4—the second most abundant mineral on the planet after feldspar, and one of the most indestructible and musical.

'It's because of its perfection, its piezoelectric capabilities.'

'Someone say pizza?' Thettie tried to cover up a yawn.

'Piezoelectric,' Doc said. 'Frankie said piezoelectric means that it's capable of converting mechanical stress or electrical force. That's why they use Quartz in watches, delicate electric instruments like sonar, and radio transmitters. It's because pure crystal sings, or cries, when you rub it, or press it, or tap it. No internal flaws to absorb the vibrations.'

Thettie had heard some of this before, but Doc didn't like a girl to interrupt him. So Thettie never got to tell him about how in America you learn in school about Benjamin Franklin's Glass Armonica, a musical instrument made of differently placed crystals, which he adapted from the ancient Greek glass harp.

Frankie told Doc that listening to sounds extracted from vibrating crystal for too long could send you mad, make you want to kill yourself. This was on account of the low frequency of the vibrations, 1000-4000 Hertz, which is not quite high enough to locate the sound in space, nor low enough to identify its source. In other words, Frankie, said, the brain has no point of reference for the unearthly sweetness of the crystal's song.

And Doc, to shut Frankie up, said, 'Speaking of sweet, I could fuck a monkey, soldier. Let's go whoring.'

Frankie did a pretty respectable crab impression for Doc to show how sand shares its oxygen arms with other components—its crystalline structure looking a little like a crab with its pincers at the top, its legs at the bottom and the two silicon atoms for eyes.

Doc laughed at the crab act, grabbed his own crotch and crab-walked toward Chicken Street.

'The thing with crystals, see,' Frankie had told Thettie, 'is that they can take a hell of an amount of pressure and just keep singing. Each of their surfaces bears a portion of the load, spreading the burden and dispersing the effects of destruction and decay. It's the Quartz which gives sand its crystalline glitter. It's hard and timeless shine.'

By the middle of that Afghani winter, Bud Wallace made even Doc uncomfortable, even if he saw potential in the HAM radio nerd and kiddie-porn hound. But the real potential for Doc lay in the polymath and drug-chemist, Corporal Francis George Washington Harpur. Doc pointed out carefully that his own medical knowledge lay a 'common ground' between them, so that Frankie understood. Doc asked Frankie more and more questions about the little backwoods lab in Triangle Gully, about their distribution network, and about the deGroots' hydroponic operation. He asked Frankie to show him the picture of Thettie again. Made sure they were cousins and nothing else, nothing at least that Frankie could put into words. Doc asked about her kids. About any husbands, boyfriends.

'You were asking Frankie to set us up?' Thettie asked.

Doc just shook his head and said, 'Ask, shmask.'

The rest of the war story, like Doc told it, was this:

Coming from the barracks one morning he passed an unfamiliar car parked outside the construction zone in the safe neighborhood from whence the Taliban had long been ousted. He was on his way to report the vehicle to his Staff Sergeant when the car blew up, setting off an explosion in the school. There were luckily no children there, just Frankie and another soldier.

Doc explained how there was no way he wasn't going to bring Frankie home alive for Thettie. He was in his civvies but he rushed in—'where angels fear to tread'—and dragged Frankie out of the rubble, bristling with shrapnel. Where Bud Wallace was at the time always bothered Thettie, but Doc talked real fast over that point—something about earning himself a dishonorable discharge in the way he knew best—and then Doc went back to his war story.

He waved his arms to mimic smoke pouring from flesh. He spread his scarred hands out to the size of the big piece of rebar sticking out of Frankie's heel.

'I did it for you, girl,' Doc said. 'I saved that crazy bastard just for you.'

And because she didn't want to hear any more about the things Doc did for her, which seemed just an excuse for Doc to talk about him and Frankie, Thettie tried to change the subject, in the usual way.

But Doc pushed her off of him and got out of bed. 'Look at me, bitch,' he said. 'And tell me what you see.'

***

It is time. Darkness is near. Thettie struts and gambols in her cage and waits for night to fall.

42. STEELERS

NEVER HAVING BEEN on a wagon, much less fallen off one, the girl proudly pulls Lee a beer. She trained for the job at the Way on Wednesday, and by the end of the week, she's an expert. She helps Avery drape the bar in black sheets, and set up orange battery-operated candles around the booths. Boner the Stiff, the Way's life-size Halloween skeleton, lurches in and out of an upright coffin. Every night Avery has to change Boner's batteries, remove cigarettes, chewing gum and condoms from between the plastic skeleton's half-melted teeth. He pulls Squeaky the Squirrel from its anal cavity, pries pizza slices from its finger joints, and once, from around its neck, a noose.

Lee worries about Habib with his hidden stash of Helotide and Doc likely to find out about it, if he hasn't already. He wants to ask Archy and Grif to arrange security for the professor, and also a distraction so Lee can search Doc's trailer for Vernon. A few Harpurs remain at camp either out of loyalty to Thettie or because they've nowhere else to go. The end of the month looms when they will be forced off the shore. The girl tells Lee how Doc had to turn his boat around yet again, halfway to the island, due to the weather.

Lee and the girl have become inseparable. He picks

her up and takes her home from work. She visits him by day, but she either works or sleeps at night. They are day friends. That's all they can be.

Like many women in Little Ridge, Avery's wife is jealous of the girl, at first. She asks him how having a disfigured Harpur behind the bar, will help business. He shrugs and says, 'Maybe as a gimmick. Times being what they are.' His wife doesn't argue. The gimmick goes off. The tavern has its busiest pre-Halloween weekend in years.

The Way began life in 1908 as a place for hunters to trade lies and exchange pelts for 'shine and ammo. Its post-prohibition highlight was when conscientious objectors stopped by on their way to Ontario, loaded with acid tabs and vials of hash oil. That pulled the young people in again for a while. Then Sunny Weeks bought the Pump Bar in the Village, had it refitted with Craft Beer on tap and since then, Avery likes to say with a sad laugh, 'It's been downhill—*all the Way.* Until *they* came back. And especially Her.'

He points to his left eye, which on the girl is still missing.

Avery turns fifty-two on Christmas morning, doesn't sleep in the same room as his wife, Irene, because of his apnea mask. Avery wears the same tortoiseshell frame glasses he's always worn, except now they're fashionable. And Irene, his bridezilla from Manila, cuts his hair like Johnny Depp.

'You're the same age, baby,' she says. 'Why not?'

Avery and Lee watch the girl with the broken eye and her plaster-white skin line up shots behind the bar.

'Takes up all the air in the room, doesn't she?' Avery says.

Lee doesn't answer because he knows Avery's not asking.

'They say she's from around here but I never seen her before,' Avery says, swiping a filthy rag over the counter. 'I want to say she looks familiar though. You get kids come through the rural areas, on their way south from Albany, Schenectady to Baltimore, DC area to Jersey. That kind of thing. Punks, runaways. They used to congregate under the Triangle Creek bridge back in the day. Every year one or two'd freeze to death, or fall off the bridge and get carried over the falls. Boyle had his share of floaters in those days, so to speak.'

'What happened?' Lee grips the edge of the bar with white knuckles.

'Remember? They closed the bridge. Put up those, whadyacallit, barriers. Razor wire.'

Peripherally, Lee takes in the crowd building behind him.

Avery raises an eyebrow at Lee. 'Hey, how come all these years I never see you here?'

Lee wipes beer off his mouth. 'I've been sober,' he said. 'Five years. Ever since my kid died.'

Avery fills his cheeks with air and blows out slowly. 'I was going to say, Bryce says she knows the crazy Harpur guy that shot Zabriskie, the one her people are looking for. She says she knows how to find him. Seems a little young for him, but who am I to say?'

The beer is soupy in Lee's mouth, hard to swallow. He wonders why she's telling everybody how tight she is with Frankie, but seeing Doc standing over by the bait fridge, he has an idea.

'Anyway,' Avery says. 'She's good for business. Not

a word of a lie there. The customers trust her. I trust her. Maybe it's the affliction.' He points to his eyes.

Avery moves across to the pass-through window, chases up an order and comes back. Lee tries to think of the last time he's eaten and what it was.

'Where was I? Fish soup. But appetites change, what can I tell you. Now it's gluten-free this and organic that. Kale and pumpkin—on pizza? That son of the dead woman, the Harpur boy. I seen him on the lake when I go out for Irene's fish. That fish soup of hers—makes you know you're alive. Clears the plumbing so to speak.'

'That'd be Archy,' Lee says.

'Steering around in circles in that little troller of his. Like crazy tight circles around a fixed point. So he comes right up to me, and yells, 'You seen it? Where is it?' I felt for him. He looked, wild, almost like he wasn't there. Like he couldn't do nothing but just spin around and around in circles. It's the grief I says to Irene. The grief is its own place, and sometimes it's the only place.'

Lee's hands begin to shake.

'Anyway,' Avery says. 'The girl's good for business. Who knows why?'

'Maybe because she's serving doubles,' Lee says.

'What? Wait!' Avery crabwalks across the bar to the girl. 'That's 80 proof, young lady, not H_2O!'

Lee likes it that the dingy little highway tavern has begun—in its own way and for its own kind—to flourish again. On Friday nights, the farmers and hands pull up in their pick-ups, bikes and Chevys, the grime scrubbed from ankle bones, muck scraped from boots, and the grease dug out from under their fingernails. Their sisters come in low cut sweaters and new haircuts to gawk at the one-eyed barmaid and to choose from the ever-changing array of cocktails she's invented. FrankenFalls (corn whisky and cranberry juice with a squeeze of lime). Super 8 (a down-at-heel mix of gin, vodka, tequila, white rum and grapefruit juice with a drizzle of blood orange). Nirvana, which seems to change every time but is your basic Mai Tai. And the Lake Monster, of course: one part Curacao—blue for remembering—to two parts Galliano—yellow for forgetfulness—served unmixed in a double-shooter.

One night, half-way through the pre-Halloween weekend, Doc and his minders corner Lee at the end of the bar where he waits for the girl to finish her shift. Archy and Grif are meant to be coming in later and they will sit where they always sit, at the haunted Harpur booth where they were all together on that last night.

Doc spits his words out of the good corner of his mouth like broken teeth. 'Your towel-head boss used to buy dope from Frankie Harpur down at Triangle Gully. You know anything about that?'

Lee inhales Doc's bad cologne and his minders' funk. 'Top of the mornin' to ye, Mr. McMurphy. So how're the excursions to the island working out?'

Lyle dances up and down on the balls of his feet and Homer pulls at the collar of his shirt. 'Never mind the island,' Doc says. 'How do you think the authorities might view some foreigner doing drug deals with a convicted felon?'

Lee makes Doc wait while he leans over and pours himself another shot. 'Firstly, Sam Habib's an

American citizen, and secondly, he had ethics committee approval for all the pharmaceuticals he obtained.' He counts off the points on his fingers, beginning with the middle finger. He feels someone behind him, a hand at his shoulder, but when he turns around there's no one there. Not yet.

Doc jabs a thumb at Lee. 'Whatever he and Frankie Harpur were up to wasn't approved by no ethics committee.'

'Look,' Lee says. 'If you're still sore about me and Thettie . . . '

'You look, lad,' Doc leans forward until his combat boots are toe-to-toe with Lee's unlaced sneakers. He's exactly the same height as Lee and his adenoidal brogue is beginning to sound like a slippery mix of Colin Farrell and Sean Connery. 'I don't give a rat's arse about you and the old lady. What I came for is some of that lizard spit the Arab's shipping across to Frankie, and I'm not going to leave without it. So tell the Arab and save us both some trouble.'

A thought crosses Lee's mind. If it *was* Doc who took Vernon, does this new desperation mean Vernon is dead, or dying? Did he hurt Vernon trying to milk the venom? The room darkens. 'Where's my lizard, Mr. Murphy?'

Homer and Lyle stiffen, and Lee can't work out if it's because they know where Vernon is or because they don't. A terrible calm descends on him.

Doc says, 'Lizard? No idea. I hope you find what you're looking for. Me? I'm good at getting what I'm looking for. Your boss can give it to me for the asking, or I can just take it, lad. Can't you just see the sad little faces of all those rent boys down in Ilium—no more visits from daddy. Shocked?' Doc brings a blistered hand to his heart. 'Not the God you thought he was? Take it from me, Lizard Man, gods never are.'

Sudden sobriety flaps at Lee like a cold towel. He grabs Doc around the collar and holds him close, so close that Doc can't move and Lee's lips are right up against the scar-ridged ear-hole. 'You go anywhere near Sam Habib, and I'll tell Archy and Grif how you set Frankie up in that raid in '05—just so you could have Thettie all to yourself.'

There is a sudden whiff of oilskin and pipe tobacco, a melodious laugh behind them.

'What's up, Doc?'

Grif shoves a Lake Monster under Lee's nose, the blue floating in a sea of yellow. Grif's voice rises and falls in a chromatic menace. Doc gives Lee's shoulders a fatherly squeeze.

'I was just saying to your ma's fella here that maybe his old boss could help us find a way to Frankie.'

Lee lifts the Lake Monster to the light. The two colors swirl around each other without blending. He drains the bittersweet cocktail, and then he wipes his mouth. 'Where's Archy?'

Grif jiggles his own drink in the direction of the girl. 'I thought Bryce was going to take us to Frankie, in return for your big-ass yacht?'

The door pushes open and it's Archy. He goes straight across to the Harpur booth.

Doc turns away slowly with Homer and Lyle just out of step on either side of him. They're like some lethal human force field, and Lee wonders how he—or the brothers—will ever get past them and into the campground to look for Vernon.

ALETHEIA

The forked vein on Grif's forehead pulses. 'Let's get a real drink.'

Back at the haunted Harpur booth, where no one else dares to sit, Archy waits surrounded by empty cocktail glasses. Little paper umbrellas and plastic seahorses float in a sticky sea of blue and green. There is a soggy pile of Vernon fliers on the seat that someone has either forgotten to hang or was in the process of taking down. Archy's hair is shorn straight across the back of his neck, and long bangs flop crazily over his forehead. He drums on the table with his ringed fingers. Grif sits on one side, leaving plenty of space, and Lee slides in on the other. Between Grif and Archy, the empty place where their mother used to sit, opens like a wound. Like a sore on a body where something's been dug out or cut off. A finger or a limb. Or an eye.

Archy bites his lip. 'We were the three-headed monster. 'Member, Grif?'

'Careful what you wish for is the message there.'

Grif's eyes are slits, the pupils submerged in blue. His wide mouth stretches in a lunatic grin and he lights his cigar and no one tells him not to. In the booth beside them sit the ever-present Emilio and Dustin with their small and committed crew, names Lee has become familiar with—Brandon, and Don, Randall and Clay.

'What's this about your old boss and Frankie?' Grif says.

There's that hummingbird in his veins again, buzzing after a shot of the Lake Monster, a villainous concoction if there ever was one. 'So, I think that somehow Doc was behind Vernon's disappearance—maybe through Jason—and maybe for the Helotide.'

'Do you think he still has him? The lizard?'

Lee presses the glass against his hot forehead. 'No. I kind of don't. He's crawled away, or died or something, I think. I think that's why Doc is sounding desperate—Plan B to get the girl to take him to Frankie, Plan C to blackmail Habib, or worse. But I still want to search for him myself.'

'We already searched the Bago.'

'If I can just get into the big trailer again. Maybe he's scared, hurt. I know what I'm looking for.'

His son had been scared. His son had been hurt. When did he know that help would never come? Lee feels a prickle at his neck—his vision turns red. Archy, Grif are dark voids and the space between them runs with red. The vision clears almost as soon as it comes.

Archy and Grif fidget with.

'The Helotide,' Grif says. 'That's the ingredient in the Killer Mix, right?'

'But why would he have needed the lizard?' Archy says. 'If he has Frankie? I mean isn't that why he wanted to get there? So he can team up with Frankie on the Killer Mix?'

Grif says, 'Doc ain't a team player now and he never was one. He wasn't going over to partner with Uncle Frankie. He was going over to get him out of the way. You know that, Archy. We both always did know it. Frankie first, then us.'

'And Vernon—the Helotide—was proof of that. What does he need with Frankie if he has his own supply of Helotide?' Lee says. 'Except now, maybe, he doesn't.'

'And you're sure of this?'

'I'm not. That's why I want to search the trailer. It's

just that why else would he be asking about Habib's supply of Helotide if he has his own? Maybe Vernon is still in the big trailer . . . '

'Don't get your hopes up.' Archy shakes his head. 'Maybe he thought Jason could help him extract the Venom or something.'

'And maybe,' Lee says, remembering the mulcher, the uncle with the just-wiped ax, 'Jason refused. Habib said he left town in a hurry.'

'So where's he now?' Archy says. 'I warrant that tweaker's too damn fried to make his own self disappear.'

But Grif was on a different track. 'Doc promised Bryce his own boat if she'd just get him over there. Sounds desperate to us. Means he's got zip.' Grif says, 'I came in from the lake that morning, saw Ma at her trailer, and helped her move her stuff to Doc's cabin. I checked it from front door to back.' He bangs on the table, his huge fist caked in cigar ash. 'I even checked her suitcase. I don't know what I was looking for, but something felt wrong.'

'Lizard shit,' says Archy.

'Coast was clear of reptiles,' Grif rubs his face, streaking it with ash. 'Nothing but a half-full bottle of Ambien and her Tampax. But I never should have talked her into moving trailers. That's on me.'

'There's no just you, Grif,' Archy mumbles, so low Lee can hardly hear him, and he wishes he had something left to say something about grief and self-blame but he doesn't.

'There's something else,' Archy scratches the inside of his thigh. Lee recoils from another dull red pulse in the darkness of the booth.

J.S. BREUKELAAR

'We were heading south on the interstate to check on Sarey,' Grif says. 'Bryce ran decoy maneuver.' They raise their eyes adoringly toward the slim boyish figure at the bar. She feels their gaze and pokes her tongue out at them, winks her good eye. They blush like schoolboys. Whatever the enmity between them over her, she has insinuated herself back into their affections like some adopted sister they secretly or not so secretly want to fuck like an animal.

'This kid—a little boy—he's hitchhiking on the side of the road. He looks way too young, so we pull over. He says he's Jason deGroot's brother and he wants to go home.'

The space between Archy and Grif is alive and running with red. A face lies under the surface of the red, trying to push through. Lee shrinks against the back of the booth, visors his hands over his eyes like blinkers. 'You're kidding.'

'You okay?' asks Archy.

'The kid with Down Syndrome,' Grif says.

Archy paws his beard and slugs one of the leftover cocktails. 'So the kid says he waits every day for his brother, gets out there as soon as he comes home from school and waits until supper time. Get that? Every fucking day. So, we ask where his brother's gone. The kid doesn't know. To work he says. Or fishing, maybe. But Jason's coming back soon. Jason has to come back. Waah-waah. The east paddock fence needs fixing. Daisy needs a hoof trim, blah-blah. Mommy's making Olly something.'

'*Olibol*,' Grif snarls. 'I looked it up. It's a Dutch donut.'

'So we say, we'll take him home. But then he says, wait, he wants to show us something. He leads us off

412

the road—kid can move like greased lightning—down to the stream running behind his farm on the south side, feeds into the Creek, I'm guessing. We hide the bikes so's the Sheriff doesn't see, and follow him.'

Grif cuts in. 'Like, it's down a rise, and there's trees, willows and aspens and other shrubs. And he takes us to this hollow log that spans both banks, like a bridge. Fishes around in it and pulls out some of his junk. Rock and dead bugs and old grass, and an arrowhead. Some nails. The usual lonely kid paraphernalia.'

'Paraphernalia?' Archy gapes at him theatrically. 'You doing Sudoku, now?'

Grif flushes. 'Maybe. Anyways. Then he gets this stick and pokes it into the log a way further and hooks it onto something and pulls that out.'

Lee reaches for a leftover cocktail, trying not to look at the swirling agate drops between them, like a consumptive cloud. Whatever's he's drinking now tastes like a combination of licorice and corned beef. From behind the paper umbrella, he watches the girl at the bar, finding him in her amber eye as it sweeps the crowd of leering faces. She turns pale at the sight of the crimson fog between the two boys, and mouths the unmistakable word: Thettie.

Archy leans forward and says in a low voice, laced with intoxication and hysteria. 'It's a Steelers' Bag, all wet and shit.'

Grif reaches under the flap of his jacket and pulls over a plastic grocery bag from the Market, tells Lee to look inside. Lee leans into the space between them. It's the same Steelers' bag he saw on Homer's shoulder the day they arrived. Same broken zipper. He thinks he might be sick.

'You want to smell it?' Archy offers.

'Why?' Lee says, swallowing. 'Would I want to do that?'

'Fat man loved that goddam bag. It had some of the team autographs on it. Ben Roethlisberger. I don't know how he got it. He said he got some kind of a locker room pass for a favor he did someone or something. No doubt, yeah? Probably killed someone for it. He carried that bag everywhere with him. Look at *mee*. Look at my *bayg*. Shit. Even if he didn't need to carry anything he carried that damn bag. Put his towel in it, or make-up, or blow-up girlfriend, or change of wife-beater . . . '

'Get to the point, Archy, you fucktard.' Grif's jaw twitches. The red and black letters float off his fingers and Lee watches them dance like lightless fireflies.

'Point is,' Archy leans drunkenly forward so his chin's almost touching the table. 'He don't have it no more.'

'Oh for fuck's sake,' Grif says. 'The point is, he lost it the night Ma . . . . you know. We even asked him about it. Hey, Fat Man What happened to your diapey-bag? And he just said, he don't have it no more. Lost it or something. Another thing gone missing. Except the kid, Jason's brother, he found it. Washed up in Triangle Creek, but down to where the deGroot stream empties. And the kid brings it back. Hides it because he knows it's important.'

'So, why would he think that?' says Lee slowly.

'So, we asked him that, too,' Grif says. 'All he said, was '*faux pas*."

Lee side-eyes each brother in turn, dimly registering that if Grif didn't know what *faux pas* meant before, he does now. 'So, I remember the bag, too. But what makes you think it's, you know, important?'

Without warning Thettie appears in the empty space between her sons. Lee's hair rises, and a scream curdles in his throat. His eyes burn. She is terrible and beautiful. Her hair is bleached almost white and falls across her eyes, which squirm with jellied worms. A blood-soaked veil covers her mouth. She extends her left arm, which is seamed with gouges in which more of the black goo twitches, the same black mercury-like matter that was on the beach.

Her sons recoil, look at each other. 'You okay? Jeezus. Is he having a stroke?'

Between them, Thettie nods to him. Her clawed fingers extend toward his and the touch sends a cold thrill all the way up his body, like dipping his hands into dry ice. He begins to shake all over.

But with her help, this is the way it comes out:

'So Doc finds out about Vernon, about how he's the source of the secret ingredient in Frankie's mix. He also finds out that Jason is the perfect patsy, not only because of his experience in handling dangerous reptiles, but also because he bears me a grudge. Jason maybe thinks Vernon should be freed or whatever, or maybe it's just money. Who knows how much Doc offers him to steal the lizard as insurance in case Frankie won't give up the formula, or ingredients. Jason thinks maybe he'll use the money to get to his mother Cassie, in LA. So he drugs and liberates Vernon the night Thettie and I are . . . together.'

The heavy black matter in Thettie's eyes drops like tears.

'So then Jason puts Vernon in his backpack, but for some reason gets wise to what Doc is planning to do to Vernon, thinks he'll try and run away with him, take him west. Which is exactly what Doc expects. Homer and Lyle cut him off at the pass—someone saw their car off him, and I don't know . . . bury the evidence.'

'You think they killed him?'

Lee tells them about seeing Fie deGroot with the axe and the scattered doll parts on the path to the barn. 'I saw that kid with the doll the first time I met him. Maybe we was leaving the doll parts there as a kind of clue, a trail to follow.' Lee didn't tell them he kept the arm.

'You think the body was in the barn that day? Like they killed their own kin?'

And Lee remembers what Habib had said about Doc being a cleaner. 'Isn't that someone who does the jobs the bad guys don't want to do themselves?

Thettie hisses, 'Cleeeeee-nerrrr.'

Lee trembles with terror, but also with want. Sweat pools in his crotch. Thettie's skin beneath the veil of blood is as pale as the stars. She pulls the veil away and smiles at him, and her tongue flicks over a double row of teeth, jagged and dripping with venom.

And then she begins to fade. Lee leans forward, far into the crimson dark.

Archy and Grif come back into focus, staring at Lee with drinks held in trembling hands. I saw her, he wants to say. *I see her. She is not gone. She did not die.* But they look at him like they already know, and then he gets that they have seen her, too.

'So . . . ' Archy falters, cracks his knuckles and tries again. 'So what you're saying is . . . that they take

Vernon from Jason, put the lizard into the Steelers' bag and take it back to the double-wide—because Ma's still in the Winnebago. By the time Ma and them switch trailers—*and* they grab their luggage—the lizard's crawled out through the broken zipper of the bag, and is, like hiding somewhere in the trailer?'

'Yes. That's what I'm saying.'

Grif shakes his head, 'Like these fools are the best Doc can do—stash the merch in a broken fucking bag. Seriously?'

"Seriously?" Archy says. 'What are you, a hipster now?'

Avery yells at the one-eyed girl to get back to work because she is staring in terror at the fading apparition of Thettie.

'I want to get into the trailer,' Lee says. 'And I want you to put someone outside Habib's place—the small villa at the south end of Main Street.'

'We know where it is.'

Thettie is just a vaporous outline between her sons now. They slurp their cocktails. Boner the Stiff lurches out of his coffin. The one-eyed girl shakes out another round of Lake Monsters, keeping her one good eye on Thettie. She readjusts her veil.

'No,' Lee says, reaching trembling hand to her. 'Don't go!'

Archy and Grif look lost again, the space between them unfillable, a wound that will never heal. The place is packed. The juke is pumping. Avery's face behind his tortoise shell frames shines with sweat as he hunts for clean glasses. Tobacco smoke wafts in from the porch and the smell of urinal cakes from the head is suffocating. Lee interlaces fingers slick with the silty black residue. Grif rubs his hands up and down the outsides of his legs, and Lee knows it's on them, too. It is on all of them now—and is all that remains of her pain except for a blue shadow between her boys, jagged, like a giant splinter that will be with them always.

Archy's cheeks are chafed and his lips are chapped from being out in the weather, 'The killer spit. What killed Ma. Doc'll be seeing a whole new world of opportunity in that.'

Grif jabs a huge finger at Lee. 'Except you don't think it was that, do you? *You* don't think it could have been the Gila. So, if that didn't kill her, and she didn't kill herself, what did?'

'Someone slipped her a Mickey, maybe, or, cut her up like that?' Spit flies from Archy's mouth.

'But what?' Grif pound on the table. 'What the hell could have done that?'

Lee shudders with revulsion and nausea but also a wild desire. Thettie reappears, summoned by her sons' rage or her lover's want, or both. Blood oozes down her face and shoulders. She brings her hand to her face, a gesture so full of false hope and monstrous sorrow that Lee moans. But the girl is suddenly behind him and her cold hand clamps over his mouth.

'Avery's selling raffle tickets for a dance with Boner,' she says. 'Any takers?'

Thettie judders before him, a blur of blood and bone. Archy and Grif reach absently for cash and the girl makes a show of ripping them perforated tickets. 'The draw's at midnight,' she says.

Thettie hisses at the girl but holds her ground. 'So, I didn't say it wasn't the venom.' Lee's voice sounds far away as if someone else is talking for him. Maybe they are. His heart pounds. 'I think it could be more complicated. We don't know exactly what the Helotide does yet. We don't know all of its effects, how the peptides work on humans.'

The lonely rage in Thettie's eyes flares once, and she is gone. In her wake, a dry corner of one the fliers of Vernon left on the table flutters. Archy stares down at the flier and smiles a strange smile. Grif looks from one to the other, 'Pizza,' he says. 'That damn lizard had a thing for pizza. It's right there, in the fliers all around.'

He lifts it up, flaps it at them. 'Ma had pizza that night.'

Archy just shakes his head and watches the girl approach the table with a tray of drinks.

They all seem to have moved toward the one thing, that Thettie's death involved great suffering and that alone seems to have moved it further along the scale of evil toward the big E.

Grif pounds a tattooed fist lightly on the table, which settles it. 'We'll get a car outside your man Habib's place. Shorty over there will keep Doc on the hop while we figure out a way to get you into the big trailer.'

Archy's knuckles whiten. 'We should have taken her home, Grif. Our own selves.'

He's standing up now in the booth, his head blocking out the light from the swinging bulbs.

You adapt, Lee tries to tell them. You grow into grief. You form lungs to breathe in it, sprout fins to swim through it. You manage your grief. You manage it by refusing to speak its name. You manage it by painting the lake inside out. By falling off the wagon. Or into a stranger's bed and all their hurt. Walking in the woods with a girl young enough to be your daughter. Waiting alone in the studio for the lake to take you. Never ever say its name. Not even a whisper.

Lee gets up next to Archy. Grif lurches to a standing position across the table. Grif raises his fist, then Archy. Lee raises both fists and bumps them back. Gently.

The important thing now is to get up and go back to the studio. Lee weaves to the bar and looks over his shoulder once, but there is just Grif and Archy alone at the booth now. Lee wants to be alone and he doesn't want to be alone. He fidgets, orders a beer he doesn't want, waits for the girl to finish work so he can see her safely home. There is an invertebrate, aquatic quality to her movements, which are as economical and tentative as a child's. Her skin in the dim light of the bar is the white of the moon. Tiny cuts and bruises—from being clumsy, she jokes—whiten or darken when she bends over, or when her T-shirt slips off her shoulder. She winks at him from behind the cocktail shaker flashing like mercury across her torso, and the clustered farmers and truckers try and get her to bend over, so they can ogle her jail bait titties. She sleeps badly, she says, has had nightmares ever since she was a child.

'Go home,' she mouths. 'It's going to be a long night.'

He obeys, not just because he likes drinking alone, although there's that. But also, because now there is a chance that he will not be alone. He looks over his shoulder as he leaves, wanting Thettie to follow and fearing that she will.

43. CHIMERA

THE **UNEARTHING OF** the Steelers' bag has extended her reach so that she is able to wander more by day. First the tooth, and then the fat man's bag—each is a key in the loosening of her iron collar so that she is even less a slave to nature than before. She glimmers in the streets in rain-streaked daylight. She is a hiss in the brown leaves, a leer in a crack of the sidewalk.

Little Ridge is lost in reverie. People lift their noses to the prevailing breeze like rabbits in the snow, nostrils quivering at the scent of blood and time. They bristle at the stink of memories that they can or will not place. The townies look at their own hands in wonder, tenderly touch faces reflected in the rearview mirror. Memories take on a vivid quality equal to physical sensation—she watches a young mother stop to throw up in a diaper bag—and past feelings are easily mistaken for present pain or sexual pleasure. The aging editor at the Village Dawn looks down at the tented crotch of his chinos in surprise.

For many of Thettie's one-time neighbors, girlhood friends, or sworn enemies, real life has taken on the quality of a dream made up of objects once lost and now found. Thettie moves through the town spreading the venom of memory, a potion that, like Bryce's cocktails, is both the infection and the antidote. And the Way is where Thettie ends up most nights, haunting the Harpur booth where she spent her last night with her sons. Bryce looks up from her work to acknowledge her because she and Bryce have come to an unspoken, unspeakable understanding. A partnership of kinds beyond pity and beyond fear.

Thettie waits for Doc, but he is never alone, never without Homer and Lyle like some weaponized twin-cam exoskeleton—Archy's words, not hers. But Jason's brother's revelation of the Steelers' bag has lifted not only her own, but also her sons' restraints. It has awakened their perception (to which she is tethered) enough to allow her to move more freely by day so as to get closer to Doc—to the point where he has begun to feel the need to look over his shoulder, to peer through the barbecue smoke, or to sniff the glacial air. Fate, she tells him. We make our own monsters, Doc. And you made me.

The townies pick up their ears to try and catch the whisper in the trees, a blue note in the call of the geese. At the bar that Saturday night, Thettie passes Avery on her way to the booth and gives him a whiff of his fifth-grade teacher's armpits reaching over him to pick up scattered crayons. Burnt Sienna. Cobalt blue. It is not how he can differentiate among the crayons—Mango Tango, Inchworm—but how the teacher's arm reaching for crayons at ten o'clock in the morning on the Thursday that Robert Kennedy will be shot is an entirely different arm than it has been or will ever be again.

For Avery, Thettie is a sensation. A pounding in his

head, a heat in his intestine, an affliction to be endured, a passenger riding shotgun. Just don't let her take the wheel. For some of the other customers she is less a presence than a perception. Sitting in the booth to be avoided because it is the (haunted) Harpur booth, she takes a drink now from the cup of their collective memory, now from that of forgetfulness. She is less an apparition than a veiled suggestion that they will, over time, inflate into the status of urban myth.

But Bryce on the other hand, is their addiction, collective and urgent and immediate. They flock to the Way to see her every night, the one-eyed priestess or maybe mad scientist, pouring out her potions. Sweet redeemer who will, for their sins, exact from the people of Little Ridge a heavy price.

Thettie bars her pointed teeth and a flap of skin loosens from her jaw. She fixes the veil and raises her shooter with the yellow and blue Lake Monster—or would if she could—to the girl, and the girl winks back behind her eye patch, or would if she could. Thettie gets it finally, the idea of being able to differentiate between that which is there and that which is not. What is left in the gap, between you (with a 'why') and I (for an eye), is the void into which Doc pushed her, the prick. She sorts through perceptions as she never could before—between those of others and those that belong in her—the way Archy and Grif would sort out their Halloween loot—sometimes trading a Baby Ruth for a Reese's but more often not. It was as important then as it is now, to see the good and the bad, to know without doubt what can be taken away from you and what must not and to guard that difference with your life. How did Doc get through her defenses?

She remembers what Cassie said that night at the motel after the deGroots filed out and Frankie drove them to Harpur Falls for what would be the last time. Cassie chain-puffing Kools in the back seat of Frankie's primer-streaked Pontiac, deGroot's seed growing inside her to make the child who would one day come back to bite them all.

'In the blink of an eye,' Cassie said. 'Everything changed.'

***

In the blink of an eye, Thettie is on the jetty over the lake. The island looms like on a conveyor belt, and Frankie waves at her from the window of the disused lighthouse.

'Why did you do this Frankie? It was you, wasn't it? Put the monster of want inside Vernon, and then come to get me. Why?' she wails. 'Look at me, Frankie. I never thought I'd die ugly.'

Frankie turns on the light and flashes one long, one short, one long, on short, two long, one short, one long.

'CQ? But Frankie, I need to remember for my boys.'

He blows her a raspberry.

'I know,' she blinks away the tears, not wanting to ask again, but forcing herself to. 'Why, this, though, Frankie? It hurts to change.'

He puts two fingers on his eyes and points at her, just to be clear. As if she didn't know the answer already, he blows another raspberry which sounds more like thunder, 'What's up Doc?'

'I got this one, Frankie,' Thettie sighs. 'Don't get your panties in a wad.'

***

Everything in Thettie that once belonged to her is coming back inside her where it belongs, just like Lee

424

said it would. But Lee haunts her with his want. The other night at the Way, his terrible, fearful need. Still, she finds it difficult to materialize at will, but practice makes perfect. So, on her way back to the camp ground early Sunday morning, Thettie stops when she sees Sunny Weeks parked outside the Zabriskie House, beneath an October sky whose blue eclipses Sunny's own weakening perception. The town benefactor steps out once again to size up the grand old butter-yellow Victorian sprawl with its twenty-six shuttered rooms, and its pagoda and gatekeeper's cottage and dusty ballroom. The blue of the sky compares unfavorably with the blue of a onesie she had her senior designer come up with for her latest American Born creation, the doll-child of Syrian refugees, against whose dark skin the blue of the onesie looks hard and chalky.

Abruptly Thettie steps out from behind the spreading maple beside the gravel drive, pulling her torn nightgown down over the scales growing across her breast. The swirls of broken capillaries on Sunny's face, which are the same stark flat blue as the sky, stand out as she pales. Thettie takes a further step away from the tree trunk, and her water-marked nightgown drags in the piled brown leaves. Sunny's legs have turned to lead, fixing her in place. The wind has come up in the barren fruit trees. Sunny lifts her purse to her chest with a robotic motion, like a wind-up doll. The naked picture of shock and terror is so insanely gratifying to Thettie that she adds a radioactive sputter to her piercing stare. The electron-blue intensity to her gaze says clearly, as if she'd spoken it, that she probably looks better in death than Sunny will ever look in life.

44. CABIN FEVER

LEE CALLS HIS contact in Ilium to inquire about getting a warrant to search the trailer Thettie died in, and his contact suggests he go back to his box set of *The Wire*. 'It's not that easy,' Detective Fabiana Brown says. 'The average Joe just can't get a search warrant whenever he wants. Why don't you just mosey over and do it yourself?'

The campground has a desolate crime-scene vacancy to it, and Lee's heart drums as he nears the trailer where she died, where she should never have been. The weeds grow rampant now in the geranium beds, a torn curtain hanging in the window. Since its unquestioned haunting, it has fallen not exactly into disrepair but into a swift and unsettling neglect. It pulsates in the starlight, its eaves sagging with the weight of its rage. Taggers have scrawled obscenities on the outer walls and doors, back and front. Someone has smashed a pumpkin on its rusting steel porch.

Lee rubs at the marks furiously with his coat sleeve, gritting his teeth through tears. He tries the door. It doesn't resist. His shoes raise puffs of dust and leave deep prints across the floor. He can smell the lake though all the windows are closed and there is also the strong smell of clean hair and cigarettes. The door closes softly behind him and he freezes at the sharp click like a tongue against teeth. Soft in his ears. Gooseflesh rises across his arms and his legs feel cold.

'Vernon,' he whispers. He shines his phone into the darkness and then he switches it off.

The only light in the trailer home comes from a small TV on a stand. But it is not plugged in, and the cord is tangled on the rug. The couch facing it pulsates in the unsourced glow. Behind that is a kitchenette. There is a note stuck to the fridge by a magnet. The note says, 'Mommy will be back soon. Eggos in the freezer.' An ashtray on the breakfast bar, a child's lunch box. As he moves into the hall, the trailer seems to expand.

Fragrant steam issues from the open door of the dark bathroom. He pushes the door open further and steps in—the tub glows in the dark like the milky way, and levitates above the floor. It's lit by dozens of candles self-affixed to the porcelain. The smell is intoxicating, exotic and heady. He approaches the tub. 'Vernon?' The water is as calm as a lake, an unearthly chalky blue, something black swimming in its depths, like a rat. Lee peers over the edge. It's a small black boat, alive and swirling beneath the sickly blue. He backs out slowly.

The smaller bedroom door to the left is ajar and Lee can hear panting. The beat of a tail on boards, the smell of wet dog. His flesh crawls. He slips on something pulpy. Shines his phone on it. It's a smashed hunk of fuzzy-rotten pumpkin. The bedroom door slams shut.

There is a light at the end of the hallway from her room, the one she died in. His chest is on fire with panic at what he'll see. Already from here he smells Vernon's reptilian funk, a flowery, slightly barf-like perfume with metallic undertones. Lee presses the tips of his fingers on the door and it creaks open. Darkness, and a bare mattress on a frame against the window. Two eyes staring at him from beneath the bed.

'Vernon!' Lee drops to his belly but there is nothing. He sweeps his hands beneath the bed, feeling for the turgid living body of his friend, but nothing. He bangs his hands on the board and sits up against the bed and starts to cry and doesn't stop. He finally and endlessly finds his tears.

He cries himself to sleep. He wakes up, curled on the floor to the sound of the TV.

He pushes himself stiffly to his feet and sits on the edge of the bed. His shirt is soaked with tears. His nose is blocked and his eyes are burning slits. The stars shine in the window, illuminating Vernon's exit route, the mark of his claws and belly is unmistakably imprinted on the dust on the floor. In the wake of his fleeing dreams, Lee is left to ponder how Vernon's path and Thettie's converged, and what, in lieu of an alternative, is the final destination to be sought.

He goes back down the hall the way he came, past the kids' bedroom. The rank smell of the dog. Toasted waffles, vaguely, undercut by bourbon. The faraway sound of an outboard. Shadows move across the television screen. A war movie. Lee sits down on the only chair, a busted La-Z-Boy. The movie is lurid color, like a B-movie. Or a cable drama. Lee hiccups, his chest shuddering off the weight of all those tears. The film shows a school being built outside of a base in Afghanistan in the early days of the War on Terror. Lee knows it must be Bagram. A car pulls up in the pre-dawn glimmer of the desert, and Doc Murphy gets out of the car. He waits in a doorway. The man he's with gets out also, but he's wearing a *kufiyah* over his face and Lee can't identify him. The man with the headdress walks away and around a corner. A Humvee arrives at first light, and two soldiers get out in blast suits. They go into the school and moments later the school explodes. Doc rushes into the flames and comes out with his clothes and hair smoking and carrying one of the men in a blast suit. Cut to the alley way into which the other man disappeared. Lee puts a hand over his mouth to hold in the vomit that spills over his knuckles. There is Bud Wallace pulling off his *kufiyah* and tossing a cell phone into a drain, leaving behind him a world in flames.

45. BOOTY CALL

NOT EASY TO keep up your self-esteem with nothing but a pair of rusty tweezers, a torn curtain for a veil over your undone mouth, and a hunk of dried face powder you find at the back of the bathroom cabinet. When your best nightgown is webbed with slime. When, running along the railway line by the shore, you're arrested en-route to a booty call by a howling attack of the uglies that sends the squirrels spiraling back into the trees.

Halloween approaches. Your sons will have to bury or burn you with your name besmirched by lies. Your flesh decaying on a slab of steel in the morgue, no earthly reason to put it on ice—case closed according to the coroner. Case closed, echo the deGroots who want you and yours gun-gun. Doc can stay. They still have uses for Doc. Especially if the Harpurs refuse to go. You will have lost. Frankie will have saved you for nothing.

You look for the missing lizard. You look everywhere but in the mirror.

Porches flutter with rubber skeletons and mulch bins overflow with pumpkin guts. Where is your family? Where is your kind? Who will oversee your revenge? All they can talk about is how to arrange for a quick burial, closed casket—so much for dying pretty.

ALETHEIA

Bryce hacks at Archy's hair on the acorn strewn grass in front of the trailer. You choke on your heart. Archy submits to the clacking shears. The strands of his hair scatter amongst the parti-colored leaved and nuts, and you gather up the hair of your son. You curse the mooncalf for over-stepping the mark and you thank her too for holding them here, for keeping them with you for a time beyond time. They may not listen to you, but they listen to her one-eyed promises, the whispered plans and schemes—and they thank her for keeping Doc on a string, and his monster-mash body guards along with him. In a voice barely audible over the snapping blades, Bryce tells Archy that if all else fails Doc thinks he can kidnap her, use her as a human shield. Something about that strikes her as so funny that she doubles up over the grass. Archy laughs uneasily, one side of this hair shorter than the other.

Human shield.

Bryce. The daughter you never had. It is Bryce who sometimes comes to visit you at night, knocks on the door, and when you let her in, it's Bryce and not Bryce, neither nor. Neither here, nor not here. She comes wrapped in a Spider Man blanket, naked beneath, a shiner blossoming on one eye. So young. So small. She holds a lantern to light her way through the dark trailer. She shines it into the sea-horse shaped space, narrow then wide, like she knows what must be found. She wants to watch TV. She sits cross-legged in front of the dead screen, wrapped in her Spider Man blanket like a kid in front of rainy day cartoons.

It is always raining. Thettie hates cartoons.

Rewind: the tooth. Rewind: the Steelers' bag. Rewind: there is more.

There is always more.
Rewind: Seek you.

***

Frankie would talk about the island like he knew. It scared him and it saw him, like a giant eye. It was the being seen that brought him to his knees. He'd disappeared for a day, came back with pine cones and feathers in his pocket, some pieces of glass—or quartz, maybe—and his mouth stained with berry juice. He'd gotten hungry, he said, and when you asked where he'd been, he said, *'I think I understand.'* He said, *'Where there's a want there's a way.'*

***

Poor Lee. Always hungry. Thettie hurtles down the path she's worn through the scrub. She has learned by heart the name and species of every plant, every vine, and the ones she doesn't know, she looks up in one of Lee's books, or on his computer. She likes thinking of him waking up to tabs he never opened. Botanical sites. Flora and Fauna. Globe flower, wild gentian. She takes note of the meteor showers over the lake. She compares them in her memory with smashed glass from a broken vinegar bottle on the kitchen floor in Triangle Gully thirty years ago and with the spray off Archy's long hair after a swim in the creek, the day before the Los Angeles jury found OJ Simpson not guilty of murder.

If you really want to get somewhere you will, Frankie had explained. You have to really want it, so much so that you have to not know exactly what it is you want. Certainty in the uncertain. A faith in the false. She sweeps past the pagoda behind the manor house bequeathed to him, and up the rise beneath the rope swinging from the old oak, and she pounds on Lee's studio window with the flat of her hand demanding he let her in, demanding what, when he stands there bleary from sodden sleep, what he wants.

Lee grinds his palms into his eyes.

'Vernon?'

No.

Her eyes are reflected in every surface around the studio, the windows, the canvases, the Perspex of Vernon's tank, her eyes telling him what she wants if only he'd understand. The blue of ice, of sky.

'The name?'

Now he's getting somewhere, but where she doesn't know except that it's not at the bottom of a bottle so she knocks it out of his hands and onto the floor and they stare at the amber puddle. Golden Brown.

From far away/stays for a day.

She'd never ask Lee to avenge her. That's not how a Harpur rolls. You want something done, do it yourself, is how it is. But there *is* something she wants of him, something she can't do herself.

'See you,' Lee kicks things aside on the floor in the studio. Books, his son's toy truck, bandages, Bryce's head phones. 'Seek you.'

Warmer, Thettie thinks.

'I tried,' he mumbles. 'I would have done anything. I didn't understand.'

'I didn't either,' she says. 'I thought if it could be done, I could do it. That no matter what it took to save the ones I loved, I had that thing in me. But what I didn't understand was the paradox—that what it took was all I had, so that in the end, the 'I' wasn't enough.'

J.S. BREUKELAAR

He doesn't hear her, not yet. But that is not what she needs from him, not now. Her hungering visitations are eased by his return to the bottle. There is his fixation on the girl, of course. But that concerns her less than she would have thought. After all, by night Bryce is trapped in her trailer like a kid on a curfew, like a rat in a cage. So, no. The nights are hers and his—when their combined yearning for love is even stronger than a combined need for forgiveness. And when Lee, lovesick with loneliness and whisky, finishes yet another painting of her and yet again throws the brushes down, splattering her colors—the dirty blues and golds—against the wall. And when he says her name—Thettie—named for Thetis, Goddess of Water, and wills her to him, which is what she wants. And with her wild halo of wheaten hair, the pale nightgown hugging her thighs and silver-freckled breasts, dark lashes framing her azurite eyes, her forked tongue moistening the red wound of a mouth— it is then that she likes to think that in death she is even more ravishing to him than she was in life. Not just in the paintings that divide and multiply around the studio, but in the summons that bring her into being. When his fingers seek the slick flesh, which is not so much immaterial as porous—a collision of mind and matter, body and soul, brain and mind. The clutch of her inside place around his telltale flesh, so swollen with love that he can't put it into words. But it is not words she wants from him now but a need to create from scratch a living dream of love, of flesh, where she waits, open to him and wet as the dew, and where they both can, with a little luck and a miracle of timing, pull it off.

46. SPLINTER

THE SPLINTER SWIMS in and out of focus. Her feet are icy from the lake. They are coated with grass clippings, twigs and scraps of rotting leaves from wherever she picked up the splinter. Beneath the grime, though, her feet are without callouses and new looking, like a child's. Being in water so much must be what makes them almost spongy to his touch, the toes soft and pliant in his seeking fingers. On the underside of the fourth toe on her right foot is a small splinter and she sits with one leg straight out and resting on Lee's knee where he is attempting to pull the splinter out with a set of curved forceps from his old dissection kit.

'Keep still,' he says, his hands shaking.

'Get rid of it! I can't move with it in.'

He's a mess after Thettie's booty call. The dream—visitation, what have you—has stayed with him, exacerbating his hangover and his sorrow and also his joy. He wishes she'd stayed away almost as much as he hungers for her return.

The girl rolls her good eye and absently scratches beneath the band of the eye patch. She shifts restlessly on the chair. With her free foot, she nudges the Tonka truck back and forth.

'How was work?' he says.

'Crazy. Boner fell on his face, broke his nose.'

'Glad that's all he broke. You bang into the bar fridge door again?'

She interrupts fidgeting with the toy truck to follow his gaze to the bruises on the calf of her straightened leg. She lifts and drops one narrow shoulder, and looks restively around the little studio.

'You've done so many paintings of her. Not too many people would have seen her naked.'

'That's not what I heard.'

She giggles, 'Arch and Grif wouldn't like you disrespecting her.'

'I mean none.'

'It doesn't bother you? What she was? You liked her. Just a little.'

Lee looks up at blearily. 'That I did.'

'Maybe more than a little.'

'Like I'm going to talk about it with you.'

'Ow.'

'Sorry.' The shard in her toe resists the tip of the forceps, sending a small electric shock through the steel. 'So, I don't know what you got in here. It's too sharp to be wood. It's white, almost. Did you step on a broken plate at the bar?'

She shakes her head adamantly.

'Do you like me, too?'

Lee concentrates with redoubled intensity on the pale shard in her foot. 'Yes. But not in the same way.'

His heart gallops, slows down and almost stops. Between heartbeats, he feels like he's floating in zero grav. His stomach grinds in a state of aggravated readiness, like a car trying to outrun its own headlights. Rain slaps against the glass walls of the studio. The wood burner pumps soporific heat. He wouldn't normally have it on so high, but she is always cold. Another side-effect of being so much in the water, she says.

'What's the latest on Doc's invasion of Nose Island?'

'He's going to give me his boat,' she says. 'He says I should tell Frankie that Doc will hurt me unless Frankie lets him on the island.'

'He *will* hurt you.'

She shakes her head, 'I'm already hurt.'

He sits back, staring at the hurt toe like a pale bud in its coat of grime. The windows fog up and he can see where she scrawled something on the inside, a blue flash to the letters. There is a half-familiar shifting in the oxygen levels, like a moan, but of pleasure or pain, it's hard to say.

She prods his thigh impatiently with her foot. He shakes off his daze, turns back to the splinter.

She nods up and down vehemently. 'I'm the wascally wabbit.'

Lee frowns. 'It's too dangerous. I don't think you should go.'

She itches her filthy hair. Lee is sure she has lice. 'Frankie won't let anything happen to me now. He promised.'

Lee peers through the smeared lenses of his glasses at the soft and wounded toe and mutters that Frankie promised that he'd take care of them, too, once. 'And Doc had to save them.'

'Doc fixed their boat.' She giggles. 'He fixed it, he fix-fix-fixed it.'

His forceps touch a nerve and they both flinch. He bites his cheek, slides roughly out from under her foot and goes to the easel and looks at Thettie lying half-naked with her face turned away from him. The shadowy figure on the island grows darker and more defined every day, but still he can't place it. He swallows blood.

'Frankie said it was our little secret,' she says. '*Shhhh.*'

She presses a filthy finger over her lips. The rain outside gets heavy. The lake guns rumble their lies.

He puts the kettle on the stove. He drinks three glasses of water at the paint-splattered sink, takes an unending piss, and returns with tea. She puts her foot back comfortably on his knee.

He sips the tea and listens to her story. How she was born with one eye, brought up in foster homes that she can barely remember. How she ran away many times and got into all sorts of trouble. She'd rather not say what. There was a terrible man. Many terrible men. She lived for a while in Ilium—she can't remember where before that. There was some bad crystal. A friend got her amped under the old bridge over Triangle Falls. She didn't feel so good. But then she had a swim and felt better. Except it got too cold, so someone came to wake her up. Someone who knew her name.

And then she met Frankie Harpur. Frankie gave her work, she says. Frankie gave her a purpose. Made her stop swimming in circles.

'What was the purpose?' he asks so quietly, he can't hear himself over the rain on the metal roof.

'I can't remember. Thettie told me, but I forgot.'

They lock eyes over her naked foot. Filthy child with a missing eye and an unspeakable name. She reaches across, takes off his glasses and cleans them on her T-shirt, returns them crystal clear.

Frankie didn't like to leave the island on account of his foot, she says. That was her job. The pain was better on the island and the stink, too. In the early days he came and went, but now, not so much. She could get him what he needed.

'And what he needed was Thettie. He needed his family back,' Lee says quietly.

The girl nods. He tried to keep them away from Little Ridge for as long as he could because this place had bad mojo, but now it was time, he said. It bothered him that they weren't safe. They were with a bad man, he said. Not a monster, but evil just the same, even if it was just evil with a small 'e.'

Frankie said he learned to shoot in the army. He could shoot anything that moved. There were things to shoot on the island. Things to hunt.

Lee has stopped prodding at the splinter, but keeps his head down to concentrate on her words, which are receding, lost in interference from the crackling wood stove, or the wind outside. He strains to hear.

There had been a monster called Bud, a different kind of monster from the lake monster, who would bring Frankie things for a while. He wasn't even a man anymore, because he ate children. He was Evil with a capital E. It made Frankie sick to think about it. Frankie said he watched the monster when it didn't know it was being watched, and saw what he threw into the lake. Parts that he didn't want, of all the children he ate. She stayed with Frankie after the monster threw the parts of children into the lake and didn't go back to the bridge. She planned to but she never got there. Frankie was her friend now, but there had been another friend, too, someone who found her under the bridge. She's forgotten his name.

She liked the island and she wanted to stay with Frankie all the time. But she could still come and go, and that was useful to Frankie. It helped him and she wanted to help him because that was her purpose.

She blows on her tea and watches Lee go back to digging around in her toe. 'I asked him why I could come and go and he couldn't and he said it was because of my name.'

'Is that the secret?' Lee fumbles the dissection forceps. Her toe keeps sliding from his grasp. He's drawing more blood than he means to.

'Frankie is afraid that if he tries to get off the island he'll forget how to get back. He's too weak, he says.'

'What about the Native American?' Lee says. 'The guy that met Doc on his Jet Ski?'

The girl nods. Kreb can move back and forth, too, like her. But he doesn't talk to her. Even when she gets lost on the island, which she still sometimes does, he never comes to find her. It is always just Frankie.

Lee's sweating under his plaid shirt and he knows he's digging too deep, hurting her. But he's so close now.

She cries out as the forceps make their blind incursion, grips the edges of her chair. 'Frankie says Doc never stopped talking with the deGroots, even down at the Landing. He says that Doc knew about Frankie's island and the Killer Fix . . . '

'Mix.'

'. . . before I came along. Frankie knew Doc would tell everyone it was me who he heard it from. That's how Frankie could send me, and no one would know. No one would know he'd gone behind their backs to help the deGroots move in on Frankie.'

Lee says. 'So, Grif was right.'

'Frankie says they were all dead meat as soon as Doc came along.' She shrugs like someone twice her age, and it's Thettie's voice he hears now, 'Frankie says it was fate.'

'You can still fuck with fate,' Lee says.

She tries to pull her leg back. 'That hurts too much!'

But he can't pull back now. The pallid tip of the splinter is almost long enough to grip with the forceps, and if he doesn't grab it now, it'll be gone forever. He is too full of the truth of what she is saying, too full of the splinter drowning in the hungry bubble of blood.

'Won't be long,' he says through gritted teeth, hating her and loving her.

She is crying, her head in her hands.

'Soon,' he says through gritted teeth. 'Soon.'

His legs feel cold. The forceps weigh heavily in his sweating hands. 'You were trying to stop me, weren't you? The night she died. You were trying to close the door.'

'I don't know what I'm doing half the time.'

'I want to see my son.'

'I feel like I'm falling,' she is sobbing. 'Most of the time, I feel that. I don't know where I am any more. Like I'm left behind.'

The splinter flees from the tips of the forceps. He stops digging and looks up at her. 'Just tell me, please. Where is he? Is he safe? Can I see him? Bryce?'

At the sound of her name, she brings her hands away from her face. It is streaked with tears and grime.

'I don't know,' her lips are running with tears because she's drowning, 'if I can?'

There is a blow torch at the back of Lee's eyeballs, and his voice is a croak. 'I'm sorry I hurt you,' he says. 'But I feel like you. Like something lost.'

He jabs blindly at the little bleeding hole, the shocks arrowing up his arm and into his heart. The forceps finally find purchase and as he slowly pulls it out, she jerks her tiny foot out from his hand. He holds aloft the forceps which clasp a pale and good-sized sliver of bone that he's pulled from her toe.

'Found it!'

She leans in, whimpering. But before he can say how maybe she got it from the pet cemetery, before he can lie again to her and to himself, she's gone. Leaving him alone with the forceps and the bone. The leaves blowing in, and the biting rain.

47. TANGLE

THETTIE DOESN'T LIKE wagons either, because they are too hard to get on and too easy to fall off.

Sarey helped deliver Archy on a rainy September dawn in 1991, five years before Thettie took custody of the nine-year-old Grif. With two boys to take care of, she decided it was time to get clean. Ten years later, Frankie was returned home to her from war, broken but alive, thanks to Doc Murphy. Doc turned up a year or so later with his medic's bag of tricks, his once red hair turned white as snow from being such a hero. It wasn't just him getting Frankie out alive, but something else about him made her feel all squishy and new again inside, juicy. Something in his deep-set eyes that said he was with her, that their meeting was predestined. That he was on her side.

The scars, maybe? He'd been burnt. A whole layer of him gone. Sacrificed for Frankie because he was on their side. That got to her, too. Caused her to reach one Sunday for one too many beers at Sarey's birthday barbecue and then later that week a bottle of honey bourbon left on Doc's dresser and then some bud. Fresh from the deGroot farm.

Doc rarely elaborated on the broken record he kept

about himself, about what he was before he was in the army, about life in Ireland (or wherever) or as a Cleaner in Liverpool for Paddy the Jew. He talked about these things with the braggart's detachment like they'd happened to someone else, like someone in a movie or a book. The stories were all the muscle he had at that time.

But there was one story he told in bits, and he only told it once from beginning to end, and she forgot all about it until now.

It comes back to her like a child's hat caught on a dark winter branch, or frozen in the ice and she picks away at it, cracking the ice, pawing it away from the tiny scrap of wool, of memory. Doc—who wasn't Doc nor Daylin but just some mother's son—waiting outside a Bingo Hall for his da, called into a back room meeting with some men he owed money to. Doc— before he was Doc, creator of worlds to destroy, and who was then just some ten-year-old-boy with a ten-year-old head full of false hope—slept that night and the next in the back seat of Da's Vauxhall. He was too scared to get out because of a chained hound outside the hall, barking without respite until it could bark no more but just kept up a frenetic rasp. Thettie never heard of a Vauxhall until now. But she can recall its dim green exterior, and how it was wood-paneled on the inside. Paddy the Hook (or Jew, depending on who you ask) came out for a smoke and saw the car. He bent in to have a look at the tearful, starving boy. Not-Doc peered back at Paddy's narrow handsome face. The beast-dog rattled its chain. Paddy got his lieutenant, Haha Malone, to break the window and lift the boy out, carried him kicking and screaming into

Paddy's Rolls Royce. Haha gently told the boy to cover his ears and not to look back, but Doc-in-the-making heard the single gunshot anyway and hears it still.

And when Thettie asked if he ever found whether the gunshot was for the dog or his da, Doc just shrugged and said he never saw either of them again. But to this day, Thettie knows that's the real reason he hates dogs and that the other war story, the one about the dogs eating his trigger fingers off? That was just a lie. Doc lost those fingers in the army hospital after the explosion in Bagram—that he actually expected them to believe he'd have been able to enlist, even as a medic, with two missing fingers?

Made men can be unmade, Sarey muttered, hating him from Day 1, but that was just wishful thinking. Frankie always said that a person had to have something no one could take away from them. That thing Thettie always believed no one could take away from her, her own self, was what Doc took. She was the one unmade.

48. SMEAR

ALL THROUGH THE last weekend before Halloween Lee wills her back. He watches Archy crisscrossing the lake, wondering what the brothers know about Doc and Frankie, and if it's his place to tell them. He waits for an answer, watching from his window as her sons move in endless circles around the point of her death.

The island.

Archy stays away for hours, sometimes all night. Lee knows it's just a matter of time before Archy turns up on his doorstep. But when he does—on a Sunday afternoon—Lee is so caught up in his new painting of Thettie that he doesn't hear Archy's approach. He has his back to the studio door, feels the cold wind and turns to a swirl of leaves. The big Harpur man-cub stands on the threshold with his huge frame filling the door, rain slanting in. Bone-white light falls across a jaw slack with grief, crumbs in his beard.

'I can't get to it.' His eyes are smears of blue, like a blurred Polaroid.

He breathes heavily through his mouth. Rainwater pools around his boots.

Lee says, 'It doesn't want you there.'

'What the fuck, Lizard Man?'

The wind flattens the nap of the grassy rise up from the shore. Its moan fills the studio. They listen for a moment to the faint report of Frankie's guns from behind the mist. Lee turns back to the canvas and licks his brush, strokes it against the part of Thettie's naked flank he's painting. 'It's got to be there somewhere.'

Archy plods soggily up to the glass. In his wake, he leaves scattered brown leaves, curled up around themselves, like clawed hands. 'Where the hell is it?

'It's there.'

Archy says ferociously, 'Bullshit.'

'The mist blocks it from view,' Lee's brush freezes on its way to blot a speck at the pale nape of her neck. 'The headland, too, depending on the angle.'

Except that's not strictly true, because no matter what the angle, sometimes the island is there and sometimes it's not. Archy closes the door behind him. He picks up the chewed doll's hand that Lee found on the deGroot farm and makes a gross-face, puts it down. He's aged, no longer the lovesick metal-head he was a few weeks ago. He looks even more dangerous now, chiseled and tragic. He nudges the big yellow toy truck, a dead child's name scratched on the underside.

'But Frankie. Frankie's there, behind all that fog.'

'So, I met Frankie once,' Lee says. He puts down his brush and pours two coffees, sloshes some whisky in them and passes one to Archy. 'Twice in fact. Once when I bought meth from him for the lab and the second time when he asked to borrow some coffee. Before he died, Zabriskie bought this place from the college, bought a few other places, too. So Frankie actually owns a good chunk of Little Ridge, and one of these days you're going to have to look into that. Being his next of kin.'

Archy has a canvas satchel over his shoulder. He drops it, and then pulls off his thermal, unleashing a smell of diesel and lake water. He reaches in the satchel for a baggie, rolls a joint and passes it to Lee.

'Chill. It's not Devil's Bud. This is just ordinary Pennsy weed.'

Lee inhales and is drawn into the intricacies of Archy's tattoos. A whole floating city on one arm, figures fornicating with cars, and Rorschach bad guys, and flayed Transformers scuttling across the ramparts of a Dr. Caligari castle. Lee smokes, mesmerized. Archy walks around the studio. His hair is unwashed, his beard tangled. The rain makes white seams through the grime on his throat. His eyes are the color of copper oxide. With an ache, Lee notices a spattering of luminous freckles like Thettie's across the boy's cheekbones. Lee passes the joint back and Archy's hand trembles so violently that he can barely bring it to his lips.

'I just don't understand,' he says.

'Maybe you don't want to,' Lee coughs, pounds with a closed fist on the area above his heart.

'Ma told me how she thought Frankie had been there before. He'd snuck across and ate some berries or something, and he was never the same after.'

'Maybe,' Lee brushes a dirty streak around the curve of her buttocks, remembering what Thettie said about how angry Sarey had been when she found out. 'Maybe he took a little piece of the island away with him when he did that. And it wanted it back.'

Until he says it, Lee isn't aware of how ridiculous

it sounds, but Archy nods gravely, like an echo, or after image of his mother.

'I don't think he wants to come home, Archy. Maybe he did once, but not anymore. I think if he did, he would. The island's where he wants to be. It's got him now. Heart and soul, is the only way I can put it.'

'But Bryce, okay? She's been there. She's met Frankie, too. Talked to him.'

'You don't know where she's been, remember?' Lee cleans his glasses on a rag, smearing dirty ice-colored paint across the lens.

'Ma said that. Used to.'

'So, she was right.'

Archy's phone rings, the one Doc bought him, and he speaks with his brother wearily and then hangs up.

'I studied to paint in juvie,' he says, turning his back to the canvas of his mother naked and far from home. 'Me and Grif did a spell down in Pennsylvania. But the paintings I did, they weren't like that.'

Lee stands back from the painting of Thettie on her stomach lying on their bed in the Winnebago with a panel of sunlight falling across her freckled back. The sheet is pulled down to the curve of her buttock and her hair is tousled and her face is turned away, but in such an angle that she seems to be looking at, or talking to someone outside of the painting, whose formless shadow seems less to fall across the floor than to be rising from it.

'What did you paint? Abstracts?'

'Yeah, they tried that with us. Cubism and whatnot. Paint your fears and such. But I didn't go for that. Nah, for me it was people. I'm a people guy. People I didn't know, but maybe I'd want to know someday. Like Beyoncé. I painted her for Ma.'

'Did you like it?'

'I liked Beyoncé,' Archy says. 'But Ma was a freak for her.'

'Painting, I mean. Do you like to paint?'

'It's okay.'

While he's talking, Archy has gone to the computer and brought up a map of Funes Lake. He bangs on the screen with his finger.

'There it is,' he says. 'On the map. So why can't I find it?'

'What you want to worry about,' Lee inhales deeply, narrowing his eyes at the illustrated man on Archy's forearm dancing in the swirling, fragrant smoke. 'Is that it doesn't find you.'

49. SCRIBBLE

SUNDAY MORNING, **1997**. After a bad run of nerves, Thettie was still asleep, dreamless in the fog of whatever Doc had prescribed for her nerves, the disease worse than the cure. Something woke her, a half-intuited absence, and she jumped out of bed to find both boys gone. It was barely six a.m. Scrappy gone, too. Her brain like peanut brittle because of Doc's medicine. Thettie and Sarey and some of the other girls searched the gully, and took boats up and down the creek, before they decided to head to the lake. Fear had burned up all the tears in Thettie's eyes. Where was Doc?

Hours of searching later, a call came through from Doctor Burlington in the town to say that the boys were with him and were fine, but the pup had drowned. The boys lucky to be alive, thanks to Mr. McMurphy.

Murphy, she could hear Doc in the background correcting him. *Doctor Murphy*

Thettie listened but not closely to Burlington tell her the boys should probably go up to Emergency for a checkup. Burlington said he'd be happy to refer her to a well-regarded parenting skill workshop series right down here at Cordell U., designed for court-mandated parents as a rule, but he could pull some strings.

Thettie dropped the receiver of the hamburger phone Frankie got her for her birthday. Its seven-degree swing will come back to her twelve years later, enabling her to calculate the exact time of the call—11:28 am—and to compare the jerking arc of the hamburger on its old retro-style cord with the arc of the rope swing behind Lee's studio when pulled by the wind. Groping along the cluttered floor for her clothes and then blindly into Frankie's Pontiac to drive to town.

Archy and Grif were waiting for her in Doctor Burlington's rooms. Doc 'What's Up' Murphy was there, too. Mrs. Burlington had washed and dried his clothes—an honor for a war hero, she'd said. Doc's eyes had flicked away when she'd tried to meet them. Thettie stroked her boys' hair, took them into her arms. Archy sobbed against her breast because Scrappy was lost at the bottom of the lake. Grif had stood to one side, tearing at his fingernail with guilt. His one obligation to his adopted Ma, to take care of all she held dear—unfulfilled. Thettie recalls, at age 8 and 12, that this was the first wedge between them. Doc offered to drive them in the SUV to the hospital. The then still young Doctor Burlington shook Doc's hand once again, and told Thettie, who he will pronounce dead from an overdose eleven years later, that he expected the boys to make a full recovery and, like Thettie, to have learned a valuable lesson besides. The lesson? That mama owed Doc as do they, and there was not a day they wouldn't know it.

Thettie's transitioning flesh ripples, remembering

how, sitting beneath the fluorescent lighting in the waiting room, a woman wearing a leatherette coat stood behind the rows of chairs by the vending machine and emitted an intermittent hissing noise—kkhkhkhkhk—from the back of her throat while Thettie tries to piece together the whole story from Doc, and the questions she tries to count off on her fingers, are A) Why does a newly fixed boat take in water so quick, B) Why a water dog doesn't swim to shore, and C) What was in the mix Doc prescribed to settle her nerves that made her sleep for a day and a night, and half of the next day, not even getting up to feed her boys? D) With her keen hearing, why would she have not woken to the sound of her own dog barking on the creek, a sound that still comes back to her after all these years?

Thettie didn't fall off the wagon again, or not entirely, and she had her stash of Ambien and sometimes Xanax to even her out. She found it hard to sleep, refused the Haldol once she found out that's what it was, but found herself relying on the pills more often than she would admit. But that was about all. No more pipes, and no more coke. No more crystal or speed.

But after the near drowning a gulf opened between her and Frankie. It was because Doc owned her now and Frankie blamed himself. Without Thettie to stop them, the voices in his head came back, and after a while, they replaced her. With Cassie gone she had no one but her boys. And they were struggling with their own separation, a wedge driven between them by Doc. Archy kept to himself now. Grif went off with other friends, unable to deal with the guilt. She told Archy that Scrappy wasn't his fault. She told Grif that it wasn't his fault, either. They were both brave boys, she said, and that she was the one who had been afraid but she wouldn't be any more.

Except in life, as in death, it takes time to change. Doc found room to move in the house he burned to the ground. He knew how to feed the enmity between men, and he gave that hunger between Archy and Grif all it could eat. He waded into the gulf of guilt and rage between them, throwing Bryce into the mix but it wasn't Bryce who got between them. It was way before that and it was Doc. That was when everything changed. From now on wherever they went, there he was. And wherever Doc was, he fed on fear to keep away whatever was left behind that Bingo Hall. Waiting for him.

After the near drowning of her boys, Thettie picked up a strange and crippling phobia of reptiles, along with a vicious tendency to melancholy. Sarey made her teas and herbal remedies and Doc invented novel ways to 'cure' her involving a rubber hose and hand cuffs. Last Christmas he gave her a bottle of OxyContin for pain—little pills that individually sell for upwards of ten dollars—which she dutifully accepted, but spat out when he wasn't looking. It was a game with Doc, and it was sometimes best to play along.

Except for when you get lost in the game. Then it's not a game anymore.

***

And now, as she rampages through her not-hometown, she watches Archy take repeatedly to the lake looking for the island, his eyes wilder each time he comes up empty. She follows Grif to the highway where he picks up Jason's step-brother to take him fishing, or buy him a milkshake at Maxine's. Thettie watches her oldest son teach this throwaway person to cast off and reel in muskies and to clean them. The small boy says something that makes Grif lift his head up and laugh. They cook and eat the fish they have caught. Their forms, one huge and the other small, are dark against the lake's bioluminescence, the disembodied tip of Grif's cigar scribbling its strange message on the night.

Sometimes she is inside of her trailer and other times she is outside. Now that the chain is gone, time jumps queasily for her. She is outside and wants to get back in but she can't and she realizes she is at the wrong trailer—her sons'. She presses her face to the outside window and sees that Doc has ordered pizza for everyone. In life he sensed her, felt her and fed off her like an obsession. Why should that change after death? So he turns around and peers out into the night. Imagines he sees her. He laughs in the face of his throwaway monster. He lunges unexpectedly toward the glass and shakes his head. He doesn't need her after all. He has Bryce—hidden in plain sight the whole time. Homer and Lyle laugh, too. Her sons try and peer over him, at whatever is making a commotion outside, a deer maybe or a fox. Homer waddles in front of them, blocking their view. They belong to Doc now— no! Thettie backs away into the woods, scratching under her armpit. Nonono. You can't know a person until you know how they can scare you.

Her only remaining fear is her last tie to the living—and it will not go quietly.

She follows Bryce to Lee's house. She follows Bryce

in the woods, where she picks wildflowers and places them in Lee's pet cemetery. Sometimes she shadows Bryce into the studio where she comes in from the cold for a cup of hot tea, or to watch Lee paint in the warmth of the wood stove. She fiddles with the knickknacks in Lee's studio. The Tonka Truck and the Spider Man figure. On the last Sunday before Halloween she watches Bryce emerge from the lake, naked and covered in filth, limping from a splinter of bone in her toe.

Sometimes, at night, Thettie accompanies Bryce to the Way and watches her work her cocktail magic behind the bar, and sometimes Thettie's boys are there, too, at the Harpur booth, and they are all together again. Afterward Thettie goes to Lee's house, and then in the early mornings she keeps vigil over Bryce in the little trailer, waiting for the return of her forgotten dream.

The night after Lee pulls her splinter, Bryce is woken early in her tiny trailer by a dream. But it's a false dream, a chimera. Dawn is still an hour away. And the false dream leads her in her leaky inflatable to the island. Thettie, having no boat of her own, must run as fast as she can to leap onto the back of the inflatable to travel with Bryce as far as the red and green warning beacon. A gap opens in the dark fog and Frankie is standing on the island.

'You're almost home,' Frankie says, and Thettie doesn't know if he's talking to her or to the Bryce.

Frankie is bald. His teeth are black and dripping, and he is lame, walking with a living cane that jumps and writhes. She's not so sure she wants to come and live with him on the island after all. A big man comes into view—Iroquois, looks like, that Thettie assumes must be Kreb, and there is a baying of dogs, but they're not dogs. They're torn, hungry things made of the same black sludge that covered the baby doll Bryce pulled out of the water, that won't wash out of Thettie's nightgown or from under her nails, and Thettie wails in terror.

'No Frankie! Please! It's me, Thettie. I'm lost!'

She bangs on the sides of the boat as hard as she can to be taken away, saved from Frankie and the island. The girl obediently steers the boat away and glides silently across the lake through the mist to Triangle Gully. She turns into the creek and steers upstream past their homes and deeper into the gully where the banks get steeper and the creek gets narrower. She slows before they get to Harpur falls. Upstream and around a hidden bend is Triangle Bridge where Bryce used to hang out.

Time stretches backward, and Thettie is younger and her claws have disappeared, her new hide stripped back to freckles and bruises. She is not wearing her bloody nightgown, but shorty pajamas and a Mets hoodie. She leaps out of the stalled boat, mad with terror. She cowers in the dead fall on the bank. The girl steers the boat across the stream where it snags in some stunted willows on the other side of the creek, a dark hostile tangle of root wads and debris coated in a thin layer of ice all year around.

Mists close over the girl and the night wind whispers through the Aspens. There is a grove of them behind Thettie on the ridge bordering deGroot land. Thettie hears wild barking but it is the howl of men, not hounds—moon-dogs baying for blood. Thettie has no defenses. She has her own teeth back, her own tongue. When she touches her skin, it feels warm, material. Her heart leaps. Is it even possible?

Thettie strides up and down the bank in agitation, waiting for the girl to reappear. 'I want to go home!' Thettie cries. 'Home!' She peers across the narrow creek. The mists part and there is a small child kneeling by the edge of the cut bank. The child is a little boy and he is naked. His attention is fixed on a hand trying to break through from beneath the ice. The shadow of the scratching, scrabbling fingers grips Thettie in terror. She tries to scream but can't. Fingers protrude through the ice, then a hand. Thettie is frozen with horror, her legs leaden. She slowly pulls one forward, then the next. There is an icy stream between them, and after all she is only human and bound by the laws of both physics and psychology. The hand breaks through enough for the little boy to lean precariously over and reach for it. He pulls its owner out, who is Bryce. Then the little boy is gone.

'Bryce?' Thettie calls hoarsely across the creek. She is livid with terror. The girl looks around confusedly. She too is naked, gooseflesh breaking out over her boyish body.

'Daddy?' the girl calls hoarsely.

But then, just as the stars begin to pale over the eastern ridge, there is a dull flash of metal at the edge of Thettie's eyes. Thettie moans. She forces her numb legs to wade through the icy sludge toward it. It is a fourteen foot Jon-boat secured in a slough and held in place by two root wads. It is made of aluminum crisscrossed with rust from its rivets and the motor is long gone, but she'd know it anywhere. It's Archy's and

Grif's from their boyhood. The one they took out to the lake to catch their ma some salmon the time Doc gave her that medicine that unmade her. Thettie's material knees buckle and she grips the side of the boat with shaking hands. Her teeth clatter. There, Scrappy's collar. There, beneath the seat across the bow, a piece of lead easy to work loose from the rusty rivet conceals a jagged slit in the base of the boat. Thettie sticks the tip of her slender finger in the slit. Man-made by a mad man. Thettie buckles Scrappy's collar around her neck and stands up, her body warm again, electric.

Bryce is back in the Zodiac, slipping on her Goodwill camo-pants and pink sweatshirt. She glides across the creek to pick Thettie up.

'This is where I was born,' Bryce says. 'And this is where I died.'

'You and me both,' says Thettie moving away from her own tangle of roots and time.

***

Later in the morning when Bryce is back in her trailer and Thettie is back in hers, and she is once again broken—immaterial—she watches Doc go to see to the boats. She watches him bend to more closely examine the black sludge sloshing in Bryce's broken Zodiac, and how it has been hastily tied and left still rocking in its own spreading, disappearing wake. But then he stands up and looks to the island and she knows, by the way he turns to summon his familiars, Homer and Lyle, and the way they know it too, that he has come to a decision and that her time is up.

50. UNTOUCHABLE

IN THE DARK of the studio Lee reads the text from Habib inviting him to breakfast the next day.

'Can't,' Lee texts back. 'Going fishing. I'll bring you some steelhead, whatever that is.'

'Trout,' Habib texts. 'Rainbow family.'

'Speaking of rainbows,' Lee texts back. 'How're the travel plans going?'

'Travel plans?'

'The travel plans you're supposed to be making in connection with the blue Impala parked outside your house this last week.'

'Mmmm. My new security detail, thanks to you. Turns out one of them is a blend man, the other's single origin. So, we alternate.'

'Not safe, Sam. Flush your stash of Helotide down the toilet and go somewhere . . . '

' . . . over the rainbow? ;-)'

Lee watches the ellipses for a while, and then he looks out to the lake, to the dim light of a small Jet Ski heading toward the shore, where it keeps going south until he can't see it any more.

***

They meet on the jetty at dawn. The slats are streaked with puddled rainbows, the apricot sky banded with dark clouds. Lee pounds his arms with opposite fists. He should have known to bring a woolen hat like Archy and Grif. They shake their hungover heads at his thin corduroy jacket thrown over his thermal, and at the Polaroid camera swinging around his neck. He wonders if they're regretting inviting him along. Maybe they only did it for their mother, like a pity play date. Grif is already on the boat. He looks for a spare hat in the hold and comes up with a Giants cap, tosses it to Lee. It's too big and flops down over his glasses, the dull ache across his nose at least taking his mind off his hangover.

Archy pulls his collar up. He takes out the saw bellies, starts chipping away the frost. Avery at the Way has said he'll buy some bass and flounder if they can get it. This, they know, is Bryce's idea—to reinstall Irene's fish soup on the Way's menu. And maybe some other dishes from the Philippines. Avery wants to try something to make the Way stand out. He's already figuring that the Harpurs won't be there forever, at least not all of them. At least not *her*.

'Dairy free x and vegan y?' Avery had dismissed these with a wave. 'Wait till they try Irene's fish soup.'

'Avery'll pay us for the catch,' they told Lee. 'Buy us some more time in this shit-hole. You coming?'

Lee had agreed, suggesting that they could drop him off at Ilium where he has a contact who might be able to help.

The best steelhead is south, in the colder water near the waterfalls around Ilium. Leave the island behind for a day is the plan.

'How did you get rid of Doc?' Lee says.

'We didn't get rid of him. He got rid of us. I think

he wants to sneak off to see deGroot. Told us to have a day off. Heard them leave early this morning.'

'Wait,' Lee stops short on the jetty, hearing the name on his tongue. 'It's not safe.'

Grif's wide mouth stretches in a grim smile. 'For Bryce? She's gotten to you, too?'

They tell him that they wouldn't even consider leaving her except she's got a double shift, and Emilio and Dustin aren't going to let her out of their sight.

'Aunt Sarey lent them one of her dogs,' Grif growls from around his cigar, all the while dragging pails and fixing lines and untying the boat. 'A big albino Rottie— mean old bitch been in the wars. Looks like hell and she's lost her voice box somewhere along the way. Maybe in a fight or caught a hunter's bullet. Sarey's always taken in abandoned animals and runaways. Well Doc took one look at it, went pale as a sheet. His boy Homer all but shat his pants.'

'Doesn't your aunt need the dog? For protection?'

'She's got a pack of them,' Archy says. 'Every time she buries one, another turns up.'

Lee turns back to the shore. Thettie stands there with one hand raised, the flesh hanging off her arm in black flaps. The black goo creeps up her shoulders and neck, separating into black scales banded in blinding light. He raises a trembling hand in reply.

'Hey Grif?' Archy glances in the direction of the island, a rocky protrusion on the chalky horizon. 'What's that?'

Grif turns to where Archy's pointing. He takes the cigar out of his mouth, holds it unlit in his tattooed knuckles. 'I don't see anything except a big-ass manor with our name on it, brother. Doc or no Doc.'

They all shiver in the wind.

Lee wipes his nose with an icy knuckle. 'You will need a lawyer.'

Archy points at some rope lying on the jetty for Lee to pick up and toss in the boat. 'Bryce told me that when Doc heard about how Frankie was rich, he tried to get Ma to make a will. And she kept putting him off. Last I overheard was him telling Homer and Lyle to fix it for proof of their de facto status. So, that means he has half and we get the other half, lawyer or no.'

'Well, I wouldn't worry about it too much,' Lee says. 'There are lawyers and there are lawyers.'

'Anyways,' Grif rumbles. 'Frankie may not have willed anything to Ma. Frankie may not even be dead. Who knows what's what.'

Detective Fabiana Brown might, Lee thinks. If we're lucky. He is last on board, turning one final time to the shore to see a stone skipping after them and no visible hand to flick it.

***

Heading south, Grif's dented Lund skims the cross-hatched surface of the water. The shore is still in night's shadow, lone lights blinking. Grif slows down and veers toward an inlet. Lee's entire face is wet, his glasses sheathed in spray. His tongue is barnacled with ulcers and it hurts to pee.

'The only hangover cure on God's green earth,' says Grif, lighting a fresh cigar. 'Fishing.'

Archy says, 'You don't have contacts or some such to wear out on the water?'

They give him a piece of line to tie around his glasses. Archy hasn't shaved since his mother died. Gray streaks his beard, which fuzzes down his jaw and neck.

'Heard you did some rafting in your time,' he says, doubtfully.

'My wife and I did. We camped and hiked some in Pennsylvania, took the kayaks with us. I got pretty good.'

'Don't quit your day job, brother.'

Lee blushes at the attention they give him. How they call him 'brother.' The dark ridge above the town recedes as they move south against the current. The mist unwinds momentarily to reveal the campus bell tower, and then winds around it again like a bandage. The campground is in darkness. Most of the Harpurs have gone to look for work and cheap housing in the surrounding towns or cities. Some have given up and gone back to the Landing. The speed boat pulls abreast of the small inlet that snakes toward a wetland. Archy's line goes taut. Grif steps alongside his brother with a net to scoop up the fish but it's a bass that's too small to eat. They toss it back.

'Heard you went to the trailer,' Grif said. 'Find anything?'

Lee wonders how he is going to tell them that he saw Doc killed Frankie, almost, in order to bring him back from the dead and be the savior to his people—how he watched that like news footage on an unplugged-in television in Thettie's cabin.

'So,' he begins. 'I didn't find Vernon, but . . . .'

'Fish on!' Archy says. Grif strides over with his net in one hand, and the burning cigar dangling from his mouth.

'Is it a brown—a big one, no—'

'It's a brown,' Archy whistles between his teeth. 'Holy huge fish.'

'Whoa Joe. You wanted to catch a brown? There's your brown.'

'Bring him in, Grif. You got him.'

'No, I don't. He got away. You see him? Damn!'

'Not as big as that one when we were kids—remember—twelve-pounder?' Grif turns to Lee with his hands spread. 'You should have seen it. Thirty inches, easy. We were like, nine or ten and it was big as he was. No one believed us. But I swear.'

'One that got away,' says Archy. 'I remember.'

They drift for while down the lake as the night pulls back from the horizon. The sun rises above the ridge, but the lake is flat as a piece of old tin foil. Grif pulls beers from a cooler.

'She never went with me,' he says. 'Bryce. It bothers you that she went with Archy?'

Lee says, 'I guess. A little.'

They've taken off their coats and Grif closes his eyes and lifts his head to the East. The weak sunlight falls across his wide forehead and across his high, fighting cheek bones.

'I miss her,' Archy says. 'And she isn't even gone.'

'She's just got that way about her,' Grif says. 'Something that stays with you.'

'I'm scared of her,' Grif says. 'But I'm scareder of myself.'

Lee says, 'None of you know any more about her? Where she's from? Where her people are?'

'Loner child. Mystery sister.'

'Told me she was a runaway, in and out of foster homes,' Archy says. 'Used to hang out under the bridge with the other punks over at Triangle Falls.'

'She told me that, too,' Lee says. 'And her eye?'

'Born that way,' Grif and Archy say together.

'I guess there's born,' Lee says. 'And born.'

Grif leans back against the side. 'What about you, Doctor Dolittle? You slept with her, too?'

Lee says, 'You want me to break another rib?'

'You didn't break shit, Lizard Man.'

'I think I broke my own ass when I fell on it.'

They listen to him laugh at himself with plenty of space to do it in. The whole lake, and not an island in sight. They drift past clusters of old-time shacks in the shadow of opulent lakeside villas. The rush of waterfalls around every bend. Some just a trickle of silver water into a crevasse. Others foaming mouths of glacial spray.

'I'm old enough to be her father,' says Lee, before he can stop himself.

The boys fidget with the necks of their beers and flash their electric eyes at each other and across the lake. 'What happened to your little boy—that's hard. Ma told us. Losing someone that way.'

The early sun is hectic on the aluminum sides of the boat, like it knows its light will be short-lived. The massing clouds give it a Polaroid quality, like a burst of light into Lee's future where there will be no Harpurs to take him fishing or get him high or slap-bang his hands or call him brother. A bleak future where he is alone again with nothing but the lake. Light pours from over the ridge and the lake rolls out before him in all its terrible beauty, not a pebble on the shore, or a frond on a willow or a stem on a cattail or a rainbow on a salmon, that does not make him want to scream. Hell is a glory, he knows, in all its seasons.

'The thing is,' says Archy, hefting his pole up

against the hard plate of his thigh. 'I know Bryce is bogus. Ma was always saying. Grif, too. And they were right. I just don't know what kind of bogus.'

'Me neither,' Grif says, turning around to face Lee. 'What about you? You're from around here, been here the whole time while we haven't. And now the two of you seem pretty tight. Don't get us wrong. No one's saying it's creepy or anything. We know you like them old, like Ma. But just wondering what's going on with the two of you? Or with her?'

Archy says slowly, 'Yeah. Like what's her angle, Lee? You're tight now? She talks to you?'

The boat passes Byrsa Falls. The roar is deafening, and the beauty takes away their talk—the plunging neck of green water, falling into the deep banded basin of rock where it froths and boils ninety feet down. Around the corner and the southernmost tip of the lake is the city of Ilium, which sprawls out ahead of them, brick and ivy and old Georgian crimes and misdemeanors.

'Over there,' Lee yells when the roar dims. 'Give me an hour, and I might have something for you.'

Archy steers into the small marina. Lee rocks awkwardly off the boat with his hands flying and his glasses slipping off and swinging from the fishing line. Archy and Grif shake their heads and call him Doctor Dolittle, and flail around the boat in gentle mockery, and Grif yells, 'One hour.'

***

It's exactly noon when they pull away, and the church bells are ringing. Lee makes his way along the pier and beneath the tattered awnings of the Commons where street-Zombies shuffle beneath blankets in the mural-painted shade of the colonial arcades and dusty New Deal doorways. Lee stops at the Hall of Justice. He pushes through the double doors and enters the foyer, where he signs in and the doorman directs him to the first floor. He gets out of the elevator and steps into a busy call room, and asks to speak to Detective Fabiana Brown.

And then he sits down to wait.

'Hey Lee.'

Lee stands up to shake the hand of the woman who took up the investigation into the disappearance, kidnapping and murder of his child. But she comes around and hugs him instead. He stiffens, then hugs her back too hard. For too long. She gently pries herself from his arms. She says she's about to have a break—they've opened up a new Papa John's. Lunch is on her.

'Can't,' says Lee. 'I'm going fishing.'

She waves him into her office but instead he stands in the threshold looking across her desk at the woman to whom he said his child's name for the last time five years ago.

'You get your search warrant?'

'Kind of,' he says.

'Good. Anything else I can help you with?'

Detective Fabiana Brown is a large athletic woman with big teeth and dyed pink hair. There is a tattoo of a bowler hat on the inside of her wrist. Lee hasn't been in the police station since they brought him in for questioning after his wife's death. Until he walks in, he doesn't know exactly why he's come. Neither does Fabiana Brown.

'Do you remember,' he begins, 'the case you were

working on at the time you took over the investigation into my son's disappearance?

His eyes burn with anxiety. His bowel knifes. He backs up against the wall. Helpless.

Brown's right hand adjusts some wild flowers in a vase, globe flowers and wild gentian. 'Remind me,' she says.

'Someone reported a body,' Lee says. 'It made the Village Dawn.'

Fabiana sits back and looks at her arrangement. 'Under Triangle Bridge. I remember. What about it?'

'It was a teenage girl. Not a local, the paper said.'

'A vagrant, probably. One of those runaways. This have anything to do with the death of that Harpur woman?'

Brown brings her hands back behind her head and crosses an ankle vigorously over her knee, and Lee remembers that she and Habib played in the same masters' soccer team for a few seasons. Habib asked Brown if she'd meet with Lee and his wife when Boyle shut the case down. There's a half-eaten muffin on the desk beside a picture of the detective's family. Two kids, a cat whose name Lee can't remember. A box of Kleenex.

Lee takes a deep breath and begins to lie. 'I'm in a show. The big one over at Ilium. I'm blocked on a painting. Something's missing.'

'Missing.'

Wrong word. 'I mean I guess it's just a little flat. Like something lacking in the vibe.'

'The vibe.'

'The mood. Or tone. So, I remembered the case. That something happened. Something weird.

Something about the body. I'm just doing a little research, try and fill out the atmosphere.'

Brown twists her mouth at him in dry smile. 'It was never found, Lee. You can look all that up over at the Library police records. The Dawn covered it. It'll be on the Internet archives. I mean it's great to see you, but I'm not sure I can help.'

'The internet doesn't give you flesh,' Lee says. 'Or blood. Real breathing life. Talking to you I thought, I mean if I could imagine. If you could describe.'

'Flesh and blood.'

His therapist used to do that. Throw his words back at him so he can hear how irrational they sound. How detached from reality. 'Because it happened at the same time as your son went missing? You really want to go back to how you were feeling then? Salt up those wounds so you can paint it in blood. That such a good idea, Lee? Any prize worth opening up that vein again?'

Stage Number Six: Reconstruction and working through. That'll be where Brown is placing him now.

'Yes,' Lee says slowly. 'It is.'

The look on her face makes it clear that she buys it. She sighs and brings her arms down, clasps her hands on the desk. 'Well there isn't much to it. We get a call from some hikers. There's a body in the willows. We get there as soon as we can. Maybe an hour later. The hikers are gone. The body is gone. Later on, we find the hikers at the Pump Bar. We bring them in. They tell us they got the skeevies waiting for us. You taking notes? Heard all sorts of noises, like someone looking for something. They tell us that they thought maybe it was her attacker coming back, so they fled the scene.'

'But there was no attacker, right?' He's sweating like a horse. 'I mean, you never found one.'

'Correct. We questioned the hikers. They were kosher. After the investigation, we concluded that she was probably one of the vagrant kids who used to hang out at the bridge. Got high and fell in, or whatever. Body carried out to the lake, went to the bottom, drifted out somewhere else. Case put on ice.'

'So it's still cold.'

'As a witch's tit, Lee. That all? Now what's going on down in Little Ridge, talking about witches. That's one stinking cauldron of shit, you ask me.'

Lee regrets lying to Fabiana who was never anything but truthful to him. Who saved him from a stinking cauldron of lies. This time he's going to have to do it for himself.

She continues, 'I remember Thettie Harpur. Her cousin lived down in the Gully with his aunt.'

Lee says. 'Frankie.'

'OD-ed and cut herself up. Bled to death, holy Christ. Clean case of suicide, according to my esteemed colleague Sheriff Boyle.' Brown spits the word 'sheriff' out, under the pretext of picking a crumb of muffin from her tooth.

'Cut and dried,' Lee says. 'They say.'

Brown inspects her fingernails. 'Self-harm's never cut and dried, is what I say. I met her once or twice. Smart woman—didn't seem the type.' Lee hears something in Brown's admiration that he can't place. 'Anyway, so someone stole that strange pet of yours. Valuable? You want me to investigate, or do you think you have this one?'

'Gila Monster,' Lee yanks his thermal off over his

head, recoils from his own unwashed reek. 'I got it, for now. But thanks.'

Brown checks her watch. Lee wouldn't put it past her to sniff around. She's done it before. Maybe that's what he wants. But he needs more time. Now he's happy to bore her. Stage one: Shock and denial is boring. Stage Two: Pain and guilt is boring. Then, Anger and bargaining is (the most) boring. Depression, rejection and loneliness are a drag. The upward turn, Stage Four, is just plain embarrassing. Reconstruction and working through, less said about those the better. Acceptance and hope, Stage Seven? A huge relief for all concerned, because grief is just so damn boring.

Lee side-eyes an aerial photograph of the lake, bunches up his thermal. 'One last thing, Detective. The missing detail in my painting. I mean not literally, but in terms of the big picture . . . was there anything at all about the body? That the hikers noticed? I mean that made them think there had been an attacker. That gave them . . . the skivvies? Anything at all . . . '

'Sounds like a creepy kind of effect you're going for here Lee.'

Little Ridge is a pretty creepy kind of place, right? I'm just trying to capture the vibe.'

'So you said,' she folds her hands together on the desk. 'Nothing else I remember. But if I do.'

He stands up. 'Anything you remember. Anything at all.'

51. THROUGH

TUESDAY NIGHT IS a Halloween party at the Way. But because Bryce has done a double shift, Avery lets her go home early. Still, by the time Thettie hears Lee drop her off at the campground it is after midnight. Thettie is unprepared but excited, not knowing exactly what lies ahead except that it is something she wants, and has been waiting for, for a long time. She lies down on the soiled mattress of the double wide and stares into the dark until the stars turn powdery and fade.

She may have fallen asleep. She is startled by a soft tap at the door, just before first light. Thettie opens it, thinking it to be the girl, as expected. But there is a child standing there instead. A small boy, maybe seven or eight, tall for his age, in a Spider Man suit.

'Wake up,' the child says.

The Spider Man suit is muddy and stained. It's torn at the helm and there are holes at the elbow. The kid's feet are filthy. Maggots wiggle between his toes, and his little face is pinched and bruised.

'Is it time?' Thettie says. 'Halloween's not for a few days.'

The child voice is muffled by the mask. 'Trick,' he says. 'Or treat.'

He waves her forward with a tiny hand, bruised and broken. Thettie grabs her curtain-veil and makes sure to shut the door behind her. She follows the child to Doc's cabin, where he knocks once again, repeating the call. Thettie waits in the shadows.

Fat Homer comes to the door, shirtless and swaying, the flesh pouched around his piggy eyes. He looks down at the child and belches, 'A little early, asshole. Hey Lyle, check this out.'

And the moment Homer turns his back to the child, Thettie is through the open door, as is her way.

The trailer living room is dark but for a dim bulb over the kitchenette sink. It reeks of excrement and pizza and stale chemicals. Lyle goes to the door, but the trick-or-treater is gone, and Homer, steps off the small porch as if hypnotized, and follows the child a way down the dim path. Lyle scoffs and calls, but Homer wanders further out onto the path, until he's just a big pale shape, flickering in the dark.

'Boo!' Lyle calls and wanders back inside the trailer.

Doc is in the bedroom with the door closed and headphones on, still surfing topographical maps of Funes Lake, YouTube documentaries on lake-effect rains, and attorneys who specialize in common law property settlements. The music that bleeds from his headphones is that classical stuff he loves, and Thettie is grateful for the headphones. She waits for Lyle to have one more pipe and pass out, restively, on the divan, half-forgetting about Homer. She has an hour of darkness left, maybe less. She waits under Homer's bed until Lyle has to pee. When he gets up she grabs him around the ankle with her mangled hand. He freezes and emits a wordless rasp. His ankle is so thin and brittle that her claw wraps around it twice and snaps the bone. He screams, but it comes out as a breathy rasp. He pisses a tobacco colored liquid that runs down her knuckles and makes his broken ankle rubbery. She pulls herself out from under the bed and purely for effect, sweeps aside all the mess off the coffee table. Lyle goes down on one knee, rummages for a knife under the mattress. Thettie lunges, rakes his chest with venomous claws right through to the erratically ticking heart. Lyle's face pales and his mouth makes a soundless 'o.' He mechanically brings a hand to the gashes over his heart and his fingers touch the beating muscle and come away on fire.

'I'll give you a head start,' she says.

He is out the door pulling on his clothes and limping down the path where he finds Homer sitting naked in a patch of poison ivy chewing on a broken doll's hand. The boy in the Spider Man suit is nowhere to be seen. Homer's curly hair has turned as white as milk, and there are bright drops of blood seeping from the scar that rings his neck. Lyle hauls Homer into the little red Ford and heads to the highway while Doc loudly snores beneath the Podcast from The Huffington Post that wakes him promptly every morning at 4 am. The rash on Homer's ass as well as his trauma-induced psychosis will outlast the stolen Ford, which gives out just after Lyle's dicky ticker does on the other side of the Ontario border. The rash will periodically flare up, causing the fat man's food to taste of silicon and deep boils to break out around his anus. Causing him, years later, to remember things he'd rather forget. His dick, for instance, which he hasn't seen since 2010. A kitten he had once, his Grandma in her dark kitchen, the canned peach-apple cobbler on Fridays in juvie. The vengeance-flushed faces of his victims—a little Indonesian dance-girl skilled in the Pilipino martial art of Kali, and her teenaged gangster brother—seated in the crowded courtroom, while he, the naked accused, must bare his throat again and again to the curved blade of the *karambit*, the floor beneath his feet molten and suppurate in the cracking flames.

52. REDEEMER

DOWN THE FIRE stairs and across the bridge, and into the nearest IHOP where Lee chases a quick beer with a quick shot, before the brothers come for him, shivering in his sweat-damp thermal. They don't ask him about it until they're in the middle of the lake again, and this time it's Grif with the line and Archy with the net. In between what they catch and what they throw back, Lee tells them that he wasn't able to find out much of anything yet, but he hasn't lost hope.

'You went to the cops?' Archy says.

Grif sniffs disappointedly.

'So, I have history with this one.'

'Don't want to involve the cops in this. They're all deGroot men.'

Lee says, 'She's not a man. She hates the deGroots and she knows Boyle's in their pocket. Plus, she saved my life once.'

'Well,' says Archy slowly. 'What did she say?'

He tells them in a roundabout way about the closing of Triangle Bridge while they were gone because of all the runaways that'd congregate there, starving or freezing in the winter months—but just talking about it seems to bring on a change of mood and weather. Grif pulls his collar up and turns the boat around.

'We better head on back, anyways. Don't like to leave Doc's psychos on their lonesome for too long.'

Lee holds onto the sides, zips his jacket over the Polaroid camera and says as calmly as he can. 'Speaking of which, what's the deal on those two? Homer and Lyle? I mean where they're from and what they're doing with you?'

Grif faces into the wind, so that Lee only gets scraps of what he's saying. 'Doc got his shady lawyer to get Homer paroled after twenty-two years, doing all day for murder. Before that, he almost got his head chopped off in the Philippines by the big brother of some little girl he tried to buy on the internet. Lyle killed a teacher down in Pittsburgh somewhere. Witnessed him robbing a Best Buy warehouse, slashed up the clerk, kid of seventeen.'

Lee shuts his eyes but opens them quickly so he won't throw up, but he lurches and almost goes over the edge.

Archy catches him by the arm. 'Easy there, brother. It is what it is.'

Grif visors his blue eyes with his hands from the glare of the lake. It begins to rain, and he sits up straighter in the boat, leans further forward, his broad, worried face straining into the distance toward the island. He turns around to say something but then the wind blows off the surface of the lake and up against the sides of the boat, and before the boys zip up their jackets Lee catches a glimpse of a sheathed blade under Grif's arm, and a holstered hand gun around Archy's waist. A lick of panic worms in his gut. Sour-smelling smoke billows out of Grif's cigar.

'I'm thinking we *should* go and have a word with

your old boss Habib,' Grif's voice has taken a mutinous turn. 'He's maybe last to see Frankie. Maybe knows a way to the island. What's nootropic anyways?'

'Neurologically enhancing.' The wind has dropped suddenly and Lee's talking too loud. 'Makes you smarter, or learn faster, or remember more, or remember different. That's another thing the peptides do.'

Archy looks bored, kills the engine.

'Peptides?' Grif says, standing up, braced across the boat on two tree-trunk legs in torn jeans.

'In Gila venom,' Lee says. 'The peptides produce a unique gene expression profile.'

'Translate?'

Lee takes out the Polaroid, and leans past Grif to focus on the island, presses the shutter. 'Meaning that the venom activates a memory gene we didn't know was there, on a neural network we didn't know was involved in memory at all.'

Grif winces into the wind, watching the Polaroid inch out, 'So, does the monster venom makes memories from scratch?'

'No. It just makes the process more efficient and faster. The genes in the brain get better at carving new paths through the forest of neurons in our brains. Paths you didn't know you could take and paths you thought you could take but discover you can't. Like between the trailer and the road except there's a poison-ivy patch in between. So, you don't go that way anymore, but the connection remains strong as a deterrent as much as anything.'

'Like a red light?' asks Grif.

'Right. Other connections grow between, say, the

elm tree to the blackberry patch across the creek or from the Indian graves by the side of the field to the shale outcrop to the lightning-split hemlock to the cabin in the woods. The positive connections are as valuable as the negative ones.'

'Blackberry patch, shit,' says Archy.

The ash drops off Grif's cigar into the lake. His blue eyes brim. 'You think that happened to Ma? You think she's out there somewhere and she can remember all this cabin in the woods shit? How she died? How she was partying with us one minute, eating pizza and doing shots, and getting attacked by a killer lizard the next? *Your* killer lizard.'

It hits Lee then, how the boys must have found her, and how, having seen her that way, they can never unsee it. The bloody smile where her mouth had been.

'Fish on!' Archy calls.

Lee's ears pop. The boys jump to their starboard positions.

'Hell yeah!' Grif grabs the pole. 'We just had a big brown, now we got a big salmon.'

'See it jump.'

'They jump all right.'

'You see that jump, Lizard Man?'

'I see. I see!' Lee is on the side now behind the boys, his heart thumping and a grin hurting his face and the wind getting behind his glasses and pulling tears out of his nose.

'Where is it?' Archy says.

'Fish be under the boat.'

Grif is straining at the line.

'Is it a salmon?' says Archy.

'Don't stab at it. It's a twenty-pounder, maybe twenty-five'

'I'm not stabbing, Grif. Keep it flat.'

'There you go. She's in.'

Archy brings the net up, the big fish flopping and glittering, drawing in light and bouncing it back out again.

'That's my biggest brown.'

'It's a salmon.'

'Damn! Biggest damn salmon.'

'Whoa, Archy! Lost the brown, now you got yourself a salmon.'

'You called it, brother. Got us our redeemer.'

'Big old redeemer. Holy salmon.'

'Hold still!' Lee lifts his Polaroid and snaps a picture of the brothers against the platinum sky with the redeemer, held still and glittering between them before they set it free.

53. DRESS REHEARSAL

ENERGY FLOWS FROM Thettie like light from an Edison bulb. Maybe because of finally banishing Homer and Lyle—and even though she could not have done it without the help of the little Spidey—she feels totally ON! Her eyes are headlights on a dark road and her body is electric, all the energy of her disembodied synapses concentrated in want. She materializes at will, fades on a click. Practice makes perfect. This must be what it feels like to go to a high school prom, instead of just giving hand jobs to strangers at the Motel 6.

She waves at the smear of Homer and Lyle's taillights. Waves until the smear is gone. Then Thettie goes back into the trailer—her little Winnebago—to wait for Doc in the dinette. He comes out of the bedroom pulling off his head phones. He looks quizzically at the negative space she occupies. He calls for his ogre and the imp. Where's his coffee? They're meant to be seeing the deGroots today, goddam it. Swears and calls for them again. He checks outside, scopes the sleeping campground. When no one comes, he does his whole military toilet but double time. Shits, showers, jacks off and shaves in ten minutes flat. Routine, he used to say, the oldest mnemonic in the book.

ALETHEIA

She follows him as he stomps uncertainly to the parking lot. When he sees the Ford is gone, he runs his hands over his face and she shimmies up and down a dead maple in glee, a blue blur at the edge of his eye. He tries to explain it to himself. Maybe they've gone off early to get supplies, or maybe snuck out whoring, and his amputated trigger fingers itch in rage. But she can tell he smells a rat and is trying not to panic. The way the good side of his mouth twitches. The overcompensating squaring of shoulders. He recalibrates. At ease soldier. About-turns with a click of his heels, facing ahead, always looking forward, the what and the what-now the only things that count. A good soldier keeps his head. Doc heads back into the Winnebago, where she has gone to wait.

'What's up, Doc?'

Because the next move belongs to her. She's not ready for it yet, but you can't always choose your timing. And whatever it is, it's important for him to see it as a demonstration, a word that was once believed to have derived from the Latin word *monstrare*—to show or display. 'Demonstrate,' Thettie now knows, actually belongs to the same etymological family that spawned the word 'monster,' which current dictionaries trace from the word *monere*—to warn with the prophetic vision of impending doom. She can't wait to talk about all this with Frankie.

'What's up, Doc?' she says again.

Doc's face drains of all color and he looks around for the source of the voice. His eyes roll in their head when she materializes. She didn't know how exactly she was going to do it but it works. His knees buckle. Still feeling theatrical, and let's face it, a little aroused after dispatching Homer and Lyle, Thettie rises a few feet above the floor and hovers in all her terrible presence.

'CQ,' she says, bringing two claws to her muddy eyes and pointing them at Doc's skull, within which lies the prefrontal cortex—site of the precious and easily compromised short-term memory.

And then she fades, not all at once, but decisively toward a conclusion of the visitation with the satisfaction of something not as well choreographed or rehearsed as she might have liked—but a good performance all the same—and one which she will maybe get the hang of over time.

54. LAST CALL

WHEN LEE RETURNS from fishing late on
Sunday there is a message on his phone from Detective
Brown. She looked back over the records, the message
says, and there were conflicting descriptions about the
face on the body found in the ice. One of the hikers said
it had no face, to speak of. That it was almost
featureless, like the face had been washed or frozen off.
But the other hiker said she remembered only half the
face was like that. Like the eye was gone, eaten away
by a groper. Or something. The message times out and
Lee is about to call her back when a text comes
through.

'When questioned, other vagrants, punk kids on
the bridge did remember a young runaway, twelve or
thirteen, with an eye-patch. But no one knew her
name.'

And when Lee tries to call her back, the phone
diverts to voice mail, and although he waits, she
doesn't return his missed call.

***

Lee comes back from the bathroom drained from both
ends. Sour, salty sweat drips off the ends of his hair.
He cleans the lenses of his glasses. He replays the
conversation with Brown. He runs through his day on

the boat with the boys, and he picks up a clean brush. He sees a body thawing in the willows with one eye. He sees it approached by small unseen feet. He sees a small hand break through the ice. He begins to paint.

55. POUND OF FLESH

BY **THE LAST** week of October, there is not a soul in Little Ridge who hasn't seen her. Drifting through the woods by the shore, picking wildflowers by the light of the moon in the deGroot fields to the East, now on campus by the vending machines in the Old Dorm Building, now at the windows of the Village Inn. That muttering sound is hers, somewhere between a hiss and a hum. So, too, is the smoky breath of tobacco in the college library, sighing for the souls of her sons, real and imagined, or her own as it begins to annihilate.

As time drags on, Thettie's will begins to corrupt. She is long accustomed to fearing no one but herself, but she can feel a change, a potential bruising of her soul. A streaking of the blue with red, and of the red with black. For the first time, she is not just fearful of— but for—herself.

At the Rod 'n' Reel, Piet deGroot arranges a new meeting with Doc on this cell, and gets a whiff, as Thettie watches from behind a rack of fertilizer, of Frankie's rotten foot. The reek wafts in from the automatic double doors like Frankie were right back in the store, instead of faraway on Nose Island where Sheriff Boyle promised the deGroots he'd be out of the way.

J.S. BREUKELAAR

Piet DeGroot has lately taken to talking to himself. He mutters how, before Frankie went to the island, you would see him at the post office picking up books he ordered online. Or at the drug store. Frankie's gaze turned inwards to his thudding pulse, the throb of his foot and lower leg, pain his only friend. He'd been attacking it again with his fishing knife. Thettie moves out from behind the shelves to stand as close to DeGroot as she dares, so that their memories infect each other—how she'd drive Frankie up to County hospital where they'd keep him for a day or two on a penicillin drip, and that would help. But a month later the painfully hot swelling would return, and with it the smell of rotting flesh and contagion of the soul. DeGroot sniffs the air in revulsion.

He's getting hot. Hot under the collar. Irradiating the store with his infected memories. It's her. Standing too close to him. She moves in closer, contaminating him with her endangered soul. He's forgotten what he was looking for, what he came to buy. He wanders out of the store, Thettie clinging to his coat.

The crystal helped Frankie. Thettie tries to make deGroot understand. You try anything. Anything that helps, and it does for a while. His own people abandon him after Doc feeds Frankie to Boyle. Boyle was under pressure from Washington, keen to make a show of cleaning up some of these small, declining towns. He was under pressure from the deGroots to get rid of the Harpurs—the deGroot's weed empire was one thing, but crystal was another.

DeGroot goes to his car, opens the door, and Thettie jumps in. He lowers himself behind the wheel, blows on his hands and starts the engine.

ALETHEIA

At first the deGroots thought Doc was just what they'd been waiting for. Someone to divide and conquer those damn hicks with their ancient smarts. He scared you with his soft, scaly face, and those thinking, fighting eyes facing straight ahead. You never could tell what side he was on. Old Man deGroot, Piet's father, said Doc was a *Zeilloos*—ravening wolf. God only knows what the hunger for a soul will do to a being born without one.

Doc drove a wedge between the Harpurs even as he set about the task of making new alliances—the old divide and conquer maneuver, oldest in the book. Doc's efforts culminated in him ratting out his sworn best friend, Frankie, to the Sheriff. Boyle got a new truck from the deGroots in return for running off the Harpurs. And Doc got the girl. But the girl wasn't all she seemed, even then. Thettie grins suggestively from the back seat. Frankie took the fall, but got early parole because some detective down in Ilium was sweet on Thettie, made some calls. DeGroot tries to remember the man's name.

'Fabiana Brown,' Thettie says. 'And she's not a man.'

DeGroot reaches into the glove box where there is a warming fifth of gin. He heads back out onto the highway where he will pick up Doc to take him to Fie's house to talk about realignments, maybe get him some muscle after all. Thettie makes herself comfortable, tries to shut a gravelly voice at the back of her spine.

'Tell me about Frankie,' she coaxes. Without her, without his people, the voices slowly came back. He had nowhere to go to with the voices but to the townies. Someone had to feel his pain. Pain so big, so consuming, that it took a village to be its witness.

Piet deGroot feels his own diabetes eat away at him. The constant struggle for a cure, the fear of relapse, the sinking heart, the way your soul comes to be vindicated by a self-perpetuating affliction. DeGroot in fact had tried to talk to Frankie. At first he took him under his wing for Cassie's sake, to try and get her to come home. They had him to the house for supper while Frankie gibbered and lamented in words Piet couldn't understand because it was the untranslatable language of pain.

Frankie taught the language to his coons and his squirrels and dogs.

'Yes!' Thettie pipes up. 'His familiars.'

DeGroot can sense her but he mistakes her words for his own chain of thought. Those critters piled up in the back of Frankie's Pontiac, or out on the boat with him when he'd reel in bass as fast as he could cast off. Returning to sell his catch at the grocery store and restaurants, he encountered locals who tried to be fair, but the stink! The townies wanted to help, they did. But their hearts weren't in it. Besides, as they pointed out to each other, he wasn't one of them, not really. He was a Harpur after all. What if his people came back? Who would he choose?

'Scaredy cats,' Thettie hisses, and when deGroot turns at the jibe, thinking a stone to have hit the side window, she notices that he's removed the headrest to give him more swivel room, 180 degrees from windshield to tray, circumvent the blind spot. Total vantage point, *ja*.

At first Frankie told everyone his family would be

back, deGroot recalls. In the back seat, Thettie claps her hands over her ears. 'Lalalala,' she sings. But after a few years, he looked as lost as he felt, with his black hair and blazing eyes. And those mutts of his, followed him slavishly wherever he went.

Even deGroot's *schadenfreude* slowed to a resentful drip. In the presence of the hair so dark it seemed to eat all the light, the flying spittle and stink, deGroot would redden. Some of the deGroot boys would gather to push Frankie around to the point where deGroot could or would not restrain them. Women standing in line at the Village Market would stare hard at the shelves when he came into the store. The room would darken in the wake of the fear he generated, the jokes at his expense. He wasn't all there, that's what they said. And if you weren't all there, where were you? The smell could be upon you before you knew it. And behind the reek, the gummy grimace, a flash of tooth-stump in a gesture half apologetic, half dangerous. Oblivious of the effect he had, eager to blather something at you about the weather, the fish, or politics. You'd flinch. Who wouldn't? Would he hit you or worse, hug you?

And the stink.

Thettie nods earnestly at deGroot in the rearview. Yeah, yeah. People like Frankie and Jason with their inconvenient stink of loneliness.

A mockery of man on one rotting leg, flies swarming around, the wound gaping and the smell halfway between a castoreum and a Motel 6 shitter.

'A castoreum?' Thettie leans forward on the seat, opens her mouth for a drop of the gin splashing from deGroot's bottle.

'Secretion from the anal sac of a beaver,' he says as if talking to himself. 'Used for marking territory, but before that in perfume. Upper classes over on the Continent couldn't get enough of that dried beaver gland.'

DeGroot warned his brothers. He warned Boyle. The Harpurs would be back. You could (and you did) burn down their houses, take their land, their women, their livelihood. It wouldn't matter because in their own minds, they were not gone. They could not die.

'You think you're a cockroach, you're a cockroach,' crows Thettie.

Cassie *was* gone, though. Piet thought—or he hoped—that if he kept Jason here, or at least tried to stop him every time he'd try and go west, she might come back. If Piet reminded the boy how useless he really was with his 'condition,' and how dollars to donuts he'd fail just like the last time—maybe not even get as far as Wisconsin this time—well, eventually Cassie would come back.

Rock star! Queen Fucking Bee! Piet pounds on the wheel and remembers how he had tried to warn her of her limitations, right from the get-go. Hell, he gave her a kid as compensation. But no. It was not enough. It was never enough for a Harpur. They never learned.

Entering into the spirit of the discussion, Thettie reminds him that as a Harpur, the things you learn are about survival. The Dutch think they've been around since the beginning. Since Old New Netherland. They think they know all there is to know about survival. But the Harpurs, they spring from the blood of ages, and rages, too. From the blood of the first people, and the people before that.

'All that history? That's in our blood but up here, too. In our brains.' Thettie jabs the back of deGroot's skull with her claw and the truck swerves onto the shoulder, sprays moonlit dust. DeGroot straightens and hits the gas.

'That's right,' Thettie giggles, thrown off the seat. 'Pedal to the metal, soldier.'

Piet deGroot and his brothers, patriots all, hated the way the Harpurs would band together.

'One heart with a mind of its own,' agrees Thettie, sucking the blood off her tongue.

Those old clans, contaminated by Indian blood, slave blood, Mexican blood, gypsy blood, Jap blood—they're all the same. The fewer of them left, the tighter they become. And what kills deGroot and his Dutch brothers more than anything is how there's always a woman on top. First Sarah Tully, then Thettie Harpur.

'Queen fucking Bee-yoncé!' Thettie squeals so that he thinks it's the brakes.

The deGroots don't go for that women-on-top baloney. Piet's old man had been a force to be reckoned with and behind him, another. Right back to a first mate called Jan deGroot on the *Halve Maen* who had been a beaver man of note back in Holland, when castoreum was used in everything from perfumes to inducing abortions. Europe couldn't get enough of those New World beavers.

'And as an antidote,' Thettie pipes up from the back 'for poisoning. Where's a good beaver when you need one?'

Frankie used to say how the deGroots are cursed with a Beaver Complex. The less they get, the more they think they're entitled to. And at last, Thettie has steered the conversation to where she's wanted it to go. Cassie Tully.

With her red-tipped rock star hair and her sapphire eyes—only way Piet deGroot was to get her to notice him was to make her.

'You left the credit card out as bait? So, she'd take it?'

'Dumb bitch!' deGroot says, swigging on his gin with one hand, driving too fast with the other.

From the back seat, Thettie gives a tearful moan. Not too loud but loud enough to silence the cold grating voice at her back, to send it back where it came from.

It is dark as pitch outside the car. The highway is empty and the fields to either side are black seas to the end of the world. DeGroot is speeding toward the turn-off to the farm.

'I loved Cassie,' he hiccups. 'I hated her, too.'

'Love can turn to hate,' Thettie says. 'It's a complex system.'

And it wasn't just that, Thettie realizes, watching DeGroot swig self-pityingly on this gin, arrested in a vision of himself as the star-crossed lover, the thwarted savior. Thettie bounces around the back seat like a dog. Tears stream down deGroot's face, and Cassie with her blue eyes and Patti Smith on her guitar, is what Thettie sees him remembering.

'It's okay,' Thettie says. 'Resistance is futile.'

He nods, licking snot off his lip. More memories fly like shards around the truck—that time at the motel. Him and the cousins, Fie and Pim, and the others, when they got the girls in there. Cassie read their palms. He can't remember the future she predicted for his brothers, but she traced the lifeline on his broad farmer's hand and showed him where it cut off.

'There is a dark highway,' she said. 'A flash of blue. And a bend in the road you won't expect.'

Thettie pops her head up so that deGroot sees her in the rearview, with her scaled neck and broken lightbulb eyes. He swerves off the road, and into a tree and the airbag inflates in time to save his heart from being crushed by the steering wheel, but not enough to prevent deGroot's neck from snapping, due to the missing headrest, with the impact.

And the last thing he sees to take down to hell is a rock 'n' roll animal with electric eyes and a rage-red mouth blowing him a kiss he will eternally want and never get.

56. CRIME SCENE

CAN'T PAINT. Lee sits on a lawn chair in the yard with his back to the lake, and beer on his chin. The cold core of the setting sun turns his blood to brittle ice. The shadow of the rope-swing's dance plays on the lawn before him. It's the Halloween weekend.

The nights are not enough. He wants her all the time. He wants his son. When will the want end? And where? Her fingers in his hair, hands on his cock, tongue at his heart—at last a new beginning. But where will it end?

He gets up, only thing he has left is to go to her one last time. To lie where she lay and maybe she'll come for him. Take him to where she is now.

He pushes himself out of the chair, gets his keys from inside the studio and drives through a world of Jack o' Lanterns and glowing plastic ghosts to the campground. He gets out and listens to the dark water lap and suck at the pylons, the boats sing on their moorings. The sweetly menacing song of a thrush calls him on, or maybe warns him off. It seems too close one moment, almost at his shoulder and high overhead the next.

He steps over the flapping crime scene tape. Goes into the trailer and shuts the door behind him.

57. DEMO

THAT WHOLE TIMING thing? She sucks at it and always has. Fresh from running deGroot off the road, Thettie comes home to find Doc in the parking lot, hotwiring Rianne's truck. Thettie's exhausted, feels she's just dodged a bullet with this whole soul thing, but no rest for the wicked, as Paddy the Hook would say.

So instead of going back to the trailer to rest, she must slither into the back of the truck, just like old times. Weary after deGroot, elated but burnt out, she tries to conserve her energy for what must surely lie ahead. Heading out on the highway at first light, Thettie jangles in the back, counting backwards from one hundred. Because it is only her visitation to *him*, that counts now. This is the one for all time—all the others mere rehearsals for opening night. She counts through the steps in her mind, the way you might rehearse what you'd say to the guy you don't want to take you to the prom. How you might let him down gently. Say it's not him, it's you.

Ninety-eight, ninety-seven.

For now, and better late than never, it's clear to her that Doc is not the guy she wants to take her to the prom. No, Doc is no freshwater fish, nor lake invertebrate and for dead sure no savior, but a shark come long ago to infest her waters and weaken her species. His eyes are so deep set and close together that they appear at times merged like the lights on a train. No viewpoint but forward. Always on the main chance, the next ride, means to an end, room with a view. If she is the beast of memory, then he is the eater of time.

And she wants it back.

So, her final visitation to him must be different than the previous ones and sure as hell different from her trivial hauntings of the town—this will not be a subtle performance. None of those blue splutters or hair-on-the-tongue effects. No. This will be a command performance, one for the ages. Not so much performed as inflicted, out of time and for all time.

Seventy-seven, seventy-six, seventy-five.

An eye for an I. Mouth to mouth. Let's be clear. Find your mark. So yes, she decides, trailing a cloud of ferrous vapor behind the truck as it races up the highway. Rock 'n' roll. Give it all you've got.

All she's got left is this want. Not to want.

He checks the rearview nervously, drums on the wheel with the stumps of both trigger fingers, the ones Paddy's dog did not bite off. Doc sniffs his Devil Dog ring. *Semper Fi,* motherfucker.

Thettie clings to the truck bed. Her bloody tongue flapping in the breeze.

Of course, she knows where he's going first, the old abortionist. To his secret cronies, the deGroots, to plead for muscle. To affect allegiance. To give them the finger. Look—he's got six left.

Doc gets out at the deGroot farm. The light has crept over the ridge and Triangle Creek sings on the other side of the Aspen wood. She counts down in the back of the truck until he is inside and then she is at the window behind the cut back hydrangeas, behind the Jack o' Lantern on the porch.

Just because you're dead doesn't mean you can hear through walls. But if she stops counting and concentrates hard enough she can make out what the men inside are saying, not at the time they are saying it but in the wake of the bad blood flowing from beneath the door, in which she dances till she drops.

The deGroot men are waiting for Piet to join them—they'd expected him to have brought Doc, not for the old sawbones to have turned up alone. He says he doesn't know where Piet is.

'So, what's up, Doc?' It never gets old, Pim says. The Dutch gin does the rounds.

Thettie's sigh shrivels the hydrangeas. Poor Doc. He reaches for the gin, but they pull it out of his reach. What Fie deGroot wants to know, what he really really wants to know is what's in it for them? Why should they give him replacement muscle? So that he can bite the hand that feeds him? They remind him how they let him back to Little Ridge in good faith and he turns up with two psychos, Fie deGroot says. Now where's the trust in that?

She listens as he explains that it was a mistake. Homer and Lyle were a speed bump, a *faux pas*. He had to let them go.

Thettie literally splits her side laughing.

He reminds them it was he who shut Frankie down in the first place by setting up that raid ten years ago at the Gully. Wasn't his fault Frankie got himself back up again. Doc brought in muscle to get past Frankie's security system, and take out Thettie's sons, the final obstacle. But he agrees that Homer and Lyle were too old-school, blames the failure on himself. Doc puts up two hands in false surrender. Guilty as charged, he admits. It might take a more sophisticated kind of approach. Black Ops. Give him one man and he'll give them Frankie on a plate.

The deGroots laugh their gallows laughs. They howl, stomp on the floor loud enough to wake the dead. Except that Thettie is getting sleepy. She yawns loudly, and a face appears from an upper story window. Jason's little brother. Thettie waves and he waves back. Then Fie gets serious. Drums on the bottle-laden table like he's thinking. Thettie hears the drumming from outside. Doc can have whatever he wants for his quote unquote Black Ops, Fie says. Over at Reservist HQ they got kayaks, night vis, the whole kit 'n' caboodle, Pim says. They tell him to make a list. Like a shopping list for the Rod 'n'Reel. But no muscle. No muscle for him to turn around like the double-crossing ungrateful Irish bastard he is, to use against them. Tell him, bring back a pound of flesh, even an ounce will do. Something with some cuts on it, so they know it's really from Frankie. Earn our trust, Doc, they tell him. No such thing as a free lunch. And then we'll give you our protection.

Doc stands at attention, brings his missing digit to his forehead in a Devil Dog Salute,

'*Semper Fi*,' he says.

At that Fie and Pim and all the Dutch uncles laugh so hard from behind their morning gins that they have to pound each other's backs and Doc seems more or less dismissed.

ALETHEIA

He shrugs his combat jacket back on and steps out into a morning which is the purple of rotten plums. Muted birdsong weary from the rain. Thettie, scuttling back to the truck, has to admit that there is still something about him that attracts and repels her. The pewter crew cut, the pug nose between those predator eyes. His shoulders are wide and lethal—he'd be on the wrong side of sixty—and his trunk as hard as a granite plinth, the long and nimble legs. He lights a cigarette and walks toward the Aspen woods where she has assembled herself and is waiting for him. At ease, Soldier.

Doc stumbles. Wipes drool from the sides of his mouth. She splutters her blue eyes at him fetchingly. He gasps with a naked fear and hunger, because after all she's a woman in her prime and a vision, she knows, even in death.

He raises a hand but this time it's not a salute. 'Hand to God, I never knew the old lizard had crawled out of the bag, Girl, when we did the switcheroo. I never would have—I loved you. Always did. It was for us I did it. In case Frankie was a goner. It was for the peptides, the Killer Mix, our insurance. And when I saw you like that, holy Jesus. I tried to save you, girl. But you were a goner.'

She puts a claw over her lips. '*Shhhhhh.*'

He fumbles his cigarette. Thettie leads him away from the watching windows of the farmhouse and through the Aspens, toward the creek. She moves through the whispering grove, and can hear by the crunch of leaves that he's following her. She puts a tick-tock in her step, her nightgown hugging her bare buttocks, the curtain-cape hiding her gash of a mouth as she looks over her shoulder, leading him toward the rushing waters. She brushes the Aspen branches with her fingers, sending down a shower of gold. Then she moves down toward the stream where the whisper of the Aspens is softer and the birdsong is muted. The silence is unnatural, the light without source. A thin layer of ice lies on the cut-banks and there are unnamed things clutched in fleshy root-wads that have never seen the sun.

He is behind her and she feels the heat of his gaze in her belly. She remembers how he found her in the jungle of a tangled Harpur history, got her clean just so he could dirty her up again, make her whole so he could take his pound of flesh. She steps up to a fallen tree that serves as a bridge and walks across it, her movements working a small rusted motor boat loose from the tangled roots of a toppled chestnut tree.

He stares at it.

'What's that then?' his voice a squawk.

Thettie turns half way across the fallen tree bridge. Doc holds his ground but peers across at her through the dark branches. It's obvious to her now, as she turns to face him—what she has achieved in death if not in life. She has extracted final proof of her being, reflected in the fearful gaze of her enemy.

'Remember?' the Aspens whisper. 'The one who got away?'

For a few electric moments, they stare at each other across the stream. She waits. She has to know.

'Frankie did the repairs on that damn Jon-boat. Don't blame me.'

She hisses.

'Okay, okay. I didn't know they'd go out so far.'

She unfurls her claws. He blanches, puts a hand to his heart. His face drained of color.

'All right. So, I did. I booby-trapped the goddam boat. What did you expect? I brought you back your Frankie, and you still wouldn't love me. Still that wasn't enough. Never enough for you. All I had left to get at you was your sons. Means to an end.'

She loosens her curtain veil. He gapes at what he sees now. Scrappy's collar around her neck, her flesh turned to scales. She brings a hand between her legs. Black matter runs down her thighs, pools at her feet and swirls around her ankles. His voice rises to a shrill scream.

'Please! I couldn't rescue the mutt! It was a goner, barking and crying, spewing up a river. Even if I could have pulled her out she'd have to be shot—what that water does to a gut. I did her a kindness. I did you all a kindness. You wouldn't even be here if it wasn't for me.'

He's yelling now. Dropped to his knees. Thettie sniffs urine.

'Bitch! Bitch-bitch-bitch!'

Thettie, in a mounting rage, silences him with a look of a hot intensity that few men of any age could resist. Doc's lips go slack. His eyes lose focus. He clutches at the dirt of the riverbank and his scars whiten against his flushed face. He fights for breath. For speech. His Semper Fidelis tattoo is stark against the shaved pallor of his chest, and the patches of shiny skin on his face turn a sickly gray. He pulls himself slowly to his feet.

'What do you want?'

This is what she has waited for. She has scrubbed

up for it, washing her nightgown in the lake so that it is clean of all but the faintest trace of pink. It billows against the fork of her thighs, her mound visible through the damp cloth. She has pulled her dislocated shoulder in at no small cost and she chokes off a scream as she straightens. She wraps the curtain back around her neck, a romantic touch, not too cheesy. She bristles a little in the rampant need in his eyes, his chalky tongue licking his lips. She doesn't know what to say. No one ever knows what they really want. Why should that change after death?

The Aspens whisper needfully, their urgent message signaled in stops and starts, like Morse Code. Long short long short long short long long short long. Hot with want, like the mating call of a monster.

'Seek you,' she says.

He hears her call and he comes. He licks his lips at the siren song of her monstrous hiss. He can't help it. She's irresistible, always was. She takes a step back. He keeps going. She smiles at him with eyes the color of hell at its coldest. Her forked tongue is tantalizingly visible between her parted rows of pointed teeth, and he feels that forked tongue on the underside of his penis, in the back of his throat, winding around his dendrites. So that when he takes her into his arms and their tongues touch and her grooved fangs scrape against his, he moans in a kind of rapture. He opens his mouth wider and her seeking tongue goes deeper down his throat and into his brain, and then she bites. Her teeth find purchase on the inside of his mouth and begin to chew. He tries to scream, but her mouth is over his. The more he tries to scream, the harder she bites.

58. ABSTRAKT

HE **WAKES UP** in the trailer and fumbles for his glasses. His palm brushes against something he missed last night. He picks it up. It's a little blue pill. He puts his glasses on. There's a tiny upper case 'A' stamped on the surface.

Lee jogs to the car, almost tripping over the branches that have swept in from the woods and litter the yard of the trailer. He turns the heat in the car on full blast and maneuvers the car slowly through the otherwise sleeping village. The old manor houses behind their sycamores and elms. The Inn and the columned library and the Lake View and Sunny's refurbished Victorian sprawl, all built on railroad or lumber or salt or gunpowder money—testament to a bunch of white guys breaking bad in the mean streets of their own making.

Lee runs from the garage to the studio, in a rush to begin painting, to map out an intersection between her dreams and his. He pokes his head into Vernon's tank by force of habit and lets the false hope go.

'Goodbye,' he whispers. 'Godspeed.'

The words cut the absence a little deeper into his heart, like that path in the dust, or in the forest, one for which the ways to and from the destination are interchangeable. He makes coffee methodically, mixes his oils without conscious thought.

And then he starts to paint. His first abstract ever, if that's what you can call it, a lyrical composition three movements of an unfinished song. One of a dirty white, the other in a blueish mottled green, and another strip of deepest earth brown pierced with painful shards of Ambien blue. So that when the canvas is all but complete six hours later, it is like waking from a dream.

59. CQ

BRYCE SLEEPS LIKE the dead. Boneless and breathless with one eye a golden crescent and the other an unsucked hole. The eye patch floats in a pool of melting ice on the night table. Thettie creeps over to the high narrow bed at one end of the trailer where Bryce lies like on a bier. How small she is, how thin, like a boy. She's naked. The sparse fuzz between her legs is a paler cinnamon color than her hair. Her nipples are small and liver-colored on a flat chest. She's covered with yellowing bruises, Thettie sees, and angry burns from the tip of something. A cigarette? A match? Her fingers are blueish white and twitch, like glow worms, with bad dreams.

Thettie sighs. A ragged, rasping exhalation. She pulls an old Spider Man sleeping bag over Bryce's body, then goes to the window with its view of the shower block. Her head slumps in her hands. She doesn't want to wake Bryce, although time is running thin. Thettie hides her face in her hands, and her tongue unfurls in bewilderment and rage.

'Breaker, breaker,' says Bryce from the bed.

'*Shhhh*,' hisses Thettie. 'It's not time.'

But in her soul, she feels the end coming. Her heart seeks forgiveness from Bryce, the dreamer, and freely overflows with memories good and bad, because the hour is upon them all. She kisses the girl goodbye, and shuts the door softly behind her. No need to lock it.

Dawn isn't far away, and Thettie must hurry. She's expecting company.

She goes back to the wrong trailer for the last time. Lee's scent floats through the toxic space like a caress. She gratefully touches the place on the bed where he lay. Where he came to know her, to learn all the truths and lies that make up a life. And then she sits to wait beside the indentation he left.

Doc comes right on cue. Thettie hears footsteps outside the trailer. The footfall is labored and is accompanied by a gluggy grunt. Thettie stands swaying. She does not attempt to materialize or dematerialize. No need now. She will always be here.

She goes to the threshold and opens the door. Doc in full camouflage points a silenced Army Issue 45 at her. She knows better than to laugh. She invites him in. He takes aim and fires at the TV. He's strangely twisted to the right at the waist and his colorless shark eyes are beady with terror, and his mouth is still swollen and bleeding from her kiss. Thettie smirks. His mouth, at least the outside, will heal. The real damage is on the inside. Where the sun don't shine.

She steps around him and blocks the door. He fires at the flicker that brings her into being.

Thettie taunts him with her laughing gash of a mouth, bars bleeding luminous teeth. 'Wherever you go, there I am.'

He screams and she leaves him screaming, shooting off rounds into the ceiling until the chamber is empty.

She can't wait to return to the little Winnebago. She has no need to pack. Everything she owns is inside her now, as Lee said it would be. She steps out of the poisoned trailer that is after all and in the end, not her destiny. She shuts the door. And throws away the key.

60. AMBIEN

LEE TURNS TO his new painting. Like all artists, he has tried to disclose the undisclosable. He starts hacking with his scraper at the top layer of dirty ice, down to the suggestion of her glacial eyes. Ambien blue to match the little pill on the easel.

Ambien. Lee sidles to his computer. Ambien is a brand name for Zolpidem, a drug used for insomnia and some mental disorders. It is, Lee reads, a non-benzodiazepine drug.

Ambien is in a class of drugs called imidazopyrdine. Not Benzodiazepine.

Lee looks up from the computer and goes to the easel. He picks up the pill. Lee now knows that some drugs (like Zolpidem) work on GABA, a neurotransmitter. For this reason, they tend to be more effective in the short term than benzodiazepine, which is why Benzos—Rohypnol and so on—are a more reliable drug if you want to rape someone. Bottom line—Benzos keep you asleep for longer, but Ambien gets you there faster. Ambien's side effects include intense hallucinations through all physical senses, delusions, insatiable hunger and PCA—Parasomnial Confusional Arousal—during which the individual remains in a transitional state between waking and sleeping.

ALETHEIA

He knows that whatever killed Thettie was no hallucination. What he doesn't know is exactly what kind of monster came out of her dreams, with no one there to save her.

61. MIRAKIL

A NARROW COLUMN of moonlit water arrows into a dark green pool ringed in a steep drop of glistening slate. The water once plunged in great foaming plumes into the pool, but not anymore. The pool is much deeper than the falls are high and is fed by a deep subterranean mineral spring. This is a Harpur secret and has been for as long as Thettie can remember which is now a couple centuries in both directions.

'Time's arrow is a whore!' She cartwheels and backflips, her nightgown riding up her immaterial bits. She is free! Doc has gone where the sun won't shine, and she—the key to her own soul—is free. She scrambles around the mouth of the pool which dips down to meet the slate wall. Thettie peers into the wet and velvety darkness for a hidden cleft in the rock. The roar of the water drowns out all other sound.

The ancient glacial water of Harpur Falls has been the secret behind their moonshine, famous for the better part of a century and a half. Even after moonshine became legit and all the rage, the water retained its secret usefulness for their salves and potions. Sarey had her own label—'Shine.' Shine Youth Serum, for example is basically just secret falls water, goats milk powder, coffee, rose-hip and salmon oil. Sarey had grinned her gap-toothed smile. 'It's a l-l-l-living.'

But there is one product—MiraKil Cream—that is the family secret, and Thettie plans to keep it that way.

MiraKil Cream is wildflower honey, spruce resin for its anti-microbial qualities, snap weed, and the Falls water in which the resin is less soluble than it is in regular water, thus increasing its shelf-life. They sold Sarey's Shine products in local pharmacies and at Farmers' Markets, but Thettie kept the MiraKil cream for her own.

There is a secret ingredient that she adds to MiraKil Cream that she reveals to no one, not even Sarey, who says she doesn't want to know, but Thettie suspects she does. And especially not to old blabber-mouth Frankie who only learns to keep his trap shut when it's too late and there's no one to listen to him anymore anyway.

Thettie crawls on all fours through the veil of spray and feels her way along the slate wall just as she used to when she was a young girl, and then a young mother, and always and forever a Harpur. Finally, her hands find what they seek. From a slit in the rock bubbles a sluggish spring of sweet, scaly black sludge, slithery and gritty at the same time. Thettie scoops some into a medicine jar and secures the lid. Licks the tarry goo off her fingers. She stands up and holds her wounded broken face to the crystal-clear falls until it heals. And then she makes her way slowly back to the campgrounds, taking her time. She hates goodbyes.

***

'Trick or Treat,' Thettie whispers. 'Bryce. Wake up. You

can sleep when you're dead, child. Wake up. It's Halloween.'

The sleeper awakes at the sound of her name, and stands naked and shivering. Thettie finds the Spider man suit and helps the sleeper to get dressed, bends down as she did with her own sons and helps with the buttons. She takes the eye patch from the side table. 'You won't be needing this anymore,' she says. She wraps it around her wrist, and promises to take care of it. She places a plastic pumpkin for trick-or-treating in the little hand.

Thettie opens the trailer door and heads off down the path, the little Spidey not far behind. They get to the shore. Bewildered townies smile at the little Spider Man who is there one minute, gone the next.

You can almost see south to Lee's beach from here and beyond that, of course, to the island, its hairy nostril clear as day. She drops a jar of her MiraKil cream into the trick-or-treat pumpkin.

'For Frankie. You tell him there's more where that came from.'

She bends down to the child, looks into his eye-socket, like a frosted over mud-puddle. 'It's okay. Don't be afraid.'

She kisses the little creature on the forehead, inhaling all the pain and fear and leaving on the cold damp flesh a promise that she knows now to be true above all else.

'We live by forgetting, child. You will be gone by light.'

62. HOUSE CALL

THE FRIDAY BEFORE Halloween Lee drives slowly down party-lit Main Street to visit Habib one last time. He flinches from the stream of oncoming headlights, the glare magnified by the smears on his glasses. At the liquor store, the checker rings up his purchase and tells him that's the second bottle of single malt she's sold this afternoon, and at a hundred bucks a pop, it's not like the stuff just walks out the door. Lee asks her if a smiling assassin bought the first bottle.

'My daughter's soccer coach? I haven't seen him for a couple weeks, truth be told. No sir. Didn't know this fellow. I want to say he was Native American. Tall, muscular gentleman. Black hair, earrings. Like that picture there.'

The checker turns and points to a faded calendar showing Bartoli's famous portrait of Handsome Lake, the Iroquois prophet and reformed drunk, who led his people to a new day.

'Except he looked a lot older than that. Looked like he'd been in the weather, too. Fishing maybe. How about the accident on the highway the other night—with old Mr. deGroot?'

At Lee's blank look, she tells him that Piet deGroot

took a wrong turn a couple of nights ago, or took it wrong—she makes a drinking gesture—and that there will be a big funeral at the Presbyterian Church sometime next week.

Lee puts the single malt in its box on the front seat of the station wagon, beside a blueberry pie from Maxine's.

The security detail is gone from outside Habib's house and the door is open. A shadow fills the door frame. Lee takes a step back to give him room. The man who emerges is easily seven feet tall, like a basketball player. Lee can see his skull beneath a receding Mohawk of a deep velvety black. Gold hoops dangle feathers from the man's stretched, flapping earlobes. Another gold ring swings from his nasal septum. He carries a small cooler, the kind used to transport plasma. He nods at Lee and keeps going around to the back of the villa. Lee dashes down the hall to the office window and watches the man clamber down the slope to the railway line by the shore, and stride down Habib's jetty to a bobbing Jet Ski. The man secures the cool cube, straddles the ride and roars off toward the island.

Lee puts the pie and the whisky in the kitchen. He finds his old friend in the basement accessed from a door in the hallway beside the furnace room. Lee sees the white plastic door of the MedSci freezer where Habib used to keep his stash of Helotide, plasma samples, sundry enzymes and reagents. The door of the freezer is open and Lee can see it's empty. Habib is ironing shirts, folding them and putting them into a suitcase. The iron hisses.

'American basements, my friend. Crucible of the

national psyche, like the Australian shed, or the Irish pub, or the Mexican *jacal*, or the . . .'

'So, you're going away?' Lee hesitates, making it sound more like a question than a statement.

'For a while. I'm thinking Spain. I've never been. Follow in the trail of the Knight with the Sorrowful Countenance.'

'Anywhere else?'

'We'll see. You can never go home again, Lee. We both know that. Would you like to come? Spain is bloody paradise for a painter.'

Lee says he'll think about it.

'I hear that Doc's security detail have been let go,' Habib says. 'Under the circumstances, I told my friends outside they could take a break. What's up with Doc? According to them, he hasn't been the same since his last parlay with the deGroots.'

'I'm heading to the campground now. I'll let you know.'

'I'd like that.'

Lee laughs for real at how, no matter what news he thinks he has for Habib, the chances are that the old spy will have the jump on him. 'The guy I just saw, what he was doing here?'

'That'd be Mr. Kreb. He made me an offer I couldn't refuse. Or maybe I made him one. I forget. I'm tired. You're right, Lee. I need a vacation.'

Habib edges the nose of the iron along a shoulder seam.

'A man's war, you know. It's never in one place. Just ask Doc Murphy.'

'Wait. You sold the Iroquois guy the Helotide? As some kind of insurance?'

'Not sold, Lee. Like I said, Mr. Kreb made me an offer I couldn't refuse.'

'Sam. No.'

'That's right,' Habib smiles. 'My very own island. No more pain, my friend. Not ever.'

'I won't let you do it, Sam.'

'Is that blueberry pie I smell? Perfect with a single malt—you're a genius. Oh Lee, calm down. I'm not going to do anything,' Habib rests the hissing iron in its cradle, and carefully slips the shirt onto a hanger. Stands back to admire his work. 'But a man has to plan for his future.'

***

Lee makes it back to the campground, managing not to fishtail on the wet highway. He pulls into the parking lot and kills the engine. He blows on his hands. The little Winnebago overhung with pine branches looks very far away, like a dream on waking.

The door opens. She steps out onto the stoop, waves across at him through the light rain. She's changing. Her injuries are fading, the shimmer returning to her skin. Her mane of coarse blond hair blows in the wind and her electric eyes signal to him. Lee waves back. He starts walking toward the trailer, where he belongs. Where she's returned. Wisps of smoke rise from the cigarette she dangles in her fingers. Closer up, his heart could burst at the firmament of freckles sparkling at her throat, along her pale arms. He keeps his hand waving, waving, and he can't feel his feet. He trips on a root lying across the path, and she grins. Lee raises a hand to her and keeps the hand out, and stumbles on toward the trailer. Her blue eyes radiate a cold flame and her breasts swell from the neck of her low-cut sweater. She points to the trailer where she died. 'Thank you,' she mouths and disappears into the Winnebago with a smile

He pulls up short. He is alongside the big trailer now. Shadows dance in the dim interior. Lee hears the clink of glasses.

A dog's water bowl lies nestled in some geraniums.

'Who's there?' The voice is Doc Murphy's but different, a different register on an unfamiliar scale, the brogue corrupted with other tongues.

'Where's the whisky, Selena?' Doc's mute bodyguard answers to a multiplicity of names. 'Make it a double for the good master. And pour one for yourself, there's a *koritsi mou. Ich gehe nicht.*'

Lee hears the rustle of heavy paper. The loud clack of a keyboard. He walks across the yard of the trailer and steps onto the small porch, waiting for his eyes to adjust to the darkness within.

'*Sláinte,*' Doc says.

There is a throaty growl and Lee turns to see the albino Rottweiler get to her feet from where she's been lying in a slice of sunlight. Lee gets a flash of yellow tooth.

Doc, his baggy shoulders and crewcut barely discernible in the dark, hunkers on a La-Z-Boy in front of the broken TV. The light from the window falls on the low table littered with maps and ashtrays and coffee cups. Lee doesn't move past the threshold, partly because the dog's lips are still pulled back and quivering. He listens to Doc begin to enumerate, in Gaelic and Hindi and English, the cases of water subsidence in the history of the state. He traces the glass of cheap hooch (his third) to the shoots, grasses and sheaves of wheat that went into its manufacture with which he compares the grassy paddock behind the Bingo Hall where he last saw his da alive, the many faces of Toeless Mears throughout the course of his protracted wake, the silent advance of dental caries and of arsenic. Doc's voice unspools from the trailer while the bitch settles back down in her patch of sun, still with one savage eye on Lee. He turns at the sound of heavy bikes rumbling and popping into the parking lot. Archy and Grif and Emilio and Dustin and others pull up, rain smearing the mud across the tire guards and fairings. They dismount and approach the trailer, assembled in the familiar spearhead formation, except this time Archy and Grif lead together, shoulder to shoulder.

'We know Homer and Lyle have bailed,' Grif says. 'He's ours now.'

'He's someone's,' Lee agrees. 'But not yours.'

'Move aside, Doctor Dolittle. This ain't your fight.' Archy wields a tire iron. His brother swings a bike chain. Their helmets are still on like the dreamers of old, and just as lethal.

Lee steps aside and there, on the shore this time, is Thettie. Ankle-deep in the heliotropic shallows of the lake, her skirt hitched up and her skin incandescent in the dusk. The wind blows her wild hair across her face, across her eyes and mouth.

Grif, huge in his helmet and black leathers, keeps his voice grave and level as a judge's. 'Let's go.'

But then the big dog heaves herself to her feet and the Harpers freeze, to a man. She growls low in her throat, blood-stained hackles up. Behind her, from the depths of the trailer, Doc's sing-song muttering continues apace. The boys waver at the sight of the beast. No wonder Sarey hadn't wanted her back. Better to assign her permanent CQ over Doc, keep him where they can all see him. Thettie giggles from the lake.

They listen for another moment or two to Doc reciting passages from the *Iliad* in Greek. Tapping at the keyboard, and moving onto the co-ordinates of Nose Island, and how a tunnel dug across from Tinkers Glen due west would most likely emerge in a subterranean cavern located just beneath the old lighthouse. The dog advances past the threshold, her tail beginning to twitch.

Doc jumps up to stand behind her with his buzz-cut in need of a trim, and blood from his nose, his middle finger itchy at the trigger of his empty 44.

'I think you've come to the wrong place, lads.'

And because the dog lifts her head and emits a voiceless but terrible howl, they agree. That yes, maybe they have.

Doc then says something about the Killer Kiss and as he's talking he reaches into his mouth and pulls out a bloody tooth. And when Lee looks around, the boys have wandered back to their trailers, and Thettie, too, is gone from the shore.

63. INK

THETTIE SITS ON the bed while her oldest son packs. He says he might go to New Zealand. He's heard the fishing is good there. A buddy of his has a YouTube channel and a Go Pro. Might start a little fishing show. Jason's little brother is a whizz on the computer.

She watches Grif thread Vernon's tooth onto a cord and tie it around his neck.

'I'll be back, maybe to finish Doc off,' he says, grins.

I think he'll manage that okay without you.

'You look beautiful, Ma.' He tucks the Polaroid of her into his wallet.

Don't forget about your brother. None of this was your fault.

There is another Polaroid on the bed. It is the one Lee took of the missing island when they were on the fishing trip. Archy used this to try and explain about the island, how it's just an externalization of memory, a shared eruption of fear and shame.

Grif said, like a curse? And Archy had said, kind of. So Grif decides to leave the Polaroid behind.

'Ma,' he says. 'About Scrappy and . . . all of it? I know. It was all Doc. The raid and Frankie left behind. Me and Arch figured Doc out from way back—not all the details—but what he was. We just didn't know how to tell you. How to save you.'

I'm sorry.

'No need.'

Grif?

'You were a good ma. You saved my life. I'd be swinging from the ceiling fan of a foster home if it wasn't for you.'

You'll come back?

He holds up two fists. The red letters that spell the word FEAR on the knuckles of one hand and the black letters that spell the word LESS on the other. His eyes meet hers in the mirror, where she will always be.

64. YELLOW

THE STUDIO FEELS different. Lee shoves his hands in his pockets. He approaches the tank at an oblique angle, not daring to hope. But of course, it's still empty. A new wet grass and shampoo smell wafts from the tank, undercut by the memory of Vernon's pukey musk. But there's something else that's missing.

It's the Tonka truck. The flash of yellow is gone. Besides the Spider Man figurine, it was the only physical relic he dared take from the house, a toy his son had already outgrown by the time he went missing. Lee had become accustomed to the soft click of its wheels moved by an unseen hand, but now there is stillness.

He would have liked to have said goodbye.

But Bryce has left him two things. The first is the words she scrawled backwards in the condensation on the window of the studio. He can peer through them on the right nights, and in the right light, he can see the island. Tonight he watches a faint light move ceaselessly back and forth along a path through the bald cypress groves, and across the same two or three trajectories. He watches the moving, dancing light on the island, hypnotized. Gradually, his eyes accustom themselves to the dark and the distance. And in a strange constriction of time and space, the island appears much closer than it is—as if lensed through gravity—which in a sense is what the letters do. The breeze pulls the clouds swiftly across the sky and in a ragged interval of their passing, the full moon's yellow wash pours down on the bunched trees that rise to a stony outcrop. A man and a boy walk along the path. He is not a bad man, not always a good man, but good enough. His name is Frankie Harpur. The boy holds a lantern for the not-bad man. Sometimes he is behind Frankie. Other times it moves in front of him, lighting the way. The little boy wears his Spider Man suit and when he hears a motor boat approaching from across the lake, he holds out his hand to Frankie so they can walk together down the path, to where the one-eyed girl will soon pull up on the shore.

In Lee's pocket is the other thing she left him. A silver dollar that disappeared with his seven-year-old son, Brice-with-an-'i.' Now returned to him.

65. MONSTER

THETTIE MOVES AT dusk between the dark and the light. In summer she sometimes joins them on the pagoda by the lake, and on some winter nights she keeps restive company in the studio. Lee is teaching Archy to paint—drives her crazy to watch. Kid paints all kinds of things. He likes to paint rock stars and characters from books. Lee tells him he's moving in the right direction, but Thettie has her doubts.

'Face looks more like that Bryce than Beyoncé,' she says.

So along with Lee's drawings of people and animals—sometimes just their hands or a face—the studio becomes filled with images of rap stars and ball players and even some monsters, which Archy is best at in her opinion. There's one in particular, a creature that's part woman, part dog, part reptile. She's got wings like a broken butterfly but no arms, and her mouth is rent with fangs. A fleshy veil hangs over her eyes. Thettie likes that picture. She likes that Lee likes it, too—had it framed and all. She circles the studio waiting to come in and tell him what she likes.

Archy goes for long rides on his bike—Thettie doesn't know where. He walks for miles, too. Sleeps under the stars on the nights that he can. He visits

Thettie's grave, sits there for hours out on the headland beneath the giant pine where they finally bury her ashes because some remains, as Thettie now knows, are better than none. Bryce is there, too, or at least her eye patch is. Lee tossed it into Thettie's grave at the last minute, and although it broke her heart to see the shine of tears on his face, she is glad he did.

Archy and Grif dragged over a pine log and engraved it with Bryce's name to put next to Thettie's headstone, and Archy likes to sit on the log and look across the lake. He comes back with a bunch of wildflowers for the studio, gentian and tiger lily and forget-me-nots. Thettie knows that he's trying to understand what Lee explained to him about Bryce, what she was and how she's not coming back—how she was never all there to begin with. But Archy prefers to think of her as all there. To remember how she came to him with her boy-hair and her bullshit and soothed his rage. The first lover he couldn't keep, the only sister he'll never have.

When Archy's up to it, they Skype Grif. They tell him about Doc's latest attempt to get the island by parachute, or the bobsled he bought on Craigslist that he's converting into a home-made submarine. Grif laughs his gentle laugh. Or the latest from the lawyers about the manor. Grif tells them to watch his latest fishing episode so they flick to his YouTube channel. Thettie's oldest son, distorted in the fish-eye lens, winks at her from the shores of Lake Pukaki in New Zealand, preternaturally blue due to the extremely fine particles of glacial silt from which it formed.

When dusk slips away, leaving uncertain night, she is a vague figure standing alone on the jetty and outlined in light. She likes to check in on Doc. Thanks to her Killer Kiss and the one or two snifters he allows himself every night, abetted by two-three Haloperidol—or three-four and who's counting—he has discovered an elaborate system of enumeration. In place of twenty-three, for example, he says *potato drive*. Other numbers are *putative lime, Amour Dure, instinct spike*.

Other nights, she haunts the Way. Doc slinks in, looking for a fix, and she calls him over with her ray gun eyes. Listens to him talk to himself, all cut up and black of tooth. Frankie, joins in sometimes from the island from where he rumbles his lake guns.

'Boom,' Doc croaks.

One day he goes out on the late Piet deGroot's military-issue kayak looking for the island, convinced it's there somewhere and that he'll find it and get Frankie to see things his way. He comes back and pesters the townies about it, or another time, he wanders across the fields at close of day— calling in on one or another of the deGroots that are still left—trying to get himself drunk or stoned enough to be able to return to the trailer, to face the Albino bitch who is his keeper now. Dutch courage, he calls it, but it's never enough.

66. ISLAND

ARCHY IS A keen art student, if an occasionally irresponsible and often absent Lord of the Manor. Lee doesn't blame him. Twenty-six rooms are too many for one man—especially one with a half dozen adoring dogs and as many girlfriends. Over a couple of beers and a tasty blunt, Lee appraises Archy's latest drawing of Beyoncé, which when viewed up close is composed of overlapping ones and zeros.

It takes a lot of explaining to get Archy to understand about the island.

'I combed the lake for years,' Lee says. 'Covered every inch. Every inlet. Every cove. Rowed out day and night. I bought diving gear from an Australian guy from Albany, Western Australia who'd been relocated to Albany, New York.'

'Well, there's a ton of Albanys,' Archy says.

'But not many people can say they've lived in one from each hemisphere.'

'I don't get it,' Archy says. 'I think I've got it but then it's gone. The concept I mean, not the island. It's neither one thing nor another. It's not here, but not *not* here.'

'From the right angle on the lake it's always just not there.'

'You can just not see it from the shore. Everyone almost just sees it.' With his finger, Archy smudges the ones and zeros along Beyoncé's jawline.

At first Lee was surprised at Archy's natural talent. Now it fills him with a quiet joy. 'I was convinced that Wallace smuggled my son's remains to the island in one of the drums of chemicals he used to load onto Frankie's boat. I painted it from every angle that it sometimes appeared to me.'

At some gut level, Archy seems to understand the never-nothingness of the island. Neither island nor not-island. They could go on, and sometime they do, accruing neither-nors all night and still Archy refuses to see the island for what it is, which is a good thing. Because once he does, it would see him back, like it did Frankie.

'After he went there, and it saw him eating those berries or whatever, you think it couldn't let him go?'

'I guess.'

'But Zabriskie knew.'

Zabriskie with his brains shot all over Sunny Weeks' future. 'I can't answer that. But it wouldn't surprise me if it had been their secret, maybe, two old warhorses. Maybe they'd each managed to get close enough in their own way to know that it was a one-way trip.'

'Some people can go back and forth.'

They are thinking of his son, whom the island did allow to come and go, and Bryce. 'It's just for a while,' Lee says. 'They never got off it, not really. Just enough to find each other beneath the ice.'

'He had to set you free. She lent him her body, and in return, he gave her his name. It was all for love . . . '

'I don't feel free.'

'But you feel different,' Archy says. 'Same thing. You're not running circles around yourself anymore.'

Lee's hands begin to shake again, as they still do when he says, or even thinks the name, and Archy turns away so he can collect himself.

'Take your time, brother.'

'Bryce with a 'y' wasn't just a body possessed, Arch. She was herself. She had her own past. Her own memories. Her own unfinished business. There was a real *she* inside that body who loved *you*. I know she did.'

Archy grows quiet. 'I loved her, too. She came to me and made me different.

'You made her different, too. You brought her home.'

Then there is just the crackle of the wood stove. They continue to work. Archy quietly laughs at the green glow of Doc's equipment out on the lake, a not uncommon sight on summer nights. The kayaker is as invisible as the kayak due to the army camouflage, complete with night vision goggles from his devil dog days. They pass the joint between them. Doc is funnier when you're stoned.

'Is Frankie free now? And Bryce? Both of them?'

Archy crosshatches Beyoncé's hair with ones and zeros. The face looks more like Bryce's than anyone's but Lee imagines that Archy knows that.

'People aren't free when they're alive. I don't see why that should change after they're dead.'

The sun drops into the lake in its usual messy rage. Archy stops to watch it, rubbing his silvered beard.

'What about,' Archy says. 'If something bad happened here a long, long time ago. Maybe human, maybe not.'

'Like a curse?'

'Maybe. And this hole opened up right here in Little Ridge,' he taps his ringed finger on the table, 'Funes Lake, so deep no one knows how deep. And from somewhere deep in its cold throat, it spat the lake monster out and the lake monster lived on the island until it got too big for it. The island is memory and the monster is the eater of memory and it belongs here. To remind us that we're never free. Time is hungry. Like ma would say, to want not to want.'

Lee opens the wood stove, pokes the flames into life. 'A curse or a blessing?'

'Both. Neither.' Archy angles back to admire his Beyoncé. 'Ones and zeros, see? Between one and zero, something and nothing, there it is.'

Night falls without warning.

'See you, kid,' Lee says, putting a hand on Archy's shoulder. Even in a thin T-shirt it is as tough and impenetrable as Vernon's dorsal armor.

'See you.'

After Archy leaves Lee waits for Thettie. In the studio rising out of spring wildflowers, or half buried beneath the snow, beneath the Milky Way, the words Bryce scrawled backwards on the inside of the window never fade. *Come home.*

Once a week, he drives over to the cemetery where he has buried a splinter of his son's bone beneath a simple marker. It is a flat piece of shale from their beloved woods by the lake, inscribed finally with the letters of his name—Brice.

67. HARD CASE

SAREY HARPUR IS still at the Gully. Thettie goes to visit her. Doc skulks off at her approach—he visits Sarey too, tries to, in order to beg or buy one of her balms or potions to cure the headaches caused by his hyperthymesia, which is slowly turning him blind. The albino bitch with the human eye, is Doc's eye now. And sometime his ears. He explains his new alphabet to her—an unending system of symbols each with their own name—different depending on the time of day, whether written or spoken—their meaning affected by their association with proximal symbols. The white dog rolls her human eye and makes a mute gasp in the back of her throat as if trying to tell to Doc that it's bullshit, exactly the opposite of any kind of meaningful system, but Doc doesn't understand or says he doesn't. His short-term memory is shot because of the venom, but he remembers every moment of every day of his life up until then, and can relive—like in a dream—the changing minutia of his own death.

He says how he sees, for example, from a great height, the future cross-Atlantic flight of a young stranger who purchases a Glock G30 pistol from a man at Newark airport hotel on arrival. This is followed by the mandatory Times Square and/or Statue of Liberty

Kodak moment cherished through the ages, foreshadowed by that of Doc's own arrival in New York from points unknown thirty years previously. He watches like it's already happened, the shooter's focused but patient inquiries at bars and billiard halls, from bag-men and corner-boys between Paterson and Poughkeepsie, before the final night ride west to Little Ridge. The shooter is the only passenger on that last leg of the journey, which will be by bus. The bus driver is a dead war veteran wearing reflective sunglasses, who will periodically emit a ghostly chuckle. Prompted by Thettie, Doc foretells the shooter arriving unnoticed and sitting quietly at the Way, or—and this is where things get a little fuzzy—the shooter could instead be waiting inside the trailer, or down on the jetty, or along a path in the woods of the Gully—Doc can't quite see that yet. But one thing he knows is that it will be anywhere but the island. So off he sets in search of it again and again, the only place on God's green earth safe from the impending arrival, certain as it is circuitous, of the hard-case widow of Toeless Mears.

Because some monsters never forget.

AFTER

THE FEMALE WAITS in the burrow. The burrow is dark. It is safe and warm. She has been waiting a long time. The male approaches after the fight, wearily and with hard-won joy. His enemies are gone. He has survived them all. He has survived science and art and maybe even God. He is old now, his sunset hide faded to mottled umber. He is a beast of memory, an exchange of light. He is home.

ACKNOWLEDGEMENTS

Thanks above all to John, my number one protagonist. Thanks to my children Isabella and Jack, for everything, which doesn't cut it, I know. But I could throw every word at you to the moon and back, and it still wouldn't be enough.

To Matt Bialer—my agent and friend—monstrous and multiple thank yous.

Thanks also to J. David Osborne for being the first responder. Your insightful suggestions and careful reading transformed 'Working Title' into *Aletheia* (and let's never mention that ending again). Inexpressible thanks also to Andiee Paviour for an early edit and for the forever friendship. To Julie-Ann Robson, for that final read—the Big Save—I am eternally grateful. Thank you also to Angela Slatter for all the sage advice, and to Angela, Paul Tremblay, Seb Doubinsky, and Richard Thomas, my humble thanks for your advance reading and encouragement.

Helen Koukoutsis and Sarah Klenbort, my sisters-in-arms—thank you both for being my writing lifeline and my home away from home.

To my real sisters, Cathy Stern and Anne Montiero, for cheering me on, for talking sense when sense seemed to have gone to hell in a handbasket—for the linked shadows we make on this forking path. Thanks to my warrior mother, Margaret Reichenberger for her love and her fight, and to my courageous aunt, Joan Stern, for her unwavering support and for reading far too much of my work than is good for her.

Gratitude in cargo-holds to Sébastien Doubinsky (again) and D. Foy for being the writers they are—my friends in need—for dragging me from the darkness into the light more times than I can say.

Thanks to Ben Baldwin for the cover art that nailed this bad girl, and to my publisher Joe Mynhardt, thank you for welcoming me to the world of the Lake.

This book is for Michael Stern, for the margaritas and the reality checks, and for being in my corner from Day 1. If there is a Tony's Jacal in heaven—and I hope there is—may your bowl of corn chips be forever full. I miss you every day.

ABOUT THE AUTHOR

J.S. Breukelaar is the author of the acclaimed novel, *American Monster* (Lazy Fascist Press), *Aletheia* (Crystal Lake Publishing), the collections, *No Bunnies*, (forthcoming from Crystal Lake Publishing), and *War Wounds*, (forthcoming from Omnium Gatherum Press). She is columnist and instructor at LitReactor, Gotham Writers Workshop and elsewhere. Her short fiction has appeared or is forthcoming in *Gamut, Lightspeed, Lamplight, Nightmare, Juked, Clarkesworld, Prick of the Spindle, Opium, Go(b)et Magazine, and the anthologies, Welcome to Dystopia (Or Books), Women Writing the Weird, (Dog Horn Press),* and *others.*

An ex-pat New Yorker, she lives in Sydney with her family, and online at www.thelivingsuitcase.com.

OTHER NOVELS BY CRYSTAL LAKE PUBLISHING

Blackwater Val
    by William Gorman

Where the Dead Go to Die
    by Aaron Dries and Mark Allan Gunnells

Beatrice Beecham's Cryptic Crypt
    by Dave Jeffery

Sarah Killian: Serial Killer (For Hire!)
    by Mark Sheldon

The Final Cut
    by Jasper Bark

*Pretty Little Dead Girls: A Novel of Murder and
    Whimsy*
    by Mercedes M. Yardley

Or check out other Crystal Lake Publishing books for
more Tales from the Darkest Depths

Hi, readers. It makes our day to know you reached the end of our book. Thank you so much. This is why we do what we do every single day.

Whether you found the book good or great, we'd love to hear what you thought. Please take a moment to leave a review on Amazon, Goodreads, or anywhere else readers visit. Reviews go a long way to helping a book sell, and will help us to continue publishing quality books.

Thank you again for taking the time to journey with Crystal Lake Publishing.

We are also on . . .

Website
http://www.crystallakepub.com/

Books
http://www.crystallakepub.com/book-table/

Blog
http://www.crystallakepub.com/blog-2/

Newsletter
http://eepurl.com/xfuKP

Instagram
https://www.instagram.com/crystal_lake_publishing/

Patreon
https://www.patreon.com/CLP

YouTube
https://www.youtube.com/c/CrystalLakePublishing

Twitter
https://twitter.com/crystallakepub

Facebook page
https://www.facebook.com/Crystallakepublishing/

Tales from The Lake Anthologies Facebook page
https://www.facebook.com/Talesfromthelake/

Writers on Writing Facebook page
https://www.facebook.com/WritersOnWritingSeries/

Beneath the Lake Videocast Facebook page
https://www.facebook.com/BeneathTheLake/

Google+
https://plus.google.com/u/1/107478350897139952572

Pinterest
https://za.pinterest.com/crystallakepub/

Tumblr
https://www.tumblr.com/blog/crystal-lake-publishing

We'd love to hear from you.

With unmatched success since 2012, Crystal Lake Publishing has quickly become one of the world's leading indie publishers of Mystery, Thriller, and Suspense books with a Dark Fiction edge.

Crystal Lake Publishing puts integrity, honor and respect at the forefront of our operations.

We strive for each book and outreach program

that's launched to not only entertain and touch or comment on issues that affect our readers, but also to strengthen and support the Dark Fiction field and its authors.

Not only do we publish authors who are legends in the field and as hardworking as us, but we look for men and women who care about their readers and fellow human beings. We only publish the very best Dark Fiction, and look forward to launching many new careers.

We strive to know each and every one of our readers, while building personal relationships with our authors, reviewers, bloggers, pod-casters, bookstores and libraries.

Crystal Lake Publishing is and will always be a beacon of what passion and dedication, combined with overwhelming teamwork and respect, can accomplish: Unique fiction you can't find anywhere else.

We do not just publish books, we present you worlds within your world, doors within your mind, from talented authors who sacrifice so much for a moment of your time.

This is what we believe in. What we stand for. This will be our legacy.

Welcome to Crystal Lake Publishing.

We hope you enjoyed this title. If so, we'd be grateful if you could leave a review on your blog or any of the other websites and outlets open to book reviews. Reviews are like gold to writers and publishers, since word-of-mouth is and will always be the best way to market a great book. And remember to keep an eye out for more of our books.

THANK YOU FOR PURCHASING THIS BOOK